Playboy Bachelors

MARIE FERRARELLA

MILLS

® and ™ are trademarks owned and used by the trademark owner and/or its licensee. Trademarks marked with ® are registered with the United Kingdom Patent Office and/or the Office for Harmonisation in the Internal Market and in other countries.

Published in Great Britain 2014
by Mills & Boon, an imprint of Harlequin (UK) Limited,
Eton House, 18-24 Paradise Road, Richmond, Surrey, TW9 1SR

PLAYBOY BACHELORS © 2014 Harlequin Books S.A.

Remodelling the Bachelor, Taming the Playboy and *Capturing the Millionaire* were first published in Great Britain by Harlequin (UK) Limited.

Remodeling the Bachelor © 2007 Marie Rydzynski-Ferrarella
Taming the Playboy © 2007 Marie Rydzynski-Ferrarella
Capturing the Millionaire © 2007 Marie Rydzynski-Ferrarella

ISBN: 978 0 263 91170 1
eBook ISBN: 978 1 472 04465 5

05-0114

Harlequin (UK) Limited's policy is to use papers that are natural, renewable and recyclable products and made from wood grown in sustainable forests. The logging and manufacturing processes conform to the legal environmental regulations of the country of origin.

Printed and bound in Spain
by Blackprint CPI, Barcelona

REMODELLING
THE BACHELOR

BY
MARIE FERRARELLA

Marie Ferrarella, a *USA TODAY* bestselling and RITA® Award-winning author, has written over one hundred and fifty novels for Mills & Boon, some under the name Marie Nicole. Her romances are beloved by fans worldwide. Visit her website at www.marieferrarella.com.

To Helen Conrad, my bridge over troubled waters.
Thank you.

Chapter One

"**W**hen are you going to get that cracked sink fixed?" Beau de la Croix asked good-naturedly as he slid back into his place at the poker table.

The question was addressed to Philippe Zabelle, his cousin and the host of their weekly poker game. Beau and several other friends and relatives showed up here at Philippe's to talk, eat and bet toothpicks on the whimsical turn of the cards. They used colored toothpicks instead of chips or money because those were the house rules and Philippe, easygoing about so many things, was very strict about that.

Philippe's dark eyebrows rose slightly above his light

green eyes at the innocent but still irritating query. Beau had hit a sore spot. Everyone at the circular table was aware of that.

"When I get around to it," Philippe replied evenly.

"Better hope that's not soon," Georges Armand, Philippe's half brother commented, battling the grin that begged to break out across his tanned face. "If Philippe puts his hand to it, that's the end of the sink."

Philippe, the oldest of famed artist Lily Moreau's three sons, shifted his steely gaze toward Georges, his junior by two years. "Are you saying that I'm not handy?"

Alain Dulac, Philippe's other half brother, as blond as Philippe was dark, bent over with laughter at the very idea of his older brother holding an actual tool in his hand. "Oh God, Philippe, you're so far from handy that if *handy* were Los Angeles, you'd be somewhere in the Atlantic Ocean. Drowning," Alain finally managed, holding his sides because they hurt.

Georges discarded two cards and momentarily frowned at the rest of his hand. "Two," he decided out loud, then looked over to his right and Philippe. "Everyone knows you've got lots of talents, Philippe, but being handy is just not one of them."

Philippe tried not to take offense, but it bothered him nonetheless. For the most part, he considered himself a free thinker, a person who believed that no one should be expected to fit into a given slot or pigeonholed because of gender or race. With the flamboyant and outspoken Lily Moreau as his mother, a woman who made the fictional Auntie Mame come off like a cloistered nun, he couldn't help but have an open mind.

Even so, it got under his skin that he barely knew the difference between a Phillips-head screwdriver and a flat-head one. Men were supposed to know these things, it was a given, written in some giant book of man-rules somewhere.

The fact that he not only couldn't rebuild an automobile engine but was pretty stumped if one refused to start, didn't bother him. Lots of men were ignorant about what went on under the hoods of things housed in their garage.

But not being handy around the house, well, that was another story entirely.

Still, he had no natural ability, nor even a fostered one. He'd always been too busy either studying or being both mother and father to his brothers because his mother had once more taken off with a show, or, just as likely, with a man. Growing up, he'd found himself taking on the role of buffer, placing himself between the endless parade of nannies and his two younger brothers. Once out of their rebellious teens, Georges and Alain had both acknowledged that even though they loved their mother dearly, Philippe was the only reason they had turned out normal. Or at least reasonably so.

That didn't stop them from teasing him whenever the opportunity arose. Their affection for the man they considered the head of the family actually seemed to promote it.

"One," Alain requested, throwing down his card first. After glancing at the new addition, he looked up at Philippe. He put on the face that Philippe knew was the undoing of every fluttering female heart at the university Alain was currently attending. A university whose tuition bill found its way into his mailbox twice a year and which he promptly and willingly paid. "Too late to change my mind and get the old one back?"

There wasn't even a hint of humor on Philippe's face. "After insulting me?"

"Wasn't an insult, Philippe," his cousin Remy assured him. Remy, a geologist, was closer to Alain in age than Philippe. "Alain was only telling it the way it is. Hey," he added quickly, forestalling any fallout from the man they all admired, "we all love you, Philippe, but you know you'll never be the first one any of us call if we find that we've got a clogged drain."

"Or a cabinet door that won't close right," Vincent Mirabeau called over from the far side of the kitchen. "Like this one." To illustrate his point, Vincent, another one of Philippe's cousins and Lily's godson, went through elaborate motions to close the closet door. Creaking, it returned to its place, approximately an inch and a half away from its mate, just hanging in mid-space. "I think you should bite the bullet and hire someone to remodel this place."

Remy put in his two cents. "Or at least the bathroom and the kitchen."

Philippe folded his hand and placed it face down on the table, his eyes sweeping over his brothers and cousins. "What's wrong with this place?" he asked.

He'd bought the house with the first money he'd managed to save up after opening up his own software design company. The moment he'd seen it, he'd known that the unique structure was for him. To the passing eye, the house where he received his mail appeared to be a giant estate. It was only when the passing eye stopped passing and moved closer that the perception changed. His house was just one of three houses, carefully designed to look like one. There was one door in the center, leading to his house. Other doors located on either end of the structure opened the other two houses. Thanks to his initial down payment, Georges and Alain lived in those. They all had their privacy but were within shouting distance if a quick family meeting was needed. Because Lily was their mother, the need for one of these was not as rare for them as it was for some families.

"Nothing's wrong with this place," Beau was quick to say. They all knew how attached to the house Philippe was. "At least, nothing a good handyman couldn't fix."

Philippe's expression remained uncharacteristically stony. "C'mon, Philippe," Remy urged, "every time you turn on the faucet in the kitchen, it sounds like you're listening to the first five bars of 'When the Saints Come Marching In.'"

Before Philippe could protest, Remy turned the handle toward the left. Hot water slowly emerged, but a strange echoing rattling noise in the pipes preceded the appearance of any liquid.

Philippe sighed. There was no point in pretending he would get around to fixing that, either. He didn't even know where to start. When it came to the faucet, his ability began and ended with turning the spigots on or off.

Tossing a bright pink toothpick onto the pile of red, blue, green and yellow, Philippe asked, "Anyone else want to bet?"

Vincent shook his head, throwing in his cards. "Too rich for my blood."

"Count me out." Remy followed suit.

But Beau grinned. "I'll see your pink toothpick," he tossed one in, "and raise you a green one."

Picking up a green toothpick from his dwindling pile, Philippe debated. Green represented five cents; he rarely went higher than that on a single bet. His father, Jon Zabelle, had been a charming incurable gambler. The man had single-handedly almost brought them down and was responsible for Lily Moreau's brief and unfortunate flirtation with frightening poverty. That period of time, long in his past and no more than three months in length, had left an indelible mark on Philippe.

It also allowed him to recognize the occasional craving to bet as a potential problem.

Forewarned, Philippe treated any obstacle head on. Since he liked to play cards and he liked to gamble, he made sure that it would never result in his losing anything more a handful of colorful toothpicks. The big loser at his table wound up doing chores to make payment, not going to an ATM machine.

"I call," Philippe announced, tossing in the green toothpick to match his cousin's.

"Three of a kind," Beau told him, spreading out two black nines with a red one in between.

"Me, too," Philippe countered, setting down three fours, one by one. And then he added, "Oh, and I've also got two of a kind." The fours were joined by a pair of queens.

Beau huffed, staring down at the winning hand. "Full house, you damn lucky son of a gun." He pushed the "pot," with its assorted array of toothpicks, toward his oldest cousin.

"Gonna cash in this time and spend all your 'winnings' on renovating the house?" Remy teased as Philippe sorted out the different colors and placed them in their appropriate piles.

Philippe didn't bother looking at his cousin. "I don't have the time to start hunting for a decent contractor."

Vincent's grin went from ear to ear. He stuck his hand into his back pocket and pulled out his wallet.

"Just so happens, I have the name of a contractor right here in my wallet."

Philippe stopped sorting, feeling like a man who'd been set up. "Oh?"

"Yeah. Somebody named J. D. Wyatt," Vincent told him. "Friend of mine had some work done on his place. Said it was fast and the bid was way below anything the other contractors he'd contacted had come through with."

Which could be good, or could be bad, Philippe thought. The contractor could be hungry for work or he could be using sub-grade material. If he decided to hire this J.D., he was going to have to stay on top of him.

Philippe thought for a moment. He knew his brothers and cousins were going to keep on ribbing him until he gave in. In all fairness, he knew the place could stand to have some work done. He just hated the hassle of having someone else do it.

Better that than the hassle of you pretending you know what you're doing and messing up, big time, a small voice in his head whispered.

For better or for worse, he made up his mind. He'd give it a go. After all, he wasn't an unreasonable man and the place did look like it was waiting to get on the disaster-area list.

He could always cancel if it didn't work out. "This J.D. have a phone number where I could reach him?"

Vincent was already ahead of him. "Just so happens,"

he plucked the card out of his wallet and held it out to his cousin, "I've got it right here."

"Serendipity," Remy declared, grinning as Philippe looked at him quizzically. "Can't mess with serendipity."

"Since when?" Philippe snorted.

Remy had an answer for everything. "Since it'll interfere with your karma."

Philippe snorted even louder. He didn't believe in any of that nonsense. That was his mother's domain. Karma, tarot cards, tea leaves, mediums, everything and anything that pretended to link her up with the past. Although he loved the woman dearly and would do anything for her, he'd spent most of his life trying to be as different from his mother as humanly possible—from both his parents.

That was why he'd turned his back on the artistic ability that he'd so obviously inherited. Because he didn't want to go his mother's route.

Lily Moreau had coaxed her first born to pick up a paintbrush in his hand even before she'd encouraged him to pick up a toothbrush and brush his teeth. If he made it as an artist, he could always buy new teeth, she'd informed him cheerfully.

But he had dug in his heels and been extremely stubborn. He refused to draw or paint anything either under her watchful eye or away from it. Only when he was absently killing time, most likely on hold on the phone, did he catch himself doodling some elaborate figure in pencil.

He was always quick to destroy any and all evidence. He was his mother's son, as well as his father's, but there was no earthly reason that he could see to admit to either, at least not when it came to laboring under their shadows.

He wanted to make his own way in the world, be his own person, make his own mistakes and have his own triumphs. And this was one of the reasons it really bothered him that he wasn't up to the task of fixing things in his own place. Neither his father, now dead, nor his mother, alive enough for both of them, could claim to be even remotely handy. If Philippe were handy, he would be even more different from his parents.

But for that to ever happen, he was going to need lessons. Intense lessons. He glanced down at the card in his hand. Maybe this would turn out all right after all.

"Okay," he nodded, tucking the card into the back pocket of his jeans, "I'll call this J.D. when I get a chance."

"Before the bathroom sink breaks in half?" Georges asked.

Philippe nodded. "Before the bathroom sink breaks in half," he promised. He picked up the deck of cards again and looked around. "Now, do you guys want to play poker or do you just want to sit around, complaining about my house?"

"All in favor of complaining about Philippe's house," Georges declared, raising his hand in the air as he looked around the table, "raise your hand."

Every hand around him shot up, but Philippe focused

his attention exclusively on his brother. Grabbing a handful of chips—the crunchy kind—he threw them at Georges. Laughing, Georges responded in kind.

Which was how the poker game devolved into a food fight that lasted until all the remaining edible material— and the toothpicks—and been commandeered and pressed into service.

The result was a huge mess and a great deal of laughter, punctuated by a stream of colorful words that didn't begin to describe what had gone on.

Hours later, after he had gotten them to all lend a hand and clean up, the gathering finally broke up and they all went their separate ways. Alain returned to his law books and Georges declared that he had a late date waiting for him, one that, he'd whispered confidentially, held a great deal of promise. Which only meant that Georges thought he was going to get lucky.

Remy, Vincent and Beau went back to whatever it was that occupied them in their off-hours. Trouble, mostly, Philippe thought fondly. Probably instigated by Henri and Joseph, first cousins and two of the more silent members of the weekly poker game.

It was still early by his old standards. But his old standards hadn't had to cope with deadlines and program bugs that insisted on manifesting themselves despite his diligent attempts to squash them. Program bugs he needed to iron out of his latest software package before he submitted it to Lyon Enterprises, his software publisher. The deadline was breathing down his neck.

He didn't have to work this hard. He *chose* to work this hard. Philippe had made his fortune on a software package that he'd designed five years ago, a package that had become indispensable to the advertising industry. Streamlined and efficient, it was now considered the standard by which all other such programs were measured. There was no need for him to keep hours that would have only gladdened the heart of a Tibetan monk, but, unlike his late father, he had never believed in coasting. He liked being kept busy, liked creating, liked having a schedule to adhere to and something tangible to shoot for every day. He wasn't the idle type.

His mother's second husband, Georges's father, had been a self-made millionaire, owing his fortune to a delicate scent that lured scores of women with far too much money on their hands. André Armand was a man who slept late and partied into the wee hours of the morning. It was because of André that they had the lifestyle they now enjoyed.

Even before André had married his mother, the man had taken to him. The moment the vows were uttered, he'd taken him under his wing, viewing him as a protégé. But Philippe quickly learned that although he really liked the man, the life André led was not one that appealed to him at all, even as an adolescent. It was because of André that Philippe had come to the conclusion that no matter how rich he was, a man needed a purpose.

He'd never forgotten it, nor let either one of his brothers forget it. He'd made sure that his brothers did their lessons and excelled in school, even when they said they didn't need to.

"You need to make a difference in this world," he'd told them over and over again, "no matter how small. Or else all you are is a large mound of dust, just passing through."

As he slipped his hands into his back pockets, the tips of the fingers of his right hand came in contact with what felt like a piece of paper. Drawing it out, Philippe stared for a second before he recalled where he'd gotten it and why.

The contractor.

Right.

Well, if he didn't make the call right now, he knew he wouldn't. Life had a habit of overwhelming him at times, especially whenever his mother was in town and rumor had it Hurricane Lily was due in soon. Details tended to get buried and lost if he didn't attend to them immediately.

Do it now or let it go, Philippe thought with a half smile.

Making his way to the nearest phone, Philippe glanced at his watch to make sure it wasn't too late to call. It was a little before ten. Still early, he thought as he began to tap out the embossed hunter-green numbers on the card.

The phone on the other end rang three times. No one picked up.

Philippe was about to hang up when he heard the receiver suddenly coming to life.

And then, the most melodic voice he'd ever heard proceeded to tell him: "You've reached J. D. Wyatt's office. I'm sorry we missed you call. Please leave your number and a detailed message as to what you want done and we'll get back to you."

Obviously this was either Wyatt's secretary or, more likely, his wife. The sensual sound of her voice planted thoughts in his head and made him want to request having "things done" that had nothing to do with reno-vating parts of his house and everything to do with reno-vating parts of him. Or his soul, he silently amended.

He was currently in between encounters. Encounters, not relationships, because they weren't that. Relation-ships took time, effort, emotional investment; all of which he'd seen come to naught, especially in his mother's life. There'd been some keepers in his mother's lot, most notably Alain's father and a man named Alex-ander Walters. But as much as his mother loved being in a relationship, loved having a man around, she had always been the restless kind. No matter how good a re-lationship was, eventually his mother felt the need to leave it, to shed it like a skin she'd outgrown. She'd left all three of her husbands, divorcing them before they'd died. Remained friends with all of the men she'd loved even years after she'd moved on.

His mother couldn't seem to function without a relationship in her life, especially when it was in its birthing stages. She loved being in love. He had never seen the need for that, the need for garnering the pain involved in ending something. He'd never wanted to be in that position, so he wasn't. It was as simple as that.

Feelings couldn't be hurt if they weren't invested— on either side. After a while, it seemed natural to have female company only on the most cursory level. To enjoy an encounter without promising anything beyond tonight and then moving on.

He didn't know any other way.

The beep he heard on the other end of the line roused him, bringing him back from his momentary revelry. "Um, this is Philippe Zabelle." He rattled off his telephone number. "I got your name from a friend of a friend. I need some remodeling work done on two of my bathrooms. I thought you might come by my place at around seven tomorrow night if that's convenient for you." He recited his address slowly. "If I don't get a call from you, I'll be expecting you tomorrow at seven. See you then."

Philippe hung up. He absolutely hated talking to machines, even ones with sexy voices. As he went up the stairs to his bedroom, he thought about how people were far too isolated and dependent on machines to do their work for them.

And then he smiled to himself. It was a rather ironic thought, given the nature of what he did for a living. His smile widened. The world was a strange place.

Chapter Two

The next morning, Philippe hit the ground running.

Usually reliable, his inner alarm clock had decided to go on strike. Instead of six-thirty, the time he normally woke up during the work week, Philippe rolled over and stared in disbelief at the digital clock beside the bed.

Burning in bright, bold red shone the numbers 7:46 a.m.

The second his brain registered the discrepancy between the time he intended to get up and the actual hour, Philippe tumbled out of bed. He then proceeded to race through his shower and decide not to bother shaving. He was down in the kitchen at exactly one minute before eight o'clock.

He would have made himself toast and scrambled eggs if he'd had bread. Or eggs. Instead breakfast consisted of the last of his coffee and a couple of close-to-stale pieces of Swiss cheese, the latter being part of what he'd served last night along with beer, junk food and conversation.

Leaning a hip against the counter as he finished the last of the unexceptional cheese, he shook his head. It was time to surrender and give in to the inevitable: he needed a housekeeper. Someone who stopped by maybe once a week, did the grocery shopping and gave the house a fast once-over. That was all that was really necessary. As the oldest and the one who often was left in charge, Philippe had learned to run a fairly tight, not to mention neat, ship. The only thing in utter disarray was the desk in his home office.

Actually, if he was being honest with himself, most of the office looked that way, what with books left open to pertinent sections and a ton of paper scattered in all four corners of the room, covering most of the available flat surfaces. He supposed, in a way, it was a statement about the way his life operated. His private affairs were neatly organized while his work looked as if he'd recently been entertaining a grade four hurricane on the premises.

Finished eating, Philippe wiped his fingers on the back of his jeans and made his way over to the telephone. Ten minutes later, he'd placed an ad in the local paper as well as on the newspaper's Internet site for an experienced housekeeper to do light housekeeping once a week.

He frowned as he hung up.

Hiring someone to invade his space, even briefly, wasn't a choice he was happy about, but he had to face it. It was a necessary evil. Business was very good and the demand on his time was high. Aside from the weekly poker games, of late he seemed to be spending all of his time working. That left no time for the minor essentials—like the procurement of foodstuff. He needed someone to do that for him.

He could have advertised for an assistant, Philippe thought as he made his way to the back of the house and the organized chaos that was his home office, but that would have meant a big invasion. He knew himself better than that. No, a housekeeper was the better way to go, he decided.

Planting the opened can of flat soda he'd discovered sitting in the back of his all-but-barren refrigerator on the first space he unearthed by his computer, Philippe flipped on the radio that resided on the bookcase beside his desk. Classical music filled the air as he sat down and got to work. Within seconds, he was enmeshed in programming language and completely oblivious to such things as time and space and earthly surroundings.

During the course of the day, when his brain begged for a break and his stomach upbraided him for abuse, Philippe made his way to the kitchen to forage for food. Lunch had consisted of pretzels, made slightly soggy by being left out overnight. Dinner had been more of the same with a handful of assorted nuts downed as a chaser. But the food hardly mattered.

It was his work that was important and it was progressing well. He'd gotten further along on the new software than he'd expected and that always gave him a sense of satisfaction, as did the fact that he handled everything by himself. He created the programs, designed the artwork and developed the tutorial and self-help features, something that was taking on more and more importance with each software package he created.

With a heartfelt sigh, Philippe closed down his computer. Rising to his feet, he went to the kitchen to get himself the last bottle of beer to celebrate a very productive, if exhausting, day.

He had just opened the refrigerator door to see if perhaps he'd missed something edible in his prior forages when he heard the doorbell. Releasing the refrigerator door again, he glanced at his watch. Seven o'clock. Both his brothers and his friends knew that he generally knocked off around seven. One of them had obviously decided to visit.

Good, he could use a little company right about now. Maybe he and whoever was at his door could go out for a bite to eat.

His stomach rumbled again.

Several bites, Philippe amended, striding toward the door.

"Hi," he said cheerfully as he swung open the door.

It took him less than half a second to realize he'd just uttered the greeting to a complete stranger. A very attractive complete stranger wearing a blue pullover sweater and a pair of light-colored faded jeans that adhered in such a way as to drive the stock of jeans everywhere sky-high. The blonde was holding the hand of a little girl who, for all intents and purposes, was an exact miniature of her.

Like the woman whose hand she was holding, the little girl was slight and petite and very, very blond. He guessed that she had to be about five or so, although he was on shaky ground when it came to anything to do with kids.

Philippe looked back to the woman with the heart-shaped face. He had to clear his throat before he asked, "Can I help you?"

Eyes the color of cornflowers in bloom washed over him slowly, as if she was taking his measure. It was then that he remembered he was barefoot and wearing the first T-shirt he'd laid his eyes on this morning, the one that had shrunk in the wash. And that when he worked, he had a habit of running his hands through his hair, making it pretty unruly by the end of the day. That, along with his day-old stubble and worn clothes probably made him look one step removed from a homeless person.

Philippe glanced at the little girl. Rather than look frightened, she was grinning up at him. But the woman holding her hand appeared somewhat skeptical as she continued to regard him. She and the child remained firmly planted on the front step.

He was about to repeat his question when she suddenly answered it—and added to his initial confusion. "I came about the job."

"The job?" he echoed, momentarily lost. And then it hit him. The woman with the perfect mouth and translucent complexion was referring to the housekeeping position he'd called the paper about this morning. Boy, that was fast.

"Oh, the job," he repeated with feeling, glad that was finally cleared up. Beautiful women did not just appear on his doorstep for no reason, not unless they were looking for Georges. "Right. Sure. C'mon in," he invited, gesturing into the house.

Philippe stepped back in order to allow both the woman and the little girl with her to come inside.

The woman still seemed just the slightest bit hesitant. Then, winding her left hand more tightly around her purse, she entered. Her right hand was firmly attached to the little girl. Philippe found himself vaguely curious as to what the woman had in her purse that seemed to give her courage. Mace? A gun? He decided maybe it was better that he didn't know.

"My name's Kelli, what's yours?" The question came not from the woman but from the child, uttered in a strong voice that seemed completely out of harmony with her small body.

He wondered if Kelli would grow into her voice. "Philippe," he told her.

The girl nodded, as if she approved of the name. It amused him that she didn't find his name odd or funny because of the French pronunciation. She had old eyes, he noted.

The personification of curiosity, Kelli scanned her surroundings. Had she not been tethered to the woman's hand, he had the impression that Kelli would have taken off to go exploring.

Her eyes were as blue as her mother's. "Is this your house?" the girl asked.

He felt the corners of his mouth curving. There was something infectious about Kelli's inquisitive manner. "Yes."

She raised her eyes up the stairs to the second floor. "It looks big."

Philippe wondered if all this was spontaneous, or if the woman had coached her daughter to ask certain questions for her. Children's innocent inquiries were hard to ignore.

Deciding to assume that Kelli was her mother's shill, he addressed his answer to the woman instead of the child.

"It's not, really," he assured the blonde. "It looks a great deal bigger on the outside, but mine is just the middle house." He spread his hands wide to encompass the area. "This is actually three houses made to look like one."

The information created a tiny furrow on the woman's forehead, right between her eyes. She looked as if his words had annoyed her. "I'm familiar with the type," the woman replied softly.

"Good."

The lone word hung in midair between them like a damp curtain.

He'd never had a housekeeper before. As a matter of fact, he'd never interviewed anyone for any sort of position before and hadn't the slightest idea how to go about it now without sounding like a complete novice. Or worse, a complete idiot. The image didn't please him.

Clearing his throat again, Philippe pushed on. "Then you know there won't be much work involved."

The woman smiled as if she was sharing some secret joke with herself. She had a nice smile. Otherwise, he might have taken offense.

"No disrespect, Mr. Zabelle," she said as she appeared to slowly take stock of his living room and what she could see beyond it, "but I'll be the judge of that." She turned to face him. "Once you tell me exactly what it is you have in mind."

He had no idea why that would cause him to almost swallow his tongue. Maybe it was the way she looked at him or, more likely, the way she'd uttered that phrase. She certainly didn't remind him of any housekeeper he'd ever come across while living at his mother's house.

"Have you done this before?" he asked. In his experience, housekeepers were usually older women, more

likely than not somewhat maternal looking. This one
was neither and if there was one thing he wanted, it was
someone experienced. But he was a fair man and willing
to be convinced.

She looked at him as if he'd just insulted her. "Yes,"
she replied with more than a little feeling. "I have references. I can show them to you once we finish talking
about the basics here."

He nodded at the information, although when he'd
find the time to check her references was beyond him.
Maybe he could get Alain or Remy to do it for him. Both
had more free time than he did.

She was obviously waiting for him to define the requirements. He gave it his best shot. "Well, I won't be
asking you to do anything you haven't done before."

That didn't come out quite right, he realized the
minute he'd said it.

The blonde reinforced his impression. Blinking, she
asked, "Excuse me?"

He must have said something wrong but hadn't the
slightest idea what. There was no clue forthcoming from
the woman's daughter either. Kelli seemed amused by
the whole exchange. Maybe she wasn't a little girl after
all, just a very short adult. Her face was certainly ex-
pressive enough to qualify.

Philippe tried again. "I mean, it'll be the usual.
Some light dusting." He shrugged, thinking. "Shopping
once a week."

The woman's mouth dropped open. And still managed to look damn sensual. It belatedly occurred to him that he still didn't even know her name. "I don't—"

"Do windows?" he completed her sentence. "That's okay, I have a service that comes by twice a year to wash my windows." There was no way he could reach the upper portion of some of them even if he did have the time, which he didn't. "I just need someone to clean up—nothing major," he assured her quickly, "because most of the time, I'm holed up in my office." He jerked a thumb toward the rear of the house. "And I'd rather you didn't come in there."

The woman shook her head, as if put off. "Mr. Zabelle, I think there's been some mistake."

He didn't want there to be some mistake. He wanted her to take the job. He couldn't see himself going through this process over and over again.

Philippe took a stab at the reason for her comment. "You're full-time, right?"

"When I work, yes."

Philippe paused, thinking. "I really don't need anyone fulltime."

"I think what you need is an interpreter." Her response confused him, but before he could tell her as much, she was saying, "When I start a job, Mr. Zabelle, I finish it."

Well, that was a good trait, he thought, but he still wasn't going to hire her full-time. "That's very admirable, but like I said, I'm only going to need someone once a week."

Rather than accept that, he saw her put her hands on her waist. "And why is that?"

Maybe this was a mistake after all. He could have gone to the store and back in the amount of time he'd spent verbally dancing around with this woman. "Because there won't be enough to keep you occupied," he told her tersely. "I'm pretty neat."

She shook her head as if to clear it. "What does your being neat have to do with it?"

"I realize you probably charge the same whether you're working for a slob or someone who's relatively neat—"

She cut him off before he could finish. "I charge according to what the client requests, Mr. Zabelle, not based on whether they're sloppy or neat."

That sounded a hell of a lot more personal than just cleaning his house.

Their eyes met and Philippe watched her for a long moment. The more he did, the less she looked like a housekeeper. Just what section had his ad landed in? And if it was what he was thinking, what was she doing bringing her daughter along on this so-called job interview?

His eyes narrowed slightly. "Did you get my number from the personals?"

He watched as her mouth formed as close to a

perfect *O* as he had ever seen. He saw her hand tightened around Kelli's.

"Mommy, you're squishing my fingers," the little girl protested.

"Sorry," she murmured, never taking her eyes off his face. She was looking at him as if she thought that perhaps she should be backing away. Quickly. "I got your number from my machine, Mr. Zabelle," she told him, her voice both angry and distant now.

Okay, he was officially lost. "Your machine?" That made no sense to him. "I called the newspaper this morning."

She cocked her head, as if that could help her make sense of all this somehow. "About?"

"The ad," he said, annoyed. Had she lost the thread of the conversation already? What kind of an attention span did she have?

"What ad?" she demanded. She sounded like someone on the verge of losing her temper.

Taking a breath, Philippe enunciated each word slowly, carefully, the way he would if he were talking to someone who was mentally challenged. "The… one…you're…here…about."

Her voice went up several levels. "I'm not here about any ad."

Suddenly, something unlocked in a distant part of his brain. Her voice was very familiar. He'd heard it before. Recently.

Philippe held up his hand, stopping her. "Hold it. Back up." He peered at her face intently, trying to jog his memory. Nothing. "Who are you, lady?"

A loud huff of air preceded the reply. When she spoke, it was through gritted teeth. "I'm J. D. Wyatt. You called me about remodeling your bathrooms."

And then it hit him. Like a ton of bricks. He knew where he'd heard that voice before—on the phone, last night. "*You're* J. D. Wyatt?"

J.D. drew herself up. He had the impression she'd been through this kind of thing before—and had no patience with it. "Yes."

He wanted to be perfectly clear in his understanding of the situation. "You're not here about the housekeeping job?"

"The housekeep—" Oh God, now it made sense. The weekly shopping, the cleaning. He'd made a natural mistake—and one that irked her. "No, I'm not here about the housekeeping job. I'm a contractor."

He thought back to what Vincent had said when he'd given him the card. "I thought I was calling a handyman."

J.D. shrugged. She'd lived in a man's world all of her life and spent most of her time struggling to gain acceptance. "A handy-person," she corrected.

The discomfort he'd been feeling grew. It was bad enough not being handy and feeling inferior to another man. Aesthetically speaking, all men might have been created equal, but not when it came to wielding a hacksaw. Feeling inferior to a woman with a tool belt? Well, that was a whole different matter. He wasn't sure he could handle it.

It felt like he'd been deceived. "What does the J.D. stand for?"

She eyed him for a long moment, as if debating whether or not to tell him. And then she did. "Janice Diane."

"So why didn't you just put that down on the card?" he asked. "You realize that's false advertising."

"My mama's not false!" Kelli piped up indignantly, moving between her mother and him.

"Kelli, hush," J.D. soothed. "It's okay." And then she looked at him and her sunny expression faded. "There's nothing false about it. Those are my initials."

"You know what I mean. By using them, you make people think that they're hiring a man."

That was the whole point, she thought. This man might look drop-dead gorgeous, but he was as dumb as a shoe—and probably had the soul to match. She spelled it out for him.

"People do not call someone named *Janice Diane* to fix their running toilets or renovate their flagstone fireplaces. They do, however, call someone named J.D. to do the same work. This world runs on preconceived notions, Mr. Zabelle. One of those notions is that men are handy, women are not. Your reaction just proved my point. You thought I was here to clean your house, not to renovate it."

She was right and he didn't like it, but he couldn't come up with a face-saving rebuttal. "Well, I—"

It wouldn't have mattered if he had, she wouldn't let him finish.

"I've been around tools all my life and I know what to do with them." She folded her arms before her. "Now, are you going to let your prejudice keep you from hiring the best handy-person you're ever going to come across in your life—at any price—or are you going to be a modern man and show me what exactly you need done around here?" It was a challenge, pure and simple. One she hoped he would rise to.

Out of the corner of her eye, Janice saw Kelli mimic her actions perfectly, folding her small arms before her.

Mother and daughter stood united, waiting for a reply.

Chapter Three

For what felt like an endless moment, two different reactions warred within Philippe, each striving for the upper hand.

Ever since he could remember, he'd had it drummed into his head—and had come to truly believe—that the only difference between men and women were that women had softer skin. Usually. His mother had enthusiastically maintained over and over again that women could do anything a man could except go to the bathroom standing up. And even there, she had declared smugly, women had the better method. At the very least, it was neater.

But there was another, equally strong reaction that beat within his chest. It was based on the deep-seated philosophy that men were the doers, the protectors in this dance of life. This notion had evolved very early in his life and had come from the fact that he'd been the responsible one in the family, the steadfast one. His mother flittered in and out of relationships, fell in and out of love, while he held down the fort, making sure that his brothers stayed out of trouble and went to school. And occasionally, when there was a need for it, his was the shoulder on which his mother would cry or vent.

He grew up believing that there were certain things that men did. They might be partners with women on a daily basis, but in times of crisis, the partnership tended to go from fifty-fifty to seventy-thirty, with the man taking up the slack.

And under that heading, but in a much looser sense, came the concept of being handy. Women weren't supposed to be handy, at least, not handier than the men of the species. Women were not the guardians of the tool belt, they were the nurturers.

Right now, as he vacillated between giving in to his pride and being fair, Philippe could almost hear his mother whispering in his ear.

"Damn it, Philippe, I raised you better than this. Give the girl a chance. She has a child, for heaven's sake. Besides, she's very easy on the eye. Not a bad little number to have around."

At the very least, it wouldn't hurt to have J.D. give him an estimate. If he didn't like it, that would be the end of that. Mentally, he crossed his fingers.

With a barely suppressed sigh, he nodded. "All right. Let me show you the bathroom."

Philippe began leading the way to the rear of the house, past the kitchen. Somehow, Kelli managed to wiggle in front of him just as they came to the bathroom that had begun it all, the one with the cracked sink.

Hands on either side of the doorjamb, Kelli peered into the room before her mother could stop her, then declared in a very adult, very disappointed voice, "Oh, it's not pretty." Turning around, she looked up at him with a smile that promised everything was going to be all right. "But don't worry, Mama can make it pretty for you. She's very good."

Philippe raised an eyebrow. "She your press agent?" he asked, amused despite himself as he nodded toward the little girl.

For the first time, he saw the woman in the well-fitting faded jeans smile. Janice ruffled her daughter's silky blond hair with pure affection. "More like my own personal cheering section."

An identical smile was mirrored on Kelli's lips. The resemblance was uncanny.

Stepping back to grab her mother's hand, Kelli proceeded to tug her into the small rectangular slightly musty room. "C'mon, Mommy, tell him what you're gonna do to make it look pretty."

Janice glanced over her shoulder toward the man she hoped was going to hire her and allow her to make this month's mortgage payment. "I don't think *pretty* is what Mr. Zabelle has in mind, honey."

Kelli pursed her lips together, clearly mulling over her mother's words. And then she raised her bright blue eyes up to look at his face, studying him intently as if she was trying to decide just what sort of creature he was.

"Everyone likes pretty," she finally declared with the firm conviction of the very young.

Philippe's experience with children was extremely limited. It really didn't go beyond his own rather adult childhood and the brothers he'd all but raised. All of that now residing in the distant past.

Too distant for him to really recall with any amount of clarity.

But since Kelli made decrees like a short adult, he treated her as such and said, "That all depends on what you mean by *pretty.*"

The smile on the rosebud mouth was back, spreading along it generously and banishing her momentary serious expression. This time, she looked up at her mother and giggled. "He's funny, Mommy."

Janice slipped her hand around Kelli's shoulders, stooping down to do so. "He's the client, Kel, and we don't talk about him as if he's not in the room when he's standing right beside us."

"Good rule to remember," Philippe approved, then decided to ask a question of his own. "You always bring your daughter along on interviews?"

Interviews. Janice had gotten to dislike the word. It made her feel as if she was being scrutinized. As if someone was passing judgment on her. There had been more than enough of that when she'd been growing up. Her father was always judging her—and finding her lacking. Besides, she took exception to Zabelle's question. It wasn't any of his business if Kelli came along or not as long as everything else was conducted professionally.

Without meaning to, she squared her shoulders. "My sitter had a date."

Philippe supposed that was a reasonable excuse, although the woman could have rescheduled. "Good for her."

"Him," she corrected. "Good for him," she added when he looked at her quizzically. "My sitter's my brother, Gordon."

Mentally, Philippe came to an abrupt halt. He was getting far more information than he either needed or wanted. If he did wind up hiring this woman to tinker and fix the couple of things that needed fixing, he wanted to keep their exchanges strictly to a business level.

But that wasn't going to be easy, he realized in the

next moment when the little girl took his hand in hers and brightly informed him, "I don't have a brother. Do you have one?"

He expected Kelli's mother to step in and admonish the little girl for talking so freely to a stranger. But there was nothing forthcoming from J.D. and Kelli was apparently waiting for him to give her an answer.

"Yes," he finally said. "Two."

"Do they live here, too?" Kelli asked. She seemed ready to go off in search of them.

He shifted his eyes toward the so-called handy-person. "Don't you think you should teach her not to be so friendly with strangers?"

Janice had never liked being told what to do. She struggled now to keep her annoyance out of her voice. The man probably meant well and he was, after all, a potential client.

But who the hell did he think he was, telling her how to raise her daughter?

She took a breath before answering, trying her best to sound calm. She was dealing with residual anxiety, as always when Gordon went out on a date. He had a very bad tendency to overdo things and shower his companions with gifts he couldn't afford.

When she finally spoke, it was in a low voice, the same voice he'd heard on the answering machine. "I don't see the need to make her paranoid if I'm around to watch her. Kelli knows enough not to talk to someone she doesn't know if she's alone—which she never is," Janice added firmly. "Besides," she continued, "Kelli's a very good judge of character."

Now that he found hard to believe. "And she's how old?"

He was mocking her, Janice thought. Probably thought she was one of those doting mothers who thought their kid walked on water. But Kelli seemed to have a radar when it came to nice people. She turned very shy around the other type.

"Age doesn't always matter," she told Zabelle. Gordon, for instance, had the impaired judgment of a two-month-old Labrador puppy. Everyone was his friend—until proven otherwise. The later happened far too often. He had a *V* on his forehead for victim and self-serving women could hone in on it from a fifty-mile radius. "Sometimes all it takes are good instincts." Something Gordon didn't seem to possess when it came to women. He fell prey to one gold digger after another. The sad part was that he never caught on. And if she said anything, her brother felt she was being a shrew.

It was hard to believe that he was the older one.

Because he'd asked and her mother hadn't answered, Kelli held up four fingers and bent her thumb to illustrate what she was about to say. "I'm four and three-quarters." She dropped her hand and then added in a stage whisper that would have made a Shakespearean actor proud, "Mama says I'm going on forty."

The unassuming remark made him laugh. "I can believe that."

"Why don't we get down to business?" Janice suggested. She wanted to wrap this up as quickly as possible, especially if it didn't lead anywhere. She hadn't had a chance to prepare dinner yet. That had been Gordon's job, but then Sheila, the latest keeper of his heart, had called and he'd forgotten everything else. When she'd come home from wrapping up a job, he'd all but run over her in his haste to leave the house.

"Good, you're finally home. Gotta run." And he did. Literally.

"Dinner?" she'd called after him.

"Yeah," he'd tossed over her shoulder. "I'm taking her out. Seems she's free after all."

Which had meant that whoever Sheila had planned to go out with had cancelled.

There'd been no time for Janice to prepare dinner before her appointment, so she'd tossed an apple to Kelli, strapped her into her car seat and driven over to the address she'd copied down. But now her stomach was making her pay for it by rumbling. She wished she'd grabbed an apple for herself.

"Fine with me," Philippe told her. He gestured toward the sink. Running the length of the sink from one end to the other, the crack was hard to miss. "I need that replaced."

Instead of looking at the sink, Janice slowly examined the bathroom, taking in details and cataloguing them in her head. Judging by appearances, no one had done anything to the oversized powder room with the undersized shower in about thirty years.

The dead giveaway was the carpet on the floor. It was very 1970s.

Finished assessing, she turned to him. "Looks to me as if you could stand to have the whole bathroom replaced."

He hadn't given any serious thought to any large-scale renovations, but he knew he wouldn't want them handled by a wisp of a woman. "Oh?"

She nodded as if he'd just agreed with her. "The tile is very bland," she pointed to the wall. "It dates the room, as does the carpet. And you're missing grout in several places." She indicated just where. "My guess is that it was probably scrubbed out over the years." She based her assumption on the fact that there didn't appear to be any visible mold. Left to their own devices, most men had bathrooms that doubled as giant petri dishes, growing several different strains of mold and fungus. "Whoever's been cleaning your bathroom has been doing an excellent job, but scrubbing does take its toll on tile and grout after a while."

He wasn't sure if she was giving him a compliment or trying to get him to volunteer more information about his personal life. In either case, he shrugged. "I just find things to spray on it—whenever I remember," he added, thinking of the last time he'd had the opportunity to go to the grocery store.

The tiny snippet of information impressed her. "A man who cleans his own bathroom." She said it the way someone might announce they'd just discovered a unicorn. "I'll have to have my brother come meet you."

That was the last thing he wanted—unless her brother was part of her crew. The second he had the thought, he realized she had somehow subtly gotten him to consider the idea of renovations rather than a simple replacement.

Still, maybe that wouldn't be such a bad thing. He looked at her in silence for a minute, then decided to ask a hypothetical question. "Okay, pure speculation."

"Yes?" she returned gamely, mentally crossing her fingers.

"If I were to do this bathroom over." And now that he thought of it, it did look pretty washed out and lifeless. "What would something like that run?"

There was no easy answer. She was surprised that he expected one—was he the type that liked having everything neatly pigeonholed? "That depends on what you'd want done."

Nothing until five minutes ago, he thought. "Nothing fancy," he said aloud. "Just replacing what's here with newer fixtures."

She glanced down at the worn short-shag carpeting that went from one wall to another. Why would anyone have ever considered that acceptable? "And tile for the floor."

That surprised him. J.D. had hit on the one thing

he'd been toying with having done—when he got around to it. He'd never cared for having a carpet in the bathroom. It got way too soggy from wet feet.

"And tile for the floor," he echoed, agreeing.

Well, at least they were beginning on the same page. "Different quality fixtures affect the total sum," she maintained.

"Ballpark figure," he requested, then amended it by saying, "what you'd charge for your labor, since I'm guessing the materials would cost me the same as you if I went and got them myself."

"More," she corrected. He looked at her quizzically. "Unless you just happen to have a contractor's license in your pocket."

He patted either pocket, causing Kelli to giggle. He realized he liked the sound of that. "Fresh out." He hooked his thumbs in the corners of his front pockets. "So I get a break hiring you?"

She didn't want to come across as pushy. People who applied too much pressure wound up losing their potential customers. It was the one thing she'd learned by watching her father. "Or any contractor."

He couldn't ask what the materials would come to until he decided on the materials. But he could ask her about her fee. He'd never liked flying blind. "Okay, what's your bottom line?"

This time the giggle needed two hands to keep it restrained—and still it came through. "Mama doesn't have a line on her bottom," Kelli piped up, her eyes dancing with amusement.

For a second, as he stared down into the eyes of the improbable woman behind the initials, he'd almost lost his train of thought. He'd definitely forgotten that her daughter was there.

Philippe laughed now at the serious expression that had slipped over what had been an incredibly sunny little face. "I didn't mean—"

"The bottom line means what things will cost," Janice explained to her daughter, speaking as if Kelli were a business associate being trained on the job.

Maybe she was, he thought, then dismissed the idea as ridiculous. It was way too soon to be training that little girl to do anything but enjoy life to the fullest and he had a sneaking suspicion those lessons had already been given.

"Oh," was all he trusted himself to say.

Janice turned toward him and after pausing a moment to take things in again and, doing a few mental calculations in her head, she gave him a quote.

He stared at her incredulously. "You're serious," he asked.

"Yes, why?"

The why was because she'd given him a bid that sounded much too low, even if it did only include her labor and not the cost of materials. "How do you stay in business with fees like that?"

She breathed a silent sigh of relief. He wasn't one of those tightwads who thought everything had to be haggled down.

"Low overhead," Janice quipped without hesitation. She ventured a little further. Once people got their feet wet, they usually decided they wanted something else done. She began with the logical choice. "Is this the only bathroom you want renovated?"

"I didn't even want this one renovated," he informed her, then abruptly stopped. The quote she'd given him was more than reasonable, coming in far lower than he would have expected. He wasn't up on the price of bathroom renovations, per se, but one of the people who marketed his software packages had just had a bathroom redone. The man had proudly given him a quote that had taken his breath away. Philippe remembered thinking that his maternal grandfather had paid less for his house when he'd bought it forty years ago than the man had paid to have his bathroom upgraded. "The other two are upstairs."

"You have three bathrooms?" Kelli asked gleefully, her eyes huge.

He had no idea why the little girl would find that a source of wonder. "Yes."

"We only have two," she confided, then leaned into him and added, "And Uncle Gordon is always in one."

Janice saw Zabelle raise his eyes and look at her quizzically. She didn't want him thinking that Gordon was strange. "My brother is staying with us while he gets back on his feet."

Kelli's silken blond curls fairly bounced as she turned her head around to face her. "Uncle Gordon gets on his feet every day, Mama."

It was an expression, but she didn't feel like trying to explain that to Kelli right now. Instead, she stroked Kelli's hair and said, "Only for short periods of time, baby."

Instinctively, Janice glanced at the man whose house they were in. She recognized curiosity when she saw it, even though she had her doubts that the man even knew the expression had registered on his face. She felt obligated to defend her brother against what she guessed this man had to be thinking.

"My brother's had a tough time of it lately." *Lately* encompassed the period from his birth up to the present day, she added silently.

Zabelle seemed to take the information in stride. "At least he has family."

The comment took her by surprise. Janice hadn't expected the man to say that. It was by all accounts a sensitive observation.

Maybe the man wasn't half bad after all.

"Yes," she agreed with a note of enthusiasm in her voice as she came to the landing, "he does. By the way," she said, leaning outside the bathroom wall and looking at him, "I noticed your kitchen."

This time, he thought, he was ready for her. Ready

to put a firm lid on this before it escalated into something that necessitated his moving out of the house for several weeks. "And?"

"Could stand to have a bit of a face-lift as well."

"This was about a cracked sink," Philippe reminded her.

It was never just about a cracked sink. By the time that stage was reached, other things were in need of fixing and replacing as well. "I thought that the oldest son of Lily Moreau would be more open to productive suggestions—even if they do come from a woman who owns a tool belt." She saw the surprise in his eyes grow. "I have access to the Internet," she pointed out glibly. "And I try to learn as much as I can about potential clients before I meet with them."

He noticed that she said the word *potential* as if it was to be discarded while the word *client* had a healthy amount of enthusiasm associated with it. The woman was obviously very sure of herself.

Even so, he didn't like having his mind made up for him.

Chapter Four

"So, are you going to do his bathrooms, Mama?" Kelli piped up as they finally drove away from Philippe Zabelle's house.

Easing her foot on the brake as she approached a red light, Janice glanced up into the rearview mirror. Kelli sat directly behind her in her car seat, something she suffered with grace. Car seats were required for the four and under set, something she insisted she no longer was inasmuch as she was four and three-quarters.

Kelli was waving her feet at just a barely lesser tempo than a hummingbird flapped its wings. Any second now, her daughter would lift off, seat and all.

Energy really was wasted on the young. "Yes. I'll be redoing them."

"And the kitchen, too?" There was excitement in Kelli's voice.

It never failed to amaze her just how closely Kelli paid attention. Another child wouldn't have even noticed what was going on. Too bad Kelli couldn't give Gordon lessons.

"Yes, the kitchen, too."

That had been touch and go for a bit, but then she'd managed to convince Zabelle there were wonderful possibilities available to him. She wasn't trying to line her pockets so much as she felt a loyalty to give her client the benefit of her expertise and creative eye.

In actuality, the whole house could do with a makeover, but she was content to have gotten this far. Three bathrooms and a kitchen. Now all she needed was to get to her computer and start sketching.

"And what else?" Kelli wanted to know.

God, but the little girl sounded so grown up at times, Janice thought. Her foot on the accelerator, she drove through the intersection and made a right at the next corner. "That's it for now, honey."

Despite the fact that she was a good craftsperson and she had a contractor's license, obtained in the days when there'd been an actual decent-sized company to work for—her father's—Janice knew she worked at a definite disadvantage. Philippe Zabelle was not the only man skeptical about hiring a woman to handle his renovations. Her own father had been like that, even though she'd proven herself to him over and over again.

He always favored Gordon over her.

She supposed she was partially to blame for that. Because she loved him, she always covered up for Gordon when he messed up, doing his work for him so that he wouldn't have to endure their father's wrath.

Even now, the memory of that wrath made her involuntarily shiver.

Sisterly love ultimately caused her to be shut out. When he died, her father had left the company to Gordon. There wasn't even a single provision about her—or her baby—in Jake Wyatt's will.

It was a cold thing to do, she thought now, her hands tightening on the steering wheel as she eked through the next light.

Gordon had had as much interest in the company as a muskrat had in buying a winter coat from a major department store. Without their father around to cast his formidable shadow, Gordon became drunk on freedom. He turned his attention away from the business and toward the pursuit of his one true passion—women. A year and a half after their father died the company belonged to the bank because of the loans Gordon drew against Wyatt Construction, and she, a widow with a young child and three-quarters of a college degree, had to hustle in order to provide for herself and Kelli.

At first, she'd been desperate to take anything that came her way. She quickly discovered that she hated sales, hated being a waitress and the scores of other dead-end endeavors she undertook in order to pay the bills. Dying to get back to the one thing she knew she was good at and loved doing, she'd advertised in the local neighborhood paper, posted ads on any space she could find on community billboards and slowly, very slowly, got back into the game.

But every contracting job she eventually landed was preceded by a fair amount of hustling and verbal tap dancing to convince the client that she was every bit as good as the next contractor—and more than likely better because she'd been doing it for most of her life. She was the one, not Gordon, who liked to follow their father around, lugging a toolbox and mimicking his every move. Dolls held no interest for her, drill bits did.

"Mama," the exasperated little voice behind her rose another octave as Kelli tried to get her attention, "I asked you a question."

Their eyes met in the mirror. Janice did her best to look contrite. "Sorry, baby, I was thinking about something else for a second. What do you want to know?"

"Is he gonna want more?"

For a second, Janice had lost the thread of the conversation Kelli was conducting. "Who?"

She heard Kelli sigh mightily. She pressed her lips together, trying not to laugh. Sometimes it almost felt as if their roles were reversed and Kelli was the mom while she was the kid.

"The man with the pretty painting, Mama."

Now Janice really did draw a blank. "Painting?" she echoed, trying to remember if she'd noticed a painting anywhere. She came up empty.

"Yes. In the living room." Kelli carefully enunciated every word, as if afraid she would lose her mother's attention at any second. "There was a big blue lake and trees and—didn't you see it, Mama?" Kelli asked impatiently.

"Apparently not."

Art was definitely Kelli's passion. The little girl had been drawing ever since she could hold a pencil in her hand. The swirls and stick figures that first emerged quickly gave way to recognizable shapes and characters at an amazingly young age. Beautiful characters that seemed to have personalities radiating from them. It was her fervent dream to send her daughter to a good art school and encourage the gift she had. Kelli was never going to go through what she had, wasn't going to have her ability dismissed, devalued and ignored.

"I'll have to go look at it the next time I'm there," she told her daughter, then paused before asking, "You are talking about Mr. Zabelle's house, right?"

Kelli sighed again. "Right." And then she got back to what she'd said initially. "Maybe he'll want you to do more when he sees how good you are."

Bless her, Janice thought. "That would be nice." To

that end, she'd left the man with a battery of catalogues, some of which dealt with rooms other than the kitchen and the bath. A girl could always hope.

"If you do more, will we have enough for a pony?" Kelli asked.

Ah, the pony issue again. Another passion, but one that had far less chance of being realized. At least for the present. But she played along because it was easier that way than squelching Kelli's hopes. "Not yet, honey. Ponies need a special place to stay and special food to eat, remember?"

The golden head bobbed up and down. "When will we have enough for a pony?"

"I'll let you know," Janice promised.

Making another turn, she looked down at her left hand. She still missed the rings that had been there. The ones she'd been forced to pawn in January to pay bills. January was always a slow month as far as business was concerned. The month that people focused on trying to pay off the debts they'd run up during the Christmas season. Room additions and renovation moved to the back of the line.

If there was any money leftover after the Zabelle job, she was going to put it toward getting her rings out of hock. The stone on the engagement ring wasn't very large, but Gary had picked it out for her and she loved it.

A bittersweet feeling wafted over her. She and Gary

had gotten engaged one week, then married two weeks later because he'd discovered that his unit was being sent clear across to the other side of the world to fight. He never returned under his own power.

She fought back against the feeling that threatened to overwhelm her. Five years and it was still there, waiting for an unguarded moment. Waiting to conquer her. Again.

But you did what you had to do in order to keep going. Pawning her rings had been her only option at the time. Bills needed to be paid. The rings didn't mean very much if there wasn't a roof over Kelli's head. After Gordon had lost the business, she was very mindful of not putting her daughter and herself in jeopardy of losing the things that were most important to them. That meant not waiting until the last minute before taking measures to safeguard home and hearth.

"Can we go out to eat, Mama?"

Trust Kelli to ground her, she thought. She felt guilty about letting herself get sidetracked. "You bet, kid. You get to pick the place."

That required absolutely no thought on Kelli's part. "I wanna go to the pizza place."

Pizza was by far her daughter's favorite food. Janice laughed. "You are going to turn into a pizza someday, Kel."

Her comment was met with a giggle. The sound warmed Janice's heart.

* * *

"Where's your cheering section?" Philippe asked two evenings later when he found only J.D. on his doorstep. He leaned over the threshold and looked around in case the little girl was hiding.

"Home," she informed him. He stepped back to let her in. "My babysitter doesn't have a date tonight." When Gordon's newest flame found out about his cash-flow problems—basically that it wasn't even trickling, much less flowing—she quickly became history. When she'd left to come here, Kelli and Gordon were watching the Disney Channel together. "Kelli wanted to come along." But this was going to involve long discussions of fees and she preferred not subjecting her daughter to that. "I think she likes you."

Walking into the living room, Janice abruptly stopped before the framed twenty-four by thirty-six painting hanging on the wall.

My God, it was so large, how had she missed that the first time?

Because she was focusing on landing this job, she thought. She tended to have tunnel vision when it came to work, letting nothing else distract her. Although she had to admit that she had noticed Philippe Zabelle would never be cast as the frog in the Grimm Brothers' "The Frog Prince."

Janice redirected her attention to the painting. It was

breath-taking. Kelli had an eye, all right. "I know she likes your painting."

"My *mother's* painting," he corrected, in case she thought that he had painted it. "I'll let my mother know she has a new fan. I know she'll be delighted to hear that she's finally cracked the under-ten set. Most kids don't even notice painting unless they're forcibly dragged to an art museum."

Forcibly dragged. Zabelle sounded as if he was speaking from experience. Had his mother forced art on him, attempted to make him appreciate it before he was ready? She'd taken Kelli to the Museum of Contemporary Art in Los Angeles when the little girl had still been in a stroller. Kelli had been enthralled.

"Most kids didn't start drawing when they are barely three," she countered.

He led the way to the kitchen table. She had paperwork for him, he surmised. He eyed her quizzically. "Drawing?"

Pride wiggled through her like a deep-seated flirtation. "Drawing."

He assumed she was being loose with her terminology. He remembered his brothers trying to emulate their mother. Best efforts resembled the spiral trail left by the Tasmanian devil.

"You mean as in scribbling?"

"No," she said firmly, "I mean as in drawing."

He laughed softly, pulling out a chair for her. "Spoken like a true doting mother."

Janice took mild offense. Not for herself, but for Kelli. Her daughter deserved better than that. "I'll show you."

"You carry around her portfolio?" he asked incredulously. When he saw her reaching into the battered briefcase that contained the contracts she'd brought with her for him to sign, Philippe realized that only one of them thought that what he'd just said was a joke. She snapped open the locks and lifted the lid. "You're kidding."

Janice didn't bother answering him. A picture, as they said, is worth a thousand words. She could protest that Kelli was as talented as they come, but he needed to see for himself. So, lifting up several manila folders and her trusty laptop, she took Kelli's latest drawing out of the case. It was of a white stallion from Kelli's favorite cartoon show.

Very carefully, she placed the drawing on top of her briefcase and then turned it toward him.

Philippe's eyes widened. "You're not kidding," he murmured.

As he admired the drawing, he shook his head. There was no way the bouncy little thing he'd met two nights ago had done this. He sincerely doubted that she could sit still long enough to finish it.

He made contact with J.D. "You did that."

She laughed softly. "I wish. My ability doesn't go beyond drawing rectangles and squares. I can do blueprints," she concluded. "I can't do horses."

Zabelle took the drawing from her. She curled her fingers into her hand to keep from grabbing it back. She was very protective of Kelli and that protectiveness extended to her daughter's things and her talent. It was a trait she would have to rein in if Kelli was ever going to grow up to be an independent adult.

Philippe gave her one last chance to withdraw her statement. "She really drew this."

"She really drew that," Janice told him proudly.

For the first half of his life, when his mother wasn't immersed in the creation of her own work or either nurturing along a new relationship or burying an old one, she had tried her very best to get him to follow in her footsteps. While he shared her talent to a degree, he had rebelled and steadfastly refused.

His reasons were simple. Art was her domain, he wasn't going to venture into it. Nor was he ready to stand in her shadow, struggling to be his own person. He needed a medium, a venue that belonged to him alone. A path apart from hers.

But that didn't keep him from admiring someone else's gift. "Can I hang onto this for a little while?" he asked abruptly.

The request caught Janice by surprise. "Why?"

The man just didn't strike her as the post-it-on-the-refrigerator type, which was where this had been until, on a whim, she'd packed it in with her contracts. She'd told herself that it would act as a good luck talisman.

"I'd like to show this to my mother the next time she flies in here."

"Your mother's out of state?" she asked, a little confused.

"No." He pulled out a chair and straddled it, resting his arms on the back. "She's right here in Bedford, California. My mother's a little larger than life and she gives the impression of flying whenever she enters a room."

"Oh, I see." She found herself wanting to meet this dynamo. Her own mother had left a long time ago, before she ever really established a relationship with her. She just remembered a tall, thin woman with light blond hair and an air of impatience about her. Eventually that impatience had led her out the door, a note on the kitchen table left in her wake. "Well, then I guess it's all right. If she asks me about it, I'll just tell Kelli that the lady who painted the landscape in your living room is going to look at her drawing."

"Why not just tell her that I have it? Why give her this longer version?"

She could see he hadn't dealt much with children. "Would you like a short person laying siege to your house?" she deadpanned. "The minute I tell her that you have it, that you thought it was good, there will be no peace," she amended, her eyes on his. "Kelli will want to know what your mother thought of it, if she liked it. She'll want to know what your mother thought was good about it. And that's only after she quizzes me about your reaction to her work. Trust me, my way is better."

She sounded as if she was speaking about an adult, a thoughtful adult. The woman was giving her daughter way too much credit. And yet…

Philippe looked down at the drawing again. He had to admit he was in awe. "I don't know all that much about kids, but your daughter seems like one very unusual little girl."

Janice laughed. Now there was an understatement. "That she is."

Reaching for her briefcase again, this time to take the contracts out, she accidentally knocked the case off the table. Half the papers flew out. They both bent down at the same time to retrieve what had fallen; they both reached for the case and folders at the exact same moment. Which was how their fingers managed to brush against each other's.

It was, at best, a scene from a grade-B romantic movie, circa 1950. There was absolutely no reason to feel a jolt, electrifying or otherwise. And yet, there it was. Jolting. Electrifying. Fleeting, granted, but still very much there. Completely unexpected and zipping its way along the skin of her arms and simultaneously swirling up along the back of her neck.

Janice caught her breath, trying to make her pulse slow down. The last time she'd been with a man was three years ago. That even had been a terrible mistake, but it seemed like the right thing to do at the time.

But this, this was deeply seated in deprivation, not anything else. Deprivation, because she'd been leading the kind of life that would have made a crusty nun proud. But this small, accidental encounter had definitely rattled her cage.

She did her best to appear unaffected, as if, for a moment, her insides hadn't just turned to jelly.

"Thanks." Straightening, she picked up the contracts—one for each room—and placed them on the table. "Let's go over these, shall we?" she asked, her throat feeling uncomfortably tight. "I want to make sure I've got everything right. I don't want you finding that you're in for any surprises."

Too late, he thought. Because his reaction to her had already more than surprised him. But he put a lid on his thoughts and smiled at her. "Don't you like surprises?"

"I do, but my clients don't—not when it comes to cost, at any rate."

He rose, crossing to the refrigerator. "Would you like something to drink?" he asked.

The room—the house from what she could see—looked exactly the same as it did the other day. The man really was rather neat. Or had he found that housekeeper he'd mistaken her for?

"Diet soda—if you have any."

"As a matter of fact, I do." He'd gone to the store

earlier today and picked up a six pack. He had no idea what possessed him to do that because neither he nor his brothers nor any of his friends drank diet soda.

Maybe he'd just anticipated J.D., he decided, returning to the table with a can of diet soda. He placed a glass next to it.

Janice popped open the can and, ignoring the glass, took a long sip before speaking. "The hunt for a housekeeper, did you find one?" She set the can back down, wrapping her hands around it.

Philippe shrugged, straddling the chair again and pulling it closer to the table. "I decided to pull the ad."

"Oh?" she tried to sound casual. "Why?"

"Well, if the house is going to look like the site of the next demolition derby, that kind of negates the need for a housekeeper right now." A beer, he needed a beer. If he was going to go on staring into eyes the color of sky, he was going to need something to fortify him. Philippe made his way back to the refrigerator. "I'll hire one once things are back to normal."

Whatever that is, he added silently.

Chapter Five

He hadn't called.

Janice sighed, staring at the calendar on the kitchen wall depicting various breeds of puppies. Philippe Zabelle hadn't called—not on her land line, not on her cell. There were no messages waiting for her. She'd checked. Frequently.

Damn.

It'd been a little more than a week since the man had signed the contracts to have work done on his house. At the time, she'd noted he took the quotes in stride, not quibbling over any of the charges for demolition, cleanup and construction.

Maybe the reason Zabelle hadn't bothered quibbling was because he'd had no intentions of seeing the project move any further beyond his signing the contracts for each of his bathrooms and kitchen.

Eight days.

She'd finished the room extension she'd been doing for the Gilhooleys in Tustin. Faced with spare time, she'd gone to St. Cecelia's and done some handiwork there, replacing a window at the school, refitting a door at the priest's residence and fixing the hole in the roof where four tiles had blown away in the last storm. She'd finished that two days ago.

Right now, she was between jobs and at very loose ends. Janice had never done leisure well, never learned how to sit still for long, especially not when there were bills to pay.

And Gordon wasn't helping any, she thought, glancing over toward him accusingly. Her big brother was part of the problem, definitely not part of the solution. At the moment, he was lying on her sofa, dozing in front of the TV set. There was a baseball game droning on in the background. The Dodgers were losing.

Welcome to the club.

She sighed. The only one being productive around here at the moment was Kelli, who had spread out her paint set on the dining room table and was painting a woodland scene.

She needed to get that girl an easel, Janice thought. As soon as there was money for things like that.

Frustrated, she walked over to the sofa and shook Gordon's shoulder. It had no effect. Her brother went right on sleeping. Subtlety was obviously not working, so she doubled up her fist and punched him in the arm.

Gordon jolted awake.

"Hey!" he cried in protest, grabbing his arm where she'd made contact.

Gordon had never been one to endure pain stoically. "I hardly tapped you."

"You have a punch like a welterweight champion," he complained, looking at his arm as if he expected it to fall off. "What's wrong with you?"

"Everything. Look, Gordon." She sank down on the arm on the far end of the sofa. "I know you're going through a rough patch right now," she acknowledged charitably, "but you're going to have to help out here a little."

"I do," he protested indignantly. When she looked at him, mystified, he nodded over toward Kelli. "I watch the pip-squeak."

Janice pressed her lips together, struggling not to point out that their financial difficulties were largely because of him. "I meant help out with the expenses."

His eyebrows drew together over the bridge of his nose. "How?"

Wow, was it really that hard for him to connect the dots? "Get a job, Gordon. Get a job."

He sighed, as if that was a goal he aspired to, but wasn't quite able to reach just yet. "I'm still trying to find myself, J.D."

"Good news," she declared. "I found you. You're on the sofa. Now get off it and get yourself a damn job, Gordon."

"And do what?" he challenged.

She threw up her hands. "Sell ties at a major department store, wait on tables at Indigo's, become a bank teller. Anything." When Gordon made no response, she added through gritted teeth, "The way I did when you torpedoed Wyatt Construction right out from under me."

The look he gave her said she'd severely wounded him by bringing the past up. "I don't want to take just anything, J.D."

Easy for him to say. He had *never* hustled for a job. On those occasions when she landed a remodeling assignment that required more than just one person, she hired him on to help and, for the most part, things worked out. But the rest of the time, he seemed content to be "looking for himself" and doing absolutely nothing. Well, it couldn't continue.

Getting up, she crossed to him and lowered her face so that it was level to his. "You like to eat, don't you? Have a roof over your head? Shower daily? News flash, big brother. The best things in life *aren't* free."

He ignored the fact that she was now in his face. "When did you get so mercenary?"

"When you abdicated the position of adult and

became my other child," she retorted. If anything, she thought of him as being younger than Kelli.

"Ouch." Gordon cringed dramatically, as if ducking a blow. "Just because you're not working, don't take it out on me."

"I'm not taking it out on you," she countered, her patience dangerously low. "I just want you to pull your load. I just—" Exasperated, she waved her hand at him. "Oh, never mind."

"Okay then—" he settled back against the pillow, stretching his legs out before him "—maybe if I try hard, I can get back to the dream you so rudely terminated for me."

The temptation to smother him with his pillow was tremendous. She struggled to calm herself down. Janice knew her brother didn't mean anything by this and he really was having a rough time of it. Gordon seemed to fail at everything he tried, but she was bound and determined to keep him from sliding into some sort of black hole and dwelling there for the remainder of his life. He needed to stand up on his own two feet—the very minute he took them out of a certain part of his posterior.

And she supposed he was right in his own strange way. She *was* taking out her frustration over her forced inactivity on him. She had a perfectly good job lined up with some very nice additions, but she was stuck in first gear until Zabelle called her.

Or she found out what the holdup was.

The best way to do that was to beard the lion in his den. And she knew where the lion lived.

Janice abruptly made her way over to her daughter. "Sweetie," she called out. After taking another stroke the little girl stopped and glanced up at her. "I've got to go out for a while. Keep an eye on your Uncle Gordon for me, okay?"

Her request was met with a sunny smile. "You can count on me, Mama."

"I know." She kissed the top of Kelli's head. "More than on him," Janice added under her breath as she left the room.

She briefly thought about changing, but then decided that there was no point. This was the way she looked when she was working and, besides, she wasn't trying to impress Zabelle with her looks, just with her talent and her ability to get the job done in record time. Which she couldn't do if she didn't get started, she thought angrily.

This was why contractors took on more than one job at a time, she decided, getting behind the wheel of her 4x4. So that they wouldn't have to waste precious days with any downtime, some contractors would sign on for two, three jobs concurrently. But that had never been the way she operated. She believed in giving each job her complete, undivided attention from start to finish, finishing it and *then* moving on, not playing musical houses and going from one job to another as if they were all part of some kind of life-size round-robin.

She'd developed all the skills needed for this kind of work—all except for the tough hide. Ignoring the needs and requirements of others to satisfy her own just wasn't her style.

Janice knew, for instance, that she should be harder on Gordon, that maybe what he needed was a swift kick in the seat to get him moving and to make him repentant for losing the company, but she couldn't get herself to do it. Besides, she didn't see how making him feel guilty about losing the company would help since it would all be after the fact and it wouldn't accomplish anything. It certainly wouldn't get the company back.

It had taken her a while to come to grips with the loss. But, as always, she'd rallied and told herself that the company was not something that the bank held a deed to, the company was her—and Gordon when she could light a fire under him and get him to help.

At the time of her father's death, the company had included eight other men, men who had since gone on to work for other contractors, or left the area or even the business. But they were just the craftsmen. She was the heart of it, she was the blood that pumped through its veins.

And she wasn't going anywhere.

"You're not kidding," she murmured to herself as the irony of the phrase hit her. She turned her truck down Zabelle's street. She'd never get anywhere if jobs kept drying up on her.

Well, she wasn't about to let this one dry up, at least not without knowing the reason why. He owed her that much.

The house where Philippe Zabelle resided was located on a through street. It was part of a community of townhomes made to resemble well-spaced single dwellings that had lawns like lush green carpets. Bedford was considered to be one of the more upscale cities within Southern California. None of the neighborhoods were allowed to run down. Everything looked new or at least lovingly cared for. There was an abundance of pride within the city that kept its homes neat and looking their best.

Parking her car by the curb, Janice marched up the dozen or so white cement stairs that led up to the front door and knocked. First once, then twice and then a third time.

Nothing.

Maybe she should have called first, she thought. But if she had called and Zabelle had told her not to come, she would have lost the advantage of talking to him face to face. She always did better in person than over the phone.

Janice raised her hand to knock one more time.

"Looking for Philippe?"

Startled, her hand still raised, she swung around and found a tall, good-looking, dark-haired man with an easy smile and kind eyes standing to her left. She hadn't even heard him approach. Belatedly, she dropped her hand, realizing that, had he been standing any closer to her, she would have wound up punching him.

"Yes," she said when she regained possession of her voice. "I guess he's not home."

"Oh, he's in there," the man assured her. "He just tends to slip into another world when he's working. Doesn't see or hear anything else but what's on the screen in front of him."

"Dedicated," she commented.

The man smiled, amused. "One way of looking at it." Taking out a key, he unlocked the front door, pushed it open, then stood back. "Go ahead," he urged, gesturing toward the inside of the house.

She hung back. "I don't know if I should just walk in."

"I do it all the time." A grin flashed as he pocketed the key and he extended his hand to her. "Hi, I'm Georges. Philippe's brother," he added.

"Oh." Realizing that she was standing there like a bump on a log, Janice slipped her hand into his and shook it.

Georges's dark blue eyes were bright with curiosity as they swept over her. There was something unobtrusive about the way he did it. She took no offense. "And you are?"

"J. D. Wyatt," she told him, then added, "I'm supposed to do some work on your brother's house."

Recognition entered his eyes. "Oh, right, you're the

one Vincent mentioned." And then, as his own words registered, he seemed to do a mental double take. "You're J.D.?"

She smiled, removing her hand from his. This was the reaction she was accustomed to. "Not exactly what you expected, right?"

Rather than look embarrassed, he grinned. The man was charming, she thought. His brother could probably stand to pick up a few pointers—not that that mattered in the scheme of things, she reminded herself.

"Only in my better dreams," he told her. "Philippe didn't mention that he actually hired anyone, only that he was thinking about it."

That didn't bode well, Janice thought. Had Zabelle changed his mind after all? He'd signed contracts, but there was always a way around that if a person was clever and she didn't have the money for a lawyer to fight him on this anyway. Served her right from not insisting on getting a check right up front, right after Zabelle had signed on the dotted lines.

"But then," Georges added quickly, "Philippe doesn't say that much of anything, especially when he's in the middle of a project."

She had a feeling that Zabelle's brother was just trying to make her feel better. She examined him more closely. As brothers, they were more different than alike, she decided. "What does he do, your brother?"

"A little bit of everything." There was no missing the

pride in the man's voice. "But officially, Philippe's a computer programmer. Right now, he's designing software packages for online advertisers."

She glanced toward the opened door. They still had not gone inside. "And he works at home?"

Georges nodded. "Turns into a regular hermit when he's in the middle of designing something." He walked in, then turned when she didn't follow him. "C'mon, let's track him down."

When she'd gotten behind the wheel, she had been completely fired up. But on the way over, some of that fire had dissipated. It was one thing to confront the man at his door and read him an abbreviated version of the riot act about wasting her time, it was another to go from room to room, looking for him and running the risk of possibly catching him in a way he wouldn't want to be caught. God knew she wouldn't have appreciated having someone skulking around her house, looking for her.

She forced a smile to her lips. "Why don't you find him for me?" she suggested. Because he was looking at her expectantly, she ventured a few steps into the house, then indicated the living room. "I'll be right here, waiting for you."

The smile on his lips washed over her, leaving no part untouched. She really, really had to start dating again. Either that or begin working out rigorously—which she'd be doing if she were working, she silently insisted, bringing the argument full circle.

"Have it your way," Georges said. Turning, he faced the rear of the house and called out, "Hey, Philippe, where're you hiding?"

Still standing, Janice knotted her fingers together, feeling incredibly awkward. She closed her eyes for a second, trying to frame her first words to Zabelle under the present circumstances.

Georges had no sooner left the area than Philippe walked in from the kitchen. He stopped abruptly when he saw that there was a woman standing in the living room. The math equations that he'd been mentally grappling with receded as recognition set in.

J.D.

That still didn't answer what she was doing here. Or how she'd gotten in. He was damn certain he'd locked the front door. "Did I miss seeing cat burglar on your résumé?"

Her eyes flew open. Surprise and embarrassment took equal possession of her features. The resulting color was rather intriguing.

"I knocked," Janice protested.

He was pretty sure he hadn't heard anyone knocking, but he gave her the benefit of the doubt. Because of where his office was located, he probably wouldn't have heard the approach of the Four Horsemen, either.

"And then broke in?" he guessed.

"No," she protested quickly. The color in her cheeks rose up another notch. "Your brother let me in."

Both of his brothers were a bit too free about coming

and going from his place, but then, he supposed he should count himself lucky. It could have been his mother and there would have been no end to her questions. To J.D.

"Which one?" he asked mildly.

"He said his name was Georges." Curiosity got the better of her. "You have more than one?"

The shrug was careless. He wasn't about to be sidetracked. "I like having a spare. What are you doing here?"

She heard the slight tone of irritation in his voice. Any apology she was about to tender vanished. He was on the offensive? He didn't have the right to take the offensive. If anything, he was supposed to be on the *de*fensive, explaining why he'd kept her dangling the way he had.

Janice forgot about being uncomfortable and invading the man's space, and thought about being made to play hide and seek with her ever-growing stack of bills.

"I'm here to find out why you're welching," she said without preamble.

He stared at her, dumbfounded. "Welching?"

Okay, maybe that was a tad too harsh. She rephrased. "We had a deal, remember?"

"Yes, of course I remember. Frankly, I was wondering why you hadn't gotten started." He'd been too bogged down with a glitch in the program to notice during the day, but at night it would hit him that she hadn't called or shown up. By the time it registered, it was always too late for him to call and investigate.

She stared at him incredulously. He was serious. Either that or playing her for a fool. For the moment, she ignored the latter and began to talk to him as if he were mentally challenged. "I can't get started until you tell me what you picked out."

His response told her that she'd guessed correctly. The man had no clue. "Picked out?"

"The tile," she prompted. "Picked out the tile." She didn't see a light dawning in his eyes. How could he be that obtuse?

Again, Philippe shrugged. The mundane had little hold on him. "I don't know. I thought you were supposed to handle all that. I was okay with the drawings," he reminded her.

That was for the redesign of the kitchen and the bathrooms. That didn't take any of the materials into account.

"Yes, you were," she enunciated each word slowly, "but I don't know what color you want. What kind of cabinets you'd like to put in or even what kind of tile you want me to use."

He looked at her for a long moment, as if the words were slipping into his brain one at a time and he was processing them. "Tile comes in kinds?"

Having dealt with this world all of her life, it was impossible for Janice to imagine that anyone was ignorant of this sort of thing. Especially anyone who appeared to be intelligent. "Have you even been to a tile store?"

"No."

"Okay, baby steps," she murmured, more to herself. She made a spur of the moment decision. "All right, I'll take you." She just needed to call home and make sure that Gordon wasn't about to run off somewhere and forget that he had a niece to watch over.

Zabelle still didn't seem to be following her. "Take me where?"

"To a tile store."

Or two or three, she added silently, keeping that to herself. She guessed that if the man were told that this was a process that took most people several afternoons, he would balk and make excuses why he couldn't go.

His eyes narrowed. It didn't look encouraging. "When?"

"Now." It was half a query, half a direct order.

He shook his head. "I can't go now. I'm in the middle of something."

"How long before you're not in the middle of something?" she asked.

Philippe thought for a second. The deadline had been moved just yesterday. He'd never been comfortable about rushing through a project. That was his name on the cover and his reputation meant a great deal to him. "End of November."

Janice looked at him, stunned. November was three months away. She couldn't stretch things out until then. "Look, if you're trying to break the contracts—"

"Go with the lady," Georges said, picking that moment to walk in. "A few hours away from the drawing board might recharge your batteries."

Philippe began to protest that Georges didn't know what he was talking about. Georges was a doctor, not a designer. He had no idea what was involved in the process. But then he shrugged. The sooner he agreed and got this over with, the sooner the woman would be busy working and out of his hair.

He looked at J.D. "How fast can you get me there?" he wanted to know.

He'd done a one-eighty so fast, she felt as if she'd just sustained a severe case of whiplash. "Fast," she volunteered. Then, because she sensed he'd appreciate it, added, "But I'll try not to break any speed limits." As she spoke, she reached for her car keys and headed toward the front door. Turning, she nodded at Georges, silently thanking him.

He winked at her in reply.

Definitely less family resemblance than more, she decided.

Chapter Six

Janice drove him to an area in Anaheim known among contractors as tile row. As far as the eye could see was store after endless store offering every kind of tile.

She had just assumed the lead since this encompassed her territory. But the short journey across the freeway, for once not hopelessly congested, had her re-thinking her decision. Zabelle sat beside her now, wrapped in silence since she'd announced, "I'll drive," and gestured him into the passenger seat of her truck.

It wasn't the kind of comfortable silence of two old friends who momentarily had run out of things to say. This was the kind of silence bound up by tension. At least, for her it was.

As she got off the freeway and turned down the first of the streets leading to their destination, Janice felt she couldn't take the oppressive silence any longer.

"Anything wrong?" she asked. When Zabelle didn't answer, she repeated the question, her voice more forceful. This time, she managed to penetrate the haze.

"Hmm? Oh, no." And then Philippe looked at her for a moment before changing his reply. "Well, yes."

The light was red. "All right, what is it?"

Since she'd asked, he gave her an honest answer. "I'm not used to sitting in the passenger seat."

Janice wasn't sure she followed him. "Excuse me?"

"I'm usually the one driving."

Funny, if asked, she wouldn't have said he had an ego thing going. Apparently she was getting to be a worse judge of character than she thought. "But you don't know where we're going," she pointed out.

"I understand that," Philippe answered. "It's just that I guess I'm not comfortable having anyone else behind the wheel."

Well, that was pretty honest, she thought. Most men would have said something about being natural pathfinders and being the better driver right out of the box. "I'm a safe driver," she told him.

He shook his head. "It's not that."

Making a left turn, she kept her eyes on the road. "You like being in control," she guessed.

That sounded obsessive, Philippe thought and he'd

never pictured himself that way. His mother had elements of obsessive-compulsive in her makeup, not him.

"No." The denial didn't taste quite right on his lips. And if he were being completely honest, if only with himself, maybe there was this one small streak that leaned toward control. "Well, maybe," he allowed, adding, "to some degree."

Janice had a feeling it was more than just that, but she wasn't about to push. Besides, they'd arrived at the first shop. She'd never come here herself, but some of the other contractors told her that the store had some very decent inventory.

"Lucky for you, we're here." With a smooth turn of her wrist, she pulled into what she believed would be the first of many parking lots that afternoon.

Instead of bolting out of the truck the way she'd expected him to, Zabelle sat on his side, eyeing the front of the store. The sign advertising the place was made completely out of black onyx. There were no windows in front. "This is the place?"

She got out, closing the door with finality, hoping that he'd take the hint. "This is one of them."

"One of them," he repeated. Slowly, without taking his eyes off the store, he got out of the truck. "How many are you planning on going to?"

She could almost hear him saying *dragging me to* in place of the words he'd used. "As many as it takes for you to find something you like." She gestured toward the other stores that lined both sides of the street. "I've never actually counted, but there are probably at least thirty or so stores along here."

"Thirty," he repeated incredulously.

"Or so," she added as a reminder.

Philippe slowly let out a long breath, as if bracing himself for an ordeal. He then squared his shoulders like a man going into battle and opened the front door. Stepping to the side, he held it for her, then glanced at her with a silent query.

For once, she could read him. "Don't worry, I'm not going to bite your head off for holding the door for me. I actually like that kind of thing."

Philippe responded to the warm smile on her lips. Given the line of work she was in, he wasn't sure if holding a door for her would somehow offend her sense of independence. Life in his mother's world had taught him to take nothing for granted about women's reactions to things.

"Good to know," he murmured.

The store looked deceptively small on the outside. Inside it was divided into fifteen or so sections, each showcasing a different kind of tile intended for every single foot of the house. Tile for the fireplace, for the pool area, for bathrooms, the kitchen and so on. There was so much to see that it was overwhelming.

Standing to the side, Janice could see that this was definitely a great deal more than Philippe had expected. Time for her to step in and be the tour guide, she thought.

Once she got started, she had a tendency to talk fast. This time Janice deliberately curbed her impulse. "I know that this can be a little mind-boggling at first. There are different grades of marble and granite, ceramic and glass—"

He seemed not to be listening. And then, just as she got warmed up to her subject, he pointed to a royal blue piece. "That one."

Janice blinked, and then looked at it. "That one what?"

"I pick that one. For the tile," he added since she was still staring at him as if he'd lapsed into an unknown dialect of pig Latin. "You can use that one for the tile." He glanced toward the door like a prisoner looking longingly at the gates leading to the freedom that was denied to him. "Can we go now?"

Janice remained speechless for exactly ten seconds before she regained possession of her tongue. "No, we can't go now," she answered in a tone she might have used on Kelli if she'd had a willful child instead of the one she'd been blessed with. "This is only the first place we've been to, Philippe, and just the first display you've seen. You have no idea what's out there," she insisted. "You might see something you like better."

It occurred to him, after the fact, that this was the first time she'd addressed him by his first name. It made the whole process seem more intimate somehow, like going out with a friend instead of an employee.

The thought had come shooting out of nowhere. He sent

it back to the same place. He was here to get this tile thing over with, not challenge himself with mental puzzles.

"I don't think so," he countered. He believed that it was entirely possible to find something he liked immediately instead of having to wade through a sea of candidates. "I don't have to see every single piece of tile to know what I like."

She'd bet anything that Zabelle was doing this because he didn't want to waste time going from store to store. Another contractor would have gone along with this, happy to have the ordeal over with. But she didn't operate that way. She liked leaving her clients satisfied with their renovations. That was what it was all about to her, matching the person to the changes, not just slapping any old thing together in order to collect her fee.

"I don't—" Janice got no further.

"If I were my mother," Philippe continued patiently, "you might have to wait six months for a decision. But I'm not like that."

Something else was going on here, she thought. But as of yet, she didn't have a clue so she could only tilt with the windmill she saw. "You can't go with the first tile you see."

"Why not?"

"Because there's so much out there that you haven't seen, that you don't know about, that you might really fall in love with," she added with feeling.

He looked at her for a long moment. So long that she

felt something inside her tighten in anticipation, although she hadn't a clue what it was.

And then, whatever it was that was going on, lessened and he said, "That sounds like my mother's philosophy about men."

She felt a little like someone who had just stepped in through the looking glass. "Excuse me?"

Ordinarily, he wouldn't have said that. Of the three of them, he was the most closed-mouth of Lily's sons. But somehow, around this little dynamo, words just seemed to slip out. "She moves from relationship to relationship, never staying long even if she falls in love." Especially when she falls in love, he added silently.

For the moment, Janice forgot about the tile. This was more interesting. "Why?"

It seemed ironic that his mother's reasoning seemed to align itself so readily with what J.D. had said about tile. "Because she feels that maybe she's settling, that maybe there's something even more spectacular out there and she's missing out." He raised his eyes to hers. "This one," he repeated. "I'll take this one."

So in some odd way, he was rebelling from behavior he'd witnessed as a child, she thought. Rebelling or not, she didn't want his bathrooms to suffer.

"You're sure you're not settling?" she prodded. An odd look came into his eyes, but she pushed forward. "Look, I realize that you're not marrying the tile, I just want you to like the finished product."

"I already told you, I like it. You can order however much you need. Can we go home now?" He repeated the question as if this time around it was rhetorical.

Philippe was surprised when she gave him an answer that was different from the one he'd assumed he would be receiving.

"No."

"No?" he echoed incredulously. How could the answer be no? "But I just did what you wanted," Philippe pointed out. "I picked a tile."

This was definitely not going to be her easiest assignment, despite the fact that the man claimed to be easy to please. She didn't want this to be something to get over with, she wanted it to leave a lasting impression on him, to catch his eye and dazzle him every time he walked into one of the bathrooms—or the kitchen for that matter.

"For the bathroom," she told him. "I won't go with the obvious, that there are three bathrooms to be remodeled—"

He cut in with a wave of his hand. "Same tile for all of them."

Janice pushed forward, pretending she hadn't heard that. "You still have to choose a slab for the kitchen counter, a backsplash, tile for all the floors, cabinets for the kitchen and bathrooms, fixtures, a tub for one, showers for the other two—"

"Wait," he cried, raising his hands as if he were

physically trying to stuff a profusion of things back into a box that had exploded before him, a box that was *not* allowing him to repack it. "Wait."

Temporarily out of steam, she paused to take a breath. "Yes?"

"What the hell is a backsplash?"

She grinned. "It's the area of the wall that runs along the back of the—"

His hand was up again, dismissing the explanation before it was completed. There was a bigger issue here. "I have to pick all those things out?"

"Well, yes." She'd shown him the blueprints. Hadn't any of this registered? Exactly how did he think this was all going to happen? "Oh, plus appliances for the kitchen."

Philippe stared at her, trying to process what she was saying and what it would cost him, not in the monetary sense but in man-hours. The latter was in short supply and he couldn't really spare what he did have available to him. At the outset, when he'd agreed to come with her, he'd expected the whole ordeal to last maybe an hour. Less if he could hurry her along. But what she was proposing would take days, days he didn't have.

This wasn't going to work out.

His first impulse was to tell her he'd changed his mind about having the rooms remodeled and pay her whatever penalty went with terminating the contract between them. An alternate plan was to postpone the work indefinitely, or at least until his own work was finished. Debating between them, he did neither.

For the same reason.

Instinct told him that J. D. Wyatt needed the money this job would bring in. So he chose another course, one that made complete sense to him. "You do it."

He couldn't mean what she thought me meant. "Excuse me?"

"You do it," he repeated.

A couple had come in with two children, the older of whom seemed to be around three and in excellent voice. He was exercising the latter and could be heard emitting a high-pitched scream from the far end of the store.

Unable to hear what Philippe was saying, Janice moved closer to her client. "Do what?"

"Pick for me," he told her simply.

"You want me to pick out your appliances." It wasn't a question so much as a stunned repetition.

"Yes. And all those other things you mentioned, too," he added.

"You have no idea what my taste is like."

He shrugged, fingering the tile he'd just selected and nodding at it as if it was privy to his thoughts. "Match it to my taste."

It took everything for her not to throw up her hands. Was he being difficult on purpose? "I don't know what your taste is like," she protested with feeling. "Other than bland."

He grinned, the corner of his eyes crinkling. "There you go."

Again, something stirred inside her, responding to the man and the moment. *Stop that,* she upbraided herself silently. "The idea is to get away from bland," she reminded him.

"I've got a contract deadline that I'm not going to make if I'm standing here in a tile store. Now it's either my way or we postpone this until I have some free time."

And that wouldn't be until November, based on what he'd said earlier. The easiest thing was to do as he said. But doing what he suggested went against her grain. Stuck, she thought for a second.

"How about this. I bring you samples and pictures of the things I picked out." She'd make sure he had a selection to choose from. She didn't mind being the go-between. It took longer, but that was part of her job and came under a heading related to hand-holding.

The thought of holding his hand created a warm wave inside her and increased her pulse rate.

Janice pushed it down and moved on. "That way you at least know you don't hate my choices."

"Sounds like a plan." He would have agreed to anything that would get him out of the store and on his way home again.

"May I help you?"

A salesman materialized behind them. Happy to see

someone he assumed would bring this all to an end, Philippe pointed to the royal blue ceramic tile he'd initially selected. "We want that tile."

The man beamed as he nodded. "Excellent choice, sir." Philippe had a feeling the man would have declared his selection "excellent" even if he had chosen something out of chewing gum. "And how much tile will you be requiring?"

Philippe shoved his hands into the front pockets of his jeans. "J.D., you're on." He gave every indication of retreating.

"That's what I like to see," the salesman declared. "A husband who lets his wife make the decisions. I'm sure you've done your homework, little lady."

Philippe stopped retreating. He didn't have to be his mother's son to know that J.D. had to find that tone offensive. He slanted a glance toward her, waiting to see her reaction.

"I have," she replied gamely, giving no indication that she would have enjoyed giving the man a swift kick for his patronizing manner. "And I'm not his wife, I'm his contractor."

The clerk seemed taken aback for a moment, but then, to his credit, he rallied. "Even better."

She was tempted to ask him why just to hear his answer. But that would be argumentative and she just wanted to move on, for Zabelle's sake. So instead, she put out her hand.

"Let me have your card," she requested easily. "We're not quite ready to order yet. I need to take some measurements first and then I'll get back to you."

It was obvious that the man felt once they were out the door, he stood a good chance of losing the sale. "We could have one of our men come by, double-check the numbers—"

"Won't be necessary," Janice assured him with a wide smile. Taking Philippe's arm, she hustled him out of the store and into the parking lot.

Bemused, Philippe looked at her as the door closed behind them. "Correct me if I'm wrong, but I thought you already had the measurements."

So he did pay attention, she thought. She inclined her head. "I do."

"Then why all that double-talk back there?" Although he had a feeling he already had the answer.

She led the way to her truck, intent on a quick getaway in case the salesman decided to follow them out to the parking lot out to make one last pitch. "I didn't like his attitude."

He struggled to keep his mouth from curving. "Is attitude that important?"

"It is in my line of work." She unlocked the truck from her side. The double click indicated that his side was open, too. "Don't worry, I saw who the manufacturer was. We can order that tile from any one of the stores I deal with on a regular basis," she promised. About to get in, she saw that he was still standing outside the passenger side. She took a guess. "You want to drive?"

That wasn't why he waited. He was watching the way a sunbeam was glinting in her hair, turning it a light shade of gold.

"No."

She thought he was just embarrassed because he was behaving so predictably. Rounding the hood, she came to his side.

"Go ahead," she urged, holding out the keys to him. "We're not going that far." The next store was only a few yards away.

After a moment's hesitation, he took the keys from her and crossed to the driver's side. Getting in, he asked, "Where's your favorite place to order tile?"

There were a couple of places she liked to frequent. Both were more than fair in price and reliability. Because there was so much competition, she liked to send business their way whenever possible.

She chose the one closest to where they were. "Orlando's. It's about a mile up the road."

"Good." Putting the key in the ignition, he started up the truck. "We'll go there."

She smiled to herself, shaking her head as she buckled up. "You just want to get this over with."

"Not that I don't find the company pleasing," he qualified, "but yes, I do."

Well, the man certainly didn't believe in beating

around the bush. And she could sympathize with dead-lines and the need to get a project done by a specified time; when she'd worked for her father's company and dealt with major businesses, there'd been penalties for going over the allotted time.

She wondered if that applied to his work as well. "Make a left out of the lot," she instructed, pointing to the open road.

"Yes, ma'am."

In the end, they went with the tile he'd first selected. But not before she managed to get him to look at a few other pieces. She convinced him to get something slightly different for each of the three bath-rooms. And just before they left the store, he'd wound up picking out the material for the kitchen counter: an impressive slab of granite known as blue pearl. It was almost black with veins of glimmering blue throughout.

"Damn," he murmured, a little stunned as he automati-cally got in behind the wheel more than an hour later. "I had no idea that there were that many different kinds of tile." She laughed and he caught himself thinking that it was a very peaceful yet arousing sound. "What?"

Her laughter had entered her eyes. "You didn't even begin to scratch the surface," she told him.

Philippe looked at her, a little stunned, wondering if that applied to her as well.

Chapter Seven

The noise didn't register until after the fact.

Somewhere, a door had closed. Someone was in the house. The next moment, he didn't have to speculate if it was one of his brothers.

One other person had the key to his house and it was that voice he heard now. Low and full-bodied like brandy being poured over ice, it filled the air, preceding her and coming at him without so much as a greeting or a preamble.

"And what is this I hear about you having the house remodeled?"

He glanced up from his computer to see her standing

in his doorway. Lily Moreau was given to dramatic entrances, even with her own family. By all accounts, she was a dramatic woman. From the top of her deep black hair, shot through with captivating streaks of gray, to the tips of her toes, polished, manicured and encased in the Italian designer shoes she favored, Lily Moreau, renowned artist, woman of passion and world traveler was the very personification of drama.

His smile was automatic. She was probably the most trying, infuriating woman in the world—she was at least in the top five—but he loved her dearly. "Hello, Mother, how are you?"

She took possession of the room and moved around like a force of nature, searching for a place to touch down, however briefly. Swirls of turquoise, at her wrists, ears and neck and along her torso, marked her path. Turquoise was one of her two favorite colors.

"Confused," she responded, pivoting to face him on the three-inch heels that rendered her five-foot-five. "My firstborn, the most stable child of the litter, has ventured into my territory without so much as a single request for input." She flounced down on the sofa, clouds of turquoise floating about her still trim hips and softly coming to rest in a circle around her. "I'd say I was more than confused. I'd say I was hurt."

Accustomed to these performances whenever his mother was in town, Philippe hardly looked away from his monitor and the equation that troubled him. "No reason to be hurt, Mother. And as for your 'territory,' since when have you been moonlighting as a handyman?"

"Handyman?" Frowning, Lily moved forward on the sofa. "I thought you were having the house redone." Although she strongly maintained that of the three of them, Philippe had inherited her artistic bent, he had always been determined to bury it. By now his flair was so far from the surface, it would have taken a crane to be resurrected. She liked being consulted on matters, liked being in the thick of things. Color schemes, textures, room dynamics, these all came under her purview.

"Not quite." He had a strong hunch he knew where his mother had gotten her information. Georges had been the one to let J.D. in the other day when she had dragged him off to those damn stores. "Tell Georges to get his facts straight."

"It wasn't Georges," she informed him, on her feet again and moving about. She stopped to finger a plant she had given him the last time she'd visited. It was two steps removed from death. On an errand of mercy, she walked into the hall, her destination the kitchen. "It was Alain."

"Tell Alain to get his facts straight next time," he called after her.

Philippe didn't bother asking how his other brother had gotten into this. He imagined it was like the old fashioned game of telephone, where Georges had taken his own interpretation of the events and told them to Alain who then put his own spin on it before telling their mother. He was actually surprised they didn't have him buying a villa in the south of France or some equally improbable scenario.

She was back with a cup full of water. Lily poured it slowly into the pot, then tried to arrange the drooping, drying leaves. "And the facts are?"

Philippe glanced at his mother. He should have known that she would want in on this. She was the one he should have sent with J.D., not gotten roped into traipsing around after the woman from store to store, selecting things that held little to no interest for him. All he'd wanted was to have a cracked sink replaced.

But to say anything on that subject would get him sucked into a conversation he didn't want. "That you don't come by enough for me to see you with a scowl on your face."

"Scowl?" The plant was completely forgotten. Lily reached for her purse and the compact mirror inside. "I'm scowling? I can't scowl, I'll get wrinkles before my big show." Mirror opened, she reviewed her appearance from several different angles, then decided that she was fine. Not twenty-two-year-old fine, but fine nonetheless.

Philippe caught the magic word. "Another big show?"

"Always another big show," she declared with gusto. It was what she thrived on, that and the men in her life. "If I can't paint, I'll just lie down and they can throw dirt over me." She tossed her head, dark ends flirting with the tops of her shoulders. "I'll be as good as dead."

She certainly had a way of phrasing things, he thought. "They throw enough dirt over you, you will be." One of the first things he'd ever learned about his mother was that, barring some crisis, there was nothing she liked to talk about more than her paintings, so he gave her a gentle nudge in that direction. "So, where and when is this big show?"

"Three weeks from Saturday at the Sunset Galleries on Lido Isle." She recited the information as if it had been prerecorded. And then she gave him a deep, pene-trating look. "You'll be there?"

Turning in his chair so that he faced her instead of the computer, he grinned. "Wouldn't miss it."

She took hold of his hands as if that was all she needed to discern whether or not he was telling her the truth. Fingers wound tightly around his palms.

"No, really, you'll be there?" She nodded absently toward the screen. "You know how you get when you get involved in your work."

"I'll be there," he promised, wiping any trace of a smile from either his voice or his face.

Lily sighed, as if getting him to agree had been an ordeal. "Good. I want you to meet him."

"Him?" Philippe eyed his mother warily. "There's another *him?*" He should have known there would be. It had been, what, five months since the last one had been sent packing? That was a long dry spell for his mother.

"Yes," Lily replied joyously. She'd moved on to the

rear of the room to gaze out at the backyard it faced. All three houses shared it as if it was one large yard instead of the culmination of three. "You need a gazebo, Philippe," she decided and then, glancing back at him, she waved her hand. "Get that look off your face, I know what you're thinking."

He made it a point to be as laid-back as she was dramatic. "I sincerely doubt that."

She was not his mother for nothing. "You're thinking, *here we go again.*"

He laughed, impressed. "Very good. I guess I'm getting too predictable."

She didn't waste words on defending her past choices. She was a woman who had always believed in moving forward. "This time, it's different."

And where had he heard that before? Philippe mused. He went back to focusing on his work, uttering a tolerant, "Of course it is."

"It is," she insisted, crossing to his desk and presenting herself behind his monitor so that he was forced to look at her. She clasped her hands together and resembled a schoolgirl in the throes of her first major crush. "Kyle is everything I've been looking for in a man. Funny, smart, youthful and vigorous—"

Philippe shot his hand up in the air to halt the flow of words. "If that word doesn't apply to the way he polishes your silverware, Mother, I really don't want to hear about it."

Lily rolled her eyes. "Oh Philippe, you know what your trouble is?"

Yes, he had a mother who had never grown up. "I'm sure you'll tell me," he replied patiently.

She took his chin in her hand, lowering her face to his. "You're not at all like your father."

Moving his chair back, he eyed his mother. "I thought that was a good thing. You left my father because he gambled away the floor from under your feet," he reminded her.

She refused to dwell on the bad. It was one of her attributes. "But first he swept me off those feet, Philippe. He had this zest for life—"

"Otherwise known as Texas hold 'em."

"Oh Philippe," she sighed mightily, "you were born old."

He didn't see it as a failing. If anything, it kept him from making his mother's mistakes and leading with his heart instead of his head. "One of us had to be and someone had to be there for the boys."

The hurricane stopped moving. Lily's expression turned serious. "Was having me as a mother so terrible?"

He wouldn't allow his mind to stray to the hundred and one shortcomings his mother possessed. The bottom line was that she meant well in her own way and she did love them. Of that he was certain. So he smiled at her and said, "You had your moments."

"I had my hours, Philippe, my days," she corrected majestically. "And I always loved all you boys to distraction." Long, slender fingers touched his cheek the way she did when he was small and needed her comforting. "I still do."

"I know that."

She dropped her hand to her side. The movement was accompanied by the sound of gold bracelets greeting one another. "I'm a passionate woman, Philippe. I need passion for my art. I *use* passion," she insisted.

This was a conversation they'd had before. Several times. "I know that, too, Mother."

She kissed his cheek, then rubbed away the streak of vivid red from his skin. Any minor disagreement that might have arisen was terminated before it had a chance to form. "Is there a reason for this handiwork you're having done?"

"Yes," he replied simply, "the bathroom sink is cracked."

"Oh." She looked exceptionally disappointed. "I was hoping that it was being done because you were finally settling down."

Philippe addressed the phrase in its strictest sense. "I'm the most *settled* out of the three of us," he reminded her.

The drama returned as Lily sighed and resumed her restless patrol of the small converted bedroom. "With a woman, Philippe, settling down with a woman." She retraced her steps and presented herself before him again. "Have you been seeing anyone?"

"Only you when I'm lucky."

Lily closed her eyes and sighed. "Use that charm on someone else, Philippe. Someone who matters."

Momentarily surrendering, he rose to his feet. He just wasn't going to get any work done with his mother here, bombarding him with questions. He might as well enjoy this visit.

"You always matter, Mother. Want some coffee?" he suggested.

She looked as if she was going to say yes, then surprised him by shaking her head.

"I don't want to take you away from what you're doing." She took exactly one step toward the threshold before she continued talking. "Just wanted to invite you to the show and to see if you had any women stashed here." The expression on her face told him that she hoped he'd do better on her next unexpected visit. "Your father always had women stashed here and there."

There wasn't very much he remembered about his parents' union when it had been official, although his mother had taken his father back for a short time between her second and third husbands. But they hadn't been married then. "Before you got engaged?"

Lily moved a stray hair from her cheek. "No, after we were married. After gambling and family, women were your father's primary addiction." She said it matter-of-factly, as if it had no impact on her what-soever. Lily might have been a cauldron of emotion, but she was never judgmental.

Philippe blew out a breath. "Not much of a prize," he commented.

But his mother's eyes were shining like two bright jewels. "Vigorous, Philippe. He, too, was very vigorous."

It was going to take him days to get the image she'd planted out of his head, Philippe thought. If he were still at a young and impressionable age, that just might have scarred him for life.

But then, if his mother's actual lifestyle hadn't done it while he was growing up, he sincerely doubted that anything at this stage possibly could. Flamboyant, ec-centric and completely unorthodox were all terms that were synonymous with the name Lily Moreau and he'd survived his childhood to become a relatively well-adjusted, successful man. If his house was a little empty at times, well, everyone paid some kind of price in life. Being alone was his.

Besides, it was a great deal more preferable than constantly making the wrong choices.

His mother still hovered over him. "I worry about you most of all, Philippe."

That was the last thing he wanted. For her to worry or, worse, to do something about that worry.

He had only one response for that. "Don't."

She sniffed, taking offense. "I may not be Norman

Rockwell's idea of the perfect mother, but I'm still a mother."

He knew she meant well. Philippe softened. "Norman Rockwell's been gone for a long time, I don't think you need to worry about him. And I appreciate the concern, Mother, but I am a grown man. We march to different drummers. You taught me that, remember?"

"Yes, but sometimes the music is the same." She pressed full lips together, thinking. And then her eyes widened the way they did when she'd been struck by an idea she liked. "Kyle has a sister—"

For a second, the name escaped him. "Kyle?"

"Yes, the reason for the smile on my face. You're not paying attention, Philippe," she admonished with a trace of impatience.

His mother's boyfriend's sister. Oh God. That was all he needed, to be coupled with a woman old enough to be his mother. That little tidbit would finally send him into therapy.

He put his hands on her shoulders, as if that could somehow push all the wild ideas she had back into her head. "Mother," his tone was firm, "Don't worry about it. Now, I do have work to do, so…"

She took her dismissal graciously enough and picked up the purse she'd dropped onto the sofa upon entry. "I'll let myself out, I know the way." She hesitated for a second. "You won't forget about the show?"

"I won't forget."

She nodded, taking him at his word. "And see if you can bring someone," she coaxed, then added with emphasis, "Someone female."

"I'll see what I can find on Amazon.com," he deadpanned.

Lily sighed. "Some things never change." Raising herself up on her toes, she kissed his cheek again. "But I love you anyway."

He smiled as she left the room. "Nice to know, Mother."

Sitting down, within moments Philippe was lost again in the details of the knotty programming problem he'd run up against.

And then he was roused out of its midst again.

"Philippe?"

He closed his eyes, summoning strength. He didn't often get impatient with his mother, there was no point. But he could get impatient at the loss of an afternoon's work, especially since he'd sacrificed an afternoon just the other day.

Taking a deep breath, he released it again before saying, "Yes, Mother?"

"You are a sneaky devil."

The single sentence, hanging in the air without preamble, begged for questions, for an explanation. He pushed away from his desk and rose to his feet, resigned to getting both.

"Why, Mother?"

There was no answer. He was about to follow the

sound of his mother's voice when the need was abruptly vanquished. Lily made a reentrance.

She wasn't alone.

His mother's ring-encrusted fingers were delicately wrapped around the small hand of J.D.'s daughter. J.D. was right behind them, bringing up the rear.

Philippe felt like the beach at Normandy on D-day.

"Where have you been hiding these two?" his mother asked with the air of someone who felt she had the right to know everything that transpired in the world of her sons.

"We're not hiding," Kelli informed her before he could find his own tongue. "We're right here."

J.D. seemed a little overwhelmed by his mother. Welcome to the club, he thought.

"Did we have a date I forgot about?" he asked. The second the word was out of his mouth, he realized his mistake. His colossal mistake.

"Date?" Lily echoed, vibrating with both curiosity and joy.

"I came for the check," J.D. explained. She was sure she'd mentioned it to him.

Lily's eyes widened. "He's paying you? Oh, Philippe—"

Janice had no idea what was going on but she just pushed ahead, hoping that somehow everything would straighten itself out if she just hung on to her part of the truth. "I didn't think you'd mind if I brought Kelli with me again." She tried to take Kelli's hand, but the woman in turquoise was in her way. "She really wanted to see you."

"He is charming, my son," Lily agreed and turned to the woman she assumed was the child's mother. "I'm Lily Moreau. It's very nice to meet you."

The next thing Janice knew, she found herself enfolded in an enthusiastic one-armed hug. Although she hugged Kelli at every opportunity, she came from a family that was light-years removed from anything demonstrative. She wasn't sure how to respond to this strange woman's embrace.

"Likewise," she murmured from within the embrace.

Letting go, Lily turned to her son again. "Philippe, out with it. Who is this lovely creature?"

"She's my contractor, Mother."

Lily laughed dryly. "You have your father's sense of humor. I would find him alone with all sorts of beautiful women. He always referred to them as his clients. Even in the dead of night when I came back from a tour and discovered him indisposed, so to speak." There was no malice, no hurt in her voice. She was simply recounting something from the past that had occurred in her life.

Still, Philippe couldn't believe she was saying this in front of a stranger. "Mother," he said sharply, glancing at J.D.

"I really am his contractor," Janice told her. "I need a check from you to make a down payment on the materials we decided on," she told him.

Kelli tugged on the woman's hand. "I'm Kelli," she informed her. And then proceeded to blow her away by asking, "Are you the lady who painted the pretty picture over there?"

Lily seemed stunned and then immensely pleased. "Why, yes, I am." She bent down to Kelli's level. "Do you like it?"

Kelli's hair bounced about her face as she nodded. "Very much." And then she added in a very grown-up voice, "I paint, too."

Lily smiled warmly. "Do you, now?" There was genuine interest in her voice, not just the sound of forced tolerance.

"Yes, she does. Very well."

The confirmation with its comment came not from Kelli or even J.D., but from Philippe. His mother looked at him with an interested expression that immediately told him he should have kept that comment to himself.

But since he hadn't, he might as well back up what he'd said. He looked at J.D. "Why don't you show my mother the drawing you carry around with you?"

Janice paused. It was one thing to show the drawing to a person she was talking to, it was another to show it to a woman who had had her paintings on display in galleries in Paris.

But Kelli gazed up at her so eagerly, there was nothing else she could do. Taking out her wallet, Janice carefully unfolded the drawing she kept tucked away there, then handed it to Lily.

Lily studied the drawing with great interest. "You did this?" There wasn't a hint of a patronization in her voice.

Kelli nodded. "Uh-huh."

Lily's smile crinkled into her eyes. "Really?"

"Really," Kelli echoed, then crossed her heart with childish fingers.

Lily looked up in Janice's direction. "This is very, very good."

Janice already knew that, but it was nice to hear a professional agree. "Thank you."

Lily studied the drawing again. It looked better to her with each pass. "Have you thought of getting your daughter some professional training?"

It was one of her cherished hopes, but it was something to address in the future, not now. "She's a little young for that."

"How old is she?" Lily asked.

Kelli responded instantly. "I'm four and three-quarters."

"Oh, four and three-quarters," Lily parroted, suppressing a smile. She glanced up at Janice. "Mozart was four when he wrote his first concerto."

"Well, he ultimately didn't wind up very well, did he?" Janice countered. She didn't want anyone treating Kelli like some oddity.

"Well-read, too." Lily nodded, looking back at her

son. Her comment, clearly about J.D., was for Philippe's benefit. "You've given me hope, Philippe."

"Remodeling, Mother, she's remodeling a couple of rooms for me."

"Four," Janice corrected. "I'm remodeling four rooms for you."

"Very promising," Lily commented. Philippe could almost see his mother's thoughts racing off to the finish line. Any protest he might offer would only make the woman believe the very opposite. This was a case of discretion being the better part of valor.

So for the time being, he kept his silence and hoped for the best. He'd survived Hurricane Lily before.

Chapter Eight

Like most people, Philippe had a temper. However, unless one of his own was being threatened, it took a great deal to nudge that particular part of his personality awake. He usually took things in stride. Being stuck in bumper-to-bumper traffic didn't faze him. But deadlines that came and went, *his* deadlines, made him uneasy. Because he felt responsible for the failure to meet this particular deadline, he'd become progressively more irritated.

And God knew, the noise wasn't helping.

Philippe looked accusingly at the closed door. He'd been in his office for the last three hours and it was just getting worse.

This was definitely not what he had bargained for.

Afraid of losing his work, he saved it, assigning the program's temporary name yet another number to differentiate it from previous versions. He laced his fingers together behind his head and leaned back in his chair.

When he'd agreed to have work done on his house, he'd forgotten to consider one important thing.

The noise factor.

Right now, the house abounded with it. How could one woman create this much noise? It seeped into every crevice of the house, taking his office prisoner.

It didn't matter if his door was open or closed. He was still very much aware of it. Sometimes the noise was loud, sometimes almost deceptively soft, making him think that perhaps he'd weathered the worst. But then it would start again. And continue.

At its best, the noise could be likened to an erratic heartbeat. At its worst, it was like the circus setting up winter quarters outside his door—with a herd of less-than-tame elephants in charge of doing all of the hammering.

It had been like this for three days.

Philippe dragged his fingers through his hair and counted to ten. And then ten again. It didn't help. His long dormant temper had gone short-fuse on him.

Abandoning his computer and its multitude of crashes, Philippe went out into the hallway and made his way to the kitchen, the source of all this ungodly noise.

He was ready to do whatever it took to get some peace.

Wearing safety goggles and wielding a sledgehammer, J.D. didn't seem to see him at first. For a second, despite the irritation that was close to the boiling point within his chest, he hung back, just watching her.

She swung that sledgehammer like a pro. Tirelessly. Splintering cabinets she'd already crowbarred from the wall.

He found the rhythmic movement oddly hypnotic. J.D. wore faded jeans that seemed to lovingly adhere to her every curve and a gray T-shirt that was damp in several places, obviously with her sweat.

Construction had never looked so good.

Something inside him stirred as he continued to watch her work.

One final swing and she broke apart the last of the cabinets. Now the mess just needed to be hauled away. The kitchen was gutted, barren, like the aftermath of a hurricane. He assumed the rebuilding would begin tomorrow. He'd never gotten around to picking out his new appliances. He'd left that entirely up to J.D. A small part of him couldn't help wondering if perhaps that had been a mistake.

She had muscles, he realized as he stared at the way they moved and flexed.

Damn, he was turned on. What was that all about? Yes, she was an attractive woman, but this went beyond just acknowledgement of that fact.

He was working too hard, he told himself. And his brain was tired.

Janice sensed his presence a moment before she retired the sledgehammer. Every single muscle in her body ached from exhaustion. One more swing and she would have dropped the hammer. Her hands couldn't hold on to the handle for another second.

She glanced up in his direction just as she wiped more perspiration from her brow with the back of her wrist. He was looking at the rubble.

"Pretty awful, isn't it?" she commented, guessing at what had to be going through his brain. Right about now, Zabelle probably couldn't envision that this chaos would, in the end, give way to something really nice.

Philippe nodded. "Yeah, that's why I'm here."

She didn't follow him and wondered if eccentricity ran in the family. His mother had all but commandeered her last week when they'd first met, absorbing much of her afternoon. The woman seemed absolutely taken with her daughter and since both Kelli and Lily shared a love of art, she had seen that as a good thing.

But there was no denying that Lily Moreau was not your ordinary woman by any stretch of the imagination. She took getting used to. And indulging.

She wouldn't have said that about Philippe, but then, she really didn't know him that well. One prolonged shopping trip did not exactly make her privy to his soul.

"All right," Janice replied, drawing out the words and hoping that Philippe would fill in the blanks.

He picked up a kitchen towel that was tossed on the table. Rather than offer it to her, he wiped away the line of perspiration that had plastered her hair to her forehead.

His hand moved in short, sure strokes along her forehead.

Their eyes met. He took a breath, realizing that his brain had vacated the premises. "I think I made a mistake."

"On your work?" she guessed. Having him this close was scrambling her insides. Either that or there was a sudden lack of air in the room.

He moved his head slowly from side to side, still gazing into her eyes. They were almost a hypnotic blue, he thought. "On yours."

"You might find you need to write in code, but talking in it is wasted on me. You're going to have to explain what you just said."

He seemed surprised. Belatedly, he dropped his hand and the towel to his side. "You know about binary code?"

She didn't see what the big deal was. After all, it wasn't as if she'd just solved the space/time continuum problem.

"I've got three-quarters of a B.A.," she reminded him, although she really didn't expect him to remember. Her educational background had been on her résumé and references.

To her surprise, Philippe did remember. "I've been

meaning to ask you, how does someone get just three-quarters of a degree?"

That was a sore point for her, but one she needed to face. "You do it by dropping out in your senior year before taking any tests."

So near and yet so far, he thought, shaking his head. "If you were that close, why didn't you stay?" It made no sense to him. He went to lean against a counter and stopped himself just in time. Another second and he would have been sitting on the floor—beside the rubble she had created.

"Because I was going to be that big." Fingers almost touching, she held them out as far as she could before her very thin, very flat stomach. "I was pregnant at the time with Kelli."

"Why didn't you go back once she was born?"

She managed to hold at bay the sadness that always came whenever she thought of that period of her life. "Because by then, I was a widow and Kelli needed to live somewhere other than inside a cardboard box." She took a breath. This didn't have anything to do with the reason she was hired. She had no idea why she was playing true confessions with this man.

"Still, I think you should go back and get your degree."

"I intend to one day, when life gets a little more comfortable."

He wondered at her definition of *comfortable*. Philippe reminded himself of the reason he'd come in search of her and scanned the gutted room. From where he stood, it looked close to hopeless. "How much longer?"

She took off her gloves and flexed her hands. Her palms still ached from gripping the sledgehammer. "Until what?"

Philippe turned back to look at her. "Until you're done."

"With the kitchen?" She refrained from reminding him that everything had already been spelled out in the contract, including dates. She watched him shifting his weight from foot to foot. He seemed restless.

That made two of them.

"No, *done* done," he emphasized. "With everything," he added when she didn't answer.

Because she loved her job, Janice worked fast but there was only so much she could do alone. Besides, the job was dependent on other people as well, people who had to get back to her with the necessary items she ordered, like the rock quarry that was going to be delivering the granite slab Philippe had ordered. She couldn't move ahead and install the sink until the counter arrived. As for the maple cabinets she'd ordered for him, they were due at the beginning of next week. She crossed her fingers mentally, hoping he would approve of them.

"Well, barring any mishaps, if all conditions are a go, I'd say you could have your house back in as little as six to eight weeks."

Philippe shook his head. "That's not going to work."

Uh-oh, here comes trouble. Well, nothing in her life

had ever been easy, why start now? She drew herself up and challenged, "Why?"

"Because I can't work with all this noise. I thought I could, but I can't."

A lot of times, people moved into a hotel when she worked on their house. But he looked unreceptive when she made the suggestion. "You could try ear plugs," she told him. "Or you could try working when I knock off for the day."

So far, she'd arrived each morning at seven and left by three-thirty. He wasn't about to set his alarm for three in the morning to work before she arrived and then start again after she left.

He shook his head. "I do my best in the morning."

Janice smiled. So they had that in common. "So do I."

Philippe thought for a moment. "Can't you work any faster?"

"I could. If I were twins." She paused, thinking. There was a way, but it involved a complication. "I could get my brother to work with me."

As he recalled, she used her brother as a babysitter. "Does he do this kind of thing?"

"Yes." It was probably his imagination, but she seemed to answer the question a little too quickly, as if she didn't want to give herself any time to think about it.

"Then get him." He saw a hesitant look pass over her face. "What? If it's a matter of more money, I'm sure we can arrive at a figure that's mutually satisfying."

"No, it's not that." She'd quoted a price and she was going to stand by it. With Gordon helping, the job would get done faster so that balanced things out. "Gordon's my babysitter. If he's working here with me, I'm going to have to bring Kelli along as well, at least until I can find someone else."

It was a little unusual, but then, nothing about J. D. Wyatt was usual. "So?"

She looked at him for a long moment, trying to discern if he was pulling her leg. "You wouldn't mind?"

"No. She seemed like a nice enough, quiet little girl." He thought of Kelli's love for painting. "We could set something up for her in the family room—the part that hasn't been invaded with groceries, dishes and small appliances," he qualified.

"All right, then—" Janice began to pivot on her heel.

"But I'm just curious about one thing."

She stopped in her tracks, waiting for the shoe to drop. "Go ahead."

"Why isn't she in preschool, or nursery school, or whatever it is that they call it these days?"

Janice had her own philosophy about that. She believed that the first few years of life should be spent around the people who love you. She'd been farmed out when she was Kelli's age. Her father couldn't deal with raising children so she and Gordon had been sent off to day care and left with people before and after school. She'd always promised herself that her own child would be raised differently, that her daughter would never waste a single moment of her life wondering if her parents loved her.

"Kelli's going into kindergarten this fall. I just wanted to keep her around for as long as possible. She has friends on the block and there's nothing she could learn in preschool that I can't cover."

He nodded, getting the feeling that he'd intruded. "Fair enough." He regrouped. "All right then, why don't you knock it off for today and then come back tomorrow with reinforcements?"

"You're the boss." The tone she used had him sincerely doubting she believed that. "You going to go back in there and work now?" she guessed.

It was getting close to noon. "After I go out to get something to eat since you've taken away my stove." He looked at the barren area where his stove had once stood. She hadn't asked him for help, the way he'd assumed she would. "How did you manage that, anyway?"

"I used a dolly and a ramp and I walked it across the floor."

"How?"

She grinned. "You move each side one at a time. First right, then left, then right and so on until you're across the room."

He and his brothers had always subscribed to the brute force method. "How did you get it on the truck?" he asked.

That had been the simplest part. "I borrowed a friend's truck. He's got a hydraulic lift."

It made sense, he supposed. It still bothered him a little that she was so much more adept at this kind of thing than he was. "Answer for everything, eh?"

The wide smile on her lips took him aback for a minute, as did the churning sensation in his stomach that came in response. "Including your lunch."

"Come again?"

"I made you something." Thinking he'd remain in his office the way he had the other three days, she'd planned on surprising him and having the meal ready on the dining room table by noon. The best laid plans of mice and men…

He stared at her incredulously. "You cook for your clients?"

This was a first, but then, Kelli had taken such a shine to him and she did feel as if she were invading his space just a little.

But in response to his question, Janice shrugged. "I made lasagna last night. I always make too much so I thought I'd bring some over." She tossed him a smile over her shoulder as she walked out to her truck.

"But I don't have a stove," he reminded her.

"There's a microwave buried on the sofa somewhere. Besides, it's good cold," she promised, leaving the room.

He was still staring at the jumbled mess on his sofa, trying to make out the shape of the microwave, when J.D. returned a few minutes later, carrying what appeared to be a large, rectangular blue and white chest made of hard plastic. It look unwieldy and he moved to take it from her.

When he did, he discovered that it was more than unwieldy, it was heavy. "You're a lot stronger than you look," he told her, bringing the chest over to the dining room table.

"I have to be," she quipped.

Setting the box down on the table, he saw her raise one eyebrow in a silent question. "I've decided to have it cold."

"Translation." She laughed. "You can't locate the microwave."

"Beside the point," he declared nonchalantly. He had, however, located two plates and he had one at each place setting now. "Join me?"

She was surprised he asked. "I thought I was being dismissed."

He supposed he had sounded rather abrupt. But he hated being stumped and the program was driving him crazy. "Is that how it sounded?"

Taking her seat at his right, she noticed that Philippe hadn't actually apologized. "You have a very authoritative voice."

He laughed, taking a seat himself. "Comes from telling my brothers what to do."

"You were a fledgling bully?" she asked. Because the lasagna was hers, she did the honors, cutting portions.

"I was the father figure. Or, I should say," he

amended, "the *stable* father figure since there were an abundance of other father figures milling around most of the time." He stopped abruptly as his words echoed back to him. This wasn't like him. "Why am I always spilling my guts to you?"

Her smile was encouraging, understanding. "I have the kind of face people talk to. I'm more or less invisible," she explained. "They don't feel that they'll see me again once the job is over, but for the duration, they have invited me into their home and since I'm there, they come to regard me as someone they can talk to." She grinned, sinking her fork into the piece she'd taken. "I'm like the family pet without the emotional investment."

That definitely was *not* the way he saw her. "We never had a pet."

"Not even goldfish?"

He shook his head. "For a while, Mother traveled around too much for us to have pets. And then when she finally bought the house and we stayed behind while she went on her tours, she made it clear she didn't want anything with fur, feathers or fins finding its way to our mailing address." Because he felt that he'd said too much again, he changed the subject. He nodded at his plate. "This is good."

"Thank you." His compliment pleased her more than she thought it might. *Careful, J.D., you've slid down this path before and all you got for your trouble is skinned knees.* "I wouldn't have brought it if it was bad."

The reply tickled him. "So, what other talents do you have?"

She didn't have to stop to think. "That pretty much covers it."

In his estimation, that was more than enough. She cooked like a house afire and could build a replacement if the need arose. "You ever think about starting your own restaurant?"

Not even for a moment. "Ninety-five percent of all restaurants fail in their first year. I need a sure thing and working with these—" she held up her hands "—is a sure thing."

He could understand her reasoning, not that the world of contractors was all that stable. "Where did you learn to cook like this?"

"It was necessity." She paused to take a bite herself. "After my mother left, it was either learn to cook or eat ready-made things out of a box."

He curbed the desire to ask her about her mother. If she wanted him to know more, she'd tell him. As for preparing things out of a box, she'd just described the way he lived. "Nothing wrong with that."

"Have you read what they put inside that stuff?"

He shrugged, then swallowed what was in his mouth before answering, "Food."

"Food whose ingredients are guaranteed to give you high blood pressure and shut down your kidneys by the time you reach middle age." Turning, she reached into the blue and white box and took out a small round bowl. "I brought you fruit for dessert." She took off the cover. "Blueberries. They're rich in antioxidants."

He laughed, shaking his head as he looked at the offering. "Anyone ever tell you that you're pushy?"

"Maybe once or twice," she allowed.

He was willing to bet it was more than that.

Philippe glanced down at his plate. Somehow, he'd managed to eat the entire portion without realizing it. The blueberries, however, held no interest for him. He moved back from the table.

"Thanks, that was really good. But you don't have to do this, you know."

"I know." She gathered up the dirty dishes, putting them back into the chest.

Philippe started to offer to do them for her and then realized that he couldn't. She'd ripped out his sink that morning. With the chest between her hands, she began to make her way to the front door. He noticed that she was leaving her tools behind.

"Don't you need to take anything else with you?"

She glanced back at the toolbox. "Why? You're my only client."

He took the chest from her, indicating that he was going to follow her out with it. "I'm sorry to hear that."

"Why?"

"Well, it means that business is bad, right?"

She shook her head. "No, it means that I only do one

client at a time." She unlocked the door and took the chest from him, placing it behind the front seat of her truck. "I was serious about that. This way, it'll get done faster."

"And with your brother working with you, it'll be even that much faster."

She was going to have to keep after Gordon, she thought. He did good work—when he was working. But given half a chance, he'd take off for a few hours or catch a nap.

"Absolutely," she promised.

Ten minutes later, J.D. had left and he was back at his desk. His appetite appeased, his brain cleared, Philippe was in a much better frame of mind to take another crack at the program.

Bathed in absolute quiet, after a few minutes, Philippe realized that he found the silence almost deafening.

With a resigned sigh, he shook his head and turned on the radio to fill up the empty spaces.

Chapter Nine

Somewhere between the time his alarm sounded and he toweled himself dry from his shower, it hit Philippe like a bullet right between the eyes.

He was looking forward to seeing J.D. Looking forward to seeing her even with the accompanying wall of noise. The realization caught him off guard. He tried not to dwell on it, tried not to attach any sort of deep meaning to it. He didn't, by definition, dislike people and she was a person. The woman had turned out to be a decent sort, that was all. No big deal.

If it was no big deal, why did he feel compelled to convince himself of that? It should have just been a given.

Making a disgusted noise that drew into service a mangled French phrase, one of the few things he had learned from his father, he focused his mind on what was important. His work.

Philippe had forced himself up early, showering and shaving a good ninety minutes before he usually left the confines of his bed. With a stale piece of toast and marginal coffee, he sat before his computer, pondering the merit of a particular equation on his screen when he heard the doorbell.

Or thought he did.

It turned out to be a false alarm. Just his ears playing tricks on him.

There was no one at the door.

Glancing around, seeing only a jogger in the distance, Philippe experienced a smattering of disappointment. He retreated. Somehow, this was all wrong, although he couldn't begin to untangle the reasons why. He had work to do.

Maybe he was working too hard. Rather than take his time or kick back, as was his cousin Beau's habit, Philippe was always doggedly at his desk, working every available moment he had. Because he believed that all work and no play not only made Jack a dull boy but also helped contribute to the death of his brain cells, he had gone out of his way to institute his weekly poker game, making sure never to miss one.

But maybe that wasn't enough. Maybe, like his

mother had said to him time and again, he needed to get out of his shell. Needed to go out. With someone of the opposite gender.

Philippe frowned.

The fact that he was even thinking like this was proof that he needed to let up a little. To let go.

Right after this baby's packed up, he promised himself.

Famous last words, he mocked. He'd thought somewhere along the same lines when he'd worked on the last program—and all he'd done was jump right into this one.

Just before he reached his office threshold, Philippe stopped abruptly. Cocking his head to the right, he listened intently.

No, this time the doorbell wasn't his imagination. Retracing his steps back to the front door, he swung it open.

And smiled.

Kelli was clearly the one who had rung his doorbell. She was standing on her toes, stretching as far as she could, about to press her small finger to the white button again. When the door opened, she offered him a smile that he imagined angels looked to as a standard by which to measure their own smiles.

"I'm here," she announced brightly.

He exchanged looks with J.D. who was standing beside her. A man in jeans and a T-shirt was behind them. His wheat-colored hair and fair complexion fairly shouted that he was related to both.

"So I see," Philippe said, turning his attention back

to Kelli. He hadn't really intended to take the girl's hand, but Kelli had other ideas. She slipped her small hand into his and then tugged him back into his house.

"I brought stuff to do," she informed him. "So I won't get in your way."

How could someone so young sound so adult? He nodded in response. "Very thoughtful of you."

She beamed. Then suddenly, as if she'd forgotten her manners, she turned around to look at the man behind her. "This is my Uncle Gordon. Mama says you want your house done faster." A little pint-sized feminine pride slipped into her narrative. "Uncle Gordon is fast, but not as fast as Mama."

Philippe caught himself wondering just how fast Mama was. Reining in his thoughts, he slanted a glance toward J.D.

Damn, but worn T-shirts never looked so good to him before. "I'll bet," he acknowledged.

Something in his tone had Janice struggling to tamp down a wave of warmth. She raised her chin a little, not certain if she should be defensive or not.

But she could be polite. She nodded at her daughter, her eyes on Philippe's. "Thanks for letting me do this."

"No problem." He glanced at the man standing behind the little stick of dynamite who still had his hand. "I'm Philippe Zabelle." He extended his other hand to Kelli's uncle. "Nice to meet you."

Gordon was nothing if not friendly. Grinning

broadly, he shook the hand that was offered to him. "Yeah, likewise." Walking toward the kitchen, he looked around as he passed. "Nice place you have here."

Philippe's laugh was dismissive. "For a bomb shelter."

Gordon turned around. "No, I mean it. You've got a really great exterior." He jerked his thumb toward the front of the house. "It gives the place a ritzy look."

Philippe supposed so, but that had never been the draw for him. The fact that he and his brothers could all lead separate lives but still be in close proximity to one another was what had sold him on the house.

That, and that the fact that the outside was painted Wedgwood blue with white trim. Most of the other houses in the immediate vicinity were painted either in shades of rust or in some drab, strange color never to be found in nature. Blue had always been his favorite color.

The clock was ticking, Janice thought. Both for her and, probably more importantly, for Philippe. She broke up the impromptu meeting.

"C'mon, Kel, let's get you settled in," she said, taking the little girl's free hand. In her other hand, Janice was carrying a large portfolio filled with several drawings and a painting that Kelli was currently working on. Pausing, she eyed Philippe hesitantly. "It is all right that we use your dining room table, isn't it?" she asked, quickly adding, "I brought this tablecloth so that it doesn't accidentally get dirty."

"Actually," Philippe cut in, "I've got a much better idea."

Kelli watched him eagerly, a kernel of corn about to pop. Janice, hearing the same sentence, felt very protective of Kelli's feelings. She didn't want anything to diminish the girl's zest. "Such as?"

He led the way to an alcove just off the living room. Yesterday, there had been a refrigerator shoved into the space. He'd moved it last night to the already overflowing family room. He had something different in mind for the space.

"I thought Kelli might like to use something else instead of just a flat surface." Walking past the living room, he gestured over to the alcove. It was empty now—except for the small easel that stood in the center.

Kelli's eyes became huge. "Look, Mama, it's kid size," she exclaimed, running over to it. She touched the easel reverently, as if afraid it would disappear once her fingers came in contact with it. And then she looked at him over her shoulder, joy tinged with a hint of hesitation. "This is for me?"

He came up to join her. It had taken him several hours to hunt this up. "This used to be mine," he told her. "But it's a little too small for me now and it's been rather sad, sitting all alone in storage. So I'd take it as a personal favor if you used it."

Excited, the girl shifted from foot to foot as if about to break into an impromptu game of hopscotch. "Where's your new one?"

He laughed, shaking his head. "I don't have one."

"You don't paint anymore?" Surprise was imprinted on every inch of the small heart-shaped face.

It was a long story, built on rebellion and not one to tell a child, even a child as stunningly intelligent as Kelli. The easel had never really been put to use and he was surprised he'd saved it. But to keep things simple, he merely said, "No."

Surprise was replaced with sympathy. It was obvious Kelli felt that everyone should experience the joy of painting. Reclaiming her hand from her mother, she patted his. "Bet you could ask your mom to get you one and to give you lessons," she told him.

It was an effort to retain a straight face. She was darling as well as intelligent and gifted. "She's a very busy lady."

Kelli nodded slowly, absorbing the excuse and its ramifications. And then suddenly, her head bobbed up, her eyes shining as she looked at him. "I could teach you." Saying it out loud reinforced her enthusiasm and she clapped her hands together. "I could. It'd be fun."

He thought of all the years in his past that he'd actively turned down every attempt his mother made to mate him with a paintbrush and a canvas. He had staunchly refused to enter her world, wanting one of his own to colonize and leave his mark on.

But with this small, eager little face looking up at him, all that melted away. "Maybe it would be," he allowed. "I'll see if I can find another easel for tomorrow."

Kelli's smile grew even wider. "Good."

God, she sounded more adult that half the people he knew, Philippe thought, completely charmed. He noted that J.D. had placed all of her daughter's jars of paint along the easel's edge and mounted the painting against it.

"Call if you need me," she instructed Kelli, then stepped away from the child. The slanted glance that came his way indicated that she wanted him to follow. When he did, she asked, "How much do I owe you?"

He'd followed her literally, but now she'd lost him. "For what?"

Her voice low, she was all but whispering. "The easel."

What kind of a person did she think he was, pretending to give a child a gift only to have her mother pay for it under the table? Maybe she was used to strings being attached to things. So he set her straight. "What I told your daughter was true. That used to be my easel. There is no charge," he informed her firmly.

She wasn't comfortable about this, didn't want him getting the wrong idea even though instinctively, part of her did like him for the gesture. Maybe that was the part that scared her. More than a little. "I know, but—"

"Just consider it a gift from me to Kelli." His eyes met hers. He saw the wariness. "No strings attached."

She took a breath, wondering if she was making a mistake, believing him. She had to work at keeping their relationship strictly professional.

Good luck with that, a voice in her head mocked. She'd

already brought him food yesterday and brought her daughter along to work today. *Not exactly proceeding according to strict professional guidelines here, are we, J.D.?*

She forced a smile to her lips, trying to quell the nervous feeling in her stomach. "That was a very nice thing you did."

"I like seeing her smile," Philippe told her honestly. He watched her mouth curve and could have sworn something tightened inside of him. "You have the same smile," he observed.

Urges began to form, swarming over him out of nowhere. Or maybe, out of a somewhere he had no business visiting. Because something told him that J. D. Wyatt wasn't just a casual date. J.D. was the kind of woman you made plans with. Solid plans. And there was nothing in his world to suggest he had a solid plan. Look at the examples he had to follow, the parents he'd had. The norm when he was growing up was here today, gone tomorrow.

He shoved his hands into his back pockets, curbing the very strong desire to touch her face, to trace his fingers along the curve of her mouth and commit it to memory. *Damn, where was this coming from?*

He cleared his throat. "I guess I'd better get back to work."

"Yeah." The words tasted like powdered spackle. "Me, too," she murmured.

Gordon reentered the room, bringing along his own

set of long neglected tools. He glanced from his sister to Philippe, then watched as the latter left the room. Setting the toolbox down, Gordon crossed over to his sister. "Something going on between you two?" he asked mildly, in the same tone he might have used if he was asking about that day's temperature projection.

The question startled Janice, throwing cold water on what might have been a moment's worth of revelry. Groundless revelry, she insisted. Trust Gordon to be blunt.

"No." She went into the kitchen. "What makes you think that?"

He laughed dryly. "Looked like a lot of chemistry and heat flashing back and forth from where I was standing."

She looked down at his shoes. "Must be some loose wiring running under your feet," she decided innocently. "Maybe you'd better examine it later just to be safe. Wouldn't want this place going up, especially after all the work we're going to put into it."

"Guy doesn't give a woman's little girl an easel because there's loose wiring in the floor," he observed.

Janice sighed, refusing to entertain the thought of what Gordon was suggesting. Philippe was her client. If he liked the job she did for him, she had no doubt he would refer other people to her. There was nothing more to their relationship. Besides, she was not about to get involved with anyone. She'd never been able to get through to her father, never had that magical moment she'd waited for where he saw how much she loved him, how much she wanted him to be proud of her. And as for her husband, well that had never had a chance to go anywhere, so she would never know. She had been a wife and a widow within six months. That had had its own set of pain attached. She didn't need to seek out more.

Besides, she had enough to keep her busy. She had Kelli and her work. There wasn't space for more than that, certainly not for another pass at having her heart broken.

"Make yourself useful, Gordon."

He grinned at her. "I thought I already was, since you can't seem to see the forest for the trees—" He scratched his head. "Or is it the trees for the forest? I always get that confused."

That wasn't the only thing he got confused, she thought. "It's the floor for the debris," she declared, pointing to the very large pile of splintered wood veneer and plasterboard, the end results of her swinging her sledgehammer at the kitchen cabinets yesterday. Philippe had sent her home before she'd had a chance to remove the debris. "Clean it up."

He could have taken exception to her tone. Once, when his father's company had been his, he'd been her boss. And even when they'd worked with their father, he had supposedly always been the one in charge. It was only after the company went bankrupt and Janice began getting jobs on her own and throwing some of the business his way that she started issuing orders.

Gordon saluted her, his expression suddenly somber. "I'm on it."

"Good to know," she murmured. She didn't want to repay Philippe's kindness by appearing to take advantage of him.

Stooping down, she filled her arms with splintered plasterboard and got started.

He wasn't in his office.

Janice glanced at her watch to check the time. It was close to eleven and she'd assumed that he'd be busy at his work. She'd deliberately gone out of her way to pass his office to talk to him.

Can't talk to an empty chair.

Had he gone out and she'd missed hearing him leave? She'd begun work on gutting the downstairs powder room and wanted to have all her ducks in a row. Or at least swimming in the right direction.

She'd brought a color chart so that Philippe could decide what color he wanted her to paint the walls.

Shrugging, she tucked the chart under her arm and went back out again. It was getting close to lunchtime anyway. She might as well collect Kelli and her brother and get something to eat. Because this was their first day on a job together, she thought she'd take them both out to celebrate the occasion instead of just bringing lunch from home.

Janice moved around the corner. She didn't have to

look to know that Kelli would be completely captivated with her work. Painting always summoned this font of joy from within her, even when it wasn't going well. With her sunny disposition, Kelli always managed to see the bright side of everything.

"Kelli, honey," she called out, "we're going to break for lunch. Would you like to be the one to pick the restaurant?"

It always made her daughter feel so grown up when she could choose where they would all go to eat. And then she laughed to herself. Before she knew it, Kelli *would* be an adult. God knew the little girl was growing up much too fast, doing ten years for every candle she blew out.

When she received no response, Janice quickened her pace and made her way through the dining room toward the alcove. The moment she came near the threshold, she could feel her heart thudding in her chest.

Could, unaccountably, feel a sting in her eyes.

Allergies, she told herself.

Philippe was standing behind Kelli, guiding her hand, giving her instructions in a low, patient voice. It was a father-daughter scene worthy of a holiday card.

Except that they weren't a father and daughter.

So what? she demanded silently. Her own father had never been that patient on the rare occasions he explained something to her. Most of the time, he'd waved her back with that trite, archaic sentiment that "girls don't need to know that." She'd learned her trade by watching, by sneaking behind her father's back to observe him in action.

Never once had he put a hammer or a screwdriver into her hand and shown her how to use it. No tips or secrets were passed to her the way they had been to Gordon. Except that Gordon wanted no part of it. He remained, pretending to listen, because he was afraid not to. But his mind was always preoccupied with the current flavor of the month he was squiring. He'd been there in body, but not in spirit.

She would have killed for a moment like this in her own life. And Kelli was obviously lapping it all up, she thought, watching the way her daughter beamed up at Philippe.

Greeting-card moment or not, she had to break this up. "Kel, we're going out to lunch."

But Kelli was completely focused on the images she was creating on the canvas and the technique Philippe was showing her. "In a minute, Mama."

She knew better than to let herself be ignored. "Now, honey."

Philippe removed his hand from Kelli's and stepped back. "You'd better listen to your mother, Kelli."

The resigned sigh was filled with disappointment. Kelli retired her brush. "Okay." And then she looked at her mother hopefully. "Can Philippe come, too?"

She had to nip this in the bud, too. "His name is Mr. Zabelle, Kelli," she reminded her daughter. "And I'm sure Mr. Zabelle has better things to do than come to eat with us."

He was about to take the excuse she tendered. He'd

already spent way too much time not doing his work. So no one was more surprised than he was to hear himself say, "Actually, I don't." He was looking at J.D. rather than the little girl. "Unless of course, you'd rather I didn't come along."

Her mouth felt like she'd been snacking on sandpaper since morning. Janice knew she should be blunt and say something about lunch being a family affair. The truth was she didn't want him around her because he made her uncomfortable—but he only made her uncomfortable because she wanted to be around him. It was a conundrum, as her father had been fond of saying.

The simplest way to avoid all that, to avoid any explanations that would probably result in her turning redder than the color of the shoes that Kelli had insisted on wearing this morning, was to say, "No, by all means, the more the merrier. Of course you can join us for lunch."

So, she did.

Chapter Ten

As it turned out, Philippe seemed to hit it off very well with Gordon and if one or the other paused to take a breath, there was Kelli, chatting like a little old lady, eager to fill in the dead air.

Consequently, Janice contributed very little to the conversation that took place over salads and seasoned chicken strips. Her exact words were: "Thank you," uttered twice and neither time to the people sitting around her at the table. The words were addressed to the waitress who brought her beverage and then her lunch.

Content to observe and listen, both with a measure of awe, Janice assumed that no one noticed her silence.

It amazed her that not only Kelli but Gordon seemed to be completely taken with Philippe. Their reasons, however, were obviously different. Kelli hung on the man's every word because she was apparently caught up in a spate of hero-worship. As for Gordon, even though he and Philippe appeared to be worlds apart, the two had some things in common.

Would wonders never cease?

So as Gordon and Philippe talked about sports and action movies, and Kelli interjected enthusiastically from time to time, Janice took in the exchange and smiled to herself. And tried not to notice the feeling of contentment that wrapped itself around her.

"You didn't talk much at lunch."

Janice sucked in her breath, startled. Preoccupied with gathering her things together, she hadn't heard Philippe come up behind her. Hadn't seen him at all for the last four hours, not since they're returned and she had gotten back to work.

Turning, she looked up into brilliant green eyes that took her breath away.

"You, Gordon and Kelli didn't leave any openings to get a word in edgewise." Her pulse was dancing, she noted. He was standing too close. "I'm surprised you even noticed."

His mouth curved just the slightest bit. "Hard not to notice things about you."

It wasn't a line. He looked incapable of grinding out lines, she decided. Which made him completely different from her brother, Gordon, and probably his brother, Georges, too, she'd wager. From his manner, and the fact that he'd winked at her as she left, she had strong suspicions that Georges was much like her own brother.

She could feel Philippe's eyes working their way along her face, studying her. Looking right *into* her.

Heat traveled up her body as a blush worked its way to the roots of her hair.

Now that had to be a sight, she thought disparagingly. A twenty-eight-year-old woman, widowed and a single mother to boot, who had, if not been around the block a few times, at least had gotten off the family stoop, blushing.

She caught herself wishing that the house didn't catch too much of the afternoon sun. There was no way the man could miss the fact that she was blushing like some adolescent school girl.

"Thank you," she murmured, acknowledging his compliment. "For everything."

"Everything?"

She elaborated. "The easel, lunch." *Hiring me in the first place.* She caught her lower lip between her teeth, debating her next words, but she didn't want him getting the wrong idea.

"You know I didn't invite you along with us to pay for it."

A surge of desire rose out of nowhere, making him want to nibble on the same lip she'd carelessly taken prisoner. Did she have any idea how delectable she was?

"As I recall, you didn't invite me at all," he contradicted. "That was Kelli's doing."

He was right. Janice shrugged. "I thought you'd be uncomfortable."

Although he wasn't as outgoing as either one of his brothers, because of the kind of life he'd led with his mother during his childhood, he was able to fit into almost any situation.

"I wasn't uncomfortable." His eyes searched her face. "Were you?"

She had been, but it wasn't the kind of uncomfortable he meant. It was the "uncomfortable" of realizing that feelings were being roused, feelings that could only lead to disappointment. But her thoughts were her own, not to be shared with someone who was, for all intents and purposes, a stranger.

She lifted her chin defiantly. "Why should I be uncomfortable?"

"I don't know." He watched her, the soul of innocence. Innocence about to go awry. "I'm harmless enough."

Had the man even *looked* in the mirror recently? She laughed shortly. "Not hardly."

He could listen to the sound of her laughter all day, even when it was aimed at him. "Care to elaborate?"

She shook her head. Tiny pinpricks of panic assaulted

her body. That was the trouble when you brought your brother and daughter with you, she thought. You couldn't just beat a hasty retreat and drive away. You had to collect them first. "No."

It was an effort to keep his hands at his sides. A stray hair along her cheek begged to be pushed back into place. "Then I was right, I do make you uncomfortable."

He made her fidget inside. Made her restless.

Made her remember that there were other things besides two by fours to put her hand to. Small, nameless desires materialized out of the mists where they'd been banished. She yearned to touch this man, to feel his muscles beneath her fingertips, his stubble against her cheek in the morning. Yearned to catch a whiff of his scent on the pillow beside hers even after he was gone.

God, but she missed being part of a twosome. She and Gary had had their problems, but it wasn't anything that couldn't have been worked out in time. She'd married him to get out of her father's house, where she felt unloved and ignored. All she'd wanted was to begin a life of her own, to matter to someone. That was her goal and she was willing to make all kinds of compromises to reach it.

But then Gary had gone and died on her. Leaving her just as her mother had. Just as her father had, in his own way, years before he died. With her parents, she'd endured emotional abandonment before they ever left her physically. With Gary, it had been physical, but this didn't lessen the pain of the loss.

There were just so many times she could expose her heart. She no longer needed approval, she was her own person. And as for love, well, Kelli loved her and in his own confused way, so did Gordon. That was enough.

Oh God, he was touching her, his fingertips moving against her face. It took everything she had not to melt into Philippe's hand, not to melt against him. Her breath backed up in her lungs.

"I don't mean to make you uncomfortable, J.D."

"Janice," she whispered.

He leaned in a little closer, his lips so close to hers, she could almost feel them moving as he asked, "What?"

It was an effort to think, to speak. "You've hired me, that means you get the right to call me by my first name."

"Janice." He nodded, repeating the name. And then he smiled. "It suits you."

"How so?" Damn it, was he ever going to drop his hand? She was having trouble thinking.

He didn't know how much longer he could refrain from acting on the impulse that kept doubling in size every second. "Short, to the point, yet feminine."

That made her laugh under her breath and she shook her head. "Been a long time since anyone called me feminine."

Very slowly, he moved his thumb along her lower lip, enticing them both. "Don't see why. You are. Under those jeans and that T-shirt, you are."

What the hell was he doing? his conscience demanded. It was like having some kind of out-of-body experience. He'd somehow stepped outside of himself and now he watched this unfold. Watched himself flirt with a woman even though any relationship would be doomed from the start. He knew he wasn't going to follow up on any of these feelings he was having, even if they were so strong they made it hard for him to breathe.

He was his mother's son, which meant that no matter what he felt now, he was going to move on. Something always seemed to stop him, made him turn away, before he became even mildly serious. Janice didn't deserve to have her life messed up like that.

He needed to stop, to walk away.

Now.

But he didn't. And he was no longer just watching, he was acting. Acting on impulse, on whim, on a desire that seemed to be bigger than he was, acting like some kind of fool.

It didn't change anything. He leaned over her trim, athletic body and brought his mouth down on hers.

Anticipation did not overshadow reality. If anything, it was the other way around. For a moment, he allowed himself to forget everything, just enjoy the moment.

Oh, my God. Everything around her, the room, the house, the world, everything faded to black and disappeared except for the incredible sensations shooting through her. Absorbing her. Breaking down from the mini-tower of strength she perceived herself to be and re-building a flesh and blood woman with needs and desires.

Without thinking, she rose up on her toes as far as she could, winding her arms around his neck and leaning into him, nerves jumping all up and down on her body. She'd never expected anything like this, never had her head turned completely around by a mere kiss.

No, not mere. Anything but mere.

"Mere" didn't make her skin sizzle or her brain go careening. But as wondrous as it was, she felt unsettled. Unsettled because his kiss opened up floodgates she was terrified of having unlocked.

And yet—

This was delicious and she didn't want it to stop. In a minute, but not now. Just a second longer and then she'd back away. She had to. No matter what her yearning was, she couldn't act on it. Because she wasn't alone.

Thank God she'd brought her brother and Kelli with her. Having them here forced her to remain on the straight and narrow path, something she strongly doubted she could have done on her own right now.

And then, as unexpectedly as it had begun, it was over.

Philippe drew his head back, his expression dazed. He took a breath, as if to steady himself. It was going to take more than a breath to do that for her, she thought.

"I'm not going to apologize," he told her.

"All right." She was fairly surprised she could

actually talk. Her lips felt as if they had the consistency of warmed honey.

"Not for the kiss, anyway."

She didn't understand, but then, it would have taken her a minute to respond if someone had asked her her name. "Then for what?"

The smile was sad and burrowed into her heart before she could stop it. "For more things than I can begin to tell you."

"You are a very complicated, mysterious man, Philippe Zabelle."

The laugh was dry with only a touch of humor to it. "You don't know the half of it."

He made her wonder. About the sadness in his eyes, about him. Had there been anyone in his life? Someone who'd hurt him? Or someone he'd hurt that he felt guilty about?

"Maybe someday I will," she replied.

Damn it, not your business, Janice. This wasn't part of the job and that was all she needed to focus on. Abruptly, she raised her voice and called out to her daughter.

"Time to call it a day, kiddo." *While Mama still had knees that functioned.*

She felt as if she'd just been dynamited off her comfortable perch. With effort she slowed her pace and left the room, trying very hard not to look as if she was hurrying away from him.

But she was.

* * *

As she carried in the laundry basket from the garage later that evening, she noticed that Gordon's car wasn't there. Still holding the basket, she passed by the window and glanced out.

The car wasn't parked at the curb, either. "Kelli, where's Uncle Gordon?"

The little girl looked up from the book of children's drawings she was paging through. "He went out."

Oh God, not on a date, Janice prayed. The only time Gordon didn't say anything about leaving, didn't call out a "see you later," he was going off on a date with someone he knew he shouldn't be seeing.

Janice set down the basket on the coffee table and sat down beside her daughter on the sofa. "Out? When?"

"A little while ago." Kelli paused to think. "The seven o'clock news lady was on. He said I couldn't go with him."

The idea of Kelli out with Gordon on one of his dates horrified her. "Well, at least he has some grain of sense," she murmured to herself, then looked at her daughter. Something wasn't adding up. "Why would you want to go with him?"

"Because he's going to Phili— Mr. Zabelle's house," Kelli amended, knowing that her mother didn't like her calling grown-ups by their first names.

Janice stared at her daughter. Okay, the two men seemed to get along at lunch, but Gordon just wasn't in

Philippe's league. Philippe had things together while Gordon was a loosely wound ball of yarn, ready to come apart at the slightest push. "Why would he be going there?"

"To play poker," Kelli volunteered brightly.

Janice's mouth dropped open. Poker? Had he gotten caught up in a new obsession? Gordon didn't do things by half measures. If he started seeing someone, he was planning marriage by the end of the first date. She'd seen him through a number of dependencies, including food and alcohol. He didn't know how to do anything in moderation—except work, she thought cynically. These days, she was working like a dog not only to pay her own bills, but to help Gordon meet his bankruptcy payments as well. The faster that was paid off, the sooner he'd be able to get on his own two feet.

A cold shiver went down her spine. That wasn't going to happen if he'd taken up gambling.

She rose to her feet, putting her hand out to her daughter. "C'mon, honey."

Kelli scooted off the sofa, taking her mother's hand. "Where are we going?"

"Well, you're going to Mrs. Addison." A grandmother three times over, the woman had made it known that she was willing to babysit in the evenings, especially if there was an emergency. This definitely qualified. "I'm going to Mr. Zabelle's house to bring back Uncle Gordon before he finds another pit to fall into."

It was obvious that Kelli didn't quite understand what

she was talking about, but she'd latched onto the one thing that was clear to her. Her mother was going to see Philippe. "Mr. Zabelle? Why can't I go with you?"

Janice grabbed her purse out of the closet. Slinging it over her shoulder, she headed for the front door with Kelli in tow. "Because Mama's going to be using some grown-up words that you're too young to hear."

"I watch TV, Mama," Kelli protested.

She locked the door behind her. "More grown-up than that," Janice told her tersely.

Her tone was far from warm, but it wasn't meant for Kelli. She was focused on Gordon, annoyed with him for blundering into yet another possible addiction. She wasn't overly thrilled with Philippe either, even though the man had no way of knowing about her brother's addictive personality.

But he would by the time the evening was through.

This was all she needed, Janice thought.

She struggled to keep her temper in-check. As she drove to Philippe's, it was an effort to keep from pressing down on the accelerator and going over the speed limit.

For most of her adult life, she'd been bailing her brother out of one thing or another. His inability to recognize that he was being taken in by a series of women who only wanted what he could give them, had catapulted him into bankruptcy, which had led him into drinking and then overeating. She'd finally, finally gotten him to come around and be her assistant on these contracting jobs. And now he was sliding backward into something new.

She pressed her lips together, trying not to swear as she eased her foot off the gas. She was doing five miles over the speed limit.

Philippe was a bright man, couldn't he see that Gordon had a weak, malleable personality?

Damn it, why did she have to be her brother's keeper, anyway? She had enough to keep her busy.

Getting over that kiss, for instance.

The second she thought of it, of her involuntary reaction, Janice felt her skin tingling.

Get a grip, Janice. You're supposed to be boiling mad, not a bowl of mush.

By the time she arrived at Philippe's door, Janice was completely worked up. Instead of ringing the bell, she knocked. Pounded was more like it. The door had taken the place of her brother's head.

Inside, Alain peered at his brother over a hand that would have gladdened the heart of a professional gambler.

Slim fingers folded the cards in his hand. Alain raised a quizzical eyebrow. "You expecting someone to come break down your door, Philippe?"

"Not tonight." The pounding continued. He sighed, folded his cards and placed them facedown on the table.

As he rose, he pointed to the hand. "Don't anyone try to mess with that, I know what I have."

"An unhealthy distrust of your relatives is what you have," Georges commented. "Philippe's blunt warning wasn't meant for you," he told Gordon. "He thinks we cheat. In reality, he's not that hot a poker player."

Gordon nodded, finding himself completely at ease in this company of men. It was a pleasant feeling, one he wasn't accustomed to.

Philippe waved a hand at Georges. "I don't cheat," he declared as he opened the door. Turning, he was surprised and not a little pleased to see Janice standing there.

Her eyes were blazing. And there was something very stirring about the image she presented. "Did I forget something?"

"Yes," she snapped, not waiting to be invited in. "Decency."

He closed the door behind her. "No, I'm pretty sure I stocked up on that the last time I was at the store." She wasn't smiling. "What's the matter?"

By now, she was no longer thinking rationally. God only knew how much Gordon could have lost. "How could you?" she demanded.

Philippe hadn't a clue. "How could I what?"

She gritted her teeth. Without her experience of plucking Gordon out of precarious situations, she might have thought Philippe was innocent. "How could you invite my brother to your poker game?"

Philippe shoved his hands into his front pockets. Eventually this was going to make sense. He just had to be patient. "Pretty easily, actually. I said something like, 'Gordon, want to come to a game I'm holding tonight?' And he said yes."

She struggled to keep her voice down. She didn't want to embarrass her brother in front of other people, but she certainly didn't want to have to bail him out any more than she was already doing.

"This isn't funny, Zabelle," she told him in a low, firm voice. "Gordon's got an addictive personality. He doesn't do anything in half measures." She was rambling, she thought and reined herself in. "I can't go into details, but this is really a very bad thing. You have to cut him off."

Philippe still looked like the soul of innocence as he asked her, "You want me to cut off his colored toothpicks?"

About to shout "yes" she stopped and stared at him. "Colored toothpicks?"

He nodded, taking her arm. Thinking he was going to usher her out, she pulled it away. "That's what we play for. Colored toothpicks."

She wasn't about to be distracted. There had to be more than that. "But they represent something, don't they?"

Philippe nodded. "Well, yeah."

To his credit, Zabelle didn't even try to lie about it.

Although that didn't change the bottom line. "Gordon can't afford it."

Very complacently, Philippe placed his hands on her shoulders. That he was so calm only infuriated her further. "Janice, calm down. If he's the big loser, he has to wash the big winner's car or clean the big winner's barbecue grill. Something along those lines."

The fire went out of her eyes. "What? You don't gamble for money?"

He shook his head. "We play for things, chores mostly. Playing relaxes us and it gives us a chance to get together." He took a breath. Maybe she'd feel better if he explained a few things to her. Ordinarily, he didn't like getting personal, but he made an exception. "My father was a professional gambler and he 'professionally' lost almost everything my mother worked for. I don't even play the slot machines in Vegas. I don't believe in real gambling, but this is just harmless fun, a way to knock off steam, get the adrenaline to kick in without any risk."

She caught her lower lip between her teeth, feeling somewhat foolish now. "Really?"

He laced his hand through hers. "Really." He nodded toward the dining room. "Come see."

"No, that's okay," she demurred. But he was already bringing her in.

Like a boy caught by his mother after curfew, Gordon looked both surprised and uneasy to see her. "What are you doing here?"

Before she could say anything, Philippe was quick to explain. "Janice thought she forgot one of her tools. I wanted to introduce her to you guys—in case any of you lugs has a remodeling job you want done." Turning to her, he confided, "All of them are as handy as dried out paste."

Georges merely laughed. "You should talk. At least I know what to do with pointy objects."

Just standing there, listening to the exchange, she could feel the love in the room. It made her envious and long for a childhood she'd never had.

Chapter Eleven

As Philippe introduced her to the other members of his weekly poker game, Janice was acutely aware of the way her brother was looking at her. As if he knew why she was really there. It wasn't because of some so-called imaginary tool she'd left behind. She wanted to check up on him, as if he were twelve and she was his mother.

It was all there in his face: annoyance at her unexpected invasion, hurt at her lack of trust. But damn it, could he really blame her? After all he'd put her through? She only had his best interests at heart.

The introductions over, Janice pressed her lips

together and mustered a smile that took in all the men gathered around the oblong table.

"Sorry, I didn't know I'd be barging in on a poker game. Please, go back to playing." Her eyes met Gordon's briefly. "I was never here." She glanced at Philippe. He made a move to follow her as she backed away from the table. "I can see myself out." Again, her eyes shifted toward her brother. "See you at home, Gordon," she added as she retreated.

Despite what she'd just told him, Philippe followed her out of the room.

She felt just awful for raising her voice and accusing Philippe of taking advantage of her brother. She wouldn't blame him if he decided to terminate their contract. But before she could tender an apology, something that never came easily to her, Philippe took her by the arm and drew her over to the side.

"Listen," he began softly, "I'm sorry I stirred things up for you."

God, when he looked at her like that with those green eyes of his, she caught herself thinking that she could forgive him for just about anything.

Get a grip, Janice. He's the guy you're working for right now, nothing else. Is that clear?

Clear as mud.

"It seemed harmless enough at the time," Philippe was saying to her. She struggled to focus on his words and not his lips or his eyes. Not exactly easy, given their proximity. "I got the feeling earlier today that your brother's struggling with a lot of problems and I thought this might help him blow off steam. It does me."

What kind of problems did Philippe have, she wondered. From everything she'd seen, he led a perfect life.

After a beat, she found her tongue and discovered that it really wasn't glued to the roof of her mouth. "You don't have to apologize to me."

The grin was quick, so was the all-but-lethal shot to her gut. "Well, apparently I do. I don't know if you realized it or not, but there was steam coming out of your ears when you got here and I think you left a perfect replica of your knuckles on my door."

Okay, so she'd overreacted. Big time. She wasn't the kind to try to bury a mistake. When she was wrong, she was wrong and she admitted it, but she wanted Philippe to understand why she'd come in looking and sounding like a possessed wild woman.

She just wasn't sure how to begin. Or how much to tell him. "Gordon's done some pretty stupid things in his time."

To his credit, Philippe didn't prod her for details. "It's a big club."

Because he didn't ask, she was more inclined to share a little more. Gordon liked to talk and she had no doubts that her brother would wind up telling Philippe the whole story sooner than later, so she wasn't violating any kind of trust by letting the man know now.

"No, I mean *really* stupid. He lets himself be led around by the nose by any woman who'll pay attention to him." She shrugged helplessly. "Could be an offshoot of our mother walking out on us. He was very attached to her."

Janice stopped abruptly, having gone further than she'd intended. The last sentence had just slipped out without warning.

Philippe nodded slowly, as if analyzing what she'd just said. "And it hit him hard when the reverse didn't turn out to be true." He stood there for a long moment, studying her. She caught herself wanting to shift beneath his gaze. It took effort to remain still. "How about you?"

Unconsciously, she raised her chin. "How about me, what?"

"How did your mother's walking out on the family affect you?"

Janice looked away and shrugged, as if it hadn't bothered her. As if she hadn't stayed up nights when she was a little girl, wondering if there was something she could have done better to make her mother stay. Guilt had been her constant companion for the first two years after the family had gone from four to three members.

"I didn't think about it one way or another," she lied. Because it felt as if his eyes were peering straight into her soul, she added, "I guess she wanted to be away from my father more than she wanted to be with us."

"We have something in common," he told her. When Janice eyed him quizzically, he said, "We both had gypsy mothers."

She'd read somewhere about Lily Moreau's bohemian lifestyle. She supposed he was trying to make her feel better about the situation. Too late, she thought, she no longer felt anything about it one way or another. "Yes, but with one difference. Yours came back."

"And left. And came back. And then left again." He laughed softly, having come to terms with it years ago. "Made for a very confused childhood. There were lots of times when we saw the nanny and the housekeeper more than we saw our mother."

If there were any problems, they must have been minor, she thought. Georges was charming and Alain seemed to be as well. And as for Philippe, well Philippe was as together and well-adjusted a person as she'd ever come across. Just a little withdrawn. But that seemed to be changing.

"You and your brothers seemed to have turned out all right."

"So did you," he pointed out. "We all do what we have to do to survive." Now that he looked at her closely, she seemed incredibly tense, like someone waiting not for the next shoe to fall but the next bomb to go off. He tried to make her feel more at ease, more hopeful. "I get the impression that Gordon's trying to come around."

She closed her eyes for a moment. *If only.* "I hope

so. I can't keep bailing him out." Philippe was smiling like he knew something she didn't.

"Sure you can," he told her. Though she might protest otherwise, he had a feeling that she was one of those people for whom family loyalty meant everything. He could readily identify with that. "You wouldn't be you if you didn't."

"You don't know so much about me."

Philippe laughed. Now there she was very, very wrong. "Sorry to contradict you, but this is the age of the Internet, Janice. I know a great deal about you."

God help her, she liked the way he said her name, as if it was purely feminine. As if *she* was purely feminine. When had she last felt that way? Other than when he kissed her, she amended.

"I know that you worked for your father at his construction company," he told her. "That he left Wyatt Construction to Gordon, not you. That within a very short period of time Gordon had to file a chapter 13 because he had borrowed so heavily against the company's assets that Wyatt Construction couldn't afford to pay its men. And then the company wound up paying penalties because it couldn't finish jobs in accordance with the deadlines in the contracts.

"I know that you have a contractor's license." She'd told him that, but he stunned her by reciting the number, something she *hadn't* told him. "And you're presently trying to regain your footing so that you can finally form your own company—after you finish paying off your brother's bills."

For a moment, there was nothing but silence in the hallway. How could there be that much information floating around about her? But then, in this paperless society, everything seemed to be drifting out there in cyberspace, waiting to be netted and pulled in like a school of salmon. Still, she couldn't get over how extensive a job he'd done.

"You looked me up?"

He nodded. "Can't just let anyone take a sledgehammer to my house," he told her. He'd investigated her after he'd hired her. Motivated, he had to admit, more by curiosity about the woman than a desire to protect himself against the possible rash actions of a stranger.

Philippe shoved his hands into his pockets, knowing she probably wouldn't like the next suggestion. But sometimes, being there for a person meant *not* being there for them 24-7. It came under the prickly heading of tough love. "Maybe Gordon should start paying off his own bills. It would probably make him feel better about himself."

Funny, ordinarily she'd resent someone giving her advice on how to handle her brother. But there was something in Philippe's eyes that told her he meant well. Besides, he was a brother, too. As the oldest, he probably knew what it meant to be there for one or both of them.

Janice shook her head. "The only money Gordon seems to make these days is the money I pay him when

I have a job that's too big for just me. Whether I hand him the money so he can pay the bills or I just pay the bills myself, it all boils down to my paying the monthly bills. Pretending it's anything else is just an illusion."

She watched, mesmerized, as his mouth curved again. Making her pulse skip. "We all need illusions to sustain us."

She sighed, knowing she didn't have all the answers. Lately, it felt as if she had very few of them. "Maybe you're right."

"I am." The quick grin went directly to his eyes. And to her central core. Janice had to concentrate not to let her breath back up. Not to allow her imagination to run away with her. "At least fifty percent of the time."

"Hey, big spender," Alain called from the dining room, "your hand's getting cold. You gonna come back and play or not?"

"You'd better go." Janice nodded toward the rear of the house, feeling guilty about having monopolized him. "Your hand is calling."

Maybe it was, but other things called to him as well, he thought. Things that had nothing to do with a hand of poker. Standing here at the threshold of his home, the lighting sparse, he was incredibly aware of almost everything about her. Aware of her close proximity, of the way her chest rose and fell with each breath.

Damn, but he had this overwhelming urge to kiss her again.

He would have acted on it, but he knew that one of his brothers, cousins or even her brother could come out looking for him. The last thing he wanted was to embarrass her. So he tightened his resolve and remained where he was, on the tip of the fence and dying to fall over to her side.

"Yeah," he murmured. "Maybe I'd better go. See you tomorrow."

She nodded, turning to go. And then she turned around again. "Oh." The single word had him pivoting on his heel, looking at her again. "I meant to tell you, about my bringing Kelli today, it's not going to be a permanent thing. I really am trying to find a babysitter for her during the day."

Philippe shook his head. "Don't."

"Don't what?"

"Don't get another babysitter for her. I think it might upset her to be left behind with someone new. Besides, it's important for a child to be around her mother." He remembered how he'd felt every time he'd seen his mother go out the door, wondering if it was for the afternoon or if he wouldn't be seeing her for weeks at a clip. Lily never liked telling him and his brothers that she was taking off. She left that up to the nanny or her husband-of-the-moment.

Years later, in an off moment, she'd confided that the disappointed expression on his face stayed with her for days, marring her joy over an upcoming show. It was easier for her just to slip away, like a mother leaving her child on the first day of kindergarten.

He'd caught on about her getaways long before she'd made her confession. Caught on and rather than confront her the next time she returned, worked at living his life without any parental support or input. He told himself it didn't matter that she took off without warning as frequently as she did.

But in his heart, in the place where secrets were locked up, he knew that it did. And that, too, made him leery of attachments. Because attachments meant disappointments.

"All right," she said slowly. She knew that Kelli would be more than happy to come along with her to work. She was relieved that she wouldn't have to face telling her daughter that she was getting a new baby-sitter, someone besides Mrs. McClonsky or Gordon. And she *really* hadn't been looking forward to the tedious round of interviews for someone suitable to watch her daughter. Her eyes smiled at him, telegraphing her relief.

"If you're sure you don't mind."

"I'm sure I don't mind," he assured her. "She's a good kid, not to mention gifted."

Janice wondered if he really believed that or if he was just saying it because every mother liked hearing such things.

Stop overanalyzing everything, she upbraided

herself. *Sometimes a raindrop is just a raindrop and not the beginning of a flash flood.*

Heartened, she drew back her shoulders and nodded amiably. "Okay, see you tomorrow."

"Hey, Philippe—" Beau called, his voice all but booming.

"Coming. Keep your shirt on." Philippe looked at her, suppressing, again, the urge to kiss her. "I'll send him back early," he promised.

And then winked.

Obviously, winking was a family thing, Janice thought as she left. Except that when Georges had winked at her, her stomach hadn't suddenly flipped over and tied itself up in a knot.

She tried not to think about that as she all but flew back to her truck.

The front door squeaked as it opened then closed. Gordon cursed under his breath, thinking for the dozenth time that he needed to oil that. The squeak prevented him from making an otherwise silent entrance home.

The second he heard the noise, he saw Janice. His sister had been stretched out on the sofa, a book housed on her chest, her eyes closed. They flew open as the squeak penetrated her consciousness. She'd always been an incredibly light sleeper. Unlike their father. But then, she didn't have a quart of wine to lull her to sleep each night the way their father had.

He might as well face the music, he thought, walking into the living room. "Look, maybe I shouldn't have snuck out of the house that way," Gordon began awkwardly, feeling like some tongue-tied teenager instead of a man talking to his sister. His *younger* sister, for Pete's sakes.

Still a little bleary-eyed, Janice stifled a yawn and sat up. It took her a second to pull herself together. She wasn't waiting up to take him to task, she was waiting up to apologize.

"I'm sorry I made you feel that you had to sneak out." Her words, she saw, surprised him. "It's just that I worry about you."

It wasn't that he didn't like her caring about him, it was just that sometimes it made him feel like he was in a straitjacket.

"Yeah, I know." He shrugged. "But I think I'm good, now. Really." He perched for a second on the arm of the sofa, right beside her. "I mean, I learned my lesson. Hell, bankruptcy, losing Pop's company. Even if I didn't like the company, I didn't mean for any of those things to happen," he told her, silently asking her forgiveness for having screwed up so badly.

"I know." Shifting over, she put her arm on his shoulder, reaching up as far as she could. "I know." She rose to her feet, tossing the book down on the coffee table. The bookmark slipped out. She picked it up and left it on top of the book, too tired to search for the passage it had been marking. "Well, I'm going to bed."

He stared at her back, dumbfounded as she began to walk away. "Don't you want to know how I did?"

Since it wasn't for money, fear had been taken out of the equation. "Okay, how d'you do?"

"I won." He was grinning like a kid who'd been awarded a lifetime supply of his favorite flavor of ice cream. "Philippe's brother, Alain, has to wash my car. Did you know he's studying to be a lawyer?" That part pleased him the most, having an almost-lawyer working for him, however briefly.

"No," she admitted, "I didn't know that." She didn't know very much about Philippe and his family. Nowhere near the amount of information that Philippe had amassed on her, she thought. Maybe it was time she put her hand to the Internet—tomorrow, she added silently, stifling another yawn.

"Maybe I should have gone to law school," he murmured under his breath, following her up the stairs to his own bedroom.

"Never too late to try," she told him as cheerfully as she could. It was a philosophy she held dear to her own heart, but right now, given her present state, it lacked conviction.

He stopped mid-nod as another thought hit him. "But then who'd help you?"

"I'd be lost without you."

Pretending to be resigned, Gordon nodded, smiling to himself. "Nice to know."

"Hey, I'd always be lost without you," she told him firmly.

Philippe was right, Janice thought grudgingly as she walked into her bedroom and closed the door behind her. The faint scent of vanilla wafted to her, coming from yesterday's pile of folded laundry that she hadn't put away yet. Her brother needed to build up his self-esteem before he could be expected to fly.

Okay, so she owed Philippe, she told herself. She'd never liked owing anyone, even people she liked. She was going to have to find a way to settle up in the near future. But right now, she needed to get some sleep if she intended to be of any use tomorrow morning.

She slept fitfully, dreaming of a man with green eyes, a magnetic smile and hair the color of the heart of midnight.

They fell into a routine, despite the fact that every day brought new challenges, new work. The routine entailed that she and Gordon, with Kelli in tow, would show up at Philippe's doorstep each morning at exactly seven. Once Kelli was set up with either her easel or a book, she and Gordon would get down to work. They kept at whatever needed doing for the better part of four hours.

More than once, she'd pass by and catch Philippe admiring Kelli's work or giving the little girl pointers regarding her art. He was also the one Kelli turned to when she couldn't sound out a word. Hungry for a father figure, Kelli quickly transferred her affections to Philippe, lapping up any attention he gave her like a hungry puppy.

Janice noted that unlike the first few days, Philippe now kept his office door open. And as likely as not, Kelli would wander in to ask a question or offer an opinion about what she saw on his computer monitor. Or just to talk. And Philippe, Kelli told them proudly over meals, would always stop whatever he was doing to listen to her.

At around eleven, she and Gordon would break for lunch. Left on her own, she would work longer, but her brother tended to flag after four hours, needing to replenish his energy. Most of the time, Philippe would join them.

That had been her doing, inviting him to sample some of the food she'd brought with her in what Kelli referred to as "Mama's picnic basket." After a while, Philippe didn't need inviting, he just joined them when eleven rolled around, to sit and eat and talk amid the dust and the debris.

At times she'd just pull back and observe what was going on, as if she wasn't part of it. It always warmed her heart and, most of all, made her wish that things wouldn't end.

Because in this present framework, she could tell herself that she wasn't falling for the man, wasn't risking too much. After Gary had died she'd sworn never to put herself out there again, never expose her heart. Crushed again. Her parents and Gary had all left her in one way or another. She refused to endure that feeling of loss again.

But each time their hands accidentally touched, or she saw Philippe take time from his incredibly busy schedule to share a moment with her daughter, she felt something. Something strong. A pull that drew her directly to him—and made her dream, wishing things were different. Wishing she weren't afraid.

But she was and it was fear she hid behind.

Philippe had asked her out several times now and each time she'd made polite excuses—just strongly enough to hold him at bay, not strongly enough to rebuff him.

What the hell was she doing? she silently demanded of herself more than once. He was going to get tired of hearing excuses and stop asking. And that, she knew, was for the best.

And yet—

And yet she didn't want him to stop asking. Didn't want him to back away.

You don't know what you want, she admonished herself. And it was true.

"You're playing games, J.D. Never knew you to play games before," Gordon commented right after lunch one day. They'd been on the job for five weeks. Philippe had gone back to his office and she was clearing away the empty pizza box.

Overhearing, Kelli was quick to come to her defense. "Mama plays lots of games."

Janice offered her daughter what she hoped was an innocent, approving smile before turning to Gordon. "We'll talk about this later."

Gordon shook his head. "I'm not the one you should be talking to." The look he gave her was pregnant with meaning. And just in case she missed it, he indicated Philippe's office with his eyes.

Before she had a chance to tell her brother that none of this was any of his business, the front door suddenly opened. Lily sailed in majestically, taking the room— and attention—as if it rightfully belonged only to her.

The second the artist entered, Kelli abandoned her easel and raced to Lily as if the woman was a favorite aunt. Or a beloved grandmother. Neither of which she had.

Rather than just fluff her off, Lily got down to the little girl's level and put her arms around her. The hug was both warm and genuine and it was difficult to determine who enjoyed it more, the woman or the child.

"Hello, everyone," Lily declared in her clear theatrical voice as she regained her feet again. She looked directly at Gordon and then at her. "Didn't mean to interrupt anything."

Janice saw the amused look on Philippe's face as he entered from the hallway. He leaned against one wall, folding his arms before him. She had a feeling that they were both thinking the same thing: that it was a lie. Lily Moreau liked nothing more than making a grand entrance and bringing everything to a grinding halt by her mere presence. The woman clearly thrived on the spotlight, even if it was only the kind cast by a child's flashlight.

Chapter Twelve

"So, you are coming, aren't you?" Still holding on to Kelli's hand, Lily looked at her son expectantly, waiting for a confirmation.

"I might," Philippe allowed. "If I knew what you were referring to."

With an audible sigh, Lily shook her head, her chandelier earrings swaying rhythmically to and fro about her perfectly sculpted cheekbones. She slanted a mock exasperated glance toward Janice.

"Men. They never seem to retain anything in their heads except for a woman's measurements." She sighed again, her attention returning to Philippe. "To my opening, of course."

He pretended to consider her words carefully. "Didn't I already go to it?"

This time, the note of exasperation was genuine. "No, you didn't already go to it—because it was postponed." She waved a bejeweled hand dismissively, as if things only happened to either impede or enhance her daily life. "Something about the gallery owner coming down with a colossal case of gastritis or some such ailment. In any event, he closed down the gallery for two weeks." She frowned at such sacrilege. "In my day, you sucked it up for art and soldiered on."

Philippe grinned. "Especially for a Lily Moreau showing."

"Exactly." And then her turquoise eyes swept over the two other adults in the partially reconstructed room. "You're welcomed to come, too." She paused for a moment, looking at the coveralls that Janice was wearing. "But it is formal."

Janice never cracked a smile as she glanced down at the faded blue denim. "I guess that means I get to wear my strapless overalls."

Lily surprised her by taking it in stride. "Very funny, dear." The woman studied her torso, circling once before nodding. "I have clothes I can lend you." She turned to her son. "You can bring her to the house, Philippe. Give her anything she wants."

Panic pricked at Janice's belly. This was getting way too personal, too social. Her first reaction was to back away, to withdraw before there were consequences. "No, wait, I really don't think I can—"

But Kelli was already tugging on her arm. One look at the small, upturned face and Janice knew what was in her daughter's heart. "Please, Mama?"

"Yes, 'please Mama,'" Lily echoed for good measure, never once assuming that it would be any other way than how she wanted it to be. "It'll be good for the child," she assured Janice. "She should have exposure to the arts."

Janice could feel her back going up. She didn't welcome advice when none was requested, especially not when it came to Kelli. "I take her to the museum," Janice countered.

Lily was obviously unimpressed. "The visual arts," she emphasized. She looked down at Kelli with tremendous approval. "You're never too young to learn what the field is all about if you're going to make a living in it."

"She hasn't entered kindergarten yet," Janice pointed out evenly. "I think it's a little early to start giving her vocational guidance."

It was evident that Lily was not of the same opinion. "She has a gift, dear," the older woman told her kindly, patting her cheek. "You shouldn't keep it from the world—or the world from her, for that matter." Lily opened her purse and took out a mauve-colored card with the gallery's name on it. She pressed it into Kelli's hand. "Bring your mommy along. If she doesn't want to come, Philippe can bring you along with him."

It still amazed Philippe that his mother never thought that people might have other plans, plans that differed from hers.

He moved closer to Janice. "That's called kidnapping in some states, Mother."

Rings glinted in the sunlight as Lily waved a hand at him. There were times he wondered if she would be able to speak if her hands were tied. "Don't be so dramatic, Philippe. Honestly," she said to Gordon, "I don't know where he gets it from." She paused, the stranger's face finally registering in her brain. Always intrigued by a good-looking man, she abruptly asked, "And you are?"

"Really fascinated," Gordon responded. He seemed overcome by this vibrant and flamboyant woman.

Without realizing it, Gordon had chosen his words perfectly. Lily smiled broadly and the years instantly melted away. She presented him with her hand. It took him a second before he came to and shook it. "Well, Really Fascinated, I hope you have the opportunity to come to the opening, too."

And then it was time to go. Lily turned to Philippe. "Tomorrow night. Don't forget. The showing begins at eight. Try not to be late." Her sweeping glance took them all in just before she crossed to the front door. "Any of you."

"Can we go, Mama? Can we?" Kelli asked eagerly the moment Lily had left the house. She clutched at her mother's hand with both of hers, fairly dancing back and forth.

"Honey, that's a little late for you."

"I'll take a nap," Kelli told her, her eyes wide with innocence. "A long one. I promise."

Janice sighed. She was really reluctant to go, but it was hard saying no to Kelli. "We'll see."

"I can pick you up," Philippe volunteered. "That way, you won't have to worry about trying to locate the gallery in the dark."

Janice lifted her chin, instantly defensive after a lifetime of having to prove herself over and over again—and never being found good enough. "I have a very good sense of direction, thank you. I can find my own way to—" She paused to look down at the name on the card she'd taken from Kelli. "Sunset Galleries."

Philippe smiled, reading between the lines. "Then you'll come."

Damn it, she hadn't meant to imply that. Janice backtracked. "Maybe."

"Mama," Kelli wailed, a pleading note in her high voice.

"Maybe," Janice repeated firmly, refusing to be pinned down or cornered by this handsome man or his larger-than-life mother.

On his way back to work in the kitchen, Gordon purposely walked by Philippe. He lowered his voice.

"She'll come. She's a pushover for Kelli even if she tries to come off tough."

Janice fisted her hands at her waist, the personification of feistiness. "I still have my hearing, Gordon."

Gordon turned around and grinned. "Never doubted it for a minute, J.D."

"I'm sorry about my mother," Philippe apologized to her as Gordon left the room. "She tends to be a little overbearing."

Now there was an understatement if she'd ever heard one. "You think?"

Over the years, he'd ceased being embarrassed by his mother's actions and had made a concentrated effort to understand her, to know the woman behind the dramatics. "But that's only because she cares so passionately. And she really does think that Kelli," he ran his hand over the little girl's silky hair, "shows a great deal of promise. I do, too. I don't have nearly the eye that my mother does, but I've never seen that kind of ability in someone so young. And in her own way, my mother's right. Exposure to an art gallery might be good for Kelli."

Janice stuck to her guns. Kelli was still four, not a junior in high school. "It's past her bedtime."

He spoke as someone who'd never had an enforced bedtime. "Kids are flexible."

She tried to summon indignation and found it was more difficult when she tried to mount it against him. Something about Philippe Zabelle disarmed her. Which frightened the hell out of her. "And you would know this how?"

The grin all but torpedoed her gut. "I put in my time as a kid. You'd be surprised what a kid can be capable of if the need arises."

She had a feeling he wasn't talking about staying up past a designated bedtime. In his own way, Philippe'd had as unorthodox a childhood as her own. Maybe even more so.

"We'll see," she repeated for the umpteenth time. "Kelli," she instructed, "go back to your drawing. As for me, I have work to do," she told Philippe. "You're not paying me to stand around and grow roots."

There was that grin again. Was it her imagination, or was he doing that a lot more lately? "I would if I could get to watch you do that."

She waved her hand at him as she turned away. But, walking into the kitchen, it was hard to keep her mouth from curving into a smile.

"Timing something?" Alain asked as he saw Philippe look at his watch for what had to be the fifth time in a very short interval.

Philippe dropped his hand to his side. "Just wondering where Mother is," he lied.

Alain grinned. "Well, Mother is probably waiting to make an entrance." He glanced toward the doorway. "You know how she is."

"He's waiting for the little fixer-upper to show," Georges interjected just before he took another sip from the glass of champagne he was husbanding. Two were his limit even though he had an evening off from the hospital. There was always a chance he'd be summoned and he liked being in control of his faculties.

Alain looked mildly surprised. His question was directed to Georges rather than Philippe. "The Wyatt woman is coming?"

Georges nodded, his attention temporarily captured by a canapé he'd snared from a passing waiter's tray. "Mother thinks her daughter has possibilities. Big brother, on the other hand," he inclined his head toward Philippe, "thinks that *she* might have possibilities." Turning toward Philippe, his train of thought halted. "Wow, did you know that you look like thunderbolts could come shooting out of your eyes? Easy, Philippe," he placed a soothing hand on his brother's shoulder, "I think this is a good thing. I haven't seen you interested in anything but a page of code for God only knows how long. Alain and I were beginning to worry about you."

He loved his brothers, but his personal life was his own. "You go out with enough women to make up for the rest of the family," Philippe pointed out.

"Hey, speak for yourself," Alain protested. "I need my own supply of women to keep me going." He grew just a tad serious. "And we're both glad that your interest's finally aroused."

He didn't mind being teased, but they had hit a sensitive spot. "What the hell do you know about my interest?" Philippe challenged. Up until this moment, he'd been fairly secure of his discretion when it came to Janice.

"They're called eyes, Philippe. Alain and I both have them and we use them on occasion," Georges told him, quickly picking up another canapé before the waiter made his way to the other end of the gallery. "We saw you at the poker game that night," he reminded Philippe. "You came to life when she showed up."

He hadn't behaved any differently before or after she'd arrived. Georges didn't know what the hell he was talking about. "You had too much beer."

"I *never* have too much beer," Georges told him. "And besides, it was the beginning of the evening."

Philippe refused to admit to anything. Not until he decided where he wanted this to go and *if* it was going to go anywhere. "Well, something definitely inhibited your perception."

"Denial is a sad thing to witness in a grown man," Alain pronounced before he took a long sip of his champagne. Georges was driving him home so he had no worries about needing to keep a clear head and, sometimes, his mother's shows were better endured just this side of inebriated.

"Speaking of grown men," Philippe neatly diverted the conversation away from himself, "how long do you think it'll take that one to reach maturity?" He nodded toward the young man who had entered the gallery with their mother on his arm.

"Long," Georges murmured, shaking his head.

This was a new face on him. "Who is he?" Philippe wanted to know.

"Mother's newest boy toy," Alain replied with resignation.

"Emphasis on *boy*," Georges chimed in.

Somewhat stunned, Philippe looked from the handsome baby-faced escort in the formal tuxedo to his brothers. "You're kidding."

"If only," Alain murmured.

"What cradle do you suppose darling Lily found him in?" Georges asked. Absently, he took another sip of champagne.

"Barely-legal-lovers 'R' Us?" Alain guessed.

Philippe frowned. They were making jokes, but this could be serious. Just how old was this newest interest of their mother? Of the three of them, he'd been the one who'd paid the most attention to the men who had paraded in and out of Lily's life. In the early days, some had been old enough to collect social security checks. Gradually, a trend took over. As his mother grew older, her lovers grew younger. For a while, her men had been the same age as she was. But in the last few years, they'd been younger. This one, however, was the first who looked as if he might be young enough to be her son.

"What the hell is she thinking?" Philippe asked.

Georges made a calculated guess. "Probably that the male of the species peaks at around nineteen while the average female hits her peak somewhere in her late thirties."

"Nothing average about our mother," Alain commented, watching the duo make their way into the center of the gallery.

Philippe shook his head. "Wouldn't it be nice if there were?"

Georges laughed. "Yes, but then she wouldn't be Lily Moreau, would she?"

"C'mon," Alain urged, setting down his empty glass on the edge of a table. "We might as well meet this one before the poor slob becomes history like all the others she's put through the mill."

Philippe hung back for a minute. Alain's words had more than a little truth to them. "Why bother, then?"

"Because she's Mother," Georges answered. "And underneath all that flamboyance is a very insecure creature who needs as much of our support as we can give her."

Philippe looked at him in surprise. "You really were paying attention in medical school."

Georges laughed. "Seemed like the thing to do at the time."

Philippe trailed after his brothers to greet not only his mother, who by now was the center of attention, but Kyle Autumn, the young man who looked remarkably comfortable and at home with all this commotion.

But just before he reached the outer circle around his mother, something out of the corner of his eye caught his attention.

Automatically glancing in that direction, he froze, his mouth threatening to fall open like some cardboard rendition of a Venus flytrap.

He recognized Kelli first.

There was no missing the bright, animated face even though she wore a deep green velvet dress instead of her customary overalls and pullover shirt.

The woman with Kelli, however, took his breath away and seriously threatened to short-circuit his brain. In one heartbeat he realized who she was.

The honey-blond hair was piled up high on her head, held there by fairy dust, magic and, he later discovered, a couple of strategically placed pins. Like the child she ushered in before her, the woman wore a dress. A dress that captured every bit of artificial light within its silvery threads, casting thin, gleaming rays that preceded her. Formfitting, it adhered seamlessly to her body from beneath her bare shoulders to the tips of her toes.

She moved like shimmering poetry.

Philippe found himself sincerely wishing that he could remember a line or two of verse that would begin to do her justice.

Wow seemed woefully inadequate somehow, but that was the only word that reached his lips, emerging in a soft, worshipful whisper.

"Wow."

Not quite sure if Philippe had said something or if he was imagining it, Georges turned first toward his brother, then in the direction that his brother was looking to see what had caught Philippe's attention so securely.

Once he did, a low, appreciative whistle escaped Georges's lips as pure admiration slipped over his chiseled features.

"Talk about cleaning up well," Georges muttered under his breath, watching the woman make her way into the gallery. He clapped his brother heartily on the back and declared with sincerity, "Philippe, I think you have a keeper there."

Only vaguely aware of what Georges was saying, Philippe began making his way over to Janice on legs that felt oddly spongy.

"You came," he said when he reached her, not bothering to hide either his surprise or his pleasure.

In response, a somewhat self-conscious smile worked its way across her lips and then faded a little. She wasn't used to dressing up anymore. It almost felt as if she had on her mother's clothes—if her mother had left any behind for her to wear. This definitely wasn't something that she'd have hanging in her closet under normal circumstances. But after Lily's comment about lending her suitable attire for the opening, she knew she had to find something that would knock the pins out from under the woman.

And if, perchance, the gown managed to do the same with Philippe, well, there was no harm in that, was there?

"Looks that way," she murmured, more pleased than she knew she should be by the look she saw on Philippe's face.

"I came, too," Kelli declared, underscoring her announcement with a firm tug on his sleeve.

There was warmth in his voice when he spoke to her. "So you did."

Bending down, Philippe picked the little girl up and was rewarded with a deep giggle and a hug. He returned the latter, then set her down again.

Try as he might, he couldn't seem to take his eyes off Janice. Because he didn't want to come off like a tongue-tied dolt, he said the first thing that came to his mind.

He repeated what Georges had said. "You clean up very well."

For a moment, she said nothing and he wondered if he'd somehow managed to insult her.

And then he saw her smile.

He wore a tuxedo, Janice noted, as did his brothers. She'd seen them first while secretly scanning the room for Philippe. Undoubtedly the tuxedos were at their mother's insistence. She had to admit that she found it rather sweet that the grown men loved their mother enough to humor her.

His brothers were good-looking in their attire, but

Philippe surpassed that. She found him breathtakingly handsome.

As if he needed any help to look that way.

"You, too," she murmured.

REMODELING THE BACHELOR

Chapter Thirteen

"She's getting too heavy for you," Janice protested to Philippe for the second time in the space of half an hour.

She, Gordon and Kelli had been there for almost three hours. For over half that time, Philippe had been carrying around a sleeping Kelli in his arms. Gordon had made himself scarce within ten minutes of their arrival, but Philippe had remained with them the entire time and Kelli had lit up like a Christmas tree whenever he spoke to her. As the little girl finally began losing her battle against drooping eyelids, he had picked her up. Kelli had been absolutely ecstatic, until she fell asleep.

But this, Janice thought, was above and beyond the

call. Despite the fact that watching him with her daughter tugged on her heart in the best possible way, she felt guilty for putting him out like this. He should be free to mingle—without a small girl in his arms.

Although she put her arms out to take her daughter, Philippe made no move to surrender his soft load to her. Instead, he merely shook his head, trying to put her concern to rest.

"I might not be a body builder," he told her, his voice low in order not to wake Kelli, "but the day I can't carry around forty pounds of sugar and spice without wheezing, I'm really in trouble. Besides," he added with a dazzling smile, "as long as I have your daughter, you can't leave."

Why was it every time she was on the receiving end of one of his smiles, something fluttered in her stomach? She was a grown woman, not some starry-eyed teenager. Reactions like that should have been long in her past.

But they weren't.

"So this is a hostage situation?" she asked wryly.

He liked bantering with her. Liked everything about her. The one exception was the very real threat to his peace of mind that she posed. But he was learning to deal with that.

"Something like that," he acknowledged. "It's working, isn't it?"

She laughed. Attending the show had been fun, but it was time for Cinderella to take her glass slippers and her coach and get home before she wore out her supply of fairy dust and midnight arrived. "Really, I think it's time I got her into bed."

Funny, the same thought had been crossing his mind. But it had nothing to do with the little girl he was carrying and everything to do with the woman whose presence made him forget the rules he'd so carefully laid down for himself.

Philippe watched her for a long moment. So long that it felt as if time had suddenly stood still. And all the while, he was debating the wisdom of what he was going to say next.

Wise or not, he couldn't stop the words. Couldn't annihilate the tiny slivers of desire that prompted him to speak.

"Far be it from me to interfere with motherhood, but could I interest you in stopping by my place for a nightcap? It's on the way," he added in case she was going to say something about wanting to go straight home.

"No. Really. Kelli. Bed." The words came out in staccato cadence as Janice allowed herself, for one moment, to entertain the idea of taking Philippe up on his offer.

And the offer she was certain lay beyond that.

It was a struggle, but she had to remain focused. She wasn't going to get involved, at least, not any further than she already was. It wasn't too late yet. The hook, the line, the sinker, they were all still within her grasp. But only if she backed away.

"You might be familiar with my place," Philippe continued as if she hadn't tried to protest. "It has extra bedrooms. The princess," he smiled at the bundle in his arms, who stirred, wrapped one small arm around his neck and went on sleeping, "is welcome to use any one of them."

Janice shifted so that her back was to the open room, creating a small, intimate pocket for herself, Philippe and her daughter. She tried not to dwell on just how intimate. "If Kelli's not in her own bed when she wakes up, she has a tendency to get scared."

"Really." He tried to look down at the face resting on his shoulder. Compassion nudged at him. He could remember Alain being abnormally afraid of the dark and Georges not being able to sleep unless the closet door was completely closed. "And I thought she was fearless."

Janice laughed softly. Kelli came off like gangbusters sometimes, but she was still a little girl, susceptible to the pitfalls of a vivid imagination. "We all have our quirks."

"Yes, we do. All right, if I can't talk you out of leaving, Cinderella, let me carry the crown princess to your car for you." When she began to protest yet again, he cut her short. "I've grown accustomed to the weight and it's a little hard to relinquish."

Janice smiled, running her hand along Kelli's head. The ribbon the little girl had insisted she put in her hair had come undone and was now drooping as much as she was. "I know the feeling." Raising her head, Janice's eyes met his. Something warm undulated through her, born of an unexpected communion and the surge of bitter-sweetness that she experienced seeing him holding her daughter like that.

The words seemed to come of their own volition. "You can come to my place."

He was almost certain he hadn't heard correctly. "Excuse me?"

Bail out. Say nothing, *and run for your life.* And yet, when she did speak, what emerged was none of that. "For that nightcap. If you'd still like to have one, you can come over to my place if you'd like."

The smile burrowed right through all the protective layers she'd ever constructed around herself. "I'd like," he said softly.

Nerves began jumping around like a compass placed in a field of magnets, warning her that she'd just taken a step into less than solid territory.

Reinforcements, she needed reinforcements, Janice thought, suddenly glancing around as she began leading the way to the front door.

"Looking for Gordon?" Philippe guessed, bringing up the rear.

She'd bailed him out so many times, it was time for him to return the favor. "I just want to tell him we're leaving."

But Gordon, it turned out, wasn't quite ready to go. He was having much too good a time. Mainly with the redhead he'd been monopolizing from the first hour he'd arrived.

Excusing himself for a moment, Gordon stepped over to the side to talk to Janice. "I'm going to hang around for a little while longer," he told his sister, then. Glancing over his shoulder toward the redhead, he added, "Don't wait up."

She knew that look. That was Gordon, smitten to the nth degree. Concerns immediately sprang up. Janice forgot that she was the one who needed help. "Gordon—"

A feeling of déjà vu washed over Philippe. This was an uncomfortable situation in the making, just the way it had been when his brothers used to go at one another when they were growing up. Time to stop it before it started.

"—Is a grown man, Janice. He's allowed to stay out late if he wants to," he pointed out.

Not expecting him to interfere, she looked at Philippe, stunned and, for the moment, speechless.

Gordon took advantage of the momentary respite and moved back to the redhead. But not before nodding his thanks to Philippe.

She supposed that Philippe was right. Gordon was a grown man, even if he didn't often behave like one. But still…

She shook her head as she started walking again. "He's only going to get hurt."

Well, at least she was talking to him, Philippe

thought. His little errand of mercy hadn't cost him that. "Maybe not. That's Electra," he told her.

They were outside now. The sky was studded with stars as she made her way to the back of the building and the parking lot where she'd left her car. "Beyond being the name of a heroine in some Greek play, is that supposed to mean something to me?"

"No, not to you," he agreed, "but to me. She's a distant cousin of Alain's—and a very nice girl," he added, hoping that would put her mind at ease.

"A distant cousin of Alain's," she repeated, stopping beside her car, "but not yours."

"No, not mine."

She began to look for her car key. For a small purse, it certainly didn't make the search easier. "And he's never been married?"

"No."

She took out her wallet and her cell phone. Holding both in one hand, she continued feeling around the bottom of the purse. "Then it's not possible."

"It is if Alain had a different father than I did."

She stopped looking. Her eyes raised to his. "Oh."

Now that he'd opened that door, he might as well open it all the way, Philippe decided. After all, it wasn't anything he was ashamed of, just something he didn't advertise. It made his mother seem inconstant—which she was but that was their business. However, something about this woman with the large soulful eyes made him want to share, to open all the doors and windows and air out the musty places that had known only darkness. "Georges did, too."

"Georges and Alain had a different father than you," she said out loud, trying to get it straight in her head.

"Why don't we take my car?" he suggested. "That way, Gordon won't be stranded. We can move the car seat," he added before she could protest.

"Okay." Opening the rear passenger door, she took out Kelli's car seat and followed behind Philippe to his sedan.

Philippe unlocked the passenger door of his car. "Fathers," he said, emphasizing the *S*. She looked at him sharply. "Different fathers." He wondered what she was thinking as she attached the car seat and then took her daughter from him, strapping Kelli in. "Mother got around," he commented philosophically. "And, apparently," he rounded the hood and got in on the driver's side, "it seems that nothing has changed in that department."

Janice pulled the seat belt around her, slipping the metal tongue into the slot. "You must have had a really rocky childhood." There was sympathy in her voice. Or was that empathy?

Either way, Philippe shrugged casually. "It was…interesting," he finally said, settling on a neutral word. He put his key into the ignition, turned it, then glanced behind him to see how Kelli was doing. She was still very soundly asleep. Like Alain at that age, he thought. He turned back around. "So, with your backup bailing out, I guess you'd rather I took a rain check on that nightcap." The car began to move.

Her sense of survival urged her to take the way out Philippe had just offered her.

But there was also her sense of competitiveness to reckon with, that edge that she'd always grasped in her struggle to make her an equal in a man's world.

She slanted a glance toward him. Philippe probably thought she was afraid of him. Nothing could have been further from the truth. If she was afraid of anything, it was herself.

Because of the feelings that had surfaced, hard and strong.

"Why?" she challenged him.

He smiled at her then, getting the very distinct impression that they were, in their own way, battling the same demon. The same fear, even if they had arrived at it by different routes.

He shrugged, easing out of the parking lot. "No reason."

Janice took a deep breath. She was going to regret this.

She couldn't stop herself.

"All right, then," she said. "Make a left at the next light."

Philippe nodded, doing as she said. He refrained from telling her that he already knew where she lived. Because he'd always believed in covering all his bases.

* * *

She lived twenty minutes away, on the far end of Bedford. Because of Friday-night traffic, it took almost twice that amount of time to reach her house from the Lido Isle gallery.

Never one to care for driving, Philippe found himself enjoying the ride. They talked about Kelli and the show. Both seemed like safe enough topics.

She lived in one of the older developments within Bedford. But there was nothing old about the house. Even in the dark, with only the porch lights to guide him as he pulled up, the two-story dwelling looked as if it had just been renovated.

Renovated inside as well as out, Philippe noted as he carried the sleeping child into the house behind Janice. She'd tried to take Kelli out of the car seat, but he had gently moved her out of the way and done it himself. He'd pointed out that she was going to need at least one hand to hold up the edge of her gown when she negotiated the stairs. Reluctantly, she'd agreed, thinking him to be an unusually observant, sensitive man.

As if he needed more points.

"Really nice place you have here," Philippe said, looking around as he followed her. He made no attempt to hide his admiration.

There were no edges in sight, no angles, other than

the windows. The walls were all rounded and the rooms fed into one another via arched entrances.

Maybe he could stand to have more work done on his house, he thought.

"Did you do this all yourself?" The place suited her, all curves and rounded shapes.

She was surprised that he was giving her all the credit. After all, she'd told him that her father had been a contractor and there was Gordon who was more than capable, once he had a fire lit under him. Philippe wasn't trying to flatter her, she realized, he was serious.

"Mostly," she admitted, doing her best not to smile smugly. Her father and Gordon were traditionalists. She'd once dreamed of being an architect.

"You're better than I thought you were—" He turned to look at her. "And that's pretty damn good," he was quick to add, knowing how sensitive she could be.

Almost embarrassed despite the surge of pride that filled her, Janice changed the subject and nodded toward the stairs.

"This way." Taking hold of her dress, she raised it and led the way quickly.

Kelli's bedroom was the second door to the left. When she opened it, Philippe stood in the doorway, awed. There were murals on three sides of the room.

Kelli was one lucky little girl, he thought. "God, this is a child's fantasy come to life."

"She helped design it," Janice told him proudly. "And she painted that one."

She pointed out the pastoral scene on the right. That hand had been a little unsteady, but it was still very impressive, Philippe thought.

He placed Kelli down on a bed shaped like a tiny Viking boat. Fairies danced on the wall behind it, all appearing to gaze down at the little girl. Sweet dreams took on a new meaning.

Removing Kelli's shoes slowly, Janice threw a light sheet over her.

He'd just assumed that bedtime would have rituals attached to it. This was almost bohemian—something his mother would have approved of. "Aren't you going to change her?"

After pausing to switch on an oversized nightlight in the shape of a teddy bear, Janice began to back out of the room. She shook her head in response to his question. "You'd be surprised how that would wake her up. I can always wash her clothes."

Though a simple sentence, she had trouble getting it out. Her lips and throat were dry, in direct contrast to her hands, which felt damp.

This was ridiculous.

She couldn't seem to talk herself out of it.

Slipping out of the room, Janice took a deep breath as she closed the door. Then, summoning courage, she glanced up at him. "You don't really want a nightcap, do you?"

Philippe moved his head from side to side, his eyes never leaving hers. The temperature in the hallway rose several degrees of its own accord. "No."

Breathe, Janice. Breathe. Superhuman effort pushed more words out. "What do you want?"

He didn't answer her.

Instead, Philippe curved his fingers lightly along her face and brought his mouth down to hers. Slowly enough for her to pull away if she wanted to, quickly enough to steal away the breath she had just drawn in.

Janice was lost from the very beginning.

Maybe even from the moment she'd decided to come to Lily's showing. Because in her heart, as she slipped on the silvery gown, she knew it would end this way. Here, in a warm, intimate circle that included only the two of them, with emotions racing through her at the speed of newly charged lightning.

Being held, being kissed, being wanted, all of it hurt because of the inevitable disappointment that waited for her at the end of the road. But for the moment, for the very vibrant, pregnant moment, it felt beyond good. It felt absolutely wonderful.

Delicious.

And then, in a heartbeat, she found herself airborne. Philippe had swept her up in his arms.

"Where's your room?" he whispered against her temple, his breath feathering along her skin.

She was melting. Melting so quickly that for a second, she couldn't focus, couldn't think. It took effort to remember where she was. Or even who. And as for all the reasons this shouldn't be happening, she couldn't recall a single one.

"There," she finally managed, pointing to the door that stood across from Kelli's room. "There," she repeated urgently. Anticipation ran through her and every inch of her tingled.

Philippe moved the door open with his shoulder, carrying her into the room without drawing his mouth from hers.

Each kiss was deeper than the last.

Each kiss rendered her a little hotter, a little wilder than the one that had come before it. The eagerness frightened her even as it overwhelmed her. Not his but her own. When he set her back on the floor, a hunger took possession of her mind, her body, disintegrating the first, commandeering the second.

She all but tore away his jacket, his shirt, his trousers as her breath grew shallow and her desire grew deep.

"There's no zipper," Philippe realized in wonder. He drew back, catching her hands in his. "How—"

Swallowing, fairly certain that she was probably never going to be able to create saliva again, Janice took his long, artistic fingers and placed his hands on either side of the swell of her breasts.

"You tug." It was more of a seductive whisper than an instruction. "Slowly."

"Your idea of torture?" A smile rose to his lips as he obeyed.

About to answer, Janice jolted involuntarily as the material left her breasts. A shiver vaulted along her spine followed by a blast of heat. It was all she could do to keep from pushing him onto the bed. Where had this appetite, this hunger come from? How could she have not known of its existence? "Yours or mine?"

"Both," he whispered, stopping as the gown dipped just below her belly button, hugging her hips.

"What's wrong?" Why was he stopping? Had he changed his mind? Oh God, she'd fall to pieces if he changed his mind.

"Nothing." He groaned softly as he passed his hands over her breasts, her waist, her belly. "Not a single thing," he told her in a voice that was equal parts awe and worship.

He wanted this to last. He wanted her to remember. And he wanted to remember it as well. Not that there was any danger that it would get lost in a myriad of dalliances. He wasn't Georges or Alain.

But even so, he wanted this to be memorable for her.

So he kissed her. Over and over again. Kissed every part of her that was exposed to his gaze until he finally drew away the last of the material. It pooled like silver rain at her feet.

They tumbled onto her four-poster canopied bed, onto a comforter that felt more like a cloud than something meant to cover a bed.

And he began to make love to her in earnest, for all he was worth. As if he'd never made love to a woman before.

Because, as far as he was concerned, until this very moment, he hadn't.

Chapter Fourteen

Janice couldn't catch her breath.

Was it because, aside from that one mistake, she hadn't made love to anyone since Gary was killed?

Was it because, until Gary, she'd been a virgin and he had been her only actual partner, her only true lover? Was her admitted inexperience with lovemaking the reason why she now felt on fire?

The pleasure came at warp speed and she found herself peaking, one of the very few times she had attained a climax. And yet it wasn't over. There was so much more, wrapped up in agonizingly wonderful sensations. More than she'd ever realized there could be.

Philippe was an expert lover, yet she had no feeling that he was doing this by the numbers. Instead, it was if he was creating something new and wondrous just for her.

Janice moaned, wanting desperately to absorb every nuance, every sensation that went spinning through her. Absorb every pass of his hand, of his incredibly sensuous mouth.

She *had* to be dreaming. *Nothing* was this good and still real.

And yet…

He did things to her she'd never had done before, aroused her by skimming places no one had touched.

After she'd climaxed again, Philippe's tantalizing breath still warm on the sensitive skin just below her belly, she felt her heart pounding in her ears, the sound so loud it was almost deafening.

How did he do it? How did he manage to weave this magic, turning her into a mass of wants and needs? This wasn't her, had never been her. She was a rock.

She was pudding.

And what was she going to be like after it was all over?

Her heart still raced madly, and she was certain that it was trying to break out of her chest.

And then everything slipped into slow motion.

Philippe drew the length of his body over hers again. Two more heartbeats and he was over her. If her body wasn't already rivaling the physical composition of dissolved ice cream, she knew she would have melted all over again.

Damn him, he was making things happen, not just in her body, but in her heart. The latter both thrilled her and scared her to death. But if he stopped now, she'd die.

Janice arched her back, raising her hips up to him in heated surrender.

Instincts had always guided Philippe. He inherently knew just how to pleasure a woman. And that was important to him because pleasure was best mutually shared.

But this, this was different. *She* was different. Janice wasn't one of those high society women he was so accustomed to: beautiful women, all planes and angles and no substance. Those were women who felt that making love was just another part of life, no different than eating and sleeping, laughing and crying. Janice's hesitant eagerness, her unabashed enthusiastic response, stirred things within him, things he was unfamiliar with. Things he was almost afraid to examine.

A tenderness emerged along with a myriad of desires and passions and it gently elbowed its way forward. Stunning him.

He wanted her. Not wanted to make love, but wanted *her.* Wanted her within his days and in his nights.

This definitely put a different kind of light on everything.

He'd always been afraid of emulating his mother, of diving into a relationship and damning the consequences, stipulating that if a union didn't work, it could be easily dissolved. You didn't enter a relationship with both hands wrapped around a safety clause, holding on for dear life. You entered into it with dreams of forever.

Forever.

A word that had come to mean nothing to so many people. But it meant everything to him. The fear of not knowing how to get there was hard to shake. He had no example to follow.

He had only his heart.

Philippe held himself physically in check for as long as he could, then, as sweet agony ricocheted through his body when he drew it slowly along hers, he paused for a moment to look into her eyes. And then he entered her. Joining with her.

And stepping into something that had heretofore eluded him.

A feeling of belonging.

They were in-tune with one another from the moment he began the dance. With hips fitted together as if they'd been created that way, Philippe slowly increased the tempo. Increased it until he thought for sure he was going to explode.

Not a single cell within his body was unaffected when he achieved the final peak with her. Clasping the euphoria to him, he enveloped Janice in his arms and held her even closer.

Feeling her heart pounding against his was empowering yet humbling at the same time. And all the while, he felt a part of something. A part of her.

That had never happened before.

As the mists slowly parted and he found himself returning to earth, Philippe realized that he hadn't shifted his weight. He was probably crushing her.

Very gently, he moved from her. But rather than just claim his own section of her bed, he continued to hold her, united in spirit if not in body. All he heard was the sound of their breathing. And then he felt Janice shrinking from him, even though she hadn't actually moved.

Oh God, what have you done, Janice? What have you gone and done? She stared at the ceiling. "I guess you'll be wanting to go."

Philippe turned his head toward her. Go? He honestly hadn't thought that far ahead, but instead basked in the incredible feeling of contentment that had found him.

"Why?"

"Because…" She licked her lips. It didn't help. They remained drier than last year's paint chips. "Because you got what you came for."

The simple statement stunned him. Philippe rose up on his elbow and looked at her. "Is that what you think? That I 'came for' this? Like I was 'borrowing' a hammer or a cup of sugar?"

Pulling the edge of the comforter to her, covering up her nakedness, Janice sat up. She kept her face averted.

If she didn't see him, maybe she wouldn't burst into tears. Where *was* all this emotion coming from?

She sighed, tamping down the urge to pull the comforter over her head as well. "Look, I don't do this kind of thing."

She heard his soft laugh behind her. "Well, for a novice, you were incredible."

She stiffened, not taking the words as a compliment. She was too scared of what she was feeling and frantically tried to shut down. Completely. "I don't sleep around."

"I didn't say you did."

She felt his breath zipping along her bare back and struggled to turn herself into stone. "But you had to think it."

"Why?"

Why, why. Was he trying to bait her? Frustration surfaced. "Because you're here. Because we made love."

"And it was great," he agreed, "but why would that automatically mean that you slept around?"

Janice dropped her head against her knees. "You're confusing me."

"That makes two of us." She felt him tugging lightly at the comforter. Her fingers instantly clamped down on it. "I've just discovered this fantastic way to make your mind go blank."

She felt his fingertips playing along her spine, causing sensations she had no defenses against. Born moving, they zipped up and down her back. She took in a deep breath, struggling for the strength to resist. "Don't."

He leaned in against her, his cheek a fraction away from her spine. She both felt and heard the words. "Do you really mean that?"

Pulse points began to throb throughout her body. Janice turned around to face him, suddenly ravenous for him. How was that even remotely possible, given how exhausted she'd felt just two minutes ago?

"No," she whispered, her body aching for his. "No."

"Good answer," he said, pulling her to him.

Philippe captured her mouth, kissing her as if he hadn't just spent the better part of an hour making love with her. As if he were insatiable.

Because, he realized just before oblivion came for him, when it came to Janice, he was.

Janice stirred, her eyes fluttering against the infusion of light.

Daylight.

Morning!

She jerked up in bed, simultaneously realizing that she'd fallen asleep and trying to pull her thoughts together. She looked around frantically. What time was it?

Time to be alone.

The place beside her in the bed was empty.

The clothes that she'd all but ripped off his body, were gone.

Philippe had vanished.

He'd left, she thought, feeling a sharp pang in her gut.

Damn it, why was she feeling like this? She'd known he'd leave, that their night was a one-time thing. Why then—

Her train of thought stopped abruptly.

What was that smell?

Janice moved her head around, sniffing. Searching for the source. Her windows were closed, so the smell couldn't be coming from outside. That meant it was inside. She took another breath, a longer one this time. The smell was coming from downstairs.

Was something burning?

Kicking aside the comforter, she hit the floor moving. Janice grabbed a pair of jeans and a sweater, pulling them on as she ran down the hall. She needed to get to Kelli and to rouse Gordon—if he'd ever made it back home.

Her heart pounded, her brain processed a hundred different things at once until she realized she was smelling coffee and bacon.

The house wasn't on fire.

Sighing, momentarily drained, Janice leaned against the wall and dragged her hand through her hair. Was she still dreaming? No one made breakfast around here but her. That's the way it had always been, ever since her mother had taken off. Gordon was completely culinarily challenged and her father had only known how to make coffee and burn steaks.

What the hell was going on here?

Barefoot, she decided to go downstairs to investigate. But not without first arming herself. Gordon's door was standing open. He obviously hadn't come home for the night. His bed was still made and Gordon could no more make a bed than he could boil water.

Her brother still played softball on occasion and his bat was leaning against the wall next to the closet. Getting it, Janice went downstairs, her heart in her throat.

With both hands wrapped around the Louisville Slugger, she made her way to the kitchen, holding her breath and not knowing what to expect.

But it certainly wasn't what she saw: Philippe, his formal dress shirt hanging open, standing barefoot beside the stove, making breakfast.

The bat slid from her fingers.

Hearing the clatter, Philippe turned toward the doorway. His expression softened into amusement and he nodded at the fallen weapon. "You usually bring a bat to breakfast?"

Feeling foolish, she picked up the bat and retired it in the corner against the pantry. "I thought you were a burglar."

His amusement heightened. He went back to cracking eggs and watching over the bacon. "People often break into your house to make you breakfast?"

Very funny. Feeling somewhat self-conscious after last night, Janice did her best to brazen out the situation.

"Nobody makes me breakfast." She joined him at the stove. "Ever."

She reached for the frying pan, but he pushed her hand away. When she eyed him quizzically, he said, "You don't have to do everything, Janice."

She frowned, reluctantly taking a step back. "I'm not used to being served."

He nodded toward the stool at the counter, indicating that she should take a seat. "And I'm not used to having a woman wield a hammer, but they tell me it's a brave new world out there. No clear-cut roles, no black-and-white rules to follow." Finished, he transferred the scrambled eggs to a waiting plate and framed it with two strips of bacon. He placed the finished product in front of her. "Enjoy. I didn't poison it, I promise."

She took a breath and drew the plate in a little closer. "When did you learn how to cook?"

"When the nanny kept burning the oatmeal." He paused for a second, collecting various scattered fragments together. "Allison was her name, I think." He pictured the woman in his mind's eye. She'd been a great deal more formidable looking than his mother. The last one anyone would suspect of shirking her duties. "She kept a small bottle of scotch in her purse. Kept that purse pretty close to her as I remember. Go on," he urged again. "Try it."

Having no other recourse, feeling incredibly awkward about being served, Janice sank her fork into the eggs and then raised it to her lips. When she drew the fork out again, she forced a smile to her face.

"Good."

The forced smile had nothing to do with what she had just sampled and everything to do with what she was feeling. She was so confused she could hardly stand it.

Janice stared down at her fork for a second before moving it again. "I thought you'd gone," she said softly as she took another bite.

Nursing a cup of coffee he'd poured earlier, Philippe looked at her. The pinch of hurt he felt surprised him. "Did you think I'd leave without saying goodbye?"

Janice shrugged, still avoiding his eyes. "My mother did. It's easier that way."

"I don't usually take the easy way." He placed his hand over hers. When she still didn't look up, he crooked his finger beneath her chin and physically raised her head until her eyes met his. "Look, Janice, I don't exactly know what's going on here," he told her honestly. "But I'm willing to find out." He paused, searching her face. "How about you?"

The inside of her mouth went dry. Mercifully, she was spared having to give him an answer because Kelli, bless her, picked that exact moment to come running into the kitchen. The expression on her small heart-shaped face was one of surprise and pleasure at seeing Philippe standing there.

Within a moment, she was next to him, looking up as if he were the eighth wonder of the world—and all hers.

"What are you doing here?" Kelli asked, her voice sounding so grown-up he couldn't help laughing.

"Well, I was in the neighborhood," he told her, "and I thought I'd stop by and make you and your mommy breakfast."

Her eyes were huge. "Really?"

"Really," he told her solemnly.

She cocked her head, her eyes narrowing. "Why are you still wearing what you had on last night?"

Janice's heart sank, but Philippe never wavered. "I was in a hurry to make you breakfast. Take a look." Picking the little girl up with one arm, he brought her over to the stove. Besides the eggs he'd made for Janice and the bacon that still remained, there were waffles beginning to turn a golden color on the griddle.

Kelli seemed duly impressed. "Wow." She turned her head toward Philippe, her hair brushed against his cheek. "I thought only Mommy could make waffles."

"They're probably not as good," Philippe allowed gallantly as he brought her over to the counter, placing her on the stool beside Janice. "But you can tell me what you think." Taking them off the griddle, he slid the waffles onto a plate and then placed that before Kelli. A fork and napkin were beside the plate a second later. "Jam or syrup?" he asked formally, as if he were a food server waiting on her.

Was it her imagination or had Kelli sat up a little straighter just then? "Syrup, please."

Janice watched Philippe cross to the cupboard and reach in. "Syrup it is."

He moved around her kitchen as if he was more familiar with it than she was, she thought grudgingly. Worse, Philippe moved around her daughter as if he was more familiar with her than she was.

With no effort at all, he was making a niche for himself in her life. And with no effort at all, he could be gone just as quickly, she reminded herself darkly.

In the blink of an eye.

That was how her life always changed. Quickly. In the blink of an eye. One minute, she was standing in her yet unoccupied nursery, picking out curtains for the windows, and the next minute, there were two polite marines in dress uniforms, telling her the man whose child she was carrying wasn't coming home under his own power, but in a box.

She couldn't do that again. Couldn't just stand around, waiting to be devastated, waiting for her world to be blown apart.

She had to get away before that happened. Had to flee. The first chance she had. To save herself and Kelli.

Chapter Fifteen

Janice didn't show up. Not at seven. Not at eight. And not at nine.

After turning up like clockwork at his house every weekday for the last six weeks, neither Janice nor Gordon made an appearance at his door the following Monday morning.

He felt like his day couldn't start until he saw her face.

His deadline was drawing uncomfortably closer, but Philippe couldn't focus, couldn't pull his brain together long enough to make any sort of headway with the program additions he was creating. Every five, seven, ten minutes his thought process would break up and reform to include Janice and *only* Janice. A restlessness pervaded through him that grew more intense with every minute.

By nine-fifteen, Philippe had abandoned all attempts at concentration and called her twice. Twice and only gotten her voice mail, both on her landline and her cell phone. Each time he was urged to leave a message.

"If you're there, Janice, pick up," he instructed, then ordered, then supplicated. None of the approaches obtained him any sort of a response. Annoyed, he'd hung up.

Where the hell was she?

Why wasn't she here?

Had something happened? And if it had, why hadn't she called to say she'd be late or unavoidably detained or there tomorrow? At the very least, if she were caught up in something and unable for some reason to call, why hadn't Gordon called in her place?

Something was wrong.

He wasn't the type to let his imagination run away with him, never had been, but it was going the distance right now. He couldn't help it. The woman was nothing if not punctual and diligent. He'd never seen a work ethic like hers before. Everyone he'd ever known who'd had work done on his or her house, even those who had been supremely satisfied at the end, said that the crew was *never* there day after day, working. The norm was that, excellent or not, they would disappear for days at a time. Maybe even for a week or more.

But not Janice. Janice was always there, determined to see the job through to its completion. That was the first thing he'd liked about her.

Well, maybe not the first thing, Philippe amended, his pacing bringing him up to the front door again, but it had certainly been among the first.

He paused to look at the easel tucked away in the alcove. Paused to look at the small painting resting there. Intended, he knew, for him.

Maybe something had happened to Kelli, maybe that was why Janice hadn't called him, hadn't left any messages. He felt a chill pass over his spine. Something had happened to Kelli.

No, that couldn't be it. If something had happened to the little girl, Janice knew he'd be there for both of them. In a heartbeat. They'd gotten too close for him to be excluded.

Too close.

Yes, damn it, he'd gotten too close. Too close when before he'd kept life, kept women, even the ones he slept with, at a comfortable distance.

But before was when he hadn't found a woman he felt he wanted to spend the rest of his life with.

The thought, the *realization*, hit him right between the eyes.

Philippe slid onto the sofa without being completely conscious of what he was doing.

He *did* feel that way about her. Oh God, when had that happened? When had forever snuck in?

That was his mistake. That was why he felt like some wild, disoriented creature. Because he'd let down his walls and however unintentionally, allowed Janice to come through. Allowed himself to believe that forever was attainable.

He knew better than that. Why should he have better luck than his mother? His mother had always been in love with love, in love with the idea of being in love. She was more than willing to risk it all and what had it gotten her? A string of ex-spouses and broken relationships.

Did that mean that he was doomed to the same?

Philippe sprang to his feet as if someone had just shoved a hot poker into the cushion beneath him. He *wasn't* doomed to the same fate, not if he could help it. Not by a long shot.

Filled with new determination, pushing down any thoughts that didn't have to do with advertising pitches, Philippe strode back into his office and forced himself to focus on his work.

That lasted all of forty minutes. A new record for the day.

Why the hell was he even pretending? Philippe flipped open his cell phone and hit the button for Janice's cell.

Ten minutes, four attempts and twenty rings later, he flipped it closed again. It was time to take matters into his own hands. It was time to get some answers.

Two minutes later, he'd locked up his house and was in his car. Had he frightened her? he wondered as he drove to Janice's house. Had making love followed up by making breakfast somehow been too much for her? Cut into her space?

He knew Janice was her own person, that she valued her independence, but after the response he'd felt the night before, he thought she was ready to share that space just as she's shared her bed and her body.

Obviously, he must have thought wrong.

With effort, he forced himself to ease back on the gas pedal. He was going fifty-three miles an hour, eighteen miles over the speed limit in this particular section of the city.

God, if he *had* scared her off, he was prepared to back-track, to reconstruct all the collapsed bridges until they could sustain his weight as he crossed them to her again.

He was willing to do anything. Anything but say goodbye.

By the time Philippe arrived at her door, he'd gone back and forth in his mind so many times he felt like a worn-out tennis player.

He barely closed the door of his car, then hurried up the front walk. He didn't bother with the doorbell, but pounded on her door just the way Janice had on his when she'd come to drag her brother away from the poker table.

That seemed so long ago now. And yet, it hadn't

been. Everything that had happened had transpired in a very short time. Maybe that was the trouble….

Sick of second-guessing, Philippe pounded on the front door again.

This time, an incredibly sleepy-looking Gordon, attired in pajama bottoms and looking very much like an unmade bed, opened the door. Scrubbing one hand over his stubbled face, Gordon obviously tried to focus his eyes. He seemed to be hanging on to the door for support.

"Hey, man, do you know what time it is?"

Philippe walked in. "Do you?"

"Yes, it's—" Gordon blinked, seeing daylight streaming in behind Philippe. Still hanging on to the front door, he looked at the clock on the mantle. "Hey, wow, it's not six, is it?"

Philippe pivoted on his heel. "No, it's not six," he snapped, then made an attempt to rein in his temper. "Where's your sister?" Janice's truck, when he'd pulled up, hadn't been parked outside and the garage door was standing wide open, allowing him to see that the vehicle wasn't inside, either.

Gordon took a deep breath, as if that would somehow help to engage his brain. Releasing it, he shook his head, then dragged one hand through his hair.

"I dunno," he admitted. "She should have woken me up for work." He looked sheepishly at Philippe. "I hate the sound of an alarm clock."

Philippe could in no way process this personal piece

of information about the other man, not right now. Every cell in his body was focused on trying to find Janice. His fear threatened to explode at any second. "Did she say anything about getting a late start today?"

Gordon shook his head. "No."

Philippe tried again. "Did she say anything about buying more supplies?"

Again the shaggy head moved from side to side in denial. "No."

He was getting dangerously close to the end of his rope. "Did she—"

"No, no, no," Gordon declared, pulling both hands through his hair. "J.D. didn't say anything about anything. She was very quiet this weekend." He looked up suddenly at his visitor as the thought struck him. "Like she was right after she found out that Gary wasn't coming home." The thought sank in and Gordon looked at Philippe. "You two have a fight?"

"No." Philippe pressed his lips together. He wasn't the kind to share, not even with his brothers. So sharing personal information with someone who was almost a stranger to him was completely foreign. But at this point he was willing to try anything to help pull the pieces of the puzzle together. "It was just the opposite." He paused significantly, hoping Gordon was clever enough to pick up on what he was saying. "I thought everything was great."

Gordon seemed a little concerned himself. "Well,

obviously something wasn't so great," he theorized. "Otherwise, J.D. would have been in my room, kicking my butt at six and telling me to get the hell out of bed." Scratching his head, Gordon realized that he was talking to himself. Philippe had left the room.

Walking into the hall, he saw that the man was already halfway up the stairs. "She's not up there, man," Gordon called after him.

Philippe made no answer, just kept going.

Maybe there was something in Janice's room that would tell him where she'd gone.

Trying to calm himself, he silently insisted that he was probably just overreacting because he valued routine so much and she had broken hers.

He stopped dead in the doorway when he reached her room. The closet doors were standing open and it was obvious that a section of clothing was missing.

"This is bad," he heard Gordon say. The man was standing behind him.

Philippe turned around. "Why?" he demanded, even though he knew damn well that missing clothing and a missing woman did not add up to a good thing. He was hoping against hope that Gordon would say something he could hang on to.

But he didn't. "Because she took some of her things. And her suitcase is gone." Gordon pointed to a space on the floor.

Just as he did, Philippe noticed a folded up piece of

paper on the dresser. When he opened it, he saw that Janice had left a note for her brother. "Gordon," she wrote, "Kelli and I had to take off for a few days. Don't worry. Please finish up for me at the Zabelle place. Love, J.D."

The Zabelle place. As if there was nothing between them. As if he was nothing more than another job.

Philippe squelched the desire to crumple up the paper. Instead, he handed it to Gordon. "When was the last time your sister just took off like this?"

Gordon stared down at the note as if the words were not sinking in. "Never."

"Do you have any idea where she'd go?"

Gordon shook his head. "No." And then he stopped, his eyes widening as a thought hit him. "Wait." He turned toward Philippe. "Maybe. Maybe I do."

Philippe took a breath, waiting. He didn't care where it was, he was going to go after her and bring her back, even if it meant going to hell and back. "I'm listening."

Gordon ran his tongue nervously along his lower lip, afraid of making the wrong call. "She could have gone to the cabin."

"The cabin," Philippe echoed. When Gordon didn't elaborate further, he pushed, "What cabin?"

"When we were kids, my dad used to rent this cabin one week a year. It's up by Whitewood," he added, citing a resort area. "I always hated going there, but she loved it."

"Can you give me something more specific than a 'cabin in Whitewood?'"

Gordon thought a minute, as if his mind had gone completely blank. And then he looked up, a relieved smile on his lips. "Yeah."

"Good," Philippe retorted between closely clenched teeth.

Gordon made the next logical guess. "You going up there to get her?"

Again, it was against his nature to let anyone in. He'd grown up holding all his emotions close, not allowing the kind of hurt he'd privately viewed his mother enduring *ever* find him. That meant keeping everything damned up. But suddenly, it was just too late for that. And he was going to need allies. Gordon was her brother, that qualified him for the part.

So he looked at the other man and announced, "Damn straight I am."

Gordon grinned and nodded his approval. "My money's on you. Got a map in your car?"

Philippe was already on his way to get it.

It took Philippe the better part of the day to locate exactly where Janice had gone. Gordon's instructions only took him so far and no further. Apparently boyhood memories for Gordon were rather hazy.

Refusing to give up, Philippe backtracked to a general store he'd seen in the area. The clerk behind the counter told him the whereabouts of the local rental agency. Philippe left a ten in his wake and forgot to take the bottle of water he'd purchased.

Hadley's Rental Agency had been there almost as long as the mountains had. Joseph Hadley, the present owner, was a heavyset man who completely filled out the chair behind his desk.

He sat in it now, rocking back and regarding Philippe suspiciously as the latter asked him if a woman with a little girl in tow had rented a cabin in the last few hours.

"Don't give out information like that, son," he announced after a long, pregnant pause. "Violates a trust."

Philippe thought of trying to bribe the owner, but Hadley seemed like a man who valued his integrity and enjoyed letting everyone else know it.

Desperate, Philippe glanced at the small older woman who occupied the only other desk in the small office. She eyed him with a touch of curiosity that appeared to mingle with sympathy.

She could be won over, Philippe thought. But only for a price. With his back to the wall, Philippe again found himself in a position where he had to share his personal business and, more important, his feelings with a stranger.

With *strangers,* he amended silently, resigning himself to what he knew he had to do.

"I'm looking for my fiancée, Janice Wyatt. She just took off this morning without any explanation." She wasn't his fiancée, but if he had to go this far, he might as well embellish and go for broke. Whatever it took to find out where Janice had gone.

Hadley's tiny eyes all but disappeared as he moved forward on his chair and squinted. "You hit her?"

"No," Philippe declared with feeling, the very thought turning his stomach. "Never raised a hand—or my voice," he added for good measure. "Her first husband was killed in the war—"

It was all he needed to say. Mrs. Hadley's imagination—or intuition—filled in the rest. "Poor thing's probably afraid to take another chance on love. Heartache's a powerful deterrent."

The second the woman uttered the words, they hit home. Philippe, prepared to humor her, looked at Mrs. Hadley in awe instead. "You're right."

"Of course I'm right," the woman said with a nod. "Don't get to sit on this mountain, watching people for close to sixty-five years and not pick up a few things." She turned to her husband. "Give him the cabin number, Joe."

"Mary Beth, that's not the way we do business," her husband growled.

She waved a hand at him dismissively. "That's not the way you do business." Walking over to the large map of the area that covered the wall behind her husband's desk, she pointed out the cabin that had been rented last. "She's right there. Go out, take the road on the right and follow it until it disappears." She smiled at him. "That'll be the backyard. You can't miss it," she promised.

Philippe thanked them both and was back in his car in under a minute.

Twilight was just beginning to tiptoe down the mountainside as Philippe slowly made his way along the winding road and first spotted her. It had taken him a lot longer than he'd first thought, but the only thing that mattered was that he'd found her.

Janice was outside, playing a game of catch with her daughter.

A rather bad game of catch, Philippe noted, amused, as he parked his vehicle and made his way silently up the path.

Kelli threw the ball to her, but it fell right through Janice's hands. She was obviously preoccupied.

Not knowing what she was liable to do, he didn't speak until he was directly behind her. "You make a lousy catcher."

Janice caught her breath. Swinging around, she almost shrieked. She half expected him to be a fabrication of her overworked imagination. But Kelli saw him, too. Abandoning the game, she ran like a shot across the grounds and launched herself straight into his arms.

"You're here!" she cried at the top of her lungs, wrapping her arms around him. "You're here!"

He rose with her in his arms, thinking how incredibly

sweet it felt, holding her like this. As he basked in her blatant adoration, he felt his heart swell. "Yes," he told her, kissing the top of her head, "I am."

It took Janice a long moment to find first her breath, then her voice. "What are you doing here?" she managed to ask.

Holding Kelli to him, he turned to look at her. Well, at least she wasn't fleeing.

"Moving heaven and earth, looking for you," he told her without fanfare. And then, in case she didn't realize just what it had taken to find her, he added, "I had to spill my guts to complete strangers to find out where you got to. Do you have any idea how hard that was for me?"

Stunned, at a loss, she stared at him. "I—"

He didn't wait for her to respond, because there were more important questions to be answered. "Why did you suddenly go on the lam?" With effort, he kept his voice upbeat for Kelli's sake.

Janice raised her chin defiantly. "Gordon'll finish your bathrooms."

His eyes narrowed. His voice was low. "That's not what I asked."

Janice glanced toward the mountain range rather than at him. Because he had gone through all this effort to find her, she supposed she owed him the truth. "Because I didn't want to be hurt again."

The woman at the cabin had been right, he thought. "Well, that's good because I don't want to hurt you."

Gently, he set Kelli down and stepped into Janice's line of vision. "Go on," he urged. "So far we're on the same page."

She shrugged, feeling lost, feeling alone and feeling very angry at being cornered this way. Why couldn't he have just accepted things and let her go? Why did he have to put her through this?

"That's it."

"That's it," he repeated incredulously.

"That's it," she echoed. Her voice took on strength as she restated her reason. "I don't want to be hurt again."

He was going to get her to see the light if it killed him. Because suddenly nothing had ever been as important as this.

"Did it occur to you that maybe the solution to never hurting again is *not* not to love but to get the most out of the love that's possible?" he asked. When she began to turn away again, he caught her by the shoulder and continued. "To enjoy and savor each day as if there's no tomorrow and to keep doing it as long as tomorrow keeps coming?"

Janice blinked. She'd heard only one thing. One word. The word that ultimately was the most important one in the world. She needed him to repeat it, to explain. Because she was afraid she was imagining things, hearing what she wanted to hear. "What love? Who said anything about love?"

"He did, Mama," Kelli piped up helpfully, dramatically pointing to Philippe.

He grinned, first at Kelli, then at her. "What she said."

But Janice shook her head. This couldn't come via hearsay or second-hand repetition. "I don't want what she said, I want to hear what you said. Are you telling me that you love me?"

He looked as if it was a surprise to him, too. But not an unwelcome one. "Yes, I guess I am." Then, trying it on for size, he said it formally. "I love you, Janice Diane Wyatt."

"And me?" Kelli asked eagerly.

"And you, too." Philippe laughed, bending over and kissing the top of her head. And then, straightening, his eyes shifted to Janice's face. For just a second, he tried to pretend he was all business. "By the way, when you do get around to finishing my place, my brothers have some renovations they want you to handle on their houses. You up for that?"

When she stared at him numbly, apparently unable to decide if she was hallucinating, he took her in his arms. Just as she caught her breath, he kissed her. Once, and then again. Deeply and with feeling.

He heard her sigh against his lips.

"Yes," she murmured, answering a question that he had silently asked with his kiss.

"Yes, what?" he asked.

"Yes, I'll do the renovations." And then she smiled broadly. "And yes, I'll marry you."

Kelli looked up at her, perplexed. She tugged on her

mother's shirt. "But Mama, he didn't ask that," she pointed out.

Delighted, euphoric, Philippe laughed as he looked down at the little girl who was going to be his daughter. "Actually, I did. I asked her with my heart."

Kelli's eyes grew wide. She stared at him as if he were magical. "You can do that?"

Janice locked her hands along the back of his neck. "He can do that," she told her daughter just before the man she'd fallen in love with kissed her again, crushing the words, "I love you, too," against her lips.

* * * * *

TAMING THE PLAYBOY

BY
MARIE FERRARELLA

To
Patience Smith
and
Gail Chasan
who make writing
the pleasure it should be.

Chapter One

The piercing screech of brakes with its accompanying teeth-jarring squeal of tires had Georges Armand tensing, bracing for what he thought was the inevitable impact.

His breath stopped in his lungs.

The unpredictability of life was something that never ceased to amaze him. Given his background and his present vocation, the opposite should have been true.

Georges Armand was the second son of the colorful, exceedingly flamboyant Lily Moreau, a living legend in the art community, both for her talent and her lifestyle. To say that his formative years had been unorthodox was like referring to the Civil War as a slight misunderstanding between two sections of the country. It was true, but a vast understatement. With his mother flittering in and out of his life like warm rays of sporadic sunshine, the one stable thing Georges could always count on was his brother, Philippe Zabelle. The rest of his world seemed to be in constant flux.

A fourth-year medical resident at Blair Memorial, his choice of career, general internal surgeon, also placed him in that same quixotic mix. It was never so clear to him as during his present stint in the hospital's emergency room. One moment, life was quiet, progressing on an even, uneventful keel. Then within the next rotation of the second hand, all hell was breaking loose.

And so it was tonight.

After putting in a double shift at the hospital, rather than electing to sleep for the hours that he was off duty to do his best to recharge his very spent batteries, Georges decided to go out. He was his late father's son and loved to party.

Handsome, with magnetic blue eyes, hair the color of the underside of midnight and a smile that pulled in all living females within a twelve-mile radius, Georges had not experienced a lack of female companionship since the year he turned ten.

From the moment he first opened his eyes twenty-nine years ago, he had been, and continued to be, a lover of women. All women. Tall ones, short ones, rounded, thin, old, young, it didn't matter. To Georges, every breathing woman was beautiful in her own way and each merited his attention.

For a short time.

Of the three brothers, Philippe, three years his senior, and Alain Dulac, three years his junior, Georges was the most like Lily, who, by her own admission had said more than once that she had never met a man she didn't like—at least for a short time.

Tonight he was off to see Diana, a woman he'd met in the E.R. a month ago when she came in complaining of acute gastrointestinal distress. It turned out to be a case of bad sushi. He prescribed medication to help her along and discharged her. And once she wasn't his patient, he dated her. Brunette, brown-eyed, Diana was vivacious, outgoing and said she was definitely not interested in any strings to their relationship. She was the kind of woman you could have a good time with and not have to worry that she was misreading the signs and mentally writing out wedding invitations. In other words, she was perfect.

As he drove his bright red sports car—a gift from Lily on his graduation from medical school—Georges was mentally mapping out the evening that lay ahead. A little dinner, a little dancing and a great deal of romance.

But all that changed in an instant.

The horrifying sound behind him had Georges swerving to the right. The nose of his vehicle climbed up against the hillside embankment. The maneuver was just in time for him to avoid being hit by the vintage blue sedan behind him. The latter was not so lucky. The black Mercedes behind the sedan slammed right into it.

His heart pounding against his rib cage, Georges looked into his rearview mirror. He saw the dark blue sedan spinning around helplessly, like a badly battered pinwheel in the center of a gale. Out of his car in an instant, Georges ran toward the car to see if he could help the passengers.

It wasn't the doctor in him that made Georges bolt out of his barely stilled sports car; it was the Good Samaritan, the instinct that had initially been instilled, fostered and nurtured by his mother. But it was predominantly Philippe who'd taught him that standing on the sidelines, watching, when you could be in the midst of the turmoil, helping, was never a truly viable option. Philippe believed in commitment, and Georges believed in Philippe.

He attributed all his good traits to his older brother, his looks to his mother and his money, of which there was more than a considerable amount, to his late father, Lily Moreau's second husband, Andre. Andre Armand was a self-made millionaire who owed his fortune to the production of a seductive yet affordable perfume. A scent, despite all her money, that Lily still wore.

The instant Georges opened the driver's-side door and was out of his vehicle, he found himself having to flatten his back against it to get out of harm's way. The Mercedes that had rammed into the sedan and had initiated this lethal game of metal tag now whizzed erratically by him. Had he not jumped back, Georges was certain that he would have wound up being the black Mercedes' new hood ornament. Or, if not that, then permanently sealed to the vehicle's shiny grill.

The figure of a dark-haired, middle-aged man registered at the same time that the vehicle zoomed by him. Blessed with incredibly sharp vision and presence of mind, Georges focused on the license plate even as the vehicle disappeared around one of the many curves that typified Southern California's winding Pacific Coast Highway.

The entire incident took place in less than a heartbeat.

Georges was running toward the blue sedan, which had finally stopped spinning. Its front end was now pointed in the opposite direction of the flow of traffic.

The driver's side was mashed against the hillside.

Now that the brakes were no longer screeching and the tires no longer squealing, Georges became aware of another noise, one that had been blocked out by the first two. Screams. The woman within the sedan, in the front passenger seat, was screaming.

Just as he reached the passenger side, Georges saw thin orange-and-yellow tongues of fire began to lick the front of the hood.

From what he could tell, there was only one other occupant in the car, the driver. The gray-haired man was slumped over the steering wheel. Georges tried to open the passenger door, but the impact from the careening Mercedes had wedged the door shut.

Desperate, afraid that any second the engine might explode, Georges tried to break the window with his elbow, swinging as hard as he could. The impact reverberated up and down his arm and shot into his chest, but the window remained a solid barrier.

The woman inside the car looked at him, their eyes meeting as shock pressed itself into her young features. Frantically, she tried to open the window on her side, working the buttons on the armrest. It was useless. There was no power fueling the buttons. The window remained in place, sealing in both her and the unconscious driver.

He needed something solid, such as a tire iron, to break the glass, but there wasn't enough time to run back to his car to get one. Georges knew that the sedan could blow up at any moment.

The Pacific Coast Highway wove its way along the coast with the ocean on one side, a sprawling hillside pockmarked with exceedingly expensive real estate on the other. Searching the ground for something heavy to use, Georges spotted a good-sized rock and quickly picked it up. Hurrying back to the passenger door, he knocked on the window until the woman looked at him again.

"Duck your head," he shouted at her, lifting the rock.

The woman did as she was told, turning her body so that she was shielding the man in the driver's seat. Pulling back his arm, Georges threw the rock as hard as he could at the window. The surface of the glass cracked and splintered in half a dozen places. Wrapping his jacket about his right hand, he punched through the shattered glass and cleared away as much as he could.

"C'mon," he ordered the woman, "You have to get out of there."

The blonde shook her head emphatically. Her arms were still around the old man. "I can't leave him," she cried.

Georges looked from her to the driver. He was old, too old, he judged, to be her husband or even her father. There was blood on the man's forehead and he seemed to be unconscious, but breathing. Georges couldn't be sure of the latter.

He was sure that if he spent time arguing with the blonde, they could all suffer the consequences. Leaning in, Georges grabbed the woman by her waist. Surprised, she began to resist.

"First you, then him," Georges told her firmly. Before she could say anything, he was pulling her through the opening he'd created. He felt the jagged edges scratch at his skin. The blonde weighed next to nothing, even as she struggled against him.

"My grandfather!" she cried as Georges deposited her on the ground.

He examined the other side of the car. It was pressed against the hillside, leaving no room for him. No way could he snake his way in and open the door on that side to get the man out. Without stopping to take into consideration that the car could blow up at any moment, Georges relied on the luck that had seen him through most of his life and crawled in through the window.

The old man's seat belt was still on. Georges hit the release button and pulled the man over toward his side. Moving as quickly as he could, he angled his body so that they could switch places. He needed the old man next to the opened window.

The blonde realized what he was doing. "Push him through," she urged. "I can hold him up."

He had his doubts about that. The blonde didn't look as if she could hold a twenty-pound sack of grain without stumbling beneath its weight. But he had no other option. Putting his shoulder against the man's lower torso, Georges pushed the old man's upper body through the opening.

To his surprise, the woman slipped her arms beneath the old man's arms and moved backward, pulling the deadweight as he pushed him out. He heard her groan and utter a noise that sounded very much like a battle cry.

The next moment, between the two of them, they'd managed to get the old man out of the vehicle.

The second the unconscious driver was clear of the door, Georges dove out, headfirst, tucking down and into his torso just before he hit the ground so that he rolled. In an instant, he was back up on his feet again. Quickly shoving his shoulder down beneath the old man's, he wrapped his arm around the man's waist.

"Run!" he shouted at the blonde.

Instead of dashing before him, the woman mirrored his movements, getting her shoulder beneath the old man's other shoulder so that both he and the old man could get away from the fiery vehicle faster.

Georges thought he heard the old man mumble, "Leave me," but he didn't know if he'd imagined it or not. In any case, he wasn't about to abandon the man, not after all the trouble he'd just gone through to rescue the driver.

They barely made it back to the front of his sports car before the blue sedan burst into flames.

Georges threw his body over the old man and the blonde just as their car exploded. After several moments had elapsed, he pulled back, suddenly aware of another problem. On his knees, Georges felt the man's throat and then his chest for a pulse. There was none.

The blonde stared, wide-eyed, barely holding fear at bay. "What is it?"

In response, Georges threaded his hands together over the man's chest and began to administer CPR. He hardly glanced in her direction, concentrating on only one thing: getting the man's heart to beat again. "I think he's had a heart attack."

"No." The word escaped her lips like a shell being fired, aimed not at Georges as a denial of his statement but at the old man lying on the ground. "No! Grandpa, do you hear me?" She scrambled closer to the man, moving in on his other side. "No, you can't do this," she told him urgently. "You can't have a heart attack."

There was absolutely no response from the driver.

"I don't think he's listening to you," Georges told her in between beats.

Mentally, he counted off compressions, then tilted the man's head back. Pinching his nose, Georges leaned over the man's mouth to blow his breath into it. Once, twice, a third time, before returning to compressions. The man still wasn't responding. Georges didn't allow himself to think about anything except the success of his efforts. Everything else, including the blonde's voice, became a distant blur.

"In my left coat pocket," he told her as he resumed compressions for a third time, "I've got a cell phone." The moment he said it, she galvanized into action, reaching her long, slender fingers into his pocket. He could feel them as they slid in.

As he fought death for possession of the old man's life, it struck him that this was one hell of a way to meet a woman. Because even in the midst of the ongoing turmoil, as he struggled to bring the driver back around, it did not escape Georges that she was one of the most attractive women he had ever seen.

"Got it!" she declared breathlessly, pulling the cell phone out of his pocket. Rocking back on her knees, she began to press the three numbers that popped into everyone's mind during an emergency.

Nine-one-one would generate an appearance of an ambulance driven by EMTs. Given where they were, the paramedics could take them to one of two hospitals, most likely County General since it had a contract with the company that most often appeared on the scene. However, Blair Memorial was just as close as County General and it was the better of the two hospitals. It was also the hospital where he put in his hours.

"Don't call 911," he told her, then rattled off the number she should call before he breathed into her grandfather's mouth.

The blonde looked at him, confused. "Why should I call that number?"

"Because that number will get you the ambulance attendants from Blair Memorial hospital and they have the better emergency room staff," he told her with no hesitation. He spared her a quick glance. "You want the best for him, don't you?"

She didn't bother answering. As far as she was concerned, that was a rhetorical question. So instead, she pressed the buttons on the keypad. Two rings into the call, the receiver was being picked up.

"Blair Memorial, E.R.," a calm, soothing voice said.

Visibly struggling to remain coherent, the blonde clutched the cell phone with both hands as she gave the man on the other end of the line all the necessary details. Finished, she followed up the information with one more instruction.

"Please hurry." With that, she let out a shaky breath and closed the cell phone again.

"I think that's a given," Georges told her.

Her eyes darted back toward the man administering CPR to her larger-than-life grandfather.

Breathe, damn it, Grandpa, breathe! I'm not ready to live in a world without you in it yet. You promised me that you'd never leave me alone. Don't break your promise, Grandpa. Don't break your promise.

Shaking herself free of the terror that threatened to swallow her up whole, she forced herself to look at the man kneeling beside her grandfather. The savior who had come to their rescue.

Replaying his last words, she blinked, trying to focus. "What is?"

"That they'll hurry."

He was sitting back on his heels. A fresh wave of terror drenched her, leaving her shivering. "Why did you stop giving him CPR?" she demanded, an audible tremor in her voice as it rose. The words rushed out of her mouth. "Why aren't you trying to get his heart going?"

He curved his mouth into a slight smile. Triumph at this point, he knew, could be tenuous and very short-lived. By no means was the man on the ground out of the woods. "Because it *is* going," he told her.

Her eyes darted back to her grandfather, searching for proof. Staring at his chest. Was that movement? "On its own?"

Georges nodded. "On its own."

Tears suddenly formed in her eyes. He became aware of them half a beat before the blonde threw her arms around his neck.

Half a beat before she kissed him.

Hard.

Like the oncoming tide, she pulled back as quickly as she had rushed forward. Georges realized that he had tasted not only something sweet when her lips had pressed against his, but something moist, as well. Tears. He'd tasted her tears on her lips. They must have fallen there just as she'd impetuously made contact with his.

They tasted salty and yet, somehow they were oddly sweet, as well.

"Thank you," she cried breathlessly. "Thank you." And then, just like that, her complete attention was focused back on her grandfather. She took the old man's hand in both of hers and held it next to her cheek. With effort, she controlled the tremor in her voice. "Now you just hang on, Grandpa, you hear me? Help's on the way." For a split second, her eyes shifted back to the man who had saved them both.

Georges felt himself getting lost in her smile as she murmured, "Some of it's already here."

Forcing himself to look back at his patient, Georges thought he saw the old man's eyelids flutter, struggling unsuccessfully to open. He took the man's other hand in his and once again felt for a pulse. He found it, albeit a weak one. Mentally, Georges counted off the beats.

The blonde looked at him quizzically, obviously waiting for positive reaffirmation.

"It's still a little reedy," he told her. "When they get him to the hospital, I think your grandfather should stay overnight for observation. They'll take some films, do an angiogram." Georges looked at the man's face. It was remarkably unlined, but he would still place him somewhere in his late sixties, possibly early seventies. Other than the gash on his forehead and the episode he'd just experienced, the man seemed to be in rather good condition. But appearances could be deceiving. "Does your grandfather have any medical conditions that you're aware of?"

The blonde laced her fingers through her grandfather's hand, as if her mere presence could ward off any serious complications. "I'm aware of everything about my grandfather," she told him. There was no defensiveness in her voice, it was simply the way things were. She took an active interest in this man who was very much the center of her world. "He has a minor heart condition—angina," she specified. "And he's also diabetic. Other than that, he's always been healthy."

Georges focused only on what he considered to be liabilities. "Those are complicating factors."

The blonde pushed back a strand of hair that had

fallen into her face. She continued holding her grandfather's hand. "Are you a doctor?"

He smiled. "I'm a fourth-year resident." He thought of John LaSalle, the attending physician that he was currently working under. LaSalle regarded residents as lower life forms only slightly higher than lab rats. "In some eyes, that makes me an 'almost' doctor."

The blonde looked back at her grandfather and, for a moment, watched the way the man's chest rose and fell in grateful silence. She was aware that she might not be watching that if it hadn't been for the efforts of the man beside her.

"There's nothing 'almost' about you," she replied softly.

It took Georges a second to realize that those were not bells he was hearing in his head but the sound of an approaching siren.

Chapter Two

One of the paramedics, Nathan Dooley, a tall, black, muscular attendant who seemed capable of carrying the patient with one hand tied behind his back, recognized Georges the minute the man climbed out of the passenger side of the ambulance's cab. He flashed a wide, infectious grin at him, even as he and his partner, a somber-faced man in his thirties named Howard, swiftly worked in tandem to stabilize the old man.

Doubling back to retrieve the gurney from the back of the vehicle, Nathan returned and raised a quizzical eyebrow in Georges' direction. "What, you don't work enough hours in the E.R., Doc? Going out and trolling the hills for business now?"

"Coincidence," Georges told him, carefully watching the other EMT work. The other man knew it, too, Georges thought, noting the all-but-rigid tension in Howard's shoulders.

"Destiny," Nathan corrected. He was still grinning, but it sounded to Georges as if the paramedic was deadly serious. He moved back as the two attendants transferred the old man onto the gurney and then snapped its legs into place.

His mother believed in destiny. In serendipity and fate, as well as savoring the fruits of all three. As for him, Georges still didn't know what he believed in. Other than luck, of course.

He supposed maybe that was it. Luck. At least, it had been the old man's luck in this case. Georges was fairly certain that if he hadn't been on this road, right at this time, traveling to see his latest— for lack of a better word—love interest, if he'd given in to the weary entreaty of his body, he would have been home in bed right now. Most likely sleeping.

And the old man on the gurney would have been dead. He and his granddaughter would have been trapped in a fiery coffin.

It was satisfying, Georges thought, to make a difference, to have his own existence count for something other than just taking up space. Moments like this brought it all home to him.

Again, he had Philippe to thank for that. Because, left to his own devices, he had to confess he would have been inclined to sit back and just enjoy himself, just as his father had before him, making the rounds on an endless circuit of parties. His father's money had assured him that he could spend the rest of his life in the mindless pursuit of pleasure.

But Philippe had had other plans for him. At the time, he'd thought of Philippe as a humorless bully. God, but he was grateful that Philippe had happened into his life. His and Alain's.

Otherwise, the petite woman beside him would now be just a fading memory instead of very much alive.

"I want to go with him," the blonde was saying to the other attendant, who, as uptight as Nathan was relaxed, clearly acted as if he were in charge of this particular detail.

Her grandfather had already been lifted into the back of the ambulance, his gurney secured for passage. Nathan was just climbing into the vehicle's cab and he nodded at the woman's statement. But Howard was in the back with the old man, and he now moved forward to the edge of the entrance, his thin, uniformed body barring her access.

When she tried to get in anyway, Howard remained where he was and shook his head. "Sorry. Rules."

Reaching for both doors simultaneously, he began to close them on her. But the action was never completed. Coming up from behind her, Georges suddenly clamped his hand down on the door closest to him. It was apparent that Georges was the stronger of the two.

It was also very apparent, especially from the scowl on his face, that Howard did not care for being challenged.

"Let her go with him," Georges told the paramedic. It was an order even though his voice remained even, low-key. "She's been through a lot."

Howard's frown deepened. This was his small kingdom and he was not about to abdicate so easily. "Look, there are rules to follow. Nobody but the patient, that's him, and the attendant, that's me," he said needlessly, his teeth clenched together, "are supposed to be riding back in—"

Georges' smile was the sort envisioned on the lips of a cougar debating whether or not to terminate the life of its captured prey—if cougars could smile.

"Have a heart—" his eyes shifted to the man's name tag "—Howard. Let the lady get into the ambulance with her grandfather."

Nathan twisted around in his seat, looking into the back of the ambulance. "Listen to the man, Howie," he advised with a wide, easy grin. "Someday he could be holding a scalpel over your belly."

It was obvious that Howard didn't care for the image or the veiled threat.

"If you get any flack," Georges promised smoothly, "just refer your supervisor to me. I'll take full responsibility."

"Yeah, easy for you to say," Howard grumbled. Drawing in a breath, he blew it out again, clearly not happy about the situation. Clearly not confident enough to back up his decision. His small black eyes darted from the woman's face to the doctor's. Survival instincts won over being king of the hill. "Okay." Howard backed away from the entrance and returned to his seat beside the gurney. "Get in."

"Thank you," the blonde cried. It wasn't clear if she was addressing her words to Howard or her Good Samaritan, or the man in the front seat behind the steering wheel. Possibly, it was to all three.

Taking her hand, Georges helped the woman get into the back of the ambulance.

But once she was inside, she didn't let go of his hand. She held on more tightly.

"I want you to come, too," she said to him. When it looked as if he was going to demur, she added a heartfelt, "Please?"

There was no more that he could do. The ride to the hospital was fast enough and once there, there would be doctors to see to the man. Besides, he still had a date waiting for him.

Georges began to extricate himself from her. "I—"

Her expression grew more determined. "You said you worked at—Blair Memorial, is it?" Georges nodded. "Then you're one step ahead of everyone else there. You saw what my grandfather went through. You treated him. Please," she entreated. "I don't want to risk losing him. I don't want to look back and think, If only that doctor had been there, that would have made the difference between my grandfather living and—" She couldn't bring herself to finish.

It was the sudden shimmer of tears in her eyes that got him. Got him as surely as if handcuffs had been snapped shut on his wrists. Georges inclined his head, acquiescing.

"I never argue with a beautiful damsel in distress," he told her. Then he glanced up at the frowning Howard who looked like a troll sitting beneath his bridge, protecting his tiny piece of dirt. "Don't worry, I won't crowd you in the ambulance," Georges promised. He jerked his thumb back at his presently less than shiny sports car. "I'll follow behind in my car." Georges shifted his glance toward the woman. "That all right with you?"

Vienna Hollenbeck pressed her lips together to

hold back the sob that materialized in her throat. She was a hairbreadth away from breaking down, and it bothered her. Bothered her because it clashed with the strong self-image she carried around of herself.

Surprise, you're not invulnerable after all.

Nodding, Vienna whispered, "Yes, that'll be fine with me."

Georges gave her hand a warm squeeze before withdrawing his own. "He's going to be all right," he promised.

With a huff, Howard leaned over and shut both doors in his face. Firmly.

Georges turned away and hurried over to his vehicle. Buckling up, he turned the key in the ignition. The car purred to life as if it hadn't come within inches of being crushed.

He'd just broken cardinal rule number one, Georges thought, waiting for the ambulance to pull away. Not the one about doing no harm. That was the official one on the books, the one that was there to make people feel better about going to doctors. He'd broken the practical one, the one that was intended to have doctors safeguarding their practices and their reputations. The one that strictly forbade them to make promises about a patient's future unless they were completely, absolutely certain that what they said could be written in stone and that their words couldn't somehow return to bite them on the part of their anatomy used for sitting.

But he found that he couldn't look into those blue eyes of hers and not give the woman the assurance that she was silently begging for.

"So I made her feel better for a few minutes," Georges murmured out loud to no one in particular. "What harm could it do? Really?"

Besides, from what he could ascertain, the old man didn't look as if he'd sustained extensive bodily injuries.

Appearances can be deceiving.

How many times had he heard that before? How many times had he learned that to be true? The old man could very easily have massive internal injuries that wouldn't come to light until after he'd been subjected to a battery of tests and scans.

Still, Georges argued silently, why make the woman worry? If there was something wrong, there was plenty of time for the man's granddaughter to worry later. And if it turned out that there wasn't anything wrong, why burden her needlessly? He always tried to see things in a positive light. It was an optimism that he had developed over the years and which had its roots in his mother's lifestyle and philosophy: never assume the worst. If it was there, it would find you soon enough without being summoned.

Georges realized that he was gripping the steering wheel a great deal more tightly than necessary. He consciously relaxed his hold. It didn't, however, keep him from squeezing through a yellow light in the process of turning red.

He kept pace with the ambulance, all but tailgating it until it reached Blair Memorial.

The hospital was an impressive structure that was perched at the top of a hill and that seemed, according to some, to be forever under construction. Not the main section, which only underwent moderate renovations every ten to fifteen years, but the outlying regions.

Beginning as a small, five-story building, over the last forty-five years, Blair Memorial Hospital, originally called Harris Memorial, had tripled in size. It owed its name change and its mushrooming growth to generous donations from the Blair family, as well as from myriad other benefactors. None of it would have been possible, however, if not for its glowing reputation, attributed to an outstanding staff.

No one was ever turned away from Blair Memorial's doors and the poorest patient was given the same sort of care as the richest patient: excellent in every way. Its physicians and surgeons thought nothing of volunteering their free time, both at Blair and in outlying regions, rendering services to people who otherwise could not afford to receive the proper medical attention that often meant the difference between life and death, permanent disability and full recovery. Georges was proud to have been accepted at Blair to complete his residency.

The ambulance made a left turn at the light, then an immediate right. Easing around the small space, it backed up to the emergency room's outer doors.

Georges was right behind it. As he brought his car to a stop beside the vehicle, a volunteer valet came to life behind his small podium and quickly hurried over toward the red sports car.

"I'm sorry, I'll have to park that for you in the other lot. We need to keep this clear for emergency vehicles." The words were hardly out of his mouth before he saw the hospital ID that Georges held up for his perusal. The valet flushed. "Oh, sorry, Doctor. I thought you were with them." He nodded at the ambulance. It wasn't unusual for family members to accompany ambulances.

"I am," Georges replied amicably. "There was an accident on PCH. I just happened to be there in time to lend a hand."

Nodding meekly, the valet faded back to his podium.

The back doors of the ambulance were already opened. Georges waited for the gurney to be lowered. Once it was, he offered his hand to the blonde to help her out of the vehicle.

Her fingers were icy, he noted.

"Thank you," she murmured, her eyes meeting his and holding for a long moment.

Georges knew the woman wasn't referring to his helping her out of the ambulance. She was thanking him for coming.

"Part of my job description," he told her.

"Trolling for patients?" she asked, repeating the words that Nathan had used earlier. She tried to force a smile to her lips.

The small, aborted attempt hinted at just how radiant her smile could be once fully projected. He found himself looking forward to seeing it in earnest.

"Helping where I can," he corrected.

The gurney was pushed through the electronic doors that had sprung open to admit it and the attendants. Georges placed his hand to the small of her back, guiding her in behind the gurney.

Warm air came rushing at them, a contrast to the cool night air outside. The next moment, the on-duty E.R. physician was coming toward the paramedics and their patient.

"What have we got?" Alex Murphy asked, pulling on plastic gloves as he approached. The next moment, he stopped, looking at Georges in surprise. The two men had crossed paths a couple of hours ago, with Murphy arriving as Georges was leaving.

"Friend of yours, Dr. Armand?" Murphy assumed.

Georges shook his head. "Hit-and-run," he replied. "Accident happened right behind me on Pacific Coast Highway. Driver of the car never even stopped." He didn't add that he had almost been hit by the same driver. Dramatics were his mother's domain; they'd never interested him. "The man had a cardiac episode. His heart stopped for less than a minute," he added when Murphy looked at him sharply. "I applied CPR."

Georges rattled off the rest of the man's vital signs. When it came to his blood pressure, Georges glanced toward Howard, who supplied the missing piece of information. The paramedic looked annoyed that he had been reduced to the role of a supporting player.

Taking it all in, Murphy nodded. "Okay, we'll take it from here."

Georges felt the woman's eyes on him, as if silently urging him to take the lead. There was no need. Murphy was an excellent physician, but to allay her fears, he turned to the doctor and said, "I'd appreciate it if you did an angiogram on him right away. He has diabetes and a heart condition."

"And this is a stranger, you say?" Murphy glanced from him to the young woman beside him. And then nodded knowingly. "Angiogram it is." Murphy turned toward the nurse and orderly who had taken the two paramedics' places. "You heard Dr. Armand." They began to wheel the old man away, but Murphy stopped them. "I want a full set of films done, as well." He fired the names of the specific scans at them. Finished, he backed away.

The nurse and orderly resumed pushing the gurney down the hall, passing through another set of double doors. The blonde began to follow behind them. Hurrying to catch up, Georges placed a restraining hand on her arm.

Startled, she looked at him, a puzzled expression on her face.

"You can't go there," he told her, then added with a reassuring smile, "Don't worry, they'll bring him back as soon as they're finished."

Murphy stripped off the plastic gloves and crossed his arms before him. "Anything else?" he asked, mildly amused.

Georges nodded. He knew how territorial some doctors could be. It was always best to ask permission rather than assume. "If you don't mind, I'd like to hang around."

Murphy glanced at the woman, who in turn was looking down the hall. Georges Armand's reputation had made the rounds and he, like everyone else, was well aware that the young surgical resident attracted women like a high-powered magnet attracted iron. "Hang all you want, Georges." He smiled wistfully. Married five years, his own romancing days were well in his past. "I'll keep you apprised," he promised.

Murphy addressed the words toward the young

woman, as well, but for the moment, she seemed oblivious. With a shrug, the physician left to attend to the next patient on his list.

"Thanks. I appreciate that," Georges called after him. Turning toward the blonde, he caught himself thinking that she seemed a little shaky on her feet. Small wonder, considering that she'd been in the accident, too.

"You know," he began, moving her over to one side as another gurney, this time from one of the E.R. stalls, was pushed past them by two orderlies, "you really should get checked out, as well."

If she stopped moving, Vienna thought, she was going to collapse. Like one of those cartoon characters that only plummeted down the ravine if they acknowledged that there was no ground beneath their feet.

She shook her head. "I'm fine. Just shaken. And worried," she added with a suppressed sigh, looking over toward the double doors where her grandfather had disappeared.

"In that case, maybe we should get your mind on other things." He saw her eyebrows draw together in silent query. "There's an anxious administrative assistant over at Registration eager to take down a lot of information about your grandfather. Here." He offered her his arm. "I can take you over to the Registration desk so you can talk to her."

Vienna nodded, feeling as if she was slipping into a surreal dreamlike state. She threaded her arm through his in what seemed like slow motion, and allowed herself to be directed through yet another set of swinging double doors.

She tried desperately to clear the fog that was descending over her head. "You know," she said, turning to look at the doctor, "I don't even know your name." The other doctor had called him by something, but she hadn't heard the man clearly. "What do I call you?" She smiled softly. "Besides an angel?"

He laughed then, thinking of what several women might have to say about that. He also caught himself thinking that he'd been right. When she smiled, it was a beautiful sight to behold. "I don't think anyone's ever accused me of being one of those."

"Well, you are," she told him. "I don't…I don't know what…I would have done if…you hadn't stopped to help." Tears stole her breath, blocking her words.

"Don't go there," he told her. "There's no point in thinking about the worst if you don't have to." He stopped walking and gave her a small, formal bow, the way he used to at his mother's behest when he was a small boy. "My name is Georges— with an *S*—Armand."

She shook his hand. "Well, Georges with an *S,* I won't think about the worst but only because I know you saved me from it. Saved my grandfather from it." She paused to take a deep breath. She wasn't going to cry, she wasn't. Tears were for the weak and she was strong. She *had* to be strong. "My name is Vienna," she told him, putting out her hand, "Vienna Hollenbeck."

Her skin felt colder than the last time, Georges thought. "Vienna? Like the city?"

"Like the city." The smile on her lips was just too much of an effort to retain. It melted as she felt herself turning a ghostly shade of pale. Perspiration suddenly rimmed her forehead and scalp. "Would you—would you mind if we postponed seeing the administrative assistant for a minute?"

"Sure. Are you all right?"

His voice was coming to her from an increasing distance. Vienna felt her knees softening to the consistency of custard. The deep baritone voice had nothing to do with it.

"I'm not… I don't think…"

She didn't get a chance to finish. Rather than sit down the way she'd wanted to, Vienna felt herself dissolving into nothingness as the world around her became smaller and smaller until it had shrunk down to the size of a pinhole.

And then disappeared altogether.

Just before it did, she thought she heard the doctor calling to her, but she couldn't be sure. And she definitely couldn't answer because her lips no longer had the strength to move.

The darkness that found her was far too oppressive to allow her to say a word. With a last rally of strength, she tried to struggle against it, to keep it at bay.

But in the end, all she could do was surrender.

Chapter Three

Georges managed to catch her just before her body hit the floor.

Scooping Vienna up in his arms, he looked around the immediate area for an open bed. He saw the nurse and the bed at the same time.

"Jill," he called out to a heavyset woman he'd met during his first day at the E.R., "I'm putting this woman into bed number seven."

Mother of four boys, grandmother of seven more, Jill Foster liked to think of herself as the earth mother of the E.R. night shift. Pulling her eyebrows together, she looked at the unconscious woman he was holding and gave him a penetrating, no-nonsense look.

"Getting a little brazen with our conquests, aren't we, Dr. Armand?"

They had an easy, good rapport, although he knew the thirty-two-year hospital veteran wouldn't hesitate to tell him when she thought he was wrong.

"She fainted," he told her, crossing over to the empty stall.

"Probably not the first time that's happened to you, I'd wager," Jill commented dryly.

On her way to answer a call from another patient, she paused to pull aside the white blanket and sheet on the bed for him. When Georges deposited the unconscious woman on the bed, Jill took off her shoes. After putting them into a plastic bag, the nurse placed it beneath the bed, then pulled the blanket up over the young woman.

"Need anything else?" she asked him. "Other than privacy?"

Sometimes, Georges thought, his reputation kept people from taking him seriously. Usually, it didn't bother him, but he wanted to make sure that the nurse understood this was on the level. "Jill, the woman's been in an accident."

Jill raised her hands to stop him before he could go on. "I know, I know, I saw her grandfather being wheeled out of here to X-ray. Orderly almost popped a wheelie moving by me so fast." Sympathy crinkled along her all-but-unlined face as she looked down at Vienna. And then the next second, she regained her flippant facade. "Well, you know where all the doctor tools are." She patted his back. "Call if you need me." As she began to walk out of the stall, Vienna moaned. Jill paused to wink knowingly at him. "Sounds to me like she's got the sounds down right. You don't want people talking. I'd leave the curtain open if I were you."

Jill left to see about her patient.

Moaning again, Vienna stirred and then opened her eyes. The second after she did, she realized that she was in a horizontal position. She would have bolted upright much too fast, but firm hands on her shoulders pushed her back down onto the mattress.

She blinked and looked up at Georges. Breathing a sigh of relief, she shaded her eyes. "Oh God, what happened?"

"You almost had a close encounter with the hospital floor." Her eyes widened. He found it incredibly appealing. Innocent and vulnerable and somehow sensuous all at the same time. "I caught you just in time."

Well, at least she hadn't made a complete fool of herself, Vienna thought. "That's twice you've come to my rescue."

He did his best to look serious as he nodded.

"Third time and you have to grant me a wish." Again her eyes widened, but this time, he thought he saw a wariness in them. Was she afraid of him? he suddenly wondered. Or had his teasing words triggered a memory she didn't welcome? "I'm kidding," he told her.

"I know that." Digging her knuckles into the mattress on either side of her, Vienna tried to get up for a second time. With the same outcome. He pushed her gently back on the bed. This time, it required a little more force than before.

She was a stubborn one, he thought. "You're not going anywhere until I check you over," he told her.

She began to shake her head, then stopped when tiny little devils with pointy hammers popped up to begin wreaking havoc. Pressing her lips together, willing the pain to go away, she looked up at him. "I'm all right," she insisted.

His eyes swept over her. Georges couldn't help smiling in appreciation. *Now there's an understatement.*

"Be that as it may, I'd like to make sure for myself." Reaching for an instrument to check her pupils, he turned on the light and aimed the pinprick directly at her right eye. "Look up, please."

She resisted, drawing back her head. "This really isn't necessary."

He pointed up to a spot on the ceiling and tried again. "Humor me."

Vienna sighed and stared up at the imaginary spot where he pointed. When he switched eyes and pointed to another area, she complied again.

Georges withdrew the instrument, shutting off the light. "Well?" she asked impatiently.

He returned the instrument to its place. "You don't appear to have a concussion."

"That's because I don't."

"But you did faint," he reminded her. And that could be a symptom of a lot of things—or mean nothing at all. He liked erring on the side of caution when it came to patients. "I could order a set of scans done—"

Vienna cut him off at the pass. "Not on me you can't." She said the words with a smile, but her tone was firm. She knew her own body and there was nothing wrong. Besides, if she was in the hospital as a patient, she might not be able to be with her grandfather and he was all that mattered. "I just got a little frazzled, that's all." Throwing off the covers from her legs, she swung her legs over the side of the bed. As she slid off the bed, she looked down on the floor and her bare feet. There were no shoes in sight. "Now if you could just tell me where my shoes are, I'll be all set."

For a moment, he thought of pleading ignorance,

but he had a feeling that being barefoot would not be enough to keep her here. Bending down, he retrieved the plastic bag from beneath the bed and handed it to her.

"It wouldn't hurt for you to stay overnight for observation, either."

Vienna took out her high heels and, placing them on the floor, stepped into the shoes. It struck Georges that he'd seldom seen anyone move so gracefully.

"Maybe not," she allowed, "but it would be a waste of time and money. I didn't even hit my head."

The hell she didn't. "Then what's this?" Georges asked as he moved back wispy blond bangs from her forehead. A nice-sized bump had begun to form above her right eye. He ran his thumb ever so lightly across it.

Vienna tried not to wince in response, but he saw the slight movement that indicated pain.

She feathered her fingers just on the outer edges of the area and shrugged. "Okay, maybe I did hit my head, but not so that I saw stars," she insisted. "It was my grandfather who got the brunt of the impact." Even as she said it, she could see the events moving in slow motion in her mind's eye. It was a struggle not to shiver. Her expression turned somber. When she spoke, her voice was hushed. Fearful. "How is he?"

"You haven't been out that long," he told her.

"Your grandfather's not back from X-ray yet." Pausing, he studied her for a second.

She shifted slightly, trying to stand as straight as she could. She did *not* want to argue about getting more tests again. "What?"

"Just before you took your unofficial 'nap,'" he said tactfully, "you were about to go to the registration desk to give the administrative assistant your grandfather's insurance information."

Now she remembered, Vienna thought. Edging over to the front of the stall, she inadvertently brushed up against the doctor and instantly felt her body tightening.

Reflexes alive and well, she congratulated herself.

Taking a deep breath, she announced, "Okay, let's go."

But he didn't seem all that ready to take her where she needed to go. Instead, he regarded her for another long moment, as if he expected her to faint again. "You're sure you're up to it?"

In response, she left the curtained enclosure. He quickly fell into step beside her, indicating that she needed to turn right at the end of the hallway. Vienna noticed several nurses watching them as they passed.

"Do you take such good care of all your patients?" she asked.

He appeared to consider her question, then deadpanned, "Only the ones I rescue from a burning car."

"Oh." A smile flickered across her lips, teasing dimples into existence on either cheek. "Lucky thing for me."

They walked through a set of swinging doors. As he brought her over to the first available space in the registration area, his cell phone began to ring.

"She has insurance information about a patient who was just brought in to the E.R.," he told the young girl behind the desk, then turned to Vienna as the phone rang again. "I've got to take this."

Vienna nodded. "Of course."

Taking the cell out of his jacket pocket as he moved away from the desk, Georges glanced down at the number. And winced inwardly.

Diana.

He'd completely forgotten about her. And about his date. He supposed if he hurried, he could still salvage some of the evening.

Georges was considering the option when he saw two policemen entering the E.R., coming from within the hospital rather than via the back entrance the way they had. By their unhurried demeanor, intuition told him the patrolmen were here to see Vienna. Since he'd seen everything that had gone down, that made him a material witness. Which meant that he was going to have to stick around to give his statement, as well.

That made his mind up for him.

Flipping the phone open on the fifth ring, he turned away from the desk. "Diana, hi. I am so sorry. I know I'm late, but I was involved in an accident—"

"An accident?" the voice on the other end repeated breathlessly. "Are you all right?"

"Yes, but the police just got here and I'm going to have to give them my statement. I've got no idea how long this is going to take." He caught himself looking over toward Vienna, wondering if she was going to be up to this. "I'm afraid that I'm going to need a rain check."

"This is Southern California. It doesn't rain here this time of year," Diana reminded him. But she didn't sound angry, just disappointed.

"We can do our own rain dance," he promised, lowering his voice.

He heard her laugh and felt a sense of satisfaction. She'd forgiven him. "That I'd like to see. All right, call me, lover, whenever you're free."

"Count on it," he told her. Ending the call, he flipped the phone closed and pocketed it again. Georges turned around just in time to see the two policemen position themselves on both sides of Vienna's chair. That same protective instinct that had had him throwing his body over hers when the car burst into flames stirred inside his chest.

He quickly crossed back to her, but he was

looking at the patrolmen as he approached. "Can I be of any help, officers?" he asked easily.

The younger of the two policeman gave him a once-over before speaking. "That all depends. You have any information about this car accident on PCH that was reported?"

Boy, have I got some information for you, he thought. Out loud, he said, "As a matter of fact, I do. But first, how did you find out about it?" he asked. He'd given Vienna the number to the hospital to summon an ambulance, not 911.

The younger of the two looked reluctant to divulge any information at all. When he remained silent, his partner said, "Paramedics called it in. Someone named Howard. Told us where to find you." The last statement was directed to Vienna.

Howard. He should have known, Georges thought. The EMT wasn't kidding when he talked about adhering to the rules.

Georges glanced over toward an alcove. E.R. doctors typically retreated there to write their reports without being disturbed. The area was empty at the moment.

"Why don't we move over there, out of the way?" he suggested, indicating the alcove. Not waiting for the policemen to agree, he put his hand beneath Vienna's elbow and helped her up from the chair.

"You a doctor?" the other policeman, older than

his partner by at least a decade, asked as he followed behind them.

Taking out the badge that was still in his pocket, Georges hung it about his neck. "Yes."

"Lucky for the people involved," the older patrolman commented. As the tallest, he stood on the outer perimeter of the space, allowing his partner and the other two to assemble within a space that normally held no more than two.

The patrolmen left half an hour later, satisfied with the report they'd gotten and armed with the make and model, as well as license plate number, of the hit-and-run driver's vehicle. The younger patrolman had even cracked a slight smile. The older one promised they would be in touch the moment there was something to report.

Vienna had held up well during the questioning, Georges thought as the two men in blue took their leave, but now she looked drained. Concern returned.

The moment the policeman walked away from the alcove, Vienna turned toward him and put her hand on his arm, securing his attention. He thought she was going to ask if she could lie down again.

Instead, she asked, "Could you go see how my grandfather's doing?"

"Sure." Glancing to the side, he saw the administrative assistant they'd initially been talking to standing in the corridor, shifting her weight from foot to foot. Rather than ask the woman if anything was wrong, Georges crossed to her and used his body to block her view of Vienna. And vice versa.

"Something wrong?" he asked, his voice low enough not to carry back to the alcove just in case the assistant had come to say something about Vienna's grandfather.

The assistant looked uncomfortable being pushy, but her job demanded it. "I still need that insurance information. All I've got is the guy's name and half an address. I need more."

Relieved that it wasn't anything more serious, Georges nodded sympathetically. "Sure you do." But in his opinion, Vienna needed a break. She'd been answering questions steadily for twenty minutes. He'd given his statement to the older of the policemen while she had been grilled by the younger one. "Look, how about I get the insurance information to you in a little while?"

The assistant hesitated, wavering. "Technically, you're not supposed to start any work on him until I have *something* for his record."

"You have something," he told her smoothly, placing his hand on hers and turning her away from the alcove and back toward her own area. "You have my word." Covertly, he read the name on her tag and added, "Amanda."

The personal touch, he'd found time and again, always helped to move things along in the right direction.

Amanda seemed flustered now, as well as uncertain. "You sure you'll get that information to me?"

Georges nodded. "Just as soon as I can, Amanda," he promised, then winked as if that made it their little secret.

Amanda was already backing away to return to her desk. "I guess it's okay."

He flashed a grin. "You're a doll." The blush that rose to the woman's cheeks told him that he had sealed the bargain.

Going back into the rear of the E.R., it didn't take him long to find Murphy. The latter was dealing with a screaming infant with colic. The first-time parents both seemed at the end of their collective emotional ropes. Flanking both sides of the raised railings of the baby's bed, they peppered Murphy with questions, one dovetailing into another.

When he approached Murphy, the physician looked relieved to see him.

"Excuse me for a moment," he said, extricating himself from the circle of noise. Moving toward the side, Murphy shook his head. "I'm going to have to have my hearing checked after tonight. I think I've lost the ability to hear anything at a high frequency."

Blowing out a breath, he glanced up at Georges. "You're going to ask me about the old man, right?"

Georges saw no point in wasting time, even though he knew Murphy wasn't anxious to get back to his tiny patient and his overwrought parents. "Are his films back yet?"

Murphy nodded. "Just. I've put out a call for an internal surgeon and I want a consult with Dr. Greywolf," he added, mentioning one of Blair's top heart surgeons.

"What's wrong with him?" Georges pressed.

Murphy rattled off the important particulars. "His spleen's been damaged, his liver was bruised in the accident and several ribs were cracked, not to mention that he did have a minor heart attack. Nice work bringing him around, by the way."

It never hurt to have one of the chief attendings compliment your work, Georges thought. "Thanks." But right now, he was more interested in the answer to his next question. "Who'd you call for the surgery?"

"Rob Schulman. He's on call for the night. I'm trying to get Darren Patterson to act as assistant on the procedures, but so far, Patterson's not answering his page."

Georges didn't even have to think about it. "I can assist," he volunteered. Murphy eyed him skeptically. All surgical residents were eager to operate whenever possible, but this went beyond wanting to put in time in the O.R. He felt an obligation to the old man to see things through. "I've assisted Schulman before. If Patterson doesn't answer by the time Schulman gets here—"

"You scrub in," Murphy concluded, agreeing. The night shift was always down on viable personnel, and they worked with what they could get on short notice.

The baby's screams grew louder again. Murphy gritted his teeth. "Any chance you want to fill in for me until Schulman shows up?"

Georges laughed and shook his head. "Not a chance. I put in my eighteen hours today."

"Then why aren't you dead on your feet?"

Georges grinned as he spread his hands innocently. "Clean living."

"Not from what I hear," Murphy responded. He turned around to walk back to the shrieking baby's stall. "Into the Valley of Death rode the six hundred," he muttered under his breath.

"A doctor who quotes Tennyson. That should look good on your résumé," Georges commented.

Murphy said something unintelligible as he disappeared into the stall.

Georges made his way back to Vienna.

The second she saw him, she was on her feet, her eyes opened wide like Bambi.

"My grandfather…"

Her voice trailed off. She couldn't bring herself

to complete the question, afraid of being too optimistic. Afraid of the alternative even more. She held her breath, waiting for Georges to answer her.

"Is going to need surgery," he told her, saying only what they both already knew. "He got a little banged up inside and we're going to fix that," he assured Vienna in a calm, soothing voice.

Relief wafted over her. Her grandfather was still alive. There was hope. And then she replayed the doctor's words in her head.

"We?" she questioned. "Then you'll be the one operating on him?"

"Dr. Schulman will be performing the surgery. He's one of the best in the country. I'll be assisting him if they can't find anyone else."

She took hold of his hand, her eyes on his, riveting him in place. "I don't want anyone else," she told him with such feeling it all but took his breath away. "I want you. I want you to be there."

"They're trying to locate another surgeon to assist, but—"

"No," she interrupted. "You. I want you." Her fingers closed over his hand. "You'll help. I can feel it. It's important that you be there for him during the operation. Please."

Georges heard himself saying, "All right," but, like a ventriloquist, she was the one who was drawing the words from his lips.

Chapter Four

The next moment, Vienna suddenly pulled back.

Georges probably thought she was crazy, she thought, and she didn't want to alienate him. But she was certain that he *had* to be in the operating room.

It wasn't that she thought of herself as clairvoyant, she just had these…*feelings,* for lack of a better word. Feelings that came to her every so often.

Feelings that always turned out to be true.

She'd had one of those feelings the day her parents were killed.

Vienna had been only eight at the time, still very much a child, but somehow, as they bid her goodbye, saying they would see her that evening, she instinctively knew that she was seeing Bill and Theresa Hollenbeck for the last time. She'd clung to each of her parents in turn, unwilling to release them, unable to make them understand that if they walked out that door, if they drove to Palm Springs to meet with her mother's best friend and that woman's fiancé, that they would never see another sunrise.

God knew she'd tried to tell them, but they had laughed and hugged her, and told her not to worry. That she was just held captive by an overactive imagination. And her grandfather's stories. Amos Schwarzwalden, her mother's father, was visiting from Austria at the time and they left her with him.

And drove out of her life forever.

The accident happened at six-thirty that evening. It was a huge pileup on I-5 that made all the local papers and the evening news. Seven cars had plowed into one another after a drunk driver had lost control of his car. A semi had swerved to avoid hitting the careening vehicle—and wound up hitting the seven other cars instead.

Miraculously, there'd only been two casualties. Tragically, those two casualties had been her parents.

It was the first time Vienna could remember ever having one of those "feelings."

After that, there were other times, other occasions where a sense of uneasiness warned her that something bad was going to happen. But the feeling never came at regular intervals or even often. It didn't occur often enough for her grandfather, who was the only one she shared this feeling with, to think she had some sort of extraordinary power. She didn't consider herself a seer or someone with "the sight" as those in the old country were wont to say.

But her "intuitions" occurred just often enough for her not to ignore them when they did happen. And even though they had not warned her of the car accident that had nearly stolen her grandfather from her, they now made her feel that if this man who had come to their rescue was not in the O.R. when her grandfather was being operated on, something very serious was going to happen. Something that would not allow her grandfather to be part of her life anymore.

Her eyes met Georges' and she flashed a rueful smile that instantly took him captive.

"I'm sorry, I didn't mean to sound as if I was coming unhinged," Vienna apologized, but all the same, she continued holding on to his arm. "But I really do feel very strongly about this," she emphasized. "You *have* to be in the operating room with my grandfather."

Georges could all but feel the urgency rippling through her, transmitting itself to him. The woman was dead serious. They were running out of time and as far as he knew, Patterson had still not been located.

"All right," Georges agreed gently. "I'll go talk to the surgeon." Placing his hand over hers, he squeezed it lightly and gave her an encouraging smile. "You sit tight, all right?"

Vienna was barely aware of nodding her head. She forced a smile to her lips.

"All right," she murmured. "And thank you. Again."

He merely nodded and then hurried away.

In the locker room, he quickly changed into scrubs. As he closed the locker door, he felt as if he was getting a second wind. Or was that his third one? He wasn't altogether sure. By all rights, at this point in his day—or night—he should have been dead on his feet, looking forward to nothing more than spending the rest of the night in a reclining position—as he'd planned with Diana.

Instead, as he headed to scrub in, he felt suddenly invigorated. Ready to leap tall buildings in a single bound. The prospect of facing a surgery always did that to him. It put him on his toes and, Georges found, instantly transformed him into the very best version of himself.

He all but burst into the area where the sinks were and after greeting the surgeon, began the laborious process of getting ready to perform the procedure—in double time.

Rob Schulman was carefully scrubbing the area between his fingers with a small scrub brush. Every surgeon had superstitions. Schulman's was to use a new scrub brush for every surgery. He glanced over toward Georges.

He seemed mildly amused at the energy he witnessed in the other man.

"Someday, Georges, you're going to have to tell me what kind of vitamins you're on." When Georges looked over toward him quizzically, he elaborated. "I saw you eight hours ago and they tell me that except for two hours, you've been here all this time. What kind of a deal with the devil did you make?" Schulman asked. He paused to rotate his neck. Several cracks were heard to echo through the small area. The surgical nurses, waiting their turn, exchanged smiles. "Why is it you're not falling on your face?"

"I scheduled that for after the surgery," Georges replied with an easy air that hid the electrical current all but racing through him. Done, he gave his hands another once-over, just in case. "I want to thank you for letting me scrub in."

Schulman laughed softly to himself, the high-pitched sound incongruous with man's considerable bulk. "You're welcome, but this time, it's more of a matter of supply and demand, Georges. Murphy told me that they can't find another assistant in time."

They could have opted to wait. Or, in an emergency, Murphy could have scrubbed in. Carefree to a fault, Georges still knew better than to take anything for granted. He inclined his head toward the senior internal surgeon. "I'll take what I can get."

Schulman concentrated on his nail beds, scrubbing hard. "They tell me you brought him in." He raised his brown eyes toward Georges for a second. "Hunting down your own patients these days?"

Georges pretended he hadn't heard that line twice already this evening and flashed an easy smile at the man.

"I was on Pacific Coast Highway," he told Schulman. "The accident happened right behind me."

"Lucky for the driver you were there," Schulman commented. Finished, he leaned his elbow against the metal faucet handles and turned off the water. Bracing himself, he looked toward the swinging double doors that led into the operating room. "All right, let's see if I can keep that luck going."

Georges nodded. Finished with his own preparations for the surgery, he followed Schulman into the O.R., his own hands raised and ready to have surgical gloves slipped over them.

An eerie feeling passed over him the moment he'd said the words. Exactly one moment after he had pointed out to Schulman that an artery the latter had cauterized wasn't, in fact, completely sealed.

With the old man's organs all vying for space, it had been an easy matter to miss the slow seepage. The surgeon was focused on what he was doing, removing the spleen and resectioning the liver by removing a small, damaged portion no more than the size of a quarter. As all this went on—not to mention the presence of various instruments, suction tubes and clamps within the small area—the tiny bit of oozing had almost been overlooked. *Would* have been overlooked had something not caught his eye in that region.

He still wasn't sure exactly what had prompted him to push back the retractor and look, but he was so glad he had. The seepage could have cost the patient his life.

I don't want anyone else. I want you. I want you to be there. It's important that you be there for him during the operation.

Had she known? Had the blonde with the intensely blue eyes somehow known that this was why he had to be inside the O.R.?

Lily believed in things that went beyond religion and beyond any reason known to man. Ever since he could remember, she made it a point to rule out nothing. Not spirits, not things beyond the realm of the everyday and the norm. Periodically, his mother would seek the guidance of a palm reader and have her future told.

According to his mother, that was how she'd known which of the men in her life to marry and which merely to enjoy. In the end, her insecurity and restlessness had her leaving all of them, husband or lover, but she claimed that her fortune-teller helped her "see" which path to take.

Both Philippe and Alain placed no stock in that, pooh-poohing her fondness for fortune-tellers as just another eccentric attribute that contributed to her being Lily Moreau. But he was inclined to go along with the that line from *Hamlet*. That there were more things in heaven and on earth than could possibly be dreamt of in anyone's philosophy.

Now, as he watched Schulman swiftly reassess the situation, he caught himself wondering about the blonde he'd left in the surgical lounge.

Was the woman clairvoyant?

He didn't know. Didn't know if he actually believed in clairvoyance—but she *had* been adamant that he be here in the O.R. And if he *hadn't* been here, her grandfather would presently be bleeding out. By the time Amos's condition worsened enough for them to reopen him again and locate the bleeding artery, it might have very well been too late to remedy the situation.

"Nice catch, Georges," Schulman was saying as he

called for more sponges to help clean out the blood
from the small cavity. Unlike some physicians, the
internal surgeon had no problem with giving credit
where he felt credit was due. "You very well might
have saved this man's life." Schulman glanced up and
his eyes above the mask were smiling as they looked
at Georges. "Again. When this is over, the man should
adopt you. Or at least put you in his will."

Georges made no comment. He was still trying
to sort things out in his head.

It was another three hours before the surgery was
finally over.

Feeling drained and spent and yet experiencing
that exhilarating high that always accompanied any
surgery he was part of, Georges untied his mask. For
the moment, he left it dangling around his neck as
he walked back to the sinks just beyond the operating room. Behind him, Amos Schwarzwalden was
being wheeled through the opposite set of doors
into the recovery room where he would remain for
the next hour or so to be observed.

As always, washing up after a surgery took far
less time than presurgical preparation. Finished,
Georges dried his hands and happened to glance
down at his scrubs. He realized that if he was going
to see Vienna, he needed to stop off at his locker and
change. His shirt had her grandfather's blood on it.

Not exactly the best way to look when he went to give her a firsthand report about the way the surgery had gone.

"Any more people you want me to operate on?" Schulman asked as he finished up himself.

"No, not tonight," Georges answered.

"Good." He glanced around the area. "Then I bid you all good night, people."

The last thing Schulman did before he left was throw away the scrub brush he'd used on his nails.

Georges hurried to the locker room for a clean shirt, not wanting to keep Vienna anxiously waiting any longer than she had to.

Vienna was the only person waiting in the surgical lounge.

Ordinarily, during the course of a normal day, the large, spacious room, with its soft lighting, comfortable sofas and large selection of surprisingly up-to-date reading material, was anywhere from half to completely full with anxious friends and relatives waiting to hear the outcome of their loved one's surgery. But at this hour of the night, the area was usually empty.

Not tonight.

Vienna had the considerable length of the room to move around in. Initially, she'd sat, first on one sofa, then another, then yet another, until she had, like Goldilocks, tried out every seat in the lounge. She'd also looked through every piece of literature in the lounge. Or attempted to.

The pages had moved, and so had her eyes, as she flipped from magazine to magazine. Not a single word had stuck during the course of her entire waiting period. So she had given up and wound up pacing from side to side, trying desperately to plumb the depth of her optimism and make herself truly believe that everything was going to be all right, just as the doctor had said.

Just as he'd promised.

But try as she may, and despite the fact that he had gone in as she'd asked him to, she still could not allow herself to fully relax. Worry became her constant companion.

Her face, a battlefield between concern and her inherent optimism, which ordinarily insisted on seeing the best in any situation, lit up the moment she saw Georges approaching in the distance. She didn't wait for him to come to her. Instead, she rushed over to him before Georges had a chance to reach the lounge.

Holding her breath, Vienna searched his face for a sign that she'd been right to beg him to go into the O.R. That the doctor fate had brought into her life so unexpectedly had saved her grandfather.

"Well?" she cried, her voice all but cracking.

He smiled at her. "Your grandfather's going to be fine," he told her.

It amazed him that yet again, a fresh wave of energy, coming out of nowhere, seemed to find him. Three was usually his limit for one twenty-four-hour period, not four.

The next moment, her face glowing with relief, Vienna threw her arms around his neck. But instead of kissing him the way she had the first time, she turned her face into his chest and began to sob.

"Hey, it's okay," Georges told her soothingly. After a beat, he closed his arms around her and slowly rubbed her back, the way he would a distraught child. "There's no reason to cry. Your grandfather came through it like a trouper." Despite the fact that Lily Moreau was the personification of drama, Georges always felt at a loss when faced with a woman's tears. Especially when those tears had nothing to do with sorrow. Why would a woman cry when she was happy? "We fixed everything that was wrong with him."

Georges held her for as long as she seemed to need it, secretly enjoying the warmth of her body against his, murmuring words of comfort. But when she finally stepped back, wiping away the tears from her cheeks and pulling herself together, he couldn't hold his question back any longer.

"How did you know?" he asked her.

Blinking back the last of her tears from her lashes, Vienna lifted her head. Though her eyes weren't swollen, her cheeks were streaked with tears. Georges reached into his pocket and found a handkerchief. Handing it to Vienna, he drew back just far enough to study her face.

"How did you know?" he asked again.

"Know what?"

Vienna let out a long, ragged breath, then drew in another one, trying to steady herself. Trying to sound normal again. For more than an hour, despite all her best efforts, she had begun to succumb to fear. She loved the old man who had dedicated his life to her, who had given up his home, his business in Austria, to come to America and be her family. Steadier now, she wiped her cheeks and looked at Georges, waiting.

"How did you know about the nicked artery?"

Vienna shook her head, silently indicating that she didn't really know what he was referring to.

"You said I needed to be there."

Now she understood. And wondered if he did.

Her eyes held his for a moment before she said anything. "And did you?"

He thought she was referring to his being in the O.R. in general. "Well, yes. The surgeon, Dr. Schulman, needed an assistant for the procedures." But she already knew that, he thought. Was there something he was missing? "But I'm talking about the fact that if I hadn't been there, Dr. Schulman would have missed the nicked artery. He'd cauterized it, but for some reason, and this is pretty rare—" he underscored that since Schulman was top in his field "—it didn't take. There was still a tiny pinprick opened and it was oozing blood. It was just enough to turn your grandfather septic if it hadn't been detected."

She nodded her head as if reviewing something that she already knew. "And you detected it."

It wasn't a question.

After a moment, Georges nodded. "Yes, I did." His eyes narrowed as he took back the handkerchief she held out to him. "You knew I would," he realized out loud. "How did you know?"

Looking away, Vienna shrugged, trying to push the question, the situation, away, as well. Without success. She knew she owed the surgeon before her more than that. He'd listened to her, come through for her. Because of him, Amos Schwarzwalden, the only living member of her family, was still alive. She owed this man more than she could ever begin to repay.

But he probably wasn't going to believe her, she thought.

Looking back at him, she shrugged again. "I don't know how I knew. I just did." Vienna moistened her lips, then indicated that he should follow her to the closest sofa. She wanted some sort of shelter, for herself and for what she was about to say.

When he sat down beside her, she continued.

"Sometimes," she confided, leaning her body into his and lowering her voice, "I get these…feelings." She raised her eyes to his face, waiting for him to laugh. When he didn't, she experienced a tremendous wave of relief. He believed her. Or, at least, he didn't disbelieve her.

Not yet.

She was serious, he thought. "What kind of 'feelings'?" Georges wanted to know.

She didn't know how better to describe it than that. "Just feelings. Premonitions," she added in hopes that the word might make it clearer for him. "Like I know something is going to happen. I don't know why I know," she added before he could ask. "And it doesn't happen very often, maybe a handful of times since I was a little girl. But when it does, I'm usually right."

It was a lie, but, in her opinion, a necessary one. She had no way of knowing how he might take the information that when these feelings came upon her, she wasn't "usually" right; she was *always* right. For the time being, she sensed that maybe this would be just a wee bit too spooky a revelation to share with the good doctor.

Even now, he seemed to be watching her a little

uncertainly. Not that she could blame him. If their positions were switched, she'd probably feel the same way.

In the end, none of that mattered. Her grandfather was going to be all right. Because Georges Armand had been in the right place at the right time. Twice.

Chapter Five

Vienna looked tired, Georges thought. Now that her grandfather's surgery was over, there was no immediate reason for her to stay.

"Why don't I take you home?" Georges suggested. "Your home," he added in case she thought he was suggesting something.

Georges was aware of the way his offer might be misconstrued because somewhere in the recesses of his mind, the thought about taking this woman home, *his* home, had occurred to him. Since she wasn't a patient of his, there was no conflict of interest—only interest, a great deal of interest—

now that the operation was behind him and he could allow himself to really look at her.

He liked what he saw. A delicate, slender blonde who didn't fold at the first sign of adversity. It was a good trait to have. Being exceedingly attractive wasn't exactly a minus, either.

But Vienna shook her head in response to his offer. "No, that's all right. I'll just stay here and wait to see my grandfather."

Maybe she didn't realize how long it would be before the old man would be moved to his room. "Most likely, your grandfather's going to be in recovery for a couple of hours."

The news didn't seem to daunt Vienna. She sounded almost cheerful as she replied, "I can wait."

"And even after they move him, he probably won't be very lucid. Most likely, he'll just sleep."

She knew the doctor meant well, but he just didn't understand. The very fact that the old man was alive heartened her. "I can watch him breathe."

Georges studied her for a long moment. "He means a great deal to you, doesn't he?"

Vienna smiled to herself, thinking how very inadequate that phrase was when it came to expressing how she felt about Amos Schwarzwalden. "You have no idea."

Well, if she was going to stay, he didn't want

her being by herself. "Is there anyone I can call to stay with you?"

Vienna didn't even pause to think. She shook her head. "We're relatively new here in Southern California. We've only been in Bedford a little over six months."

The late hour had done nothing to abate his curiosity about her. Was there a husband in the wings? A significant other she didn't want disturbed?

"By 'we'…" He allowed his voice to trail off, waiting for her to fill in the blank.

She smiled at his fishing. "I mean my grandfather and me."

It wasn't the most common combination when it came to family members. He heard himself asking, "Where are your parents?"

He saw a little of the color leave Vienna's face and knew he'd stumbled onto ground he had no business crossing.

"Both gone," she told him, doing her best to sound matter-of-fact. She didn't quite pull it off. "They died in a car crash when I was eight. My grandfather was visiting from Austria at the time and staying with us." She tried not to think as she spoke. Even after all these years, it still hurt. "When the accident happened, he sold his business in Vienna and stayed in America with me." She looked up at him, wanting Georges to understand why the man meant so very much to her. Why she would do anything for him. "He turned his whole world upside down for me because he didn't want to take me away from the home where I'd always lived."

Selflessness was a rare thing. The closest he'd come to it in his own life was Philippe. His mother, bless her, went by a whole other set of rules. It didn't make her a bad mother, just different. "Sounds like your grandfather is a hell of a man."

"He is that." Leaning toward him, Vienna placed her hand on top of his. But it was her eyes that seemed to touch him, her eyes that said more than her words could. "Thank you for saving him."

He'd never had a problem accepting gratitude. To him, it was all part of the field he was in. But he couldn't remember ever seeing it look or sound so eloquent and yet so simple.

"You've already thanked me," he reminded her.

Vienna slowly moved her head from side to side. "Never enough." And then she grinned as she withdrew her hand from his. "You're entitled to free baked goods for life."

He could have sworn that he still felt her fingers against his skin. "Excuse me?"

"We moved to Southern California for his health," she told him, "but my grandfather isn't the kind of man who can stand doing nothing. So he opened a bakery in Newport Beach. He was a pastry chef in his native country," she said proudly. "In this country, too. When he came to New York to raise me, he opened up a small bakery off Fifth Avenue. After a while, so many people started coming, he had to buy out the store next to him and expand." By the time he sold his bakery, it was a tremendous cash cow. "I'm sure that once he's back on his feet, my grandfather's going to insist that you come by— on a regular basis, most likely."

Georges rolled the idea over in his head. He had to admit, this did open up possibilities. He wouldn't mind seeing the blonde again after her grandfather checked out of the hospital.

"You work with him?" he asked.

She nodded. "I run the business end of it for him." And had since she graduated with a business degree from Columbia University. "But he's taught me a little about baking. I can't hold a candle to him—his pastries have to be tied down to keep them from floating away off the plate—but you won't have to run to the medicine cabinet for mouthwash after eating one of mine."

Not if her pastries were anything like her kisses, Georges caught himself thinking. "Well, I'll have to come by, then." And then he realized he was missing one crucial piece of information. "What's the shop called?"

"Vienna's Finest." When he looked at her, amused,

she blushed. He found the added shade on her cheeks intriguing. "Grandfather was born in Vienna and it was his favorite city when he was a boy. My mother was born there, too," she added. "She and my father met when he was in the army stationed near there."

"How did you come to be named after the city?" he asked.

"My mother said she wanted to do something to make her feel closer to her father, so she named me after his favorite place. You have to admit, it's better than calling me Amos," she added with a fond smile.

There was a sadness in her eyes, Georges noticed. A sadness he found himself drawn to even though, at the same time, he wanted to erase it from her soul.

He changed the subject. "So there's no one I can call for you?"

Vienna shook her head. "Grandfather knows a lot of people and they're all very fond of him, but there's no one to rouse out of bed at one in the morning."

Even if there was, she wouldn't have allowed it. She couldn't think of anything worse than getting a call in the middle of the night, saying someone had been hurt and was in the hospital. The call about her parents' accident had come in the middle of the night. It had taken that long to identify them. To this day, she cringed whenever the phone rang after she went to bed.

"I'll be fine," she assured him with feeling. "I'll just curl up here—" she nodded toward the sofa "—and wait until they take him to his room."

"Well, then I guess you'll want some coffee." He stopped in his tracks and turned around to give her another choice. "Or some chicken soup. They have some in the vending machine by the nurses' station on the second floor. I can bring you back a container. It's surprisingly not bad."

She noticed that he didn't say *good* and laughed. "Not exactly a ringing endorsement," she observed. "Doctor's orders?"

"Yeah, maybe." If that's what it took to get her to eat or drink something. As he recalled, she'd had neither since she'd gotten to the hospital. "If you're going to play Florence Nightingale, you're going to need to keep your strength up."

She supposed that made sense. Vienna nodded, making her choice. "Chicken soup, then. But I can get it. You need to go home, or wherever it was that you were going before we all but crashed into you and pulled you into our lives."

"It's too late for 'wherever.'" If he were being honest with himself, he no longer had a desire to see Diana tonight. He'd gotten too wrapped up in the surgery to wind down enough for the kind of evening he shared with her. "And I can always go home. Besides—" he glanced at his watch, a Rolex that was a gift from his late father "—at this point, I'm closer to my next shift than not."

Vienna frowned. The man should have been asleep hours ago. "Now you're making me feel bad." At least, for him. But then, if he hadn't been there, her grandfather might not be in the recovery room right now.

"No reason." He hadn't said what he had to make her feel guilty; it had just been a fact, duly noted. "Didn't you know? Doctors run on batteries the first ten years of their careers." He began to walk toward the back elevators. "I'll be right back," he promised.

She nodded, settling back against the cushions. She tried not to sigh. "I'll be right here."

When he returned fifteen minutes later, true to her word, Vienna was exactly where he'd left her: sitting on the sofa closest to the entrance.

But her eyes were shut and she appeared to be dozing. Very quietly, Georges placed the container of chicken soup on the circular table in front of the sofa and within her easy reach once she woke up. Straightening, he wondered if he could borrow a blanket from the emergency room in order to cover her. Without the warm press of interacting bodies, the hospital felt cold.

As he began to tiptoe away, heading toward the E.R., he heard her say, "There's no reason to tread so softly. I'm not asleep."

Georges turned back around to face her. "You're eyes were shut."

She stifled a yawn, pressing her lips together until it faded. "I was just resting them. I might not be a doctor, but I don't need much sleep, either. Especially when my nerves are all in knots."

She'd taken off her shoes and had tucked her feet under her on the sofa. She stretched out now, swinging them down. Her bare feet brushed against the indoor-outdoor carpeting as she reached for the container he'd brought back for her. Vienna pressed a perforated square on the plastic lid and slowly took a sip.

"Mmm, good," she commented. Savoring her first taste, she smiled fondly. "Grandfather always says there is nothing like chicken soup to make you feel better." She paused, as if debating telling him the next part. "I drank a lot of chicken soup that first year after my parents died," she added softly.

She raised her eyes to his as she cradled the container between her hands. There was sympathy in his eyes. Or was that pity? Sympathy was all right, but she didn't want pity. That was what she got for opening up like that, Vienna silently upbraided herself.

"No word yet, right?" She punctuated her question by nodding in the general direction of the O.R.

"No," he confirmed. "And no news actually *is* good news in this case. We want your grandfather's progress to be unremarkable—and steady."

She'd drink to that, she thought.

Vienna raised her container slightly, like someone giving a toast. "To unremarkable and steady." For a second, Vienna's eyes shifted over toward him. "And to the remarkable and steady doctor who came to Grandfather's rescue."

Georges shifted to her sofa and took a seat beside her. At this proximity, the bump on her forehead was visible enough for him to examine again.

"Sure I can't talk you into getting a scan of that?" Very lightly, he touched her forehead so she knew what he was referring to. "On me," he added in case she had no medical coverage available.

"A CT scan, the gift for the girl who has everything," Vienna quipped, just before taking another sip of her soup. And then she laughed even as she shook her head. "Not necessary, Doctor. Even my headache's gone." Or almost gone, she amended silently.

He looked dubious. "That could just be shock, masking it."

"Or it could be nothing," she countered. She didn't want him fussing over her. If anything, she wanted him fussing over her grandfather. "I'm very resilient, Doctor."

And then, out of the blue, she thought of her heart and the way she'd had to put all the pieces together after Edward had walked out of her life. Two years gone in a puff of smoke, just like that, without so much as a backward glance. All because he couldn't allow anyone else into the narrow world he'd defined for them, not even her grandfather. Not even after he knew how much the man meant to her. She'd misspent those two years. But it didn't help her heal any faster.

"I've had to be," she added softly, saying the words more to herself than to him.

He looked at her for a long moment, curbing the desire to lose his fingers in her hair. "That sounds like it has a story behind it."

She raised her eyes to his and tried to smile as she banished the memory away. "It does."

"But you're not going to share it," Georges guessed after a beat.

"Not tonight." And then she smiled, adding, "Not until I know you better."

The words echoed within the all but empty room.

They had *future* stamped all over them. It surprised him to realize that he rather savored the unspoken implication. Ordinarily, when someone made any sort of definite plans that involved him and went beyond the weekend or, in rare instances, the following week, alarms would go off in his head, ringing loudly and urging him to end it because he had to move on.

Time to get out of Dodge and head for the next sunrise.

But there were no alarms, no warning bells. Instead, he found himself wondering about the woman beside him. Wondering and wanting to know things about her. Wanting to fill in the myriad of blanks dancing in front of him.

This, too, shall pass, he promised himself. It was just something different, that's all. *She* was something different, he amended. And different had always intrigued him.

"Something to look forward to," he said to her. It earned him another smile. One that seemed to burrow right smack into the middle of his chest.

In a little while, after the soup had been finished and the coffee grown cold, he went to check on Amos's progress.

The sleepy-eyed night nurse informed him that his patient had responded so well to the surgical procedure, the attending physician had decided to move him out of recovery a full half hour before Amos was scheduled to leave.

Georges returned to share his findings with Vienna.

The moment he did, she was on her feet, heading toward the recovery room's outer doors. They arrived just as Amos was about to be transported.

Vienna felt tears gathering in her eyes as she looked down at her grandfather. She didn't bother wiping them away.

Clutching the heavy-duty plastic bag that contained her grandfather's clothes, Vienna walked beside the gurney as the orderly wheeled the sleeping man to the back of the hospital and the service elevators. Georges accompanied them to the third floor, which, for the most part, was designated as the surgical wing.

Every second light was turned off, giving the area almost an eerie atmosphere as, once off the service elevator, they made their way down the corridor.

Amos was placed in a single care unit that was only marginally larger than his space in the recovery room had been. Still, with the right finagling, some space could be found.

"I can have a cot brought in," Georges offered, looking at Vienna, "so you can stretch out a little."

Vienna placed the plastic bag with her grandfather's things into the closet and shut the single door. Her slender shoulders rose and fell in a shrug to Georges' offer. "Stretching out is highly overrated." She nodded at the padded beige chair by the window. "I'll be fine in this chair."

It seemed pointless for her to spend the night in the chair, even though he knew that the heart was not subject to logic. "He's probably not going to wake up between now and morning."

She knew that. Knew that it was better for her grandfather to sleep through what was left of the night. "I don't need him to wake up, Doctor. I just need him to be."

Georges sighed, shaking his head. "Are all Austrians this stubborn?"

Her mouth curved. For the first time, he saw a smile enter her eyes, as well. It took him a second to extricate himself.

"I'm Austrian and one quarter Italian," she informed him. "But yes, to answer your question, they are. And so are Italians."

Georges took the information in stride, nodding. "Then I guess that I haven't got a prayer of talking you out of this."

"'Fraid not."

Vienna moved closer to the bed. Standing over her grandfather for a moment, she brushed back a few gray strands that would have been in his eyes had they been open. Her grandfather had a full head of gray hair, still thick and rich. It was one of the things he was proud of. That and the fact that, at seventy-four, he was still pretty much as strong as an ox, albeit a more mature ox, she'd often teased him.

Be that ox now, Grandfather. Come back to me.

And then she turned to look at Georges. "I will, however, let you get that extra blanket for me if you like."

Georges watched her for a long moment. He'd thought about getting the blanket when she'd been in the surgical lounge, but— "I never said that out loud," he told her slowly. "Are you going to tell me that you read minds, too?"

Her smile was like quicksilver. "I'm not going to say anything of the kind."

Was that because she didn't want to spook him, or because she didn't think she could? It struck him that this whole night was a little on the surreal side. "Then how…"

Vienna casually lifted her shoulders and let them fall again. "Elementary, my dear Watson. You look like the type who likes to take care of people. Covering a sleeping person with a blanket just seems to make sense," she explained.

It was plausible, of course, but he couldn't shake the feeling that he had just stumbled into something that was different. Something he couldn't explain away all that easily.

In addition, he thought as he walked out of the room, in search of said blanket, the way that Vienna seemed to intuit things about him made him feel a little uneasy. Uncertain. He took care of people because he was a doctor, but she made it sound as if what she sensed about him went deeper than that. As if it had roots in something more.

She seemed to know him better than he knew himself.

The next moment, he dismissed the thought, bunching it under the simple truth that he was tired and nothing more.

It seemed like a reasonable enough explanation.

Chapter Six

Ultimately, Vienna dozed for perhaps thirty minutes. Perhaps less.

Restlessness roused her and she wound up shrugging off the blanket and just sitting in the chair, watching her grandfather sleep. And talking to the man who insisted on keeping her company.

Just before dawn, Georges was finally able to convince her to go home. Not to get some well-deserved rest, which would have made sense, but to make sure Vienna's Finest opened on time. It was the only thing that finally got her to consider leaving her grandfather's side.

Her grandfather, Georges pointed out, wouldn't want the customers who came in for their early morning pick-me-up to be disappointed and go away empty-handed. He managed to appeal to her sense of loyalty and to what he surmised was her equally, very deep-seated sense of responsibility.

The idea came to Georges as he heard her make a call on the phone beside Amos's bed at around 3:00 a.m. The call was to someone named Raul who apparently was the baker and made the different confections. From what Georges could piece together, Raul had moved here from New York after they had relocated because he was unwilling to work for anyone else besides Amos.

Raul seemed highly excitable. His voice became very audible on the other end of the line when Vienna told him that she and her grandfather had been in a car accident.

"He's all right, Raul," Vienna assured him quickly, repeating the words several times and striving to sound soothing despite her weariness. "There was a doctor on the scene and he brought us to the hospital."

"On the scene?" Georges heard the man's heavily accented voice fairly shout over the line. "What do you mean, on the scene? Was this doctor the one who caused the accident?"

Vienna glanced over toward Georges and smiled. "No, he was the one who saved my grandfather's life. I just need you to open up the bakery this morning. Can you do that, Raul?"

There was a long pause before Raul answered. When he did, he sounded highly skeptical. "I don't know. Customers…" His voice trailed off for a moment. "I bake, I don't sell."

There was no way to avoid hearing. Georges tapped her on the shoulder. When she looked at him, he suggested, "Why don't you go in and open up the bakery, get things started?"

She thought for a moment. It had been a long time since she'd been behind the counter, not since she'd graduated college. But she supposed it was like swimming. You never quite forgot what to do with your hands. She finally nodded. "I can keep it going until Zelda comes in."

"Zelda?" he asked.

"A part-timer. She comes in around nine to help behind the counter." Vienna turned her attention back to the receiver. Raul could be heard calling to her, asking if she was still there. "Yes, I'm still here, Raul. Business as usual. Just go in and do what you'd do on any other day. I'll be there by six-thirty to handle the rest."

Which was how Georges got her to finally leave the hospital.

* * *

It was just as her newfound knight in shining Armani was turning into the driveway of her house that it suddenly hit her.

Covering her mouth with both hands she uttered a stifled, "Oh God."

Georges nearly swerved, thinking he'd hit something or was about to, most likely some meandering neighborhood pet too low to the ground to see easily. But the driveway stretched out before him debris-free, with not so much as an overzealous grasshopper to squash.

"What?" he demanded a little more sharply than he'd meant to.

She sank back against the back cushion, figuratively and literaly flattened by the weight of her sudden epiphany. "My purse was in the car."

Which was now toast, Georges thought. By the time the fire department had arrived on the scene, on the heels of the ambulance from Blair Memorial, the flames around the car were retreating, leaving a burnt shell in its wake. He'd been so intent on getting her and her grandfather out, he hadn't even thought of anything so trivial as a purse.

Maybe he should have, he thought now. "What was in it?"

She looked devastated, he noted, as she gave him an answer that was universal to women everywhere except for the darkest recesses of the African and South American jungles.

"Everything." With a gut-wrenching sigh, Vienna closed her eyes, momentarily feeling overwhelmed by this latest development. "My wallet, my driver's license, my cell phone, my car keys." Opening her eyes again, she looked at the house and then turned to him. "My house keys."

Parking, Georges pulled up the hand brake and turned the engine off. "You don't keep a spare near the front door?"

The very idea was completely foreign to her. "I'm from New York. We double lock everything. We don't keep keys hidden under a planter so that someone can break in." Still sitting in the car, she looked at the door again. "Oh God, what am I going to do?"

He was thoughtful for a moment. "I think you already covered it."

When she glanced back at him again, she could have sworn that she saw the curve of a smile on his lips. "What?"

"Break in," he replied simply.

She thought of her neighbors. This was a very quiet neighborhood.

"You mean like break a window?" At the first sound of breaking glass, especially at this time of the morning, she had no doubt someone would be on the phone, calling 911.

Georges was already out of the car on his side, his attention riveted to the front door. "Something a little less messy than that."

She wasn't following him. At least, not mentally. She hurried up the walk behind him as he approached the front of her house. "Like what?"

He didn't answer her immediately. Instead, he took out his own keys. On the chain he also had two very thin pieces of metal no thicker than the lead used in a mechanical pencil. As she watched, he inserted both into the lock, keeping them at an angle to one another. He wiggled them around and she half expected him to say something like "Hocus-pocus" because, in less time than it took to observe what he was doing, Georges had opened her front door.

He gestured toward the interior of her house. "This," he replied, answering her question.

Rather than walk in, Vienna stared at him, a little confused about the kind of man she was with. "Is that your fallback career if this doctor thing doesn't work out for you?" she asked. "You're training to be a burglar?"

He grinned. "I hadn't thought about that, actually."

"Seriously," she pressed, "how did you manage to do that?" She'd seen it done in movies and on police dramas, but she thought that was just writers taking liberties with the truth. Apparently not.

He waited for her to walk in first. "I used to hang

out with the wrong crowd for a while—until Philippe yanked me out."

"Philippe?" They'd talked in the hospital, but mostly about her grandfather.

"My brother. My older brother," Georges added. And then, because he felt that he might as well give her the whole picture, he amended the label, even though there was nothing *half* about Philippe. "My older half brother."

The way he said it made her think there were more. "You have others?"

"Just one. Alain." Although he knew that his younger brother would take umbrage about the word *just* used to describe him. In his own way, Alain was every bit as flamboyant as their mother was. As blond as she was dark, Alain was the newly minted lawyer in the family, as well as playboy par excellence. There were times when the youngest of Lily Moreau's boys made him feel as if he were a saintly altar boy.

"Is he a half or a whole?"

He grinned. "A half."

Finally crossing the threshold, Vienna looked around. Nothing seemed to have changed. But it had. And it could have for the worst. What a difference a few hours made.

Trying to get her bearings, she turned around to face Georges. "Any sisters? Half or whole," she added for good measure.

"Not that I know of." Of course, what with two stepfathers and his own father in the mix, he could never be certain. None of the men had been monastic in nature. But no small voices, crying out in the wilderness had been heard from—so far. "At least, none that my mother had."

Vienna smiled. It had been so long, she hardly remembered what it felt like to have a mother. "Sounds like an interesting woman."

He could only laugh in response. "You don't know the half of it." When she raised an eyebrow, he said, "Maybe you've heard of her. Lily Moreau."

Vienna's mouth dropped open. "Of course I've heard of Lily Moreau." There'd been an article on her in a national magazine just last month. She'd read it in the dentist's office. "She's that wildly beautiful Bohemian artist. The one who says she always paints best when she's in love." She couldn't help staring at him, looking for similarities. "Lily Moreau is your *mother?*" she finally asked in disbelief.

He was used to getting that kind of a reaction. "When she can find the time to be," he replied with an air of someone who long ago had accepted the fact that his was not like all the other mothers. His burst in, larger than life, then disappeared in a flash, off to another showing, another gallery somewhere halfway around the world. Another man who promised to love her in exchange for basking in her aura. When he was younger, he'd resented both her lifestyle and her men, but eventually it no longer bothered him. She was just being Lily.

Vienna didn't know whether to envy him because of his famous mother or pity him for the same reason. It couldn't have been easy, having a personality as flamboyant as the celebrated artist as a mother, she thought. Aside from the recent article, Lily was in the news every so often, her paintings and her men earning almost equal lines of print.

"You seemed to have turned out all right." The words were uttered before she thought to hold them back. God, was that as judgmental-sounding as she thought? She hadn't meant it to be.

He grinned and inclined his head. "Except for the wild teen period," he allowed.

That had been his crossroads and it could have gone either way for him—had Philippe not physically wrestled him for possession of his confused soul the night he'd bailed him out of the local jail for shoplifting. Lily had found the lawyer who had gotten him off, but after that, Philippe was the one who had policed him like a newly paroled prisoner, making sure that he had no further contact with the boys who thought that robbing was a rite of passage and that eluding the police was the supreme challenge.

All his priorities and basic values had gotten reorganized that summer. It was also the last time the sound of approaching sirens had made him nervous.

Standing now within Vienna's small residence, Georges scanned the room. They were in the living room and he could see the kitchen just beyond. It was a nice, homey house, he thought. Something Lily would have instantly begun redecorating.

Love lived here. He could all but feel it permeating from the walls.

Turning around, he looked at the woman who had inadvertently caused him to take a mental stroll down memory lane and revisit the less-than-stellar portion of his past.

He had to be going. Even so, he was reluctant to leave her alone like this.

"You'll be all right now?" he asked her, his eyes holding hers.

His concern made her smile. Kindness was never unappreciated. "Believe it or not, I really can take care of myself."

"Didn't mean to imply that you couldn't." Even though she did stir protective feelings within him. He nodded toward the door. "I'll be going now."

She surprised him by placing her hand on his arm and detaining him. "I'll see you again, won't I?" He saw her catch her lower lip between her teeth, as if she felt she'd just made a blunder. "I mean, at the hospital. My grandfather—"

Vienna's voice trailed off. She had no idea how to finish the sentence gracefully without making it seem as if she were trying to corner him. The last thing she wanted in her life was any kind of male-female entanglement. Just that there was something about him that made her feel everything was going to be all right. And she needed to feel that.

Technically, the man wasn't his patient, he was Schulman's. But he was Schulman's surgical resident, so that made him part of the team. "I'll be looking in on him," Georges promised.

She breathed a sigh of relief. "I'd appreciate that." Vienna walked the three steps with him back to the front threshold. "Thanks again." She put out her hand and then, impulsively, as if deciding that wasn't personal enough, she suddenly dropped her hands, framed his face with them instead and kissed him.

It felt as if something magical had touched him.

Just like the first time.

Georges caught himself wanting to extend the moment, the sensation. Wanting to sample a kiss in earnest, existing for its own sake rather than as an extension of her gratitude.

But that would be taking too much for granted. So he savored the brief, sweet contact and allowed her to back away.

"My pleasure," he murmured. And then he

left. As he made his way back to his car, he ran his tongue lightly along the outline of his lips. Sealing in her taste.

"Burning the firecracker at both ends again, Georges?"

The question came from his left. About to get back into his car after a quick shower and change of clothes, Georges had hurried by without realizing anyone was out yet.

He looked now toward the man standing several yards away from him, a newly fetched newspaper in his hand. Philippe raised the newspaper in a kind of salute.

Close as children, closer as adults, Georges and his two half brothers now lived in three separate houses built by a clever architect to look like one large, sprawling estate. One imposing door in the front, two on the opposite sides, all leading to different residences.

Philippe had the one in the middle, while he and Alain lived in the houses that flanked the central one. "Separate but equal" was what Philippe had said when he'd initially found the property. It was evident that Philippe still thought of himself as the patriarch and wanted to be close by in case he was needed.

It hadn't been a hard sell. Both he and Alain had liked the look of the houses and there was something subconsciously comforting about having your brothers close by, just not so close that they got into your business if you didn't want them to.

After graduating from medical school and four years into his residency at Blair Memorial Hospital, he would have thought that Philippe would have realized his little brother didn't need someone watching over him. Still, he supposed, old habits died hard. The parade of nannies notwithstanding, during their formative years Philippe had looked after both him and Alain when their mother was away, which was more than half the time.

Philippe was eyeing him now, waiting for some sort of a response.

Georges spread his hands innocently. Ordinarily, Philippe would be right. He did have a habit of going out after a grueling, endless shift. Some people recharged sleeping; he did it in the company of beautiful women. But not this time. At least, not exactly.

"Work-related," Georges told him.

Philippe moved closer. He made no attempt to hide the fact that he was giving him the once-over. "Dressed a little fancy for work, weren't you? I saw you come in earlier."

It struck him that in another life, Philippe might have made his living as an interrogator instead of the software genius he turned out to be. He saw no reason to lie. "I *was* on my way to see Diana."

Philippe nodded, as if he'd thought as much. Not

that he knew who Diana was, but Diana, Stella, Angela, it didn't matter. The names were all interchangeable. By the time one was learned, Georges had moved on. But it was always a woman who lured him out to play.

Amused, Philippe asked, "And that turned into work how?"

Georges shut his door. This might take a while. He had a few minutes to spare. "When a hit-and-run driver sideswiped the car behind me, trapping the passengers inside and sending the car spinning up against a hillside on PCH."

Philippe's eyes narrowed as he scrutinized his brother. He had no way of knowing that Georges' smoke-damaged clothing was stashed on the floor of his closet. But despite the time lapse and the shower, there was still the slight smell of smoke about Georges' dark hair. Knowing Georges, he wouldn't have hesitated when it came to saving lives.

"Anyone hurt?" Philippe asked, even as he continued to check Georges over for any indication that the hurt person might have been Georges himself.

Georges knew Philippe wouldn't be satisfied with a yes or no answer. His older brother might not talk much, but he expected his brothers to fill in the gaps.

"The man behind the wheel suffered a minor heart attack," he told Philippe. "The doors were sealed shut. I had to break a window to get inside and get him and his granddaughter out. I had her call Blair for an ambulance while I did CPR on the old man."

Philippe nodded, taking it all in. "How is he?"

"Fine now—so far," he qualified, then explained. "He needed emergency surgery."

Georges had mentioned that there'd been two people in the car. "And the girl?"

Georges wasn't aware that'd he frowned when he answered, but Philippe was. "A little banged up, but she refused to let herself be admitted. Stayed at the old man's side for most of the night."

"And you stayed by hers." It wasn't a guess. When it came to his brothers, Philippe had gotten good at filling in the blanks.

Georges nodded, then tried to sound modest as he added, "When I wasn't operating on her grandfather." There was no missing the pride in his voice.

Philippe looked at him with genuine surprise. He was aware that Georges routinely attended surgeries, but he didn't know that his brother was operating on patients. "They let you scrub in?"

Georges shrugged, doing his best to contain the excitement that scrubbing in as an assistant had generated. "They were short internal surgeons."

Philippe draped his arm around his brother's shoulders. "Sounds like you had a pretty eventful evening. Not as eventful as it might have been had you gone out with Diana," he surmised, teasing him, "but still, eventful. I take back what I was thinking."

Georges arched an eyebrow. "And what were you thinking?"

"That you're a hopeless playboy."

"Hey, we all can't be as steadfast as you, big brother. Zeroing in on one woman and pledging commitment without really taking the time to see what else is out there."

In direct contrast to their mother, Philippe seemed almost reclusive when it came to his social life, preferring the company of good friends to the dating field. But it was because he'd watched their mother go from relationship to relationship, all but fleeing when things became serious, that caused him to believe there was no use in searching for someone to spend his life with.

Until Janice and her bright-as-a-newly-minted-penny daughter had come into his life.

"I don't need to see what else is out there, Georges," Philippe informed him evenly, then smiled. "Some things you just know."

Georges folded his arms before him, waiting. "Like what?"

He wasn't one to profess love out loud, or make his feelings public. But loving Janice had changed some of that. "Like the fact that Janice is the one for me." He looked to see if his brother understood what he meant. "Janice is a once-in-a-lifetime woman."

Georges laughed at the sound of that. "Sounds like some kind of sect."

The best thing in the world that he could wish for Georges, for both his brothers, was to find someone like Janice. "It means, little brother, a woman like that comes along once in a man's lifetime and he had better be on his toes when she does. Because if he misses his chance, if he lets her slip through his fingers because he's too blind, he'll never see her like again. And the rest of his life could be spent looking for someone who even came close to her."

"Very poetic." Straightening, Georges unfolded his arms. He had to get going. "Don't get me wrong, Philippe. I think the world of Janice. Until she came along, Alain and I were afraid that you'd wind up some bitter old man we were going to have to share custody of. Sitting by the fire, rocking and uttering insane platitudes every so often." He grinned, clapping his brother on the back. "But now with Janice around, we don't have to worry anymore."

"Touching."

Georges was inclined to agree. "I thought so."

Philippe shifted, watching his brother open the driver's-side door. "So when are you planning on getting some sleep?"

Georges got in behind the wheel. "Don't worry, I have it penciled in for a week from Friday." He waved as he drove away.

But that was just the trouble, Philippe thought, heading back to his own house, he *did* worry. And would continue to do so until Georges found his own once-in-a-lifetime woman.

Chapter Seven

Georges was busy even before he entered the hospital. Parking his vehicle in the lot designated for hospital personnel—doctors had a closer lot, but he would not qualify for that until he completed his residency—he was about to walk through the main entrance when a woman stumbled right in front of him. He steadied her as best he could. She looked to be about ten months pregnant with a great deal to steady.

Helping her inside, he brought the woman to the admissions desk. English was not her first language. Because of the travels his mother had taken him and his brothers on, Georges knew a smattering of a handful of languages. Trying them out on the pregnant woman, they came together over French, enough so that he could put her at her ease and, more importantly, find out her name and the name of the doctor she was coming to see.

Once she was situated, Georges dashed over to the east wing, where he was supposed to have been on duty for the last half hour. His attending, John LaSalle, was not pleased about his being late and made no effort to hide the way he felt. But then Dr. Sheila Pollack, the head of the maternity ward, came by to personally thank him for helping with her patient. The woman's husband had been called and would be on his way in time for what appeared to be a very fast-track delivery.

After that, LaSalle retracted some of his harsher words, and Georges was left to take on his regular duties. Two more hours were eaten up.

He didn't get a chance to swing by Amos Schwarzwalden's room on the third floor until just a little before eleven.

Georges knocked softly in order not to disturb the man if he was still asleep. Opening the door, he saw that the old man was not alone. Her back to the door, his granddaughter was sitting beside Schwarz-walden's bed, just as she had been last night.

Vienna twisted around in her chair to see who

opened the door. The smile that greeted him instantly spread warmth all through his chest.

Her hair was piled up on her head and pinned haphazardly, with tendrils descending here and there. She looked younger somehow, more vulnerable now than she had last night, he thought.

Coming into the room, he caught the scent of something warm and tempting. He would have said it was her, but there was a dash of cinnamon mixed in. He doubted that she dabbed cinnamon behind her ears.

That was when he saw the open white box at the foot of her grandfather's bed. Streamers of entwining blue and pink were embossed on the sides, obviously a logo of some sort. The box was crammed full with pastries.

Fresh from the oven from the smell of it, he thought.

Vienna rose to her feet and crossed to him. "Hi." Was it possible for a single word to all but vibrate with sunshine? he wondered. "He's still unconscious," she told him needlessly.

"Not unusual," he assured her. "His body needs the time to heal. This is the best way. Don't worry, your grandfather'll come around." He glanced at the open box. She'd probably brought that so he would see something familiar when he opened his eyes, Georges surmised. Too bad. "But when he does, he really can't have those right now."

"I know." Picking up the box, she presented it to him. "I made them for you."

He held the box as if he meant to pass it back to her. "Me?"

Her smile grew wider as she nodded. "I'm not as good as my grandfather," she freely admitted, "but he did teach me a few things." Very gently, she pushed the box back toward him. "It's just my way of saying thank you—other than paying the bill." Her eyes were shining with humor and it took effort to draw his own away.

When he did, Georges gazed down at the box in his hands. There had to be over a dozen assorted pastries and cakes in it, maybe more. Each looked lighter and more delectable than the last.

Ever since he was a little boy, he'd never been one to stop for a morning meal. That was because he was never hungry before noon, no matter what time he got up. Breakfast for him these days was an extra-large container of coffee. Caffeine rather than nutrition saw him through his morning hours. A bad attitude for a doctor, he knew, but he had yet to run up against the age-old saying of, "Physician, heal thyself."

However, there was something about the box of mouthwatering confections that prompted him to take a small sample. Breaking off a tiny piece of one, he popped it into his mouth. Once he did, he wanted more.

The experience was not unlike his reaction to Vienna's kiss last night. Or had that been this morning? The hours were running together for him at this point, and he'd lost his markings.

But his memory was sharp when it came to remembering the impact.

"Good," he murmured with enthusiasm, licking a drop of frosting from his index finger.

"Of course she is good."

The reedy-sounding affirmation came from the patient in the bed. Georges and Vienna looked at each other, wide-eyed, before approaching the man in the bed.

"She is my granddaughter." Amos's eyes all but disappeared as he smiled at her. "Everything she does is good."

Georges nodded. The comment seemed to come out on its own. "I have no doubt."

Vienna hardly heard him. Her heart hammered very loudly in her ears. "Grandpa, you're awake." Overjoyed, she took his hand and pressed a kiss to it, careful not to dislodge any of the lines attached to him.

"Why shouldn't I be awake? The sun is up." And then he became aware of his present surroundings.

Amos frowned at the various tethers he saw attached to his body. Two different IVs ran into his arm, one for nutrition, one for medication, as well as a clear tube beneath his nose supplementing his oxygen. A wide cuff was wrapped around his other arm, periodically measuring his blood pressure, heartbeat and various other vital signs.

"Why am I tied down like this?" he asked Vienna. Then he turned toward the man he didn't recognize. Maybe he had an explanation for all this. "What have I done?"

Vienna fought back tears of joy. She feathered her fingertips along the old man's finely lined brow, lightly brushing back his hair. "Nothing, Grandpa. You've lived. Survived."

"Do you remember anything that happened, sir?" Georges asked. It was not uncommon for people involved in an accident not to remember anything for several hours, sometimes days, after the accident.

Amos paused for a long moment, as if to scan the depths of his mind for a scrap of information that somehow didn't belong there. But in the end, he slowly moved his head from side to side.

"No," he confessed and it looked as if the admission troubled him. "What is it I should be remembering?"

Vienna wrapped her hand about her grandfather's, as if to temporarily give him her strength. He'd always been her rock. Now it was time to return the favor.

"There was an accident, Grandpa. A drunk driver hit us. The Pontiac spun out and wound up hitting the side of hill."

The news had him clutching her hand harder as he scrutinized her face. "You? You are hurt?"

She smiled. He always thought of her first, never himself. "No, Grandpa, I'm not." She nodded toward Georges. "Thanks to Dr. Armand."

The lines in his forehead became more pronounced as Amos's frown deepened. "I don't understand."

Georges left the explanation up to her. He had a feeling that the old man would understand it better if it came from Vienna.

"He saw the accident and risked his life to save ours. He got me out of the car and then dragged you out." Her voice quivered just a little as she added, "You had a heart attack."

Amos's face was immobile. "No."

"Yes," she contradicted gently. "You did. Dr. Armand gave you CPR and then had the ambulance bring you here." Her eyes shifted to the man's chest. Amos wore the customary hospital gown assigned to everyone, but that didn't keep her from visualizing the long, fresh surgical cuts beneath. "You had to have emergency surgery."

"All this and I do not remember?" Uttered in awe, it was a question, an appeal to both her and the man beside her to help him recall the events.

Very lightly, she ran the back of her knuckles along his cheek. A tad of his color was returning, she thought with relief.

"You were unconscious, Grandpa. But now you're back. And I'm ever so grateful." She shifted her eyes toward Georges to underscore her feelings before she looked back at her grandfather again.

Amos nodded slowly, trying to assimilate the information coming at him. He raised his eyes to her face. "What about the car?"

"Gone," she told him. "It burst into flames just as Georges got you out."

"Georges?"

"Dr. Armand," Vienna corrected herself.

She'd lapsed just then. The man's profession demanded that respect be accorded him. And yet, after all they had been through in such a short space of time, it didn't seem quite right being so formal. He'd given both her grandfather and her their lives back.

"I see." The words left Amos's lips in slow motion. "We'll need a new one."

"Yes, we will." She smiled at him fondly, her heart feeling so full she could barely breathe. Was there ever a time when her grandfather didn't look forward, didn't push toward the future rather than lament the past? He was going to be just fine, she assured herself.

"What about the shop?" Amos realized suddenly. He attempted to sit up. "I should be there."

"You should be here." With gentle but firm hands, she pushed her grandfather back onto the bed. "Raul is in the back, baking. Zelda is in the front, taking care of the customers. Everything's running smoothly for now." Vienna looked at the old man pointedly, not about to stand for an argument. She could be tough if she had to be. He had taught her that. "We all just want you to get better."

Georges had stood off to the side, feeling that the old man needed this, needed to have his granddaughter refresh his parameters for him and help him orient himself. He sensed it would make the man feel better and ultimately be more cooperative when it came to his treatment.

But now it was his turn. He had rounds to make with Schulman soon, and he didn't want to miss this opportunity to check out Amos's condition before he had to get on with his work.

So he came now to stand by the man's bed, doing his best not to seem threatening in any way. There were people who had almost a pathological fear of doctors. "How do you feel, Mr. Schwarzwalden?"

Amos leaned back against his pillows and exhaled dramatically. "Like elephants have been dancing on my body." He slanted a look at the younger man and smiled. "And please, you saved my granddaughter. Call me Amos."

Georges inclined his head, smiling back. "All right, Amos." He got down to business, keeping in mind that he didn't want to alarm his patient. "These elephants, do you feel like they're pressing on your chest?"

Amos considered the question and watched Vienna, who was holding her breath, waiting for him to answer. "No, all over."

Then it wasn't his heart, Georges thought. Just a general achiness, which was to be expected. Had the pain been isolated to the man's chest area, it could have been an indication that more heart trouble needed to be addressed.

Picking up the chart, Georges made several notations before resting it on the bed. Rather than rely strictly on the machine readings, he checked over Amos's vital signs on his own. Measuring his blood pressure, taking his pulse, listening to his heart and lungs.

Finished, because he had verified it for himself, he felt a sense of relief at the outcome.

"Your pupils are fine," he told Amos, shutting off the light he'd shone into the man's eyes. "No indications of a concussion. Your heartbeat is strong, your blood pressure remarkably low for a man your age."

The grin on Amos's face was completely reminiscent of his granddaughter's expression. "That is because I am not a man my age, Doctor. I am a man much younger than my age."

Vienna felt she needed to explain that to Georges

before he thought that her grandfather was lapsing into some sort of childish babble.

"Grandpa believes that everyone has to get older, but no one has to get old." It was a saying Amos attributed to the late comedian George Burns. Her grandfather had made it his own, repeating it as often as he felt was necessary. She secretly felt that it was more of a case of self-hypnosis than anything else because he certainly was a true believer these days.

Georges grinned, retiring his stethoscope. "Great philosophy to have." He looked at the pastry chef. "I think you'd get along very well with my mother."

Despite his condition, interest seemed to instantly pique on Amos's face. "She is single, your mother?" he asked.

Georges thought of the man currently squiring his mother around. Kyle something-or-other. A would-be artist some twenty-five years younger than Lily. She claimed being with Kyle made her feel like a schoolgirl again. He'd always believed in live and let live, but he had to admit that he and his brothers were not happy about this one. His mother had brought him around several times, secretly, he was certain, seeking their approval.

But much as he didn't like the way she was running her life lately, it was her life and he had no right to interfere. "Not at the moment."

Amos has a keen ear. He dispensed advice along

with his baked goods at his store every day. "Oh? It does not sound as if you approve of this person in your mother's life."

Georges shrugged casually, as if he really didn't have a hard-and-fast opinion on the matter. "She's done better."

"His mother is Lily Moreau," Vienna interjected for her grandfather's benefit.

"Lily Moreau?" Complete surprise and then keen interest washed across Amos Schwarzwalden's still very pale complexion. "The famous artist?"

"One and the same," Georges replied with a weariness that caught him off guard. He hadn't meant to sound like that when admitting to their connection.

Try as he might, Georges couldn't remember a single time when someone didn't instantly know who his mother was when her name came up in the conversation. Most of the time, he was proud of her, proud of her work and even of her Bohemian bravado. But lately, he found himself wishing she would settle down again. Just not with someone young enough to be her son.

"You must bring her to the shop," Amos told him with enthusiasm, then added with a resigned note, "Once you let me go back to it."

He wasn't about to fall for that sorrowful face, Georges thought. He had a feeling Amos could get people to do what he wanted. He was one of those endearing people you hated saying no to.

"That all depends on you, Mr.—ah, Amos," Georges stopped, correcting himself. And then, because the man's attitude seemed so positive, he gave him something to be positive about. He gave him the good news. "But if you keep going the way you are, I don't see any reason why we won't be discharging you in a few days."

"A few days?" Amos echoed. Rather than be happy, the old man seemed somewhat disheartened. "I was hoping to be released in a few hours."

"You had a lot of internal injuries, Amos. Ruptured spleen, bruised liver, cracked ribs." He didn't bother mentioning the heart attack. He didn't want the man to feel overwhelmed. It was enough that they all knew one had happened. "You need time to heal. We just want to make sure everything's mending properly before we set you loose again." Removing the stethoscope from around his neck, he put it in his deep pocket. "Why don't you take this opportunity to rest. According to what your granddaughter says, you haven't had a vacation in years."

Amos laughed under his breath. "No disrespect, Doctor, but this is not exactly a place I would choose to have my vacation."

Neither would he, Georges thought. "Luck of the draw, Amos, luck of the draw." Closing the chart, he hung it off the foot of the bed again. "I'll stop by later to look in on you again," he promised.

Amos nodded, looking less than happy about the scenario. "Unfortunately, I will be here."

"You'd better believe it," Vienna told her grandfather with feeling.

"I raised her to be tough," Amos confided to Georges. And then he frowned as he looked at Vienna again. "Perhaps that was not such a good move."

Georges couldn't help the admiring grin that rose to his lips as he eyed the man's granddaughter one last time. The word *knockout* ran through his mind. "It was from where I'm standing."

"I like him," Amos told Vienna the moment the door was closed again and Georges had left.

Absently, Vienna agreed. "So do I."

Despite his condition, Amos was instantly alert. "Oh?"

She could read him like a book, an old, beloved, well-read book. "Get that look out of your eye, Grandpa. I meant as a doctor."

The smile on his lips was positively mischievous. "I didn't." He gave her a long, penetrating look. "It is about time you forgot all about that Edward person. He was not worthy of you."

He'd get no argument from her, not after the final scene between them. She didn't do well with ultimatums, and Edward had made it clear that she had to choose—her grandfather or him. It wasn't a fair contest. Edward hadn't even come close—because her grandfather would have never asked her to choose between them.

"You're right, he wasn't. But I'm not looking to replace him right now." She took her grandfather's hand in hers. "All I want right now is for you to get better." Her eyes misted as she said, "I don't know what I'd do if anything ever happened to you."

"You would continue, Vienna. You are strong. Like your mother was, and her mother before her." It was a source of pride within the family that the women on the family tree were made of unbendable mettle. "But," he went on to allow, "it does not hurt to have someone in your life who is looking out for you."

How had they circled back to this? "Stop right there," Vienna warned him. "If that someone isn't you, I don't want to talk about it."

He sighed, resigned. For now. "Very well. Tell me about the shop."

His mistress, Vienna thought fondly. Her grandfather loved the shop the way few men loved their wives. "The customers all want to know where you are."

The questions about what had happened had come so steadily from his crowd of regulars that she's stopped to print up a short, detailed account of the accident and posted it on the outside door. All it had done was generate more questions. Which was why it had taken her so long to get here.

"They all send their good wishes for a speedy recovery."

Amos smiled, pleased. "That is nice." And then he looked at her intently, sobering. "You are sure that you are all right? That you were not hurt?"

"I'm sure. Georges insisted on checking me out last night."

He nodded knowingly. "And this checking out, it was nice for you?"

Vienna laughed and shook her head. "As a doctor, Grandpa, he checked me out as a doctor."

"I saw the way he looked at you when he was here. Not just as a doctor, Vienna, but as a man. Men know these things," he informed her solemnly. "And this I can tell you, he is a nice man, to risk his life for strangers."

Not that she was playing devil's advocate, but she really didn't want her grandfather making something out of nothing. "He's a doctor, Grandpa. He's supposed to help people."

"In the hospital or his office, yes," he agreed. "Burning cars are another story." And then, before she could say anything to counter him, Amos sighed. He seemed to fade into the bed. "I am tired right now, Vienna. Maybe I should rest, like he said."

"Maybe," she agreed fondly.

Her grandfather was asleep before the second syllable had faded away.

Chapter Eight

"You're a big hit with the nurses," Georges told Vienna when she walked out of her grandfather's room a few minutes later.

He'd purposely hung around the area, taking his time finishing up a chart just in case she ventured out of the room. But she was holding her purse, which meant she was leaving. That surprised him. After the way she'd kept vigil at her grandfather's side last night and early this morning, he hadn't expected her to be leaving so soon. He wondered where she was going. And when he would see her again.

Vienna eyed him quizzically and he realized that

he had gotten ahead of himself again. It was a habit he'd picked up from his mother. His mind was always moving, juggling a hundred thoughts at once. Sometimes, when he spoke, it was in the middle of a thought. He backtracked now.

"The pastries you brought," he explained. The box he nodded at was completely empty. "I believe the consensus was that they were 'to die for.'"

"Oh." She glanced down at the empty box. Because neatness was ingrained in her, she picked it up and flattened out the sides, then dropped it into the wastebasket she saw by the side of the desk. "I thought you'd take them home and eat them yourself." If she'd known that he was going to pass them around, she would have brought more.

"That's just the trouble, I would have." He patted his middle, which was flat by design, not through an accident of nature. "And then I'd have to buy a whole new wardrobe."

"No, you wouldn't. That's my grandfather's secret." Other ingredients were substituted for the more fattening ones, drastically reducing the caloric composition of the pastries he prepared. "His pastries aren't as fattening as you think they are."

She began to move toward the elevators and he fell into step with her. "Eating twelve of anything at one sitting is fattening," he assured her. "You're leaving already?"

Glancing at her watch out of habit, she nodded. "Have to." Losing her purse in the fire had created a lot of time-consuming, annoying problems for her. She'd had to call and order replacements for her credit cards. But that wasn't the worst of it. "I can't rent a car until I can show the rental agency my driver's license, and I don't have a driver's license to show them until I can get it replaced. Which means—" she sighed "—I have to go and wait in some endless line at the DMV. Meanwhile, I'm stuck calling cab companies." Reaching the elevators, she pressed the Down button.

Georges suddenly thought of a way out for her. "Do you have a cab waiting for you in the parking lot?" he asked.

Vienna shook her head. She was going to call one when she got to the lobby. "Not yet."

The elevator arrived, but he drew her aside. "Why don't you hang on a second?"

She followed him gamely over to the side of the corridor. "What do you have in mind?" His smile told her that maybe she'd just asked a loaded question.

Banking down the first response that rose to his lips, he went with a far safer one as he took out his cell phone from the depths of his pocket. "I might be able to pull a few strings to keep you from having to wait in that endless DMV line."

The thought of *not* having to spend the next two

hours shifting from side to side and occasionally moving forward on a spiraling DMV line sounded like heaven. "You know someone?"

"Technically, my cousin Remy knows someone." Georges flashed her a reassuring smile as he pressed a number on his keypad and then placed the phone to his ear. "But I know my cousin Remy, so, by association, yes, I know someone."

"But will he—"

She didn't get a chance to complete her question. His cousin had obviously come on the other end. Georges had raised his hand, indicating that she should refrain from saying anything further.

Five minutes later, after asking her a few questions and passing the answers to his cousin, giving the man all the necessary information, it was settled. Remy had assured him that a copy of Vienna Hollenbeck's original driver's license would be messengered to her house by late afternoon.

When he told her, Vienna thought it was nothing short of a miracle. But then, she was beginning to think Georges Armand was in the business of miracles. "I didn't think you could do that."

He winked, slipping the phone back into his pocket. "There are ways around a great many things if you just take the trouble to find the right path."

Her grandfather had taught her to be a dreamer, but there was a practical bent to her, as well. Whenever possible, she tried to be prepared for all contingencies. "But what if his friend finds he can't get a copy of my license?"

Georges glanced down at the pocket where he'd deposited his cell phone. "If that rings in the next few minutes, then Remy's friend hit a snag. If it doesn't, you're home free."

She eyed his pocket, then raised her eyes to his face. "I must say, you certainly are a handy man to have around."

When she looked at him like that, he could feel the very breath stopping in his lungs. He'd never had anyone look at him quite like that before. It took him a second to get his wits back about him.

"I have my moments."

Now there was an understatement, she thought. How was she ever going to pay this man back? Crossing back to the elevators, she pressed the Down button again.

"I just keep slipping deeper and deeper into your debt."

He moved so that she could look at him. "Have dinner with me and we'll call it even."

Dinner. That wouldn't make them even by a long shot. But it would open a door she wasn't sure if she wanted to open.

"Dr. Armand, Dr. Schulman is looking for you," a nurse called out to him as she came down the corridor from the nurses' station. "He was just called down to the E.R. and he wants you there to evaluate a patient."

Georges knew better than to stall, even for a moment. Blair was a teaching hospital, and he was still a student. If he wanted to do well here, he couldn't afford to get on the wrong side of the surgeon.

"Thank you." The elevator arrived just then. "I'll ride down with you," he said to Vienna.

But to his surprise, she stepped back. "I forgot something in my grandfather's room."

The doors began to close. "Dinner?" he pressed, placing his hand between the doors to keep them from shutting before he got his answer.

But she was already hurrying down the corridor back to her grandfather's room. "I'll get back to you," she promised, throwing the words over her shoulder.

The next moment, the elevator doors closed and he was gone. Vienna stopped. Watching the doors for a second, she retraced her steps back to the elevator bank. She let out a long, ragged breath as she pressed the Down button for the third time.

There was no denying that she would have loved nothing more than to say yes to the doctor's invitation. But that was just the problem. She would have *loved* to. And that was dangerous. There was something about Dr. Georges Armand, something that pulled at her, something that, at the same time, warned her that if she said yes to his invitation, that if she met him outside the protective four walls of the hospital, she would wind up getting involved with him. Passionately.

The last thing she wanted right now was to get involved with someone, passionately or otherwise. Her grandfather needed her. And she needed to sort out her life, which still felt as if it were a shambles despite the structure she'd given it lately. She'd put her whole heart and soul into caring for the wrong man. Coming to that realization had shaken her up. It made her doubt her instincts, at least her instincts when it came to making any sound judgments about men.

There was no denying that the sight of Georges' wicked smile made her heart flutter in double time, but acting on that might have some consequences attached to it. She had no room for serious heart-ache. For the time being, she just wanted to purge any and all memories of Edward and go on with her life. Slowly.

Something told her that if she went out with Georges, tempting though it was, things would proceed at a rate far from languid and slow.

This was a lot better, she thought, stepping into the elevator. The nurse had interrupted them just in time, sparing her from having to turn Georges down. She didn't want to hurt him; she just didn't want to be hurt herself.

Arriving on the first floor, Vienna fished out the phone number of the taxicab company she'd copied down before leaving for the bakery this morning. Since Georges had rescued her from having to endure the DMV, she needed to get back to the bakery to make sure that Raul hadn't let his temperament get the better of him. Raul and Zelda got into it over some trivial thing almost every day.

Love had to be in the air, she mused, walking over to a lone public phone.

Georges made it a rule never to push. Pursue, yes, but never push. If he had to wear a woman down to get her to say yes, then it wasn't worth it. God knew that practically from the day he was born, he'd all but had to beat women off with a stick and he never lacked for companionship. All he had to do was smile and there would be willing women beside him. It was just the way things were.

When he was barely a teenager, Lily had laughed and said she was afraid that he might become a professional ladies' man. But Philippe had kept after him, always making him mindful of his potential and the real need, since family and position were merely an accident of birth, for the *haves* to give a little something back to the *have-nots*.

But his philosophy notwithstanding, Georges caught himself wanting to push. Wanting to convince Vienna to have dinner with him. Because he had a feeling that once they broke bread together, other pleasing events would follow naturally.

And he wanted them to follow.

Wanted to discover what the texture of her skin felt like beneath his fingertips. Wanted to explore all the different tastes and flavors that went into making up this particular woman.

It had been five days since he'd first met her. Four days since he'd suggested dinner. Their paths crossed regularly in her grandfather's room, but she said nothing to indicate that she wanted to take him up on his offer. So he didn't offer again.

But he wanted to.

She'd infiltrated his mind, something that never happened. Oh, he thought about women, thought about them a great deal, but only when he wanted to. Their faces did not suddenly come, unbidden, materializing before his mind's eye.

Hers did. He had no idea what to make of it. Or what to do.

Georges frowned as he sat at the circular table at his older brother's weekly card game, completely oblivious to the cards he was holding. His thoughts were drifting again. And they were drifting toward the blonde who hadn't taken him up on his invitation.

What the hell did all this mean?

"Fold," he heard his cousin Vinnie Mirabeau,

who sat opposite him, announce just as he dropped his cards facedown on the table. Vinnie pinned him with a knowing look. "You're doing that on purpose, but I'm not falling for it."

Roused, Georges eyed him curiously. He hadn't a clue what Vinnie was going on about. "It?"

"Making that face," Remy chimed it, following suit and tossing his cards down. "Like you don't like what you see. You don't have a poker face, Georges. Everything you think is normally right there, but even you know better than to frown at your cards. So if you're frowning, that means you're trying to put one over on us because you've got one hell of a hand."

Philippe laughed, shaking his head at Remy. "I think you're overthinking this and giving him way too much credit. Georges is preoccupied. His eyes weren't even on his cards when he frowned."

That was a little too close to home. Not to mention insulting. "Georges is right here, you know," Georges pointed out, looking at his older brother. "You don't have to talk about me as if I were some cardboard place holder you stuck on a chair."

"True," Alain allowed good-naturedly. "A cardboard place holder might present more of a challenge." He flashed a confident smile. "I'll see your ten and raise you five more," he told Georges.

Alain counted out a total of fifteen toothpicks,

some yellow, some blue, the different colors designating different point values rather than different dollar amounts.

They never played for money, Philippe made sure of that. His father, Jon Zabelle, Lily's first husband, had been a reckless gambler, hopelessly addicted to any and every game of chance ever created. He very nearly cost Lily everything she had until she put a stop to it by putting a stop to their marriage.

Suspecting he'd been bitten by the gambling bug, as well, Philippe sought to assuage his urges to bet by hosting this game and playing for the big win—which amounted to the big loser of the week having to do chores of some sort for the big winner. Chores varied with the winner, but no one had complained so far. At least, not genuinely. A little bit of griping was expected.

The poker game was a weekly affair that usually took place in Philippe's house and included all three brothers, as well as an assortment of cousins and friends who came and went from the table. Exchange of conversation and information was always the most valued by-product of the evening.

Gordon, Janice's older brother and his soon-to-be-brother-in-law, sighed as he tossed in his own hand. There weren't too many toothpicks left in his personal pile. "This is getting too rich for my blood. All I've got is a pair of sixes."

Philippe's expression was solemn and completely unreadable as he nodded. Looking around at the faces about his table, he asked, "Any more bets?" Everyone but Georges and Alain had dropped out.

Alain was the picture of confidence as he glanced down at his cards. "Nope."

"Not me," Georges replied.

It was time to end this. "Okay, I call." Philippe looked at his youngest brother first. "What have you got?"

Alain grinned and shrugged. It was obvious that he'd been hoping to bluff his way through. He laid his cards on the table. "Three of a kind," he answered, grouping his three jacks together.

"Too bad, I have a straight," Philippe told Alain.

Georges raised his eyes in surprise. "Me, too," he announced.

Remy laughed as he shook his head. "Put 'em down, boys," he prompted. "Let's see whose straight's the higher one." Philippe and Georges put their cards down at the same time. Looking from one set of cards to the other, Remy snorted, then hit the back of Georges' head with the side of his hand the way he used to when they were boys together. "Dummy, that's a straight flush you have."

Georges blinked, looking down at the cards as if this was the first time he was seeing them. He was every bit as preoccupied as Philippe had pointed out. "Oh, yeah, I guess it is." Raising his eyes to look around the table, he couldn't resist asking, "Does that mean that I win?"

"No, that means we'll just let you hold on to the toothpicks for tonight," Alain retorted in momentary disgust. "I say, if he doesn't know he's won, he doesn't deserve to win." But since that didn't hit a responsive chord with Philippe, Alain sighed and shook his head. Then he looked at Georges more closely. "Just where the hell are you tonight?"

Nowhere he wanted to admit, Georges thought ruefully. So he merely shrugged as he gathered together the colorful slivers of wood and drew them over to the pile he already had in front of him.

"Just a little off my game, so to speak," he said, addressing his answer to the table in general. "Had a tough case today at the hospital." It was a good, all-purpose excuse, one that he felt wouldn't be questioned by the others.

Vinnie snorted at the revelation. "And that, ladies and gentlemen, is why I don't trust hospitals." He glanced toward Georges. "Doctors are always re-thinking their decisions."

"Well, in your case," Georges commented cheerfully, "they're probably just trying to figure out the best way to treat whatever it is you are." His humor returned as he successfully banked down any further teeth-jarring thoughts of bright blue eyes and a wide, inviting mouth that pulled into a smile all too easily. A mouth that kept tempting him every time he thought about it.

About her.

About kissing her.

An uneasy edginess threatened to recapture him. This wasn't like him, all but mooning over a woman. He never let thoughts of *any* woman interfere with either his work or the downtime he spent with his brothers and cousins. It was as if something had short-circuited inside of him.

"Well, while you're thinking, how about we play another hand?" Remy asked, gathering the cards together and shuffling them. It was his turn to deal. "Or is that too much multitasking for you?"

Georges watched as Remy all but made the cards dance for him. Of all of them, he was the handiest when it came to cards. "Just shut up and deal. I'm feeling lucky."

"Oh, what's her name?" Alain laughed as he turned to look at Georges.

"Never mind, don't tell us," Vinnie begged. "It'll be someone else by next week. I've given up trying to keep track of you and Alain over here." And then he looked over at their host. "Philippe here has the right idea. Find yourself one decent woman and settle down."

"You're only saying that because you can't even find one," Alain responded.

"Well, if you and Georges weren't systematically trying to go through the entire female population of Southern California, the rest of us might get a break," Remy responded.

"Speak for yourself, Remy," Vinnie told his cousin. "Me, I'm doing just fine." And then he grinned. "I hear congratulations are in order, Philippe."

"They are?" Georges looked at Philippe. "Why?"

"He'd making an honest woman of Janice," Vinnie replied, then slanted a glance toward Gordon. "No offense, Gordon."

"None taken. That's great news, Philippe. About time, too," Gordon added. "J.D. could stand to have some happiness in her life."

"What makes you think Philippe's going to do that?" Alain asked. "Trust me, I lived with the guy for eighteen years. He didn't make me happy."

Philippe blew out a breath. "Just be happy I let you live. Now, are we going to play poker, or are we going to sit around like a bunch of useless old men and gossip?" he asked.

"I'm dealing," Remy declared obediently. "I'm dealing."

Philippe nodded as he began to pick up the cards that were coming his way. "That's better," he murmured in approval.

Chapter Nine

Amos Schwarzwalden frowned. It wasn't an expression ordinarily seen on his jovial face. He watched his examining physician remove the stethoscope from his ears.

Amos sighed sadly. "And here I thought I liked you, boy."

Georges smiled. He made no attempt to correct his patient, or point out that he had not been a "boy" in a very long while. At Amos's age, he surmised the man thought of everyone under the age of fifty as young enough to merit the label of "boy" or "girl." Besides, he could well understand the man's disappointment. In his place, he would be tugging at the invisible restraints, eager to leave the second he was conscious. He knew the good that could be accomplished at a hospital, but psychologically, as Dorothy had once chanted, there was no place like home.

"I'm sorry," Georges apologized with feeling, "but this is really for your own good."

Amos's frown deepened until it seemed etched in. "Keeping me here instead of letting me go home? How is that for my good?"

"Well, there is that code blue incident," he needlessly reminded him. It had transpired just as he was about to go off duty last night. At the elevator, about to get in, he heard the alarm sound and somehow just *knew* it was Vienna's grandfather. He'd run all the way back to the room. One application of the paddles and the man's heart regained its rightful rhythm. Luckily, Vienna hadn't been there to witness any of that. "You gave us quite a scare." Slipping the stethoscope from his neck, he put it in his pocket. "Your heart stopped beating again. We need to know why."

Amos seemed completely unfazed as he shrugged his wide shoulders. "That is simple," he told Georges. "It doesn't like the food here. Let me go home and everything will be fine."

There wasn't a chance in hell that the man was going to leave today. Not unless Amos tied the bed sheets together and slipped out through one of the windows. "I'm afraid we need the pleasure of your company for another day, Amos."

Amos eyed him closely. "Just one more day, then? And then I'm free?"

Georges knew better than to promise. He made one last notation on the man's chart, then replaced it at the edge of the bed. "With luck. If your tests all come back negative—"

Amos shook his head, amused. "I am seventy-four years old, boy. The tests won't be negative. At seventy-four, there is *always* something wrong. All they need to be is better than the next seventy-four-year-old's tests."

"He's just thinking of you, Grandpa."

Georges turned around and saw that Vienna had come into the room. She looked like sunshine, he thought, feeling a warmth materializing out of nowhere to wrap itself around him.

Amos laughed, shaking his head as he waved away the thought. "Let him think a little more about you and less about me."

Embarrassed, Vienna gave her grandfather a warning look that should have silenced him. "Grandpa."

Think more about her? Georges' brain echoed. Not possible. This last week alone, Vienna had been on his mind to the exclusion of everyone else in his life. Thoughts of her had infiltrated his mind to the point that it almost got in the way of his work.

Not something he was accustomed to, Georges thought. It gave him more than a little concern. He figured the only way he was going to get past this was to make love with her and put it all behind him. Once the exhilarating thrill of the hunt was gone, things would start getting back to normal for him.

"I'm sorry," she apologized without looking in Georges' direction. He noted that her complexion looked a little rosier than it had a moment earlier. "My grandfather tends to be a little blunt at times."

"I do not hide what is on my mind, if that is what you mean," Amos told his granddaughter. His eyes shifted toward Georges. His eyes, Georges thought, were almost as hypnotic as hers. "That would be a waste of time and I do not know how much longer I have." His eyes locked with Georges'. "I want to be sure there is someone to look out for Vienna."

Okay, enough was enough. In another minute, he was going to be accepting offers of beads and horses in trade for her.

"Grandpa," she admonished fondly, "women don't need men to look out for them anymore."

"Of course they do," Amos told her matter-of-factly in that voice the didn't allow for any argument. Before she could refute his words, he said, "Just like men need women to look after them." He turned toward the only other person in the room with them. "Am I right, Georges?"

He wanted to beg off before he was drawn into a family argument, however calmly advanced it might be. But something inside of him had him agreeing with the old man's philosophy. So he smiled at Vienna and said, "Sounds about right to me."

Her eyes met his. There was that wariness again in them despite the easy smile on her lips.

"You don't have to humor him," she told Georges. "Lord knows, I do plenty of that on my own."

He had no doubt. Amos Schwarzwalden looked to be a lovable man, but he also struck him as someone who wasn't easily manipulated and could stick to his guns if need be.

He wondered if that ran in the family.

"Could I see you for a moment?" Georges asked Vienna.

She seemed surprised by the request and then nodded. "Sure."

"If he tries to talk you into agreeing to make me stay here longer than tomorrow," Amos called out to her, raising his voice, "the answer is no."

"Yes, Grandpa," she returned patiently. She picked her battles carefully and never raced into the field prematurely. If her grandfather had to stay in the hospital longer than tomorrow, then tomorrow was time enough to let him know about that.

Right now, she was curious as to what the doctor wanted to tell her away from her grandfather's bedside. Instincts told her it had nothing to do with the man's health.

Georges drew her aside right outside the door. He kept his back to the corridor, creating their personal pocket of space. "You never gave me an answer."

Vienna raised her eyes innocently to his. "To?"

She was stalling, he thought. And right there, that should have been his answer. But something within him resisted. He didn't want to take no as her final decision. "Having dinner with me."

A smile teased the corners of the mouth she tried vainly to keep straight. "Didn't I?"

"I was called away before you could give me an answer," he reminded her.

She pretended to remember. In reality, the scenario had never been far from her thoughts. She didn't know whether to view it as an opportunity she'd let slip away, or a bullet she had dodged. Because something told her that in the sum total of things, any time she spent with this man was going to matter.

"Oh, that's right. You had to hurry off to a patient."

She wasn't fooling him for a second. She hadn't forgotten, he thought. "And what were you about to say just before I 'hurried off?'" he prodded, then, to forestall a negative response, he quickly added,

"Now before you answer, let me just tell you that dinner can be anywhere you choose. In the middle of Huntington Gardens if you want." Just in case she was afraid he'd come on to her—which he very much wanted to, but at the same time, knew he could hold himself in check indefinitely. "I would just very much like to have dinner with you."

Oh God, me, too.

She knew she was in trouble. "Why?" she pressed. Humor curved her mouth, but her eyes were serious, probing. Maybe he'd say something to turn her off and then she'd be safe instead of feeling as if she were sinking. Quickly.

"Because I like your company," he told her simply. "I like talking to you. Here," he volunteered, holding his hand out to her. "Touch me. See if there's an ulterior motive. See if you don't find that saying yes isn't a mistake."

When she made no move to place her hand on his, he did it for her, placing her hand on top of his.

Touched, amused, Vienna smiled as she shook her head. "It doesn't work that way," she reminded him. "I told you, I'm not clairvoyant. I just get…feelings…sometimes." And boy, were there feelings rumbling through her now. But none of them were her usual kind—like the one that begged Georges to be in the operating room with her grandfather.

His eyes held hers. "And you have no feelings about me?"

Her knees felt funny, as did her stomach. "That isn't quite accurate," she allowed, the words leaving her lips slowly.

"Oh?"

The smile that curved his lips found its target immediately. Her queasy stomach swiftly acquired knots that stole her breath.

She forced herself to sound calm and in control. It was her only hope. "Dr. Armand, you have an entire harem of women to select from. What do you want with me?"

He didn't like the way that made him sound, like a womanizer governed only by self-gratification. That wasn't him. "Who told you that?"

She noted that he wasn't denying it. "I've been coming here for over a week now. I hear the nurses talking." Amusement rose to her eyes. "It's amazing, given the social life you're reported to have, that you have time to fit in any doctoring."

Being a doctor had never taken second place in his life. "Number one, people exaggerate, you know that. Number two, I haven't been out with anyone since I pulled you and your grandfather out of the car." And he hadn't. He and Diana had never gotten together for that evening he'd canceled and he had absolutely no desire to pick up where he'd left off.

Vienna had taken center stage and there were no understudies.

God help her, she believed him. "Is that because we had a moment?" Vienna asked wryly.

"I'm not sure what we had," he told her honestly. "But we had something. I just want to find out what that something is. And I thought that dinner might be a good place to start." And then he did smile. "Besides, I think it might make your grandfather happy."

Her grandfather was the kind of man who could take an inch, stretch it out and build a freeway on it. He'd done it before. "What would make my grandfather happy is if I was married with six kids."

Not so unusual, Georges thought. And her saying this didn't make him want to run for the hills. The thought of running didn't enter his mind.

"Every journey starts with the first step," he told her, then put his hand out to hers. He sensed he had an advantage and he pressed it. "How about it? Tonight? At seven?"

Vienna regarded the hand, but held back from taking it. "And I get to pick the place?"

"Absolutely."

"The cafeteria."

His eyes narrowed as he tried to follow her. "What cafeteria?"

As if it were a done deal, she placed her hand in

his, sealing a bargain he hadn't yet agreed to. "The one in the basement."

"You want to eat in the hospital cafeteria." He repeated the words, too stunned by the choice even to form them into a question.

Her eyes shone as she nodded. There were reasons for her choice. She told him the most obvious one. "This way, if anything comes up with my grandfather, you won't be far away and neither will I."

Georges was fairly confident that nothing would come up. Yesterday's code blue had been an aberration. All of Amos's vitals looked good today. "You know, I can afford better than the cafeteria."

"I'm sure you can," she replied. "But I sampled some of the cafeteria food from my grandfather's tray the other day. It's not bad."

There was a challenge in her voice. If he tried to argue her out of her choice, he had a feeling she'd change her mind and decline the invitation altogether.

Better than nothing, Georges told himself. "If that's what it takes to have dinner with you, then the cafeteria it is."

He could have sworn that the smile on her face was a wee bit nervous around the edges.

His day over, Georges changed and then made his way over to Amos's room. He was early and

Vienna wasn't waiting outside the room, or inside it once he walked in.

Since he was there, he decided to recheck the old man's vitals one more time. Nurses came by to do a periodic update, but he had never liked being idle.

Greeting the man, Georges began to take his pulse.

Amos eyed him closely. "I hear you're taking my Vienna out for dinner."

He nodded, releasing the man's wrist. "Just to the cafeteria."

"The cafeteria?" Amos repeated incredulously. The old man looked at him as if he'd lost his mind. "This cafeteria? The one in the hospital?"

Georges laughed and nodded. "Afraid so."

Amos hit the controls on his handrail, raising the back of his bed a little more. He stared at the younger man, confused. "Listen, boy, if it is a matter of money, I can—"

Georges stopped him before the man could make an offer and embarrass him. "Thank you for the thought but it's your granddaughter's choice. She wants both of us to be close by in case you need us."

Amos opened his mouth to protest, then closed it again. And then he smiled. Broadly. "She is one in a million, that girl." Amos looked at Georges, his blue-gray eyes all the more imposing beneath tufts of gray eyebrows. "You do know that, do you not?"

She was certainly different, Georges thought,

he'd give her that. He couldn't think of a single woman he'd ever been with who would have been satisfied with being taken to a cafeteria. "I am beginning to get that impression."

Amos looked at him for a long moment, as if debating saying what he was about to tell him. And then he made up his mind. The man needed to know just how unique Vienna was. "Not everyone breaks up with their fiancé because they put family first."

The information caught Georges off guard. And made him feel oddly hollow. "She's engaged?"

"Was," Amos corrected firmly. "Six months ago. Before we moved here from New York." He didn't know how much Vienna had told the young physician. Probably not much, if he knew Vienna. She was friendly and outgoing, but closemouthed at the same time. Not an easy feat. "My doctor said I needed to come out here for my health, get away from the cold, wet winters before they got the better of me," he explained. For a moment, he closed his eyes. "It meant starting over again at my age."

Georges had no doubt that the man had probably been up to it, but still, it seemed like a lonely proposition if he had to do it by himself.

"Vienna would not hear of me coming out alone. She wanted us to move as a family. Me, her and Edward." By the way he said the name, Georges had the feeling that Amos was not too keen on Edward. "Edward refused and told her it was about time she grew up and made an adult choice." He fairly beamed. "So she did." And then his smile receded as he clearly relived the scenario. "I did not want to stand in the way of her happiness and told her I would be fine, but she wouldn't listen. Said that since I did not ask her to choose, she picked me."

He leaned in closer to Georges. "To tell you the truth, I am glad. Not because I love her company or because she has a wonderful business head on her shoulders, but because that Edward was not any good for her. He did not appreciate the girl that she was."

"Doesn't sound like he did," Georges agreed. It earned him a wide, approving smile from Amos.

"Everything was always about him, never about her," Amos continued. "You can not love someone if you do not put them first." He looked at Georges for a long moment, as if to see if his words had penetrated. "Do you understand what I am saying?"

Lessons in love from a seventy-four-year-old, Georges mused. He did his best not to grin. "I do."

"Good," Amos pronounced. He was about to say more, but the door to his room opened. Wearing a simple blue sheath and her hair pinned back from her face, Vienna entered.

She looked suspiciously from one to the other. "What are you to talking about?" she asked.

"I was just telling him to let an old man rest," Amos informed her, never missing a beat. He waved a thin hand toward the door, then closed his eyes. "I am tired."

She crossed to the bed. "Don't you even say hello?" she asked him.

He opened one eye for a moment. "Hello. Goodbye." His eyes were shut again.

With a laugh, she leaned over and brushed her lips against his cheek. "Good night, you old devil."

She thought she heard him chuckle as she left the room with Georges.

The elevator was crowded. Georges and Vienna made their way to the rear, claiming a space as best they could. She stood in front of him. He was aware of the scent of her hair, aware of her body as it pressed against his.

Georges lowered his head so that she could hear him. "Not too late to change your mind about eating here," he told her as the elevator made a stop on the second floor. "I hear I can still get a table at McDonald's without having to book it first."

She turned slightly, brushing her hair against his lowered face. "The cafeteria is fine," she told him. "I have very simple tastes, Doctor." They stopped at the first floor and most of the elevator emptied. Taking advantage of the space, she took a step to the side and turned to look at him. "This isn't about the food, anyway."

The scent he'd detected earlier seemed stronger somehow, wrapping itself all around him. "What is it about?"

"Getting to know each other." Her eyes searched his face to see if he agreed. "That's why people go out, isn't it?"

It would have been simple to coast and go along with everything she said. But something about her demanded the truth from him at all times. "Sometimes."

"And other times?" The elevator doors opened in the basement and they stepped off, along with a nurse and another person.

He took her arm. "And other times, it's just a prelude to the real point of the evening."

They made their way down the winding corridor to the cafeteria doors. Subdued noise greeted them as they entered. She turned toward him. "Which is?"

He laughed shortly, shaking his head. Maybe he should have just agreed after all. "You don't make this easy, do you?"

She stopped short of entering the food service area. "It can be as easy or as hard as you like, Doctor. But I really do value honesty."

He plunged ahead before he could weigh his options. "All right, here's some honesty for you.

You've been on my mind since I first pulled you out of the car. For some reason, I can't stop thinking about you and that's saying a lot since, as you seem to know already, I don't exactly live like a monk.

"I postponed a date to remain with you," he continued, drawing her aside as another couple made their way into the cafeteria, "which isn't unusual. But then I didn't reschedule, which is." The more serious he became, the lower his voice grew. "I haven't wanted to see anyone else since I met you, which is *definitely* unusual for me. You kissed me that first evening and ever since I keep wondering what it would be like to make love to you. I think about it almost all the time, even when I don't want to be. I have to admit that I'm not really happy about it because I never wanted to commit to anything but my work—and now…I don't know anymore."

For a very long moment after he finished, she said nothing. She wasn't exactly sure what she'd expected him to say, but this was far more than she'd been prepared for. He'd overwhelmed her. Overwhelmed her and taken her breath away.

It took her a moment to find it. And to make up her mind.

Vienna smiled up at him. "You weren't kidding about being honest, were you?"

"No, and I'm not kidding about anything else, either," he told her.

"All right." Slowly, she nodded her head, her eyes never leaving his. "All right," she repeated, turning away from the food service area.

He'd blown it, Georges thought. A feeling of desperation, of wanting to fix what had been broken, washed over him. But he hadn't a clue where to start. He could only ask numbly, "All right what?"

She touched his face before answering, her fingertips lightly gliding along his skin. Her heart hammering wildly in her chest. "All right, we'll go to my place. So you can stop wondering what it would be like to make love with me."

Chapter Ten

It took Georges several seconds to regain use of his tongue, which, along with the rest of him, had momentarily gone numb after Vienna's invitation. He stared at her now, wondering if he'd misheard. "You're kidding."

Nerves shimmied up her spine, but she'd come too far to back down. "I never kid about something like that."

Georges continued looking at her, somewhat uncertain. It wasn't like him to refuse an offer like this from someone he was interested in. But the offer itself confused him. Perhaps for the first time in his life, he felt like a man standing on the middle of a tightrope without a clue about how he'd gotten there.

He wanted to make sure he hadn't misunderstood. "You're sure?"

She sighed and laughed at the same time, confusion reigning supreme. "God, no."

The laugh was a nervous one. The mystery deepened. Was he missing something? "Then why…?"

She took a breath. "Because I know it just has to be."

"Another 'feeling?'"

For lack of a better way to explain it, she agreed. "Something like that."

But her feeling had nothing to do with touching him and that ensuing sensation that sometimes carried a premonition. There was no premonition here. She just had a need, an overwhelming, stunning need she couldn't ignore, even though this would probably turn out badly for her.

And yet, she couldn't make herself walk away. Couldn't make herself run and hide, to wait this out. Because if not tonight, then tomorrow, or the day after that, when she least expected it, she'd succumb. She'd wind up making love with him. This way, while her grandfather was still in the hospital for one more day, she could call the shots.

Sort of.

Okay, he thought, this was good. This was better than good. Working hard to keep his brain from scrambling, he tried to remember his manners. "Do you want to have something to eat first?"

She pressed her lips together. Committed, she needed to see this through. "No."

He'd assumed that she'd suggested the cafeteria because the noise and people were, in a way, a protective shield for her. To keep their relationship from moving forward. Now that they were all but racing to the finish line, there was no more need for that kind of barrier. "I mean in a really decent restaurant."

Vienna didn't say anything. Instead, she gazed at him for a long moment. The longing she felt inside, the hunger eating away at her, grew to almost unbearable proportions.

Maybe it was because of everything she'd been through these last few days. Maybe it was fueled by the emotional turmoil she'd endured, confronted with her grandfather's mortality.

Or maybe it just had to do with the extremely magnetic connection she felt whenever she was around this larger-than-life heroic doctor. She didn't know. All she knew was that *this* really needed to happen between them. "No."

Well, he'd tried, Georges thought. And to be honest, eating was the furthest thing from his mind right now. Calmly breaking bread in a five-star restaurant might be more than he could manage to pull off at the moment.

"All right, then," he agreed. "Your place."

Her eyes held his for a flickering of eternity. "My place," she repeated.

Vienna's hand was trembling as she tried to put the large silver key into her front door lock. Trembling so hard that her first attempt to open the door failed. The key ring slipped from her hand and fell with a jarring clang to the blue-and-gray welcome mat.

Before she could pick them up again, Georges stooped down beside her and retrieved the keys. He selected the right key and unlocked the door for her.

But even as he placed his hand on the doorknob, he refrained from turning it. Instead, he whispered to her, "You don't have to do this, you know. We can just turn around and—"

Placing her hand over his, Vienna pushed down and opened the door. She entered her house and swung around in the foyer in one smooth motion.

The next moment, her mouth was sealed against his lips.

Sealed as closely as her body was to his, filling every space between them until there wasn't enough left for a whisper of air.

Something suddenly ignited between them. Within them.

It occurred so fast that whatever breath Georges thought he had left was stolen away. He'd never had that happen with a woman before. Oh, he'd been breathless before, but always by his own design and calculation. And he had always, always been in control of the situation, of the moment.

Here, he was free-falling without a single recollection of how it had begun.

Only that it was.

He liked to make love to a woman at his own pace, but with Vienna, he was losing control. There was an urgency that spurred him on, running like a flame along fuel that had been spilled on the ground, speeding to encompass every inch.

Within moments of slamming shut the door, holding Vienna's supple form trapped between the wall and his body, Georges swiftly stripped her. She did the same for him. Shirt, pants, dress and assorted undergarments went flying in all directions, a flurry of material and colors left to fend for themselves.

Georges wanted her with a fierceness that made his teeth ache. It would have scared the hell out of him if he'd taken so much as a microsecond to pause and consider. But he couldn't. All he could do was hold on for dear life.

Hold on and savor.

God, could he savor, he thought, his lips traveling up and down the length of her throat, the breadth of her breasts. Thoughts and desires all swirled into one another as he methodically worked his way down her torso.

Then, dropping to his knees, he continued to hold her against the wall as best he could while moving downward, ever downward.

He heard her whimper and thought he would dissolve in a cloud of vapor.

Small, almost animal-like noises escaped from her lips. His tongue caressed her in all the places that his hands, his mouth, touched. Her whole body felt as if it were vibrating. Throbbing.

She could hardly breathe as she wound her fingers through his hair, pressing him against her. Urging him not to stop even as her body jerked and trembled. The sensation that exploded within her as his tongue found her inner core caused the world to go dark just for a heartbeat. Weakened, she all but sagged down to her knees beside him.

But then he pushed her back, weaving the magic more forcefully, more urgently this time until another climax found her. Rocked her. Sounds, almost guttural, rose in her throat, lodging there, fighting for space with her ragged breath.

With her last bit of strength, her fingers digging into his shoulders, Vienna managed to drag him back up to her level.

Or maybe he came of his own volition, she wasn't sure. All she knew was that the next moment, he was kissing her and their bodies were entwined.

She could feel him harden against her. Jumping up, she wrapped her legs around his torso, her invitation clear. With a sob, she cried out his name as Georges drove himself into her.

Her head spun.

She began to move against him, more and more urgently. His arms tightening around her so hard she could hardly breathe. All the while, their lips slanted over and over again in kiss after endless kiss. They reached the apex together. She thought his lips would be forever imprinted upon hers.

And then, suddenly, they were tumbling onto her sofa, their bodies covered in a slick sheen of sweat as exhaustion drenched them both. His back was to the cushions and she was on top of him and far too spent to notice.

She was never going to draw a normal breath again, Vienna thought as her chest continued to heave. But that was all right, she told herself, because her head was lost in the stars.

As was the rest of her.

After what seemed like an eternity, Georges opened his eyes and looked up at her. "You are a surprise, Vienna Hollenbeck," he marveled fondly.

Vienna felt a smile spreading in response.

"You're not." She took a moment to draw more air into her lungs. Would there ever be enough again? "You're exactly what I thought you'd be."

Well, that made one of them, he thought. Because he'd even surprised himself with the level of sensations that had telegraphed through him. With the desire that had all but torn him in half as it rammed itself into his body. As for his level of exhaustion, well, even at his most vigorous, he'd never felt as if he'd just run a twenty-six-mile marathon.

Shifting, he continued to hold her against him, feeling her warmth seeping into his body. Arousing him. Was that possible at this point? If he was half-dead, did that mean he was half-alive?

He felt her smile against his side. Georges raised an eyebrow as he looked into her face.

"Is this cuddling?" There was amusement in her voice. Had that ex-fiancé never held her as if she were something precious? While the thought took form, he felt the sting of something unpleasant.

Jealousy?

"This is called holding on for dear life until the room stops spinning," he informed her whimsically, using humor to hide the fact that his own reactions had left him shaken.

Vienna dug herself out of the pocket he'd created for her. Propping herself up on her elbow, she looked down at him. The tips of her blond hair skimmed lightly, teasingly, over his chest with each word she spoke.

He began to feel his stomach tightening in anticipation.

"Does this mean that you don't want to do it again?" she asked.

More than he wanted to breathe, he thought. But there were limitations.

"There's a world of difference between desire and execution," Georges told her. "I'm afraid that you're going to have to give me a few minutes so I can pull myself together."

Hand planted on his chest, she pushed him back against the cushions. Leaning over his face, her lips grazed his so lightly it was almost more of a promise of a kiss than an actual kiss.

"How few?" she whispered, her breath caressing his skin. Smiling, she glided just the very tip of her tongue along the outline of his mouth, moving back out of reach when he tried to kiss her. There was laughter in her eyes.

He could feel his blood quickening, could feel the adrenaline surging as the anticipation of another wild ride began to form.

Craning his neck up away from the sofa cushion, Georges cupped her face between his hands and brought it down so that his mouth captured hers. He kissed her long and hard as all systems came back on line, declaring their readiness to go at will.

"This few," he said against her mouth before he kissed her again.

They went slower this time, but still fast enough to all but set the sofa cushions on fire.

Their positions were reversed. While she had been the one to take the initiative before, only to have him steal the reins from her, this time around Georges began their intimate dance only to have her suddenly take over the lead.

Vienna feasted on his body just the way he had on hers earlier, driving him crazy with desire until he was fairly certain he would have given her anything she asked for.

He knew he'd willingly given her his soul.

They made love twice more until, both spent beyond all reason or measure, Georges and Vienna fell asleep in each other's arms.

Georges slowly stirred. It took him a moment to realize that his eyes were shut. He'd fallen asleep. The same moment that occurred to him, what had preceded came back to him in vivid color.

Vienna, lighting his world the way it had never been lit before.

Vienna.

The emptiness beside him registered even before

he opened his eyes. As did an incredible feeling of abandonment. That was something he'd never felt before. Something he was quick to bank down. Because it was so unlike him, he attributed it to the strange way the evening had unfolded.

"Vienna?"

There was no answer. He scrubbed his hand over his face, trying to pull himself together. Trying to get his brain back in focus.

Light came in from the hallway. It was still dark outside. That meant not too much time had lapsed. How much was not too much? He couldn't make out the numbers on his wrist watch.

Getting up, Georges quickly pulled on his pants. For the time being, he left everything else off. He needed to find out where Vienna was before he thought about mundane things like socks.

The moment he left the bedroom, he heard noise coming from below. Someone was up and about downstairs. He padded down the stairs, his bare feet brushing against the raised design of the gray carpeting.

Rather than call out her name again, he decided to silently investigate her whereabouts.

To his relief and somewhat surprise, he found Vienna in the kitchen. Her back to the entrance, she was wearing a coverall apron that draped loosely over a pair of jeans and a blue pullover sweater.

He would have preferred seeing her in just the apron alone.

As he crossed the threshold, he saw that Vienna had slipped something into the microwave oven. She pressed a combination of buttons on the keypad, then Start. The light went on inside the microwave and the turntable rotated.

Georges snuck up behind her, then slipped his arms around her waist, pulling her against his chest. She didn't squeal in surprise.

He had a feeling she'd probably seen his reflection in the shiny surface of the toaster that stood next to the microwave. "I thought you weren't hungry."

She placed her hands over his, not to remove them but, for the moment, to press them even more tightly against her. Absorbing his strength.

"I didn't say that." And then she turned in the circle of his arms until she faced him and could look up into his eyes. "I was just more hungry for something else."

Before Georges could teasingly make reference to her other appetite, she rose on her toes and brushed her lips against his. Once, twice and then a third time, each pass lasting a little bit longer than the last. And then, wrapping her arms around his neck, Vienna kissed him long and hard.

She was smiling when she finally drew her head back to look at him again.

"What?" he asked.

Her smile was positively wicked as her eyes dipped down to just below his waist. "It feels as if you want to play again."

He laughed, holding her closer again. She made him feel carefree and yet serious at the same time. "Is that what you call it now? 'Playing?'"

Vienna nodded her head. Playing. That was the label she had to put on it. Because, she sensed, calling it anything more serious might scare him off. Georges was not a man who played for keeps, he was a man who merely played.

And she, well, she wasn't altogether sure what she was right now. A little while ago, she would have said that when she played, it was for all the marbles. Because making love with someone was very serious to her. But being with Georges even this one time had changed all the rules on her. It didn't, ultimately, make her want any less, but it made her willing to settle for less.

Because wanting more, asking for more, would only give her nothing. She was going to have to take this man on his terms—drawing them out a little more each time, until perhaps, just perhaps, his terms and hers met somewhere in the middle. Until then—if *then* ever came—she was more than willing to dance this strange dance whose music she found filling her head.

"Uh-huh," she murmured just before he deepened the kiss she had initiated.

And then, as he came up for air, Georges grinned as he looked into her eyes. "You've got my head spinning so much, I could swear I hear bells ringing."

"You did," she told him, her mouth curving. When he looked at her, puzzled, she explained, "That's the microwave." Vienna nodded her head toward the counter. "I think it's done."

"But I'm not," he told her just before he lowered his mouth to hers again.

Chapter Eleven

Amos Schwarzwalden gripped the arms of his wheelchair, not for support but because he couldn't wait to be free of it. He'd insisted that he could walk across the hospital threshold to his freedom, but Shelly, the cute day nurse he'd been flirting with for the last few days, had informed him that use of the wheelchair was mandatory hospital policy. No one was released from an overnight stay at Blair Memorial unless they were wheeled out.

He'd promised not to sue, no matter what happened, but the nurse just continued to look at him until he finally got off the bed and reluctantly lowered himself into the wheelchair.

Watching the exchange, both verbal and silent, Vienna gave serious thought to kidnapping the young woman and bringing her home with them. Shelly seemed to be able to handle her grandfather a lot better than she could.

Much to Amos's obvious dismay, Shelly was not the one taking him down to the front entrance. But he lit up again when he saw who was.

Georges.

That made two of them, Vienna thought, returning the greeting the doctor tendered to first her grandfather, then to her. Was it her imagination, or had his eyes lingered on her a little longer?

At times like this, it was hard to remember that she was a grown woman with one lengthy relationship, not to mention engagement, behind her. Especially when her pulse insisted on racing.

"You are taking me out of here?" Amos asked, craning his neck to look at Georges more closely.

Georges took hold of the wheelchair's handles. "I insisted." He glanced again in Vienna's direction. "Ready?"

"I am," Amos declared, as exuberant as a schoolboy about to embark on his first day of summer vacation.

Georges began to push the chair out of the room and down the hallway. "Then we're on our way."

Vienna fell into place beside him. She wore that perfume of hers again, he noted. The one that instantly drugged him and brought intimate images into his mind. It filled the empty service elevator just enough so that he couldn't concentrate. Amos was talking to him and he hadn't heard a single word.

"Do not be a stranger, now," Amos said as they left the confines of the elevator car. Georges took a deep breath, trying to counteract the effects of Vienna's sensual scent. "Remember, I want you to feel free to come by the bakery at any time." They took the shortest route to the front entrance, making their way down a newly recarpeted corridor. "There will always be a box of pastries waiting for you." Turning again in his seat, this time to the other side, Amos glanced slyly at his granddaughter. "Among other things perhaps."

She'd been pushy enough for both of them last night, Vienna thought. Georges didn't need her grandfather applying pressure, as well. The man was as subtle as a cave-in.

"Grandpa," she admonished, "Dr. Armand has more important things to do than spend his free time hanging around Vienna's Finest."

Amos was not easily daunted. "Every man needs to relax a little."

Vienna laughed shortly. "This from a man who refuses to even lie down when he's sick."

"I am not sick," Amos insisted with feeling. "I am healthy, right, Georges?" He turned his head toward the younger man for backup. "Otherwise, they would not be letting me go from this fine establishment." He waited for agreement. "Am I correct?"

"Absolutely," Georges told him, doing his best to look somber. Satisfied, Amos turned back around to face front. Georges caught the concerned look in Vienna's eye. "Just remember not to overdo it," Georges warned.

Amos nodded his head. "I will remember."

A small "Ha!" escaped Vienna's lips. When he looked at her, she pointed out, "Notice that my grandfather promised that he'd remember, not that he wouldn't overdo it." Her grandfather was well versed when it came to artfully dodging any appeals regarding taking life a little easier.

Amos sighed, clasping his hands in his lap. "I have you for that."

"You'd better believe it," Vienna assured him with feeling. She intended to be his nurse and his keeper until she was satisfied that he had fully recovered.

Georges pushed the wheelchair across the threshold as the electronic doors drew open for them. The late-morning air was welcoming and

sultry. Just like Vienna, he caught himself thinking. Georges brought the wheelchair to a stop on
the wide rubber welcome mat just beyond the
threshold.

Amos shifted so that he could see him. His smile
was warm, appealing. Another trait he shared with
his granddaughter, Georges thought.

"Well, my young friend, I cannot say it has
not been interesting." Leaning forward, he took
Georges' hand and instead of shaking it, held it in
both of his. Despite the various conditions that had
stricken him, he was still a short bull of a man with
powerful hands. "And I am very glad that you have
come into our lives, mine and Vienna's. Very glad,"
he underscored, still clasping the doctor's hand. He
beamed. "I will see you again."

"Count on it. I want to see you back here for a
checkup with Dr. Schulman in two weeks." He raised
his eyes to Vienna's face for a confirmation. She
nodded, but it was Amos who answered. His tone
was less than glowing when he spoke of the surgeon.

"Ah, yes, Dr. Schulman. The man who does not
smile." Amos shook his head, as if he pitied anyone
who found life so somber. Vienna had mentioned
that her grandfather had been a boy in Austria
during World War II and had endured a great many
hardships, only some of which he shared with her.
That the man found the will and the strength only

to look at the bright side of life was an amazing tes-
timonial to his character. "I will see him, too. But
you, you are the one I *want* to see."

Georges nodded and slowly extricated his hand.
For a moment, he made no comment. Instead, he
looked over toward Vienna. He'd left her house in
the wee hours of the morning instead of staying the
night. He'd wanted to, God help him, but it was
something, as a rule, he never did.

Looking at her, he felt regret rippling through
him, surfacing out of the shadows. A first, he thought
as he felt a warmth spread over him because he was
looking at her. Nothing more.

Another first. He was going to have to get hold
of himself, he silently promised.

But for now, there were last-minute instructions
to give. "A home health care nurse will be calling
you this afternoon," he told both of them. "I've seen
to the paperwork myself." And he had, calling in a
favor so that Amos would be given the maximum
amount of care for a minimum cost. He'd promised
to take care of the rest, making sure no one told
either the old man or Vienna.

"Make sure she's young," Amos requested with
a wicked wink. "And pretty."

"Make sure she's fast," Vienna added. She smiled
fondly down at her grandfather. "He's pretty quick
when he wants to be."

"I'll pass that along," Georges said, then asked, "Can I speak to you for a moment?"

"Sure."

Securing Amos's wheelchair so that it wouldn't roll away, Georges stepped over to the side. Vienna followed, then waited, holding her breath. Afraid that he was going to say something he didn't want her grandfather to hear, something about Amos's health that he hadn't been apprised of.

"Yes?" she pressed when he didn't say anything immediately.

Georges took in a subtle breath. "I'd like to see you again. Once your grandfather's settled in and there's a routine in place," he added quickly. Damn it, he was tripping over his tongue. When was the last time that that had happened? To his recollection, never. It was her doing, all hers.

Run, an urgent voice in his head ordered. *Run now, while you still can.*

It *was* something he didn't want her grandfather to hear, Vienna thought, a smile blossoming on her lips. But an entirely different something than she'd initially thought. A lovely something. She was so relieved, she could have cried.

"I'd like that," she answered softly. "Why don't you take him up on his invitation? Come by the house, say tomorrow night for dinner?"

Georges could see that Amos was trying very

hard to hear what they were saying and still appear not to be listening. He found it hard not to smile. "His invitation was for the bakery," he reminded her.

"Bakery, house, there's not much difference. My grandfather practically lives at the bakery and I'm sure he will again, once he's well."

He liked the idea of seeing her again. And the idea of having a chaperon might help keep things in check until he figured out just what was going on here. "What time?" he asked.

That was purely up to him, she thought. "When can you make it?"

For a second, Georges tried to remember his schedule. Most of the time, it was up in the air. His shift could get switched around at any time, entirely at the discretion of the attending physician or anyone else who outranked him.

"I'm going to have to get back to you on that later today," he confessed.

She began to reach into her purse. "You need my cell number?"

He put his hand on hers, stopping her. Or maybe it was his smile that did it. She couldn't think when her bones were melting faster than snow in July. "Still have it from when you gave it to me at the hospital the first time."

"Okay. Good." She nodded, pleased more than she could possibly say. Her grandfather was coming home and Georges had just indicated that last night wasn't just a glorious one-night stand but perhaps something with a little more substance. God was in His heaven and all was right with the world. "Can you wait with my grandfather while I bring up the car?" She caught her lower lip between her teeth as she waited for his answer.

Georges felt his gut tighten. He wanted to kiss her. But he was good at keeping his true thoughts from showing on his face. So he nodded and gave her the easy smile that everyone always associated with him.

"My pleasure," he told her.

"Thank you. Be right back." Vienna hurried across a crosswalk out to the aboveground parking lot located on the far side of the hospital grounds.

"Wonderful girl," Amos commented as his granddaughter disappeared from view. He turned to see if Georges was watching her.

Not so much a girl as a woman, Georges thought. A woman who'd managed to set his world on its ear. "That she is."

"Do not know what I would do without her." And the old man meant that from the bottom of his soul. It seemed ironic to him that somewhere along the line, the tables had gotten turned and the little girl he'd taken care of was now taking care of him. "But I would give her up to the right man," Amos told him, still craning his neck so that he could study the face of the man standing behind him.

Meaning me? Georges couldn't help wondering what the old man would say if he knew about his reputation.

At this point, he honestly didn't know if he should follow his needs or go with his instincts. The latter told him to stop this before it got out of hand. Before he lost his heart to this woman and suffered the consequences.

Before, that same voice mocked. Too late for that.

Was this what his mother felt? Fear? Fear of being out on that limb, only to find himself abandoned.

His mother left lovers before they could leave her. Years ago, he'd realized that it was because she was afraid of giving her heart to someone who would either abuse her love or break her heart in two. Despite all her fame, Lily Moreau had been through a great deal.

He and his brothers generally agreed that Philippe's father had been the love of her life, but he'd also been a hopeless gambler, far more enamored of Lady Luck than he was of Lily. He all but gambled away the very roof over their heads. Had she not taken drastic measures to save them, he would have. After that, she never put her faith or trust into one man, although she'd been twice tempted, with his own father and with Alain's. But both marriages were tempestuous and relatively short-lived. No man was a match, it seemed, for the dynamic and larger-than-life Lily Moreau.

Because there was no stability for him to use as a compass, Georges had picked his way through life much the way his mother had, enjoying the company of the opposite sex and then, when the threat of something more serious was in the offing, he would move on. Life had been free and easy with no strings, no pain hiding in the shadows, waiting to seize him when he least expected it.

And there was no lasting love hiding to capture him, either.

Lasting love. Was there such a thing? he wondered as he stood there, watching Vienna pull up to the curb in her vehicle. At this point, he didn't know.

"Okay, your chariot awaits, Grandpa," she announced, swinging her legs out of the driver's side.

Vienna came around the back of the vehicle to help him out of the wheelchair. From what she had seen, he was still a little wobbly on his legs and she didn't want to risk having him hurt himself.

Between her and Georges, they managed to successfully lower Amos into the passenger side of the front seat. Georges drew away the wheelchair, locking the wheels so that it wouldn't suddenly go rolling down the winding path. With that out of the way, he closed Amos's door. Vienna rounded the front of the vehicle and he looked at her over the roof.

"I'll call you," he repeated.

Something in Georges' voice, a vague distance she hadn't heard before, planted a seed of doubt in her head. Worse, in her heart. But she told herself she was just imagining things. So she smiled at him and nodded.

"Until then," she replied warmly. Secretly hoping that was enough to make him want to keep his word.

"Don't you look at your messages?" Georges heard Philippe's voice in his ear as he answered his cell phone more than a week later. There was suppressed irritation in his brother's tone, simmering just beneath the surface.

Georges was feeling too good to get defensive. Life had been hectic, but progressing rather well these days. As promised, he'd secured the nurse for Amos and it had turned out to be a perfect match. The old man still hadn't gotten to the point where he could go back to the bakery for anything but a short visit, but he was progressing well.

Things were progressing well between him and Vienna, too, he thought. So well that he caught himself waiting for a mythical shoe to drop.

Or maybe the bottom to fall out.

But most of the time, he refused to allow himself to think about it beyond the moment. There was safety in ignorance, he thought.

Georges knew what his brother was referring to. Not messages left on his cell phone, but on his computer. Philippe had made his money and a name for himself developing software for large companies. He lived and breathed the computer.

The same was not true of him.

"E-mail is not something I usually have time for," Georges told him. "I don't know about you, but I'm still connected to the rest of the world by phone. Now, what is it I was supposed to have read and, I'm guessing, responded to?"

"Mother's having a show tomorrow. She wants all of us to be there."

By all, he knew Philippe was referring to not just him and his other brother, but Philippe's fiancée and Janice's daughter, Kelli, a five-year-old Lily doted on. Gordon, Janice's brother, had gotten pulled into the circle, as well, plus assorted cousins. Alain usually brought his date of the moment with him. He, on the other hand, never did.

He was outside of Blair, taking one of his rare breaks. Georges leaned against the wall, the cell phone to his ear. "You know, when we were kids, all her shows were usually located halfway around the country. We practically had to make appointments to see her. Now she's here much more than she's not. Why the change?" he asked.

Philippe, as always, had all the answers. He laughed softly. "Age."

"Mother doesn't age," Georges reminded him. Other people's mothers aged. Lily Moreau had her portrait hidden somewhere in someone's attic. *It* was aging while she did not.

"She wishes," Philippe said with a laugh. "No, I'm serious. I think somewhere along the line, it finally hit her that she'd missed out on a lot on the home front, flying around the way she did while we were growing up on her. Probably, in her mind, she's trying to make up for lost time."

Georges had another theory about what could've brought about this change in their mother. She'd always been a loving mother in her own way, but she'd never stayed in their lives for such a long stretch of time before. "I think it's you getting married that probably triggered all this."

There was silence on the other end as Philippe considered his words. "Maybe," he allowed. "At any rate, no matter what brought this on, bottom line is she wants us to show up."

Georges hesitated. He was on duty in the evening for the rest of the week. "I can't unless I find some-one to trade hours with—"

Philippe laughed. Their mother was way ahead

of him on that. "The chief of surgery at Blair's a friend of Mother's. She's already made sure you have the evening off."

Typical, Georges thought. She might have seemed like a hurricane blowing into town, but Lily always liked being in control, always liked calling the shots. "Why couldn't we have had the kind of mother who liked to put on an apron and bake cookies?"

"Because then she wouldn't have been Lily Moreau—and for all we know, if she followed that kind of lifestyle, you and Alain might have never been born. She would have stuck by my father through thick and thin."

Philippe had a point. In any case, they'd never know. "So, what's so special about this showing? She just had one a few months ago."

"This one's for Kyle. They're his paintings."

Kyle, their mother's so-called latest "companion." Now that he thought of it, Georges remembered her saying something about Kyle having a great deal of potential. So, she was talking about his ability to paint, not something else. But could he paint well enough for a show? "The boy toy?"

"One and the same, except I think Mother sees him as something more than that."

Georges suppressed a groan. While "Lily in love" was more like a force of nature, he didn't exactly relish this particular choice she'd made. "She's had countless 'companions' since Alain's father died. What makes you think that this guy in short pants is so important to her?"

There was another pregnant pause on the other end, longer this time, as if Philippe were composing his thoughts. "You haven't noticed the resemblance?"

Georges had no idea what he was talking about. "To who?"

"To my father."

For a second, Georges was speechless. Until Philippe had said it, there had only been that vague recognition echoing in the recesses of his mind, the kind that haunted people when they saw someone they thought they knew, but weren't sure.

"Oh God, you're right."

Philippe's father was the only one of their mother's partners and lovers with whom she ever reunited on an intimate basis. After she divorced his own father, she took Philippe's back for a while, although they didn't get married the second time around. But the reunion was short-lived. The final straw came when she discovered that his gambling affliction was worse than ever.

Despite the turbulent nature of their last breakup, she was inconsolable when she discovered that the man had died, taken by a brain aneurysm that had suddenly ruptured.

"Do you think that's why she's with him?" Georges asked.

"That's part of it. The other part is that our eternally young mother wants to remain that way. I think that Kyle is her second chance at being twenty-five again."

A thought suddenly pushed its way forward, stealing Georges' breath away. "You don't think she's going to wind up marrying him, do you?"

"Hard to say. This is Mother we're talking about, a woman who has never played by any rules known to the ordinary man."

Philippe was right. Of all of them, he was the one who knew her best. "What do you think of him?"

"He's young."

"Other than that," Georges said impatiently. He got to the heart of the matter. "Do you think that he's after her money?"

"Personally, I think he's as dazzled by her as the rest of the world is. She needs that right now, needs to be the center of someone's universe."

"She could have been that by being more of a mother and less of a celebrity when we were growing up."

"Can't change the past," Philippe told him. "Can only work with the present and the future." He had to get going, and he still didn't have the answer he wanted. The least emotional of her three sons, he was still very protective of his part-time mother. "So, are you coming?"

It sounded as if his showing up was important to Philippe. "Are you asking?"

"I'm asking."

He owed Philippe more than he could ever possibly repay. "Then I'm coming." He hesitated for a moment, debating asking, then decided he had nothing to lose. "If I bring someone with me, do you think that'll cause any ripples?"

"Are you bringing that woman you've been seeing?"

Georges picked up the inference in his brother's tone. Defensive instincts kicked in. "I never mentioned a specific woman."

"You didn't have to. Do I think it'll cause ripples? Probably. But as long as it's not a tsunami, you'll survive. Bring her. I think I'd like to meet the woman who finally nailed my brother's hide to the wall."

Georges anticipated the repercussions. He changed his mind. "Forget it. I'm coming alone."

Philippe's laugh said that he knew better, but for now, he'd play along. "Suit yourself. See you at the gallery tomorrow night."

Chapter Twelve

Georges smiled to himself as he closed his cell phone and put it back into his pocket. Good old Philippe. His brother always knew that the fastest way to get him to do something was to tell him not to. That much about their relationship hadn't changed.

While the inclination was still fresh, he'd placed a call to Vienna and caught her at home instead of the bakery. She was having lunch with her grand-father. He kept the conversation short and asked her if she wanted to come with him to the show at the gallery.

The words were barely out of his mouth before

she eagerly accepted the invitation he'd tendered. It was only after he'd terminated the connection that he began to wonder what he was letting himself in for and why he was doing it in the first place.

No quick answers came to mind. And those that did he wasn't up to contemplating.

Tomorrow night was going to be one hell of an interesting evening.

"Are you sure you're going to be all right, Grandpa?" It was the third time in as many minutes that she asked the question.

Vienna was dressed in a shimmering electric-blue cocktail dress that flirted with the middle of her thighs. Georges was close to mesmerized by the way the hem moved and swayed along her skin. She'd been ready to leave now for more than ten minutes, yet couldn't quite get herself to go.

No premonition kept her from leaving with Georges, who looked so dashing tonight in his black tux. It was just that her grandfather's color was so pale, she was afraid something would happen to him while she was away.

"Better question is will Silvia be all right?" Amos replied, summoning a deliberately salacious expression as he eyed the evening private-duty nurse that Georges had sent over from the agency. And then the older man appealed to Georges. "Get Vienna off my hands, will you, boy? If I give her half a chance, she will be cutting my food for me."

Georges laughed and slipped his arm around her waist, gently urging Vienna toward the door. He handed her the purse that was on the side table. "As long as she doesn't offer to chew it for you."

Amos made a face and shivered.

"We'll be back early," Vienna promised her grandfather just before crossing the threshold.

"Then I will be very disappointed in both of you," Amos declared with feeling. "Besides—" the old man raised and lowered his eyebrows comically "—if you come back too soon, you might be interrupting something."

Georges took that as an exit line and closed the door behind them. He led the way to the curb where he'd parked his newly detailed, gleaming red sports car.

Vienna's thoughts were still back in the living room. She frowned slightly. "I hope he's not too much of a handful for Silvia."

"Don't worry, she knows how to handle herself. She'll be fine." Lowering his mouth so that it was next to her ear, he assured her, "He'll be fine."

God, she hoped so. She looked at Georges, wanting desperately to have her mind set at ease. "Is that your professional opinion?"

"It is. Get it while it's hot." His smile widened as he opened the passenger-side door for her.

"Speaking of hot—" his eyes swept over her "—you look sensational in that dress."

Color rose to her cheeks. She got into the car. "Thank you."

She would look even more sensational without it, Georges caught himself thinking as he got behind the wheel. He glanced in her direction as he buckled his seat belt. Her belt was secured and her fingers were wrapped around her purse, allowing it to live up to the description: clutch purse. Her knuckles were all but white.

"He'll be all right," he repeated, turning on the ignition.

Vienna paused to blow out a breath before answering. "I'm not worried about that." It was a lie, but not a very big one. She knew she was being overly concerned about her grandfather and overly protective. But he *was* her only living relative and she did love the old man dearly. Independent though she was, she just couldn't picture life without him in it.

Georges wove his way out of her development. "Then what?"

There was no sense in lying about it. Even though she was looking forward to meeting the famous Lily Moreau, she couldn't help wondering what the woman would think of her. After all, she was sleeping with the woman's son—or, at least, had slept with him. Even though Lily didn't know that, it didn't change anything. She wanted the artist to like her.

But she couldn't say any of that to him. It would sound as if she were assuming too much. One step at a time.

"It's not every day I get to meet a living legend," she answered. Shifting in her seat to face him, she asked, "What's she like?"

"Mother?" Living legend. Funny, he had never thought of her in those terms. Even when he occasionally read stories about her, her shows, her three-day parties, he didn't really associate that person with the woman who, whenever she was in town, would tuck him into bed. "She's just Mother." Amused, Georges turned his head for a moment and smiled at her. "Don't worry, she doesn't eat people for dinner," he teased. "Only for breakfast."

"Very reassuring," she said wryly. And then her nervousness resurfaced. "No, really, tell me. What's she like?"

"A little larger than life, I guess. Enthusiastic. About everything," he added because it was true. He'd never known his mother to take things lightly or not jump into things with both feet. "You know that old classic line from that Bette Davis movie?" He fished for the title. "*All About somebody or other*—"

"Alice," Vienna supplied, then quickly amended, "No, I mean Eve. *All About Eve*." She'd heard of it, but she'd never seen it. Was his mother shrewish and self-centered like the main character was supposed to be?

"Right," he said. "Anyway, in the movie Bette Davis says something like, 'Buckle up, it's going to be a bumpy night.'" He grinned. "I think Bette Davis knew my mother. With Mother you just never know what to expect."

"In other words, expect the unexpected."

"You've got it." As he got onto the freeway that eventually led to the gallery, Georges glanced at the woman in the passenger seat. She *did* look nervous, he thought. Maybe he shouldn't have invited her. Too late now. There was nothing left to do but try to reassure her. "Mother doesn't care for most women too much, but she'll love you."

"Why?"

He laughed then and the rich, mellow sound warmed her. "How could she not?"

Her breath stopped traveling again. It seemed to be a regular occurrence every time she was around him. Or thought about him. Vienna looked at his profile to see if he was joking, or just turning on the charm that came to him as easily as breathing did for some.

They came to a red light and he pressed down on the brake. As if sensing that she was studying him, Georges spared her a long glance.

He seemed serious, she realized. Was he? Or was

that just his way of putting her at her ease? In either case, she was appreciative. But she needed more.

"You won't leave my side?" she asked.

"Stick to it like glue," he vowed. "Unless, of course, you want to use the ladies' room. If I go in with you, there might be a problem." He grinned again, and her stomach flipped.

The light changed and he moved his foot back on the accelerator.

Just the sound of his voice was reassuring, she thought. "What if I go into the ladies' room and your mother walks in after me?"

He never hesitated. "Run."

And then he laughed, making her feel infinitely better. As if she could do anything, face anything. As long as he was there with her. How had he become so important to her so quickly? A few weeks ago, she hadn't even known he existed. Moreover, she'd been firm in her resolve to leave things like love hidden away on some back shelf, completely out of sight.

And now…

And now there it was, she realized, front and center. Love.

Oh my God—she loved him?

The realization—the very thought—had nerves jumping through her again. It took a great deal of effort on her part to bank them all down before they finally reached the gallery.

* * *

The Sunrise Gallery was one very large room that faced the street. It had cathedral ceilings and stark white walls that were repainted on a regular basis. The snow-white walls acted as a dramatic backdrop for the paintings that continually found their way through the front door.

Right now, the gallery was crammed with patrons, would-be patrons and Lily's well-wishers. It was a gathering of the famous, the not-so-famous and the wealthy unknowns. Smoking had long since been banned from the city's buildings but the air was thick with voices.

When Georges opened the front door for her, the wall of sound hit Vienna hard. She was tempted to hang back. "I didn't realize that there'd be so many people," she confessed.

Georges took her hand and crossed the threshold. The door closed behind them, sealing them in. "Neither did I. Looks like Mother went all out spreading the word."

Slipping his hand around her waist reassuringly, Georges guided her away from the entrance and toward the displays.

Vienna looked at him curiously. "Can't imagine why she'd have to. The very mention of her paintings would bring people in."

"Oh, this isn't a showing of her paintings."

Vienna didn't understand. She looked at the small grouping of abstract paintings closest to her. "Then whose—"

"Her…friend's." Stuck for the right term, he pulled the all-purpose label into service. "Kyle Winterset or Summerfield or some such name involving one of the seasons."

"Autumn," Alain said, coming up behind them. He clamped down one hand on his brother's shoulder. The other held a glass of champagne. A half-empty glass of champagne. His eyes shifted to the woman beside his brother. The interest was impossible to miss. "His name is Kyle Autumn."

Georges didn't remember hearing that last name. Had to be a last-minute decision of his mother's. "You're kidding."

Wearing a tuxedo like his brother, Alain lifted his broad shoulders in a careless shrug. "That's what Mother says." He gestured toward a far wall with his glass. "Some of his efforts aren't half-bad." Taking a sip of champagne, he smiled into his glass. "Of course, his efforts with Mother are spectacular." Lowering the glass again, he looked at Vienna. "Hello. My uncouth brother seems to have completely forgotten his manners and lost the ability to speak, so while he's just standing there, posing for the park's next statue, let me do the honors and introduce myself. I'm Alain Dulac, Georges' younger brother." Lifting her hand, he brought it to his lips in the courtly fashion of an era long gone. And then he raised his eyes to hers. "And you are…?"

"Not impressed," Georges informed him before Vienna could reply. Taking possession of his younger brother's arm, he drew Alain away from Vienna.

"Territorial," Alain commented, nodding with approval as he looked from his brother to the woman in shimmering blue. "Sounds promising." Moving closer to her, Alain said in a stage whisper, "He's never brought any of his ladies to one of Mother's shows."

Georges took matters into his own hands. If he didn't, he had a feeling that Alain would feel tempted to monopolize Vienna all night. Not that he could blame him.

"Go fill up your glass, Alain," Georges urged. Turning his brother away from Vienna, he placed both hands on Alain's shoulders and propelled him toward a waiter. The latter was moving through the crowd, offering glasses of champagne to those without liquid libation. "Alone" again, he focused on Vienna. "Don't mind Alain," he told her. "He likes to run off at the mouth. He's a lawyer, so it's pretty much an occupational hazard."

She'd liked Alain, she thought. And the two got on like typical brothers. An only child, she envied Georges a little. "He seems nice."

Georges made a sound that was swallowed up by the crowd's noise. "Operative word here being *seems.*"

Well, one hurdle passed without incident. But Alain wasn't the main attraction. Vienna drew in a breath. "When do I get to meet your mother?"

"Now." He barely had time to utter the single word—or was it more of a warning?—before Lily swooped down on them.

Vienna swung around in time to see a diminutive, shapely woman with raven-black hair and eyes the color of violets in the spring materialize behind her. Her nails and lips were scarlet. The rest of her was all in black.

On her, black seemed like a lively color.

"Welcome, welcome," Lily declared with the dramatic intonation she was famous for. Not standing on ceremony, she enveloped Vienna in an embrace, pressing her against an ample chest that would have been more in keeping with a far larger woman. "I'm Lily and you must be…?" She looked from Vienna to her son, waiting for a name. Wanting to have been filled in yesterday.

"Vienna Hollenbeck," Georges said, which was good because she seemed to have temporarily lost her voice.

"Vienna," Lily echoed. And then she nodded her approval. "What a charming name." Releasing her, Lily took half a step back and extended her hand to her. "Well, I'm Lily Moreau," she said needlessly, as if she could be anyone else. "Georges' mother."

Not foremost, Georges thought. Lily had never been just a mother to any of them. It had always seemed more like a footnote, an afterthought, even though she'd always been careful to see that they were well cared for. But he was beginning to think that maybe Philippe was right. Lily seemed to be trying to make up for a huge amount of lost time.

Well, if anyone could do it, Lily could.

Turning away from them for a moment, Lily extended her hand to someone just behind her, beckoning to him with her fingertips. Scarlet spiders moving through the air.

When he joined her, she slipped both her arms through his and smiled. Damn, but she seemed content, Georges thought. When had she last looked like that?

"And this is Kyle Autumn," she was saying to Vienna. "My protégé."

So that was what they were calling it these days, Georges thought. Kyle was tall and thin, with jet-black hair. He wore a black turtleneck sweater and black slacks, looking for all the world like a throwback to the beat era of the fifties. But his mother had a penchant for black and he had a feeling that Kyle did everything in his power to please her and remain on Lily's good side.

He refused to think about how far Kyle's efforts extended.

Kyle towered over the famed artist. "And she is my muse, my angel," Kyle told them. The statement was punctuated by a light kiss pressed against the top of Lily's head.

Georges experienced a sudden desire to punch that very good-looking jaw, but refrained.

Oblivious to her son's thoughts, Lily seemed appropriately pleased by Kyle's words. "Kyle, you know my son, Georges. This—" scarlet fingertips gestured toward Vienna "—is Vienna Hollenbeck, his…"

Lily let her voice trail off, waiting for one of them to fill in the glaring blank she'd left open.

Instinctively, she knew that Georges would want to avoid any labels being thrown at whatever it was they had between them. So Vienna took the conversation in a different direction. "Dr. Armand is my grandfather's doctor. He saved his life," she told Lily, then added, "And mine."

Very carefully sculpted eyebrows narrowed over dramatic eyes. Lily seemed to be looking right into her. "Is that figuratively, or literally?"

Both, Vienna thought. But out loud, she replied, "Literally."

The answer seemed to please the mother in Lily.

"I need to hear all about it," Lily declared, slipping her arm through Vienna's.

Georges almost laughed. For a fleeting moment, the expression on Vienna's face looked as if she were being kidnapped by a hoard of Vikings and whisked off to the deck of their ship as their booty.

"Shouldn't you be mingling with your other guests?" Georges suggested tactfully. He glanced at the so-called guest of honor. "Introducing them to Kyle's work?"

To his surprise, when his mother glanced at him, there was gratitude in her smile.

She thinks I've accepted him, Georges realized. When had his opinion, or the opinion of his brothers, mattered to her? He loved his mother and he was certain, in her own fashion, she loved all of them, but he had never thought of her as the garden variety mother who wanted to matter to her children or who sought their approval, however covertly. This was something new.

Lily clapped her hands together, suddenly struck by a thought, her subtle interrogation of Vienna, for the moment, placed on hold. "I almost forgot, Georges. I have a gift for you."

He looked at her, a little stunned. "A gift? Why? What's the occasion?" Gifts came on birthdays and Christmas. Tons of them. Sometimes even in the right size. Lily was generous and lavish, though thoughtful rarely ever entered into it.

"Your graduation from the residency program," she declared, her expression asking how he could have possibly forgotten that.

"That's not for another few months, Mother," he tactfully reminded her.

Undaunted, she waved her hand at the reminder. "So, I'm a little early. Why wait until the last minute?" She turned toward the tall, handsome man beside her. "Kyle, be a darling and bring me the box from the back room."

Georges knew for a fact that the "back room" was actually the office where the owner of the gallery conducted his day-to-day business. But, as they all knew, when his mother moved in, she commandeered everything in her path and it all became hers.

He watched as his mother looked after Kyle as he disappeared from view. Like a schoolgirl watching her first crush, he thought. He wondered how concerned he and his brothers should be.

Kyle returned quickly, carrying a large rectangular box before him. When he brought it to her, Lily shook her head.

"Not to me, to him." She pointed at her son. Shifting, Kyle presented the large box to Georges. "Open it," Lily coaxed, sounding very much like an eager child on Christmas morning. "Open it."

Curious now himself, Georges did as she requested. Silver wrapping rained down to his feet as he tore it away. Vienna held the bottom of the box for him as he lifted the lid and found himself looking down at—

"A defibrillator?" he asked, looking up at Lily quizzically.

His mother nodded. "You want to be a heart surgeon, don't you?" she asked, obviously proud that she remembered. And then uncertainty entered her eyes. "Or have you changed your mind?"

"No, I haven't changed my mind," he assured her, looking back down at the box and its contents again. Heart surgery was his eventual goal, but that was going to require two more years of residency, hopefully again at Blair.

"Then this is perfect for you," she declared, then flashed a pleased smile.

They had the same smile, Vienna thought.

"This way," Lily was saying to him, "if my heart stops beating, you can zap me back to the land of the living without my having to go to that wretched hospital." To Lily, all hospitals were wretched and meant to be avoided at all costs. She beamed at him. It was the most expensive one she could find. "Do you like it?" she wanted to know. "Tell me you like it. If you don't, I can always exchange it for—"

He didn't even want to imagine what was running through her head. "I like it, Mother, I like it," he told her with the feeling he knew she required. Holding on to his gift, he stooped to kiss her cheek. "You're one of a kind."

"Yes, I know," she replied, looking pleased with herself. Forgetting about the inquest she'd wanted to conduct, Lily turned to Kyle. "Now we can go and mingle, my love."

Still holding the box with the defibrillator in it, Georges eyed Vienna to see how she'd weathered her first encounter with his mother.

"She's a little like a hurricane," he repeated his earlier description. "If you're left standing in her wake, you're doing well."

That, Vienna thought, was a gross understatement.

Chapter Thirteen

Once she realized that there was nothing to be nervous about, Vienna had a wonderful time at the gallery.

She had an even better time afterward.

Given Georges' careless-charmer reputation and the intimate level of their present relationship, it surprised Vienna that he took nothing for granted when it came to her feelings. After spending a good twenty minutes saying goodbye to his mother and her protégé, his brother Alain and the man's date, and his brother Philippe, who was there with his fiancée, Janice, as well as Janice's sparkling jewel of a daughter, Kelli, Georges escorted her out of the gallery. Taking her arm, he hustled her across the parking lot and to his sports car.

Just as he unlocked and opened the passenger-side door for her, he surprised her by whispering against her hair, "I know you want to get back to your grandfather, but why don't you make a call to Silvia and see how he's doing?"

"Why?"

She searched his face, wondering if he knew something she didn't. Had Georges gotten a call from the nurse while she was talking to Janice or one of the other patrons at the gallery? Had he kept it to himself, not wanting to spoil her time? The nerves she'd successfully eradicated earlier came rushing back.

But Georges seemed untroubled. "Because I thought if he was doing well, maybe we wouldn't have to call an end to the evening so soon."

Relieved, she glanced at her watch. "It's not evening anymore. It's very early morning."

"Semantics," he responded, amused. Once inside the vehicle, he looked at her to gauge her feelings. "Does that mean you don't want to stop at my place for a nightcap?"

She wasn't interested in a nightcap, but she was interested in his place. She'd never seen where he lived before. The fact that he wanted to bring her there was a large step forward.

"Maybe just for a few minutes," Vienna allowed, doing her best not to sound as excited as she felt. As she took out her cell phone, she saw that he was grinning. "What?"

"What I have in mind might take a little longer than just a few minutes." His eyes were teasing her as he buckled up. "Unless we *really* hurry."

She couldn't have restrained the smile that rose to her lips even if she'd been sucking on a lemon. "Maybe for more than a few minutes," she amended.

He put the car in gear. "Sounds good to me."

And it was good. Oh, so good. For both of them.

So good, she thought later, that the very word needed a new meaning, one that took in the presence of flashing lights, electrical currents flowing through limbs and a complete spectrum of adjectives that bowed before the altar of ecstasy.

They'd made love now more than a few times, and each time was better than the last. Almost different from the last. It still surprised her that she could experience this heightened state of pleasure. Lovemaking with Edward had been nice. Satisfying most of the time, but after the first time, it had become almost routine to the point that she worried about her own response. She knew what to expect. Edward made love by the numbers.

If Edward played the kazoo, Georges was the

whole damn orchestra, she thought. She'd quickly discovered that she never knew *what* to expect. There was always the promise of something new, something wondrous each and every time they made love together.

He taught her that she could climax in a myriad of ways, enjoy a myriad of sensations, all slightly different from one another. And she never, *ever* knew which she would experience.

Or for how long. Some climaxes tiptoed in before pouncing, others exploded with a teeth-jarring crescendo and then softly slipped away. Still others seemed to go on and on for so long, she thought she was going to expire from sheer sweet agony.

But covertly woven through the pleasure was the dreaded realization that a man like this was not going to stay. A man like this would, sooner or later, find himself straying to new ground, in search of new conquests.

Vienna was on borrowed time, and she knew it.

The knowledge made her try to savor everything as much as she could, to make love with him in the fullest sense of the word. It helped her not to think about the future.

She couldn't help but think of the future.

Turning toward her on his bed as the euphoria of their last joining began to fade away, Georges saw the sadness in her eyes before she had a chance to bank it down. "What's the matter?"

Vienna forced a smile to her lips, but it was just that. Forced. "Nothing."

He traced the outline of her lips with his fingertip. "Nothing was making you frown, hence it has to be something."

When she said nothing in response, Georges pressed his lips to her bare shoulder. She had to struggle not to shiver, not to turn into him and just cling. The last thing a man such as Georges wanted was someone clinging to him like some hapless damsel in distress. Besides, that wasn't her, she silently insisted. What was going on? She was more independent than that.

Wasn't she?

Because he was still waiting for an answer, she gave him a half truth. "You know when you're very, very happy and you feel it just can't last? That something is going to happen to take that happiness away from you?"

She was thinking of her grandfather, Georges thought. Afraid that the yin and yang of life would take the man from her because she was enjoying herself too much. It wasn't a philosophy he ascribed to.

"It doesn't always have to be that way," he told her, slipping his arms around her waist and pulling her body into his. He did his best to look serious.

"There are documented cases of some people experiencing happiness for decades."

"You're making that up." And she loved him for it, she thought. Loved him for trying to joke her out of it, for trying to make her feel better instead of annoyed that she was marring his own enjoyment.

"You'll have to torture me to get me to admit that," he told her.

"All right," she agreed. "How shall I start?"

Vienna got no further in her teasing. He'd framed her face with his hands and brought her mouth down to his, stealing her breath—and her heart—away again.

Maybe he was right, Vienna thought two weeks later as she glanced over her shoulder toward the dining room. Maybe Georges had actually been right, even though he'd been teasing, and there were cases of happiness that had lasted for decades. Because God knew, she was close to deliriously happy and fervently praying that she would remain that way.

Moving about the kitchen quickly, Vienna deposited the empty beer bottles into the recycling bag and gathered together another eight bottles from the refrigerator. She placed them on the tray.

Voices crisscrossed over one another from the other room, warming her.

Holding her breath, she picked up the tray and walked slowly into the dining room, which had been commandeered tonight by Philippe, Georges, Alain, Gordon and three of their cousins whom she'd met at the gallery show last week: Vinnie, Remy and Beau. Seemingly out of the blue, Georges had suggested to her that he and the others bring their weekly poker game over here. Specifically to her grandfather. He'd broached the idea within Amos's hearing range. The old man had perked up considerably and was overjoyed at the prospect of having so much testosterone gathered together under his roof.

She, on the other hand, although thrilled by the thought of her grandfather having company, hadn't exactly been keen on the idea of having him gamble. He wasn't really all that good. But then Georges had explained that they bet with toothpicks, not money, and that the big winner collected a prize, a chore of his choosing performed by the big loser of the evening.

That was right up her grandfather's alley.

Miraculously enough, Vienna noted as she set down the tray on the side table, her grandfather seemed to be winning. She began to distribute the bottles, wondering if her grandfather's winning streak was due to luck or design.

"How's it going?" she asked cheerfully, placing

an opened bottle before Philippe and then another before Alain.

Georges frowned as he made a show of studying his hand. "You didn't tell me that in another life, your grandfather was a riverboat gambler."

"Just lucky." Amos chuckled. He looked as pleased as a child at Christmas who'd discovered Santa Claus's bag of toys.

She paused in her bottle distribution to plant a kiss on the crown of his snow-white head. "You always were that," she agreed affectionately.

Looking back at the table, he patted the hand that had dropped to his shoulder. "I was to have gotten you as my granddaughter."

Taking a last long look at his hand as Amos placed another bet, Alain blew out a breath and folded his cards. "Well, I'm out."

Vinnie followed suit, tossing down his hand. "Me, too."

"Call," Philippe said, tossing in the same number of toothpicks that Amos had used to raise the stacks.

A show of the remaining cards around the table had Amos being the big winner again. The old man beamed as he drew the colorful assortment to toothpicks to himself, adding to his pile.

Smiling to herself, Vienna took her empty tray and retreated to the kitchen.

"I'm going to sit the next hand out," Georges announced, rising.

Walking into the kitchen, he found Vienna working at the counter, making another batch of sandwiches. She'd been feeding them all night. He'd already told her that she didn't have to do that, but he couldn't seem to get her to pay attention. The lady had a mind of her own, he thought fondly.

"Need any help?" he asked.

Taking a long serrated bread knife, she cut the sandwich she'd just completed in half. She noted Gordon had been wolfing them down as if he hadn't eaten in days. Losing made him hungry, she thought.

Placing the sandwich on a plate, she turned from the counter and reached for a towel to wipe her fingers. "You've already done plenty," she told him.

"All I did was lose a bunch of blue and green toothpicks. And a couple of gold ones," he recalled. Coming up behind her, he slipped his arms around her waist, enjoying the way they seemed to fit together no matter what the angle. Resting his cheek against the top of her head, he paused to inhale the fragrance of her shampoo. It made him think of wildflowers. "Your grandfather's one sharp player."

Vienna laughed shortly. "And you, sir, are one really poor liar." Discarding the towel, she turned around to face him, her body brushing against his, sending electrical pulses through them both. "I would have thought that a man with a harem of women in his past history would be a better liar than that."

"Whoa, what harem?" he asked, looking properly indignant. "No harem, Vienna. I'm as innocent as a lamb." Georges did his best to look simple and unworldly.

She only laughed. The man had probably ceased being innocent the second he'd hit puberty. Rather than strands of jealousy, she felt only affection.

"The hell you are." She threaded her arms around his neck. Ever so subtly, her body leaned into his. "You've made him very happy, Georges. I can't tell you what that means to me."

He nodded solemnly. "There are times when words fail." And then, unable to keep a straight face any longer, he laughed as his eyes shone. "Maybe you can show me later instead."

"I'd be happy to."

The counter at her back, Vienna rose up on her toes, her eyes never leaving his. She kissed him then, long and hard and with an endless gratitude that seemed to spill out and go on spilling. When they drew apart for a breath, she could still feel her heart swelling with the affection she felt.

"I love you." The next moment, to her horror, her

words came echoing back to her. Her eyes widened in shock as she looked up at him, trying to read his reaction. God, but she hadn't meant to say that. Nothing drove a man away faster than hearing those words prematurely. "Sorry," she apologized quickly. Vienna could feel her throat tightening up as a panic threatened to set in. "That just slipped out. I tend to say 'I love you' when I'm very happy. It doesn't mean anything, really," she assured him with a wee bit too much feeling.

Didn't it? he wondered. Looking into her eyes, he found he couldn't tell. She'd suddenly masked her feelings from him.

"That's a shame," he told her. "Because it sounded nice."

He'd never had a woman tell him that before. That she loved him. Partly because, he surmised, he had never stayed around long enough for a woman to feel the kind of emotions that would prompt her to say that. Until this very moment, he'd always thought himself lucky not to be entangled in that sort of web, where basic feelings came out to play and wound up complicating everything they came in contact with.

Maybe he was wrong, Georges thought now as he looked down into her face.

Maybe he hadn't been lucky not to hear it. Because hearing her say she loved him had stirred something inside him, something that had been dormant—possibly forever.

He wasn't really sure what to do with this new feeling, but he knew it bore closer scrutiny.

Had she upset him? Was he serious? She hadn't a clue. Her best bet, she decided, was to be philosophical, because she had absolutely no idea what kind of ground she was standing on, whether it was rock solid or oatmeal soft.

"Well, it certainly does sound nicer than hearing someone shout, 'I hate you,'" she agreed. The tips of her fingers grew damp. Time to change the subject quick, she thought, before there turned out to be no way out.

She cleared her throat and nodded toward the large rectangular box she had on the far end of the counter. She'd brought it home with her from the bakery. Very carefully, she removed her arms from around his neck and took a step away. She picked up the sandwich she'd just made for Gordon. "Since you want to help, why don't you carry that box in for me?"

He went to do as she asked. The box was huge. Georges glanced at her over his shoulder. "Another defibrillator?" he teased. "I've still got the one my mother gave me in the trunk of my car."

He'd been meaning to put it away since the night at the gallery, but somehow, he never thought of it until well after he was already home and in bed, usually exhausted beyond words after putting in double shifts at the hospital.

"No, something some people might say necessitates having a defibrillator in the trunk of your car." She paused to point at the logo on the side of the box. It was a drawing of a girl munching a jelly donut. Her grandfather had once told her he'd given a photo of her at age four to an artist and this was what he had designed. "Pastries," she told him.

He picked up the box, ready to follow her out. "I knew that."

Coming back into the dining room again, Vienna was greeted by the sound of her grandfather's laughter as the man responded to something Philippe said to him. It warmed her heart.

"Thanks," Gordon said heartily as she placed a roast beef sandwich before him.

She smiled her response, then looked at the other faces around the oval table. "All right, gentlemen," she announced, "whenever you're ready, there are pastries from my grandfather's bakery awaiting your pleasure." Once Georges placed the box on the side table, she removed the lid to expose more than twenty different kinds of confection.

She could almost hear everyone's mouth watering.

"*Our* bakery," Amos corrected, raising his voice as he looked at her pointedly. "Everything that's mine is yours, Vienna, you know that."

She pretended to eye the colorful mass of toothpicks gathered on the table before him. "Including your toothpicks?" she teased.

Without realizing it, she slanted a look toward Georges. If she were the evening's big winner and he the loser, she knew exactly what she'd ask for as her prize.

A huge, pleased grin slipped over her grandfather's face. His color had completely returned and he looked exactly the way she always thought of him, exactly the way he had looked when he had first come into her life to take care of her.

"*Almost* everything," Amos amended. And then he took on his rightful role as host, gesturing toward the box of pastries. "Please," he urged his guests, "eat up and then we will continue playing." His expression was positively mischievous as he added, "I have leaves in my gutters that need removing."

His mouth full of a cruller, Vinnie glanced at Vienna. "Is that some kind of Austrian idiom?"

"Only for those Austrians with rain gutters," she deadpanned.

And then she laughed as Georges came up behind her and wrapped his arms around her in a bear hug. Out of the corner of her eye, she saw the contented look on her grandfather's face as he sat back in his chair, observing them.

He looked happy, she thought. Maybe happiness *could* go on indefinitely.

At least she could hope.

Chapter Fourteen

"He's in his element, and he's happy."

Abruptly breaking the silence and the rhythm of slow, easy breathing that came after lovemaking, Vienna began talking to Georges about her grandfather.

Though he'd asked after the man's health, Georges hardly heard her. His own thoughts were filling up the spaces in his head.

They were lying on his bed. An initial outing that had the preview of a new, Broadway-bound play at its core had somehow morphed into this, another wild, tempestuous meeting of the body and the soul.

It was not the first time they'd gotten sidetracked like this. The exceedingly enjoyable interlude just further fueled the realization that, after six weeks together—hardly a lifetime—Vienna Hollenbeck was swiftly becoming the center of his universe, something that had never happened to him before, and certainly not to this degree.

It also brought home the fact that he needed to get out—now—before there was no turning back. Before he stood there naked in the town square, waiting to be incinerated. Because he knew, by example, that it could happen.

"But I can't help feeling that he's doing too much," Vienna was saying. "He refuses to take things slow, no matter what I say. He went back full-time last week, working hours like he used to. All his customers were thrilled to see him, and he looked like a kid at Christmas." She caught her lower lip between her teeth, still staring up at the ceiling, trying to find a way to bank down her fears. About everything. "Ordinarily, I'd say that was the best medicine in the world for him, but—"

It took a beat for him to realize that she'd stopped talking. That, her voice trailing off, she'd turned to look at him.

She was waiting for him to say something. He replayed her words in his head as best he could. There were gaps. "You're worried about him."

"That's what I've been saying."

Georges' response bothered her. He wasn't here tonight, she thought. Even at the height of their lovemaking, when she felt as if the very walls were catching fire, she'd had this distant, uneasy sense that part of him wasn't there with her. That hadn't happened before.

The beginning of the end? Vienna wondered.

All along, amid her happiness, she'd been dreading this. Anticipating this. Pretending it wasn't going to come, knowing that it would because he was who he was. She was a nester and he was a man who moved from hotel to hotel. In her heart, she'd always known that she was just a stop along his route.

When in doubt, make doctor noises, Georges thought. Besides, though the last exam had been excellent, Vienna might have a point. Her grandfather might be having some kind of relapse. No sense in taking a chance.

"Bring him by the hospital tomorrow," he said. "I can have a few tests done." He smiled at her. "Put your fears to rest."

Not that easy, she said silently. In either case. But out loud, she only focused on one concern. "He'll say he's too busy."

Georges smiled. "If anyone can make him, you can. Besides, I'm his doctor. And he likes me."

She did her best not to let him sense the tension that all but snapped through her veins. "Yes, he does."

And so do I, God help me. So much that I can hardly breathe. How am I going to stand it when you go?

Georges took in a long breath and glanced at his watch. "Well, our little detour cost us the play. Sorry about that," he apologized. "No sense in walking in on the last third—unless you want to," he tagged on, giving her the option.

But she shook her head. "No, that's all right," Vienna murmured.

"We still have late reservations at the restaurant," he remembered. "We could easily make that."

Whatever appetite she'd had had fled in the wake of this uneasiness. "No, I'm not really hungry. Maybe we should just call it a night."

If he'd had his head caught in a cement mixer, he would have still picked up on the desolation in her voice. Georges sat up. "Something wrong?"

Now there's an understatement. The smile that curved her mouth was the epitome of sadness even though she tried hard to lock her feelings away. "Depends if you're you or me."

Something was very wrong here, Georges thought. Was she clairvoyant despite her protests? Had she picked up on something, on the thoughts shuffling through his head? He didn't want to hurt her for the world. He just didn't want to hurt himself, either. "I'm not sure I follow."

"Because you don't follow, you lead." Vienna sat up, too, and as she did, she reached for the clothes that had been haphazardly tossed aside in the frantic quest for fulfillment and fleeting ecstasy. "Look, we both know that this is just an interlude." She got out of bed. "A wonderful, wonderful interlude, at least for me, but it's not the beginning of something." Vienna turned to face him, regal in her stance despite the fact that the only clothing she had on was what she was holding against her. Her eyes held his for a moment. "When this is over—" she couldn't bring herself to pronounce its demise just yet "—I want you to tell me. I don't want you here a moment longer than you want to be."

He wished he could somehow reassure her even as he wanted to back away. "What brought this on?"

"You." Vienna held her clothes tighter, as if that could somehow keep her from crying. "I can feel you withdrawing."

God, she knew him better than he knew himself, he thought.

Very softly, she told him, "I just want you to know I understand." Vienna looked away, afraid that she was going to break down. There was an emptiness hovering on the edges of her being, threatening to leap forward and swallow her up if she didn't keep moving, didn't keep sidestepping it somehow. "I'd like to go home now, if you don't mind."

Vienna didn't wait for his answer. Instead, she went into his bathroom and shut the door. When she came out five minutes later, he was already dressed. He wasn't trying to talk her out of it. Wasn't even trying to deny what she'd guessed. Which meant that she was right.

It was over.

She was making it easy for him. She knew that. But then, she didn't want to cling to him. It wouldn't mean anything that way. The only way she wanted him in her life was if he truly wanted to be there. And it was obvious that he didn't.

The ride home was filled with music from the radio, but it didn't block out the silence within the car. The silence encroaching like a malevolent force, feeding on itself.

Vienna was painfully aware of it. Painfully aware that for the first time since she'd met him, Georges wasn't talking to her, wasn't making her laugh or feel better about a given situation. His silence was agreement. She'd never hated being right so much in her life.

The ache inside her grew with every passing moment, every passing mile. And then they were at her door. He pulled the car up at the curb in front of her mailbox.

She had her hand on the door handle, ready to leap from the car. "You don't have to come out," she protested, but he did anyway.

He still wasn't sure what had happened, how this had evolved out of some of the most satisfying love-making he'd ever experienced. Either he was transparent to her, he decided, or she really was clairvoyant.

In either case, he wasn't just going to eject her out of the vehicle and take off. "I'm walking you to your door," he told her firmly.

Maybe this was a mistake. Even though part of him was grateful to her for making it so easy for him, for giving him an escape hatch, part of him felt an incredible, overwhelming sadness descend over him, the magnitude of which he'd never dealt with before. The sadness told him that maybe it already was too late. Maybe this one had come to mean more to him than anyone before her and that he'd be a fool to leave her.

Damn, up was down and down was up, and he'd lost his compass.

His course of action with women had always been so clear-cut, so natural for him before now. He'd never been confused before, never had his emotions tied up in knots before. Because no one had ever meant more than just having a good time and living in the moment.

He wanted more. He wanted lots of moments.

Damn it, go! Go before you make the biggest mistake of your life, a voice in his head ordered urgently, even as he walked her to the door.

"I was serious about you bringing him in tomorrow," he told her.

Vienna nodded, valiantly trying to concentrate on her grandfather and his health, and nothing more. Amos Schwarzwalden deserved nothing less from her and she was going to wrap herself up in her responsibilities and duties, using them to help her get over this.

She tried her best not to allow her voice to sound shaky. "I'll get in touch with you after I have a chance to talk to my grandfather."

Georges nodded. Guilt, indecision and sorrow dueled madly within him, gluing him in place.

"Vienna—" he began, not knowing what he was going to say after that.

There was no need to worry. She was already turning away. A second later, she'd let herself into the house, closing the door behind her.

Georges stood for a moment, staring at the door, wondering if he should make an excuse to knock and ask her to let him come in. But then he took a breath and turned away. He began to walk to his car.

It was better this way. Better for him, for her.

Better that he should—

He heard the door swing open and then bang on the opposite wall as Vienna screamed out his name. His heart froze.

Instantly, he came running back to her. He knew without being told that the look on her face had nothing to do with what had just happened between them.

"It's my grandfather." Her throat was so tight with fear, she could hardly get the words out, hardly get any air in. "This way—"

Clamping on to his hand, she ran back so fast, she was all but dragging him in her wake.

Amos was in the kitchen, lying facedown and unconscious on the floor.

"He's not breathing," she sobbed. "I tried to make him breathe, but I can't."

Dropping to his knees, Georges dug into his pocket. He threw her his car keys. "I've still got that defibrillator in the trunk of my car." Silently he blessed his mother. "Get it," he ordered as he began manual CPR.

Trembling, Vienna missed the keys when he threw them. Picking them up, she dashed outside. She was back almost before she left.

"Here," she cried, dropping to her knees beside him with the defibrillator in her arms. "Do something," she begged. "Bring him back." She knew how unreasonable that sounded, but she didn't want to be reasonable; she wanted to be a granddaughter. Amos's granddaughter.

"I'm trying, Vienna, I'm trying. Plug it in," he told her.

Once the defibrillator was sufficiently charged and up and running, Georges picked up the paddles.

"Call 911," he told her. "He's going to have to go back to the hospital."

For a split second, she felt paralyzed. She could only stare at what Georges was doing. "But he's going to be all right, isn't he? Isn't he?" she demanded.

"I'm doing my best," he shouted. "Now make the damn call!"

By the time she'd gotten the dispatch's promise to send an ambulance right away, Georges had gotten her grandfather's heartbeat back.

Rocking back on his heels, feeling more drained than the man lying before him, Georges told her, "It's beating again."

She didn't realize she was crying until then. Her cheeks were wet and a teardrop fell on her collarbone. She wanted to throw herself over her grandfather, to hold him close to her and will her life force into his. But she was afraid if she did, the jarring motion might do something to change the status quo.

She was afraid to even breathe.

Moving forward, she took the old man's hand in hers. "You live, you hear me, old man?" she instructed through gritted teeth. She had to blink twice in order to see him. Her eyes were filling up with tears. "You can't leave me to handle everything, Grandpa. It's not fair. I need you. You have to live. I need you," she repeated, her voice breaking.

She could have sworn she saw the tiniest of smiles curve the old man's lips just then.

He'd heard her, she thought, clinging to that thought as if it were a life preserver in a choppy, erratic ocean. He'd heard her. He was going to live. Never once had her grandfather denied her anything she'd asked for.

Her grandfather was going to be all right. She wouldn't let him not be.

The diagnosis came as no surprise. Amos had had a massive heart attack. Although they'd gotten his heart to begin beating on its own again, the coma he'd slipped into continued, mocking every effort Georges attempted to bring him around.

One day came and went, bringing another in its wake. There was no change in Amos's condition. Vienna sat by his side, keeping vigil. Other people came to the hospital to visit him, a great many people. Raul had put out the word that the friendly

Austrian baker had taken a turn for the worse after seemingly being on the mend.

Because Amos had been placed in the coronary care unit for proper monitoring, visitors were supposedly restricted to two per hour for a total of five minutes each. No one paid attention to the rules. The nurses complained to them, to Vienna and to the doctor, all to no avail. Eventually, since the visitors were quiet and respectful, if persistent, the nurses surrendered.

And through it all, there was a growing concern not only for the comatose patient, but for the young woman who sat, waiflike, holding his hand, talking to him and praying.

Unable to cast a blind eye to what was happening before her any longer, the head day nurse, Chantal Reese, a twenty-six-year hospital veteran, not to mention the grandmother of five, decided to voice her opinion. Placing her ample figure in his path before Georges could walk down the corridor to Amos' sroom, she completely stopped him in his tracks.

He looked at her quizzically. "Something wrong, Chantal?"

"Yes, something's wrong. It's that girl."

"Girl?" he repeated.

"The old man's granddaughter." Before he could ask what she was talking about, she told him. "Dr. Armand, in the last three days, she's hardly moved out of that chair. Lord knows I haven't seen her eat anything, just drink a little water now and again. She's going to need one of our beds herself soon if she keeps this up." Though the other nurses swore the woman ate new hires for lunch on a regular basis, there was nothing but compassion in Chantal's wide, dark face. "Can't you talk any sense into her?"

He'd been concerned about Vienna himself. But every time he thought of telling her to go home, something in her eyes forbade him from making the suggestion. Over the last three days, she had been getting progressively more fragile.

"I can try," he told the nurse. "But she's a very stubborn young woman."

Chantal snorted, waving a dismissive hand at his protest. "Never known any woman who wouldn't listen to you once you got that sweet tongue of yours in gear, Dr. A." She gave him a knowing look.

"You give me way too much credit," he told her as he began to walk away.

"Not from what I hear." Her words followed him down the corridor.

That, he thought, was all behind him. Though he hadn't had much interaction with Vienna these last three days, except at her grandfather's bedside, he found himself in a kind of limbo. Free to resume the life he'd once led but with absolutely no inclination to do so.

Georges walked into the small cubicle allotted each patient within CCU. There was hardly enough room for proper maneuvering. At the moment, space was being taken up by a myriad of machines that kept tabs on every vital function the human body offered up for viewing.

Vienna was in a chair beside her grandfather's bed, holding his hand just the way she had been every other time he'd walked in. For a moment, she seemed oblivious to him. She was talking to Amos as if he was just asleep rather than comatose.

Chantal was right, he thought. Vienna's face appeared to be getting gaunt.

Just as he was about to say something to her, Vienna raised her eyes to his. "He won't wake up," she told him. Her voice was so incredibly sad that it threatened to break his heart. Letting out a ragged breath, she gazed back to the old man in the bed. "I shouldn't have left him." Each syllable was so pregnant with guilt.

"When?" According to Chantal and the other nurses on duty, Vienna hadn't left the old man's side for more than a few minutes in three days.

She pressed her lips together, trying to gain control over herself, over her voice. "The night we were supposed to see the play. I shouldn't have left him," she repeated. Despite her best efforts, a tear slipped down her cheek. She wiped it away with the back of her hand. "If I'd been there—"

"He would have still had his heart attack," Georges told her firmly.

He refrained from putting his arms around her, although the urge was strong. Ever since her grandfather had been brought there, it was as if she was steeling herself against any human contact. All her energy seemed to be focused on being with her grandfather. On willing him to health.

"But I could have gotten help for him faster. Who knows how long he was on the floor like that before I found him?" she sobbed.

Precious minutes could make the difference between life and death. She'd heard that over and over again. She'd been berating herself these last three days, wondering when her grandfather'd had his attack. Was it when she was making love with Georges? When he was undressing her? When they lay there in each other's arms?

If he died, she was never going to forgive herself for failing him. For putting her pleasure above his health. She'd known he wasn't well yet.

"You're not to blame for this," Georges told her sternly.

Oh, but she was, she thought.

Her eyes were tortured as she turned to him again. "Can't you find a way to get him out of this somehow?" she begged. "Give him a shot, inject him with something that'll bring him around?"

"Maybe the coma's for the best right now. Think of it as being off-line. The body is trying to heal itself," he told her. "Once it does, it'll be on line again." He felt as if their roles had become reversed. The realist had become the optimist and the optimist had fallen victim to pessimism.

Making note of the vital signs and checking them out for himself, Georges did what he could. He could feel Vienna watching his every move. But there was precious little to do. Nothing had changed.

She couldn't continue this way indefinitely, he thought. "Why don't you go home, get some rest? I can have—"

But she was already shaking her head. "I'll rest when he opens his eyes again," she told him fiercely.

There was nothing he could do, short of physically carrying her out. And who knew? Maybe having her here was the best medicine he could prescribe for Amos. So for now, he retreated.

"I'll be back in an hour," he promised.

"Thank you," she murmured without looking up. She continued holding her grandfather's hand, holding on for dear life. Willing him back among the living.

She heard the door closing as Georges slipped out of the cubicle.

"He is right, you know."

Her eyes flew open. Had she just imagined that?

Imagined her grandfather's voice because she wanted to hear it so badly? But his eyes were open and he was looking up at her.

"Oh Grandpa—" Her voice choked and she couldn't get any more out.

She saw his mouth move, but nothing audible came out. Vienna leaned in closer to hear him. But even then, her heart was pounding so hard, it was difficult to make out his words.

Out of nowhere, a feeling slipped over her. Frantic, she pressed the buzzer for the nurse with her other hand. Hard.

"You need to rest," Amos whispered hoarsely against her ear.

She blinked back tears. The feeling inside her grew more ominous. "And you need to get better."

He was struggling with each word. But even so, his thin lips curved in a weak smile. "Even when I am dying, you argue."

"You're not dying," she cried fiercely, but even as she did, she knew it was true. "You hear me? You're not dying, I won't let you."

Georges came rushing in. He'd just passed the nurses' station when he saw the light from Amos's cubicle go off. Fearing the worst, he'd doubled back.

"I…need to…say…this," Amos insisted, each breath audible. "I…love…you. You have been… the…sunshine of…my life…I don't… want…

you…changing." He tried to turn his head and couldn't. But his words were meant for the young man who had come into his life just in time. "Take…take care…of…her for….me…Georges."

"Nobody is going to take care of me but you, Grandpa. You hear me? Only you. Grandpa? Grandpa? Grandpa, please. Don't go," she pleaded. "Don't go."

But Amos's eyes had closed again and he made no answer to her pleas. She felt his fingers go lax in hers.

Vienna's heart broke.

Chapter Fifteen

Once Raul and Zelda had spread the word at the bakery, Vienna had expected that her grandfather's funeral wouldn't be one of those soul-wrenching, solitary affairs where only she and the presiding priest would attend. She'd always known that, no matter where they called home, everyone loved her grandfather. He was just that kind of man.

But she hadn't expected the church and then the cemetery to be overflowing with people the way it was. Every pew in the small church of St. Thomas Aquinas had been filled and people were rubbing elbows at the Peaceful Passage Cemetery.

And, more than that, she really hadn't expected Georges and his entire family, including his sister-in-law-to-be and her daughter and brother. Vienna knew that the other people, the regular customers and their families, had come because of her grandfather. They'd come to pay their respects and to honor a hardworking man who had gladdened the heart of every person his life had touched.

But Georges and especially his family had come because of her. Not because they knew Amos Schwarzwalden and liked him, but because they knew her. And because they felt that she needed the support.

Had Vienna been able to feel, she would have been greatly touched by their gesture and their kindness.

But she couldn't feel. Not anything.

She'd purposely frozen her heart, throwing herself headlong into not just the details of making the funeral arrangements but in running the bakery. She refused to close it after his death, not even for the three days of the wake. She divided her time between the funeral parlor and the bakery, something neither Raul nor Zelda could talk her out of.

The idea behind it all was that she keep moving to outdistance the pain, to dodge and weave and, at all times, to keep several steps ahead of it. If she stood still, if she allowed herself time to think of *anything* but tiny, cluttering details, she knew in her heart that she was going to fall apart.

That was why, even after the funeral, when a large group of the mourners adjourned and followed her from the cemetery to the house she'd shared with her grandfather—the house that was now so very, very empty to her—Vienna did her best to be everywhere. No detail escaped her. None was too large or too small. She made sure that the trays of food found their way to a buffet table and that everyone's glass was always at least halfway filled. She kept an eye on the napkins and the paper plates, making certain that the supply didn't run out.

Though he wanted to help her, Georges had deliberately stood back and watched Vienna at the church, at the cemetery and now here. He knew that he had to give her space. Had to allow her to deal with her grief as she saw fit.

But she wasn't dealing, she was running. He knew the signs. Having done it himself for a number of different reasons, Georges knew the signs well: you didn't stand still long enough for your emotions to catch up and find you. It was the only way to stay invulnerable, to elude the jaws of pain.

But in Vienna's case, the pain *would* come, *would* find her. Most likely when she was least ready for it. And then, then she was going to implode in a million tiny pieces and cave in.

She couldn't continue this shadow dance, Georges decided.

So, as Vienna scooped up an empty tray that had

held an assortment of macadamia chicken and all but aimed her body toward the kitchen in order to replenish the supply, Georges moved directly in front of her, blocking her swift exit.

"I'll get that," he offered. His hand was on the tray, ready to take it from her. But she wouldn't relinquish her hold.

"No," she told him firmly, pulling the tray back. And then, realizing that she'd practically snapped, she added, "Thank you. But no, I have to do it."

He searched her face, looking for an opening. It was as if she'd just dammed up any access to the person inside.

"What you have to do is stop being so stoic," he told her.

She pulled back her lips in a patient smile. It didn't reach her eyes. "There, good Doctor, you're wrong. I *have* to be stoic."

Out of the corner of her eye, she saw Lily coming toward her. She wanted to run, but it was too late. It wasn't that she didn't appreciate what Georges and his family were trying to do, she just didn't want them doing it. Didn't need them doing it. The kinder they tried to be to her, the harder it was to maintain her barriers. And she desperately needed those barriers to keep back all the pain that threatened to find her. To undo her.

Lily's majestic eyebrows narrowed as she took

in what was happening. "Georges, take that tray from her." Her tone left no room for argument.

Vienna held on to the tray as if it were a lifeline. "No, really." She held the tray closer to her. "Please. I *need* to do this."

But Lily was not to be ignored. Very gently, she peeled away Vienna's fingers and physically took the tray away from her. Once in her possession, she thrust the tray to her middle son.

Eyes the color of newly blossoming African violets remained on her. They were filled with compassion and understanding.

"I know," was all she said. "I know." And then, despite the young woman's initial effort to pull away, she enfolded Vienna in her arms.

Realizing that there was no getting around this, that if she resisted, Lily would only continue and that it would draw attention to them, to *her,* Vienna appeared to surrender and allowed herself to be held. Her face buried against Lily's shoulder, Vienna bit her lower lip, trying to keep the walls inside her from crumbling.

Her mind went elsewhere. She forced herself to try to remember how many small sandwiches she'd ordered and then, that failing, she tried to remember all the movements of the last waltz that Strauss had written.

Strauss's compositions had played at the church during the service and then she'd had them piped in over the loudspeaker at the cemetery. Her grandfather had always loved Strauss. Her earliest memories of him were associated with his very old, scratchy record collection. As a gift one Christmas, she'd given him an entire CD collection, meant to replace the old vinyl records. But she caught him playing the latter anyway. He'd said that playing them reminded him of her late grandmother, who'd felt as he did that waltzes were the only melodies worth listening to.

Hearing the notes today had both gladdened her heart and all but torn it in half. At one point, she'd very nearly lost her resolve.

Just as she was in danger of losing it now.

Lily stepped back, releasing her with a resigned sigh. The woman was savvy enough to know that she hadn't accomplished what she'd set out to do. Vienna was still walled in.

"I'm here if you need me," she told Vienna, squeezing her hand.

"That goes for all of us," Georges told her, leaning in as his mother moved away. His eyes held hers for a moment. "Especially me."

Taking the tray back from him, she pressed her lips together and nodded. "I know."

"Do you?" he questioned. She looked at him, confused. It was a simple enough statement that she had uttered. Why was he challenging it? Challenging her? "Do you realize that you're not alone?" he pressed. "That you don't have to be alone?"

Vienna tried her best to smile, to really smile because he knew the difference, but it was a half-hearted effort.

"Oh, but I am," she whispered.

The next moment, she hurried away, to see to the tray, to see to a thousand and one tiny details that mattered to absolutely no one, but the execution of which kept her sane for a minute longer.

It was how she managed to string together her day and all the days that had come between her grandfather's death and now. One scrambling minute after another until an hour faded and then another and another, forming a day.

Vienna leaned against the door, sighing as her eyes fluttered shut for a moment.

It was over.

The people who had attended her grandfather's funeral and the ceremony at the cemetery were finally gone from the house as well. A wave of relief and fear washed over her at the same time. Relief because she no longer had to pretend for anyone that she was all right, and fear for the same reason.

Because she no longer had to pretend.

Because the rest of her life was staring her in the face and she felt so completely, so devastatingly alone. All these years, ever since her parents had died, it had been just her grandfather and her and in her heart, she'd always hoped to expand those numbers. To fall in love, marry, have children and all the while, have her grandfather there as part of the whole.

She wanted him to know how much she appreciated what he had done for her taking care of her all those years. She wanted him to be proud of the way she'd turned out and to know how grateful she was that he had loved her all those years and been there for her whenever she needed him. And sometimes, during her rebellious years, when she'd insisted that she didn't.

Those were the times when she'd needed him most of all, she thought.

Except for now.

Now she needed him. God, but she needed him. Needed something to block all this emptiness dwelling within her. But he was gone.

Busy, get busy, she silently ordered herself. She'd keep busy until she'd drop from exhaustion and fall asleep. It was the only thing that gave her hope.

Feeling like a sleepwalker, Vienna began to pick up the empty paper plates from the table, gathering them from the various surfaces where they had been left.

Janice and Lily had offered to stay and help. She had politely but firmly refused. She wanted to be alone, she'd said.

She'd gotten good at lying, Vienna thought.

"So where would you like me to start?"

A scream escaped her lips as she swung around. The paper plates she'd been holding slipped from her fingers, landing facedown, dirty side against the carpet.

"I guess there," Georges decided, bending down to pick up the plates and the forks she'd dropped.

Vienna pressed her hand over her heart to keep it from breaking out of her chest. It was pounding hard enough to mimic a drumroll.

"What are you doing here?" She could have sworn there was no one in the house. "I thought you'd left with the others."

"Really not all that memorable to you, am I?" he quipped, continuing to gather together the discarded plates. "So much for having an ego." And then he smiled at her, his eyes softening. "I thought you might need some help—"

"I already told your mother no—"

"—and some company." Georges meandered through the living room and the small dining room beyond, stacking plates and cups wherever he found them.

She raised her chin, the lone defender of an abandoned fort. "I said no to that, too."

He paused for a second to pick up a glass that had been left under her grandfather's baby grand piano. "Yes, I know you did."

She circumvented the piano, following him through the room. "So why are you here?"

He placed the stack he'd made on the buffet table. "Because I don't believe you."

She wasn't going to get pulled into a duel of words. Everything was meaningless, anyway. "It doesn't matter what you believe. It's what I want that matters."

Georges turned from what he was doing to look at her. His eyes seemed to hold hers prisoner. "Exactly." His intonation indicated that he was seeing past the barricade of words she'd thrown up and instead, delving into her soul.

Her eyes narrowed. A surge of anger, red-hot and completely out of the blue, with no rhyme nor reason, overtook her. "You're telling me you know my mind better than I do."

If she meant to get into a fight with him, she failed. He looked completely unflappable. "In essence, yes."

Marching over to the front door, she pulled it open, then stood, waiting. "I want you to leave."

He crossed to her, then caught her off guard by slamming the door shut. It vibrated as it settled into its frame. "No, you don't."

"Yes, I do." But when she tried to pull the door open again, he put his hand over hers, preventing her. Her eyes were shooting angry sparks as she looked at him. "Damn it, why are you doing this to me? You know you don't want to be here."

Where the hell had that come from? And then he knew. She was referring to the last time they'd been together, just before she'd discovered her grandfather. But he no longer wanted to swim the waters he'd been testing then. She needed to know that, he thought.

"I've never wanted to be anywhere so much in my life," he contradicted.

No, she wasn't going to believe him. It was a ruse, however well intended, Vienna thought. "You're saying that because you think I'm hurting."

But Georges slowly shook his head. "No, I'm saying that because without you, I'm hurting."

She began to turn away but he caught her by the shoulders, holding her in place. Needing her to listen.

"I won't deny that I wanted to run. That's been the plan all along. Whenever things looked as if they might get serious, I left." She tried to jerk out of his hold, but he only tightened his hands on her shoulders. She needed to hear all of this.

"But a funny thing happened to me on the way to my next escape. I kept putting it off, until I didn't want to go at all." He searched her face to see if she believed him. "You've taken me prisoner and I don't want to leave."

She blew out a breath, wishing he'd let her go. Wishing he'd stop touching her. Her strength ebbed and she needed him to leave before it did. "You've just described the Stockholm syndrome."

He grinned at the mention of that. "I've always wanted to go visit Stockholm," he confessed. "Maybe we can do it together."

"Sorry, too busy." This time, she did manage to break his hold. Turning her back on him, she retreated into the living room.

He kept up, moving faster so that he got ahead of her. "Not if it's a honeymoon. You'd clear time for a honeymoon, wouldn't you?"

He saw her eyes widening in dazed confusion. He had her, he thought.

Georges pretended to consider the matter as if this hadn't already crossed his mind three times over today. "Can't be right now, but we could schedule it for the summer. They take the shackles off me at the hospital in the summer."

"Wait, wait," Vienna pleaded before he could continue, leaving her gasping in the dust. "What honeymoon?"

He looked at her as if he couldn't understand her confusion. "Our honeymoon."

"Our…" Her voice trailed off. She stared at him as if he'd lost his mind. "You can't have a honeymoon unless you're married."

If his grin had been any wider, an extra mouth would have had to be pressed into service to accommodate it. "Exactly."

All right, he was pulling her leg, having fun at her

expense. Vienna crossed her arms before her. "And when did we get married?" she asked sarcastically.

"We didn't." His eyes met hers. His were infinitely warm, teasing. "Yet."

Okay, enough was enough. "Look, if this is some off-the-wall plan to get me to break down and cry because you think I need closure or some such nonsense, it's not going to work."

He stopped her before she reached the kitchen, blocking her way in. "No, it's some off-the-wall plan to get you to say you'll marry me. Does that work?"

Her mouth fell open. "You're asking me to marry you?"

Very slowly, Georges nodded. "Yes."

He didn't mean that—did he? Oh God, did he? "Seriously?"

"Well, I'm smiling," he allowed, then was as serious as he could be, "but yes, seriously."

The next minute, she realized what had to be going on. "Is this a pity proposal? Are you asking me to marry you because you feel sorry for me and this will snap me out of whatever it is you think I have?"

Damn, this woman could come up with more weird road blocks, more excuses to stop him in his tracks than anyone he'd ever known. But then, like Philippe had said, she was a once-in-a-lifetime woman, and women like that were unique in every way.

"The only pity that's involved is if you say no and

then I should be on the receiving end of that pity, not you. But yes, I do want you to snap out of this invulnerable, iron wrap you've spun around yourself." Because otherwise, he was never going to get through to her, he thought.

Georges tried to take her into his arms, but she shrugged his hands away. But he refused to be put off. He'd stood by, gave her her space for these last four days, and that hadn't worked. Now he was doing it his way, the way his heart told him to. And he wasn't about to back off until he'd won her over.

"Your grandfather wouldn't want you to be like this, Vienna. And he wouldn't want you to turn me down." Georges raised his eyebrows, doing his best to look innocent and affable. "He liked me, remember?"

"You're doing this because of Grandpa?" It all suddenly came together for her. "Because he asked you to take care of me."

The look he gave her said she should know better. "I liked that old man a great deal, Vienna, but trust me, I wouldn't marry someone just because a man I admired asked me to. There's such a thing as free will." He let the words sink in before continuing. "And I'm laying down my free will at your feet." He slipped his arms around her. This time, she didn't push him away. It gave him hope. "Marry me, Vienna."

"Why?" she asked. "Give me one good reason why."

Georges didn't say anything for a moment. Instead, he placed his hands on her face, framing it. "Because I love you."

The moment he said them to her, the moment the words penetrated the armor around her heart, Vienna's eyes welled up. The tears she'd been holding back since her grandfather's death, the tears that had gathered in her soul when she believed that she and Georges were through, broke out.

Vienna began to cry. "That's the reason," she whispered.

His hands were still framing her face and he looked intently into her eyes. "Are those tears of joy, or tears of frustration?"

"Will you stop asking me questions?" Vienna raised her mouth to his.

Her lips were so close, he brushed against them as he said, "Just one more." Vienna drew back her head and looked at him, waiting. "Will you marry me? You haven't answered me yet."

"Yes," she cried. "Now shut up and kiss me."

"I can do that."

And he could. And very, very well, too.

* * * * *

CAPTURING THE MILLIONAIRE

BY
MARIE FERRARELLA

To
Debby, Amy, Maria
And
all the other wonderful volunteers at
The German Shepherd Rescue of Orange County,
thank you for Audrey

Chapter One

It wasn't supposed to rain in October. Not in Southern California, anyway.

Alain Dulac was pretty sure it was a law written down somewhere, like the requirements for Camelot. As he tried to steer his sports car, a vehicle definitely not meant for this kind of weather, he found that his visibility was next to zero. Because, as the old song from the sixties went, it never rained in California—but it poured.

And that's what it was doing now. Pouring. Pouring as if the entire Pacific Ocean had gotten absorbed into the black clouds that were hovering overhead and were now dumping their contents all over him. He would have been alert to the possibility of a flash flood—if he could see more than an inch or so in front of him. He wasn't even sure where he was anymore. For all he knew, he could have gotten turned around and was headed back to Santa Barbara.

By the clock, it was a little after 4:00 p.m. But to all appearances, it looked like the beginning of the Apocalypse. There was even the rumble of thunder, another unheard of event this time of year.

His windshield wipers were fighting the good fight, but it was obvious they were losing. A few seconds of visibility were all their efforts awarded him.

Alain swallowed a curse as the car hit a pocket of some sort and wobbled before continuing on its road to nowhere.

It would have been nice if the weatherman had hinted at this storm yesterday, or even early this morning, he thought darkly. He gripped the steering wheel harder, as if that could afford him better control over his car. If there had been the slightest indication that today was going to turn into something that would have made Noah shudder, Alain would have postponed going up to Santa Barbara to get that deposition until the beginning of next week.

Archie Wallace certainly looked healthy enough

to hang around until Monday. At age eighty-four, the former valet—or gentleman's gentleman, Alain believed the old term was—looked healthier than a good many men half his age. Alain could have waited to get the man's testimony instead of risking life, limb and BMW the way he was right now.

That's what he got for going into family law instead of criminal law. Not that, he'd discovered, there weren't a host of criminal activities going on behind the so-called innocent smiles of the people who came into his firm's office.

For the first time since he'd left Archie's quaint cottagelike home, a hint of a smile curved Alain's lips. Nothing wrong with camera time, he thought. As he turned the notion over in his head, he found that he liked the idea of getting his own spotlight instead of being in one by proxy. Heretofore his main claim to fame was being the youngest of Lily Moreau's sons. His mother, God bless her, was as famous for her lifestyle as she was for her exotically colorful paintings. At times her lifestyle overshadowed her work.

Alain had no doubt that the reporters who'd come to cover her last show were as interested in the dark, handsome, quarter-of-a-century-younger man at her side as they were in the latest paintings that were on display. Kyle Autumn was Alain's mother's protégé and, to hear her talk about him, the love of her life.

At least for this month.

The fact that Alain and his two older brothers each had a different father bore testimony to the fact that Lily loved her men with a passion. But that passion was anything but steadfast.

She was a better mother than she was spouse, and, luckily for the art world, a better artist than she was either of the two.

Alain had no real complaints on that score, though. Long ago he'd realized that Lily was as good a mother as she could be, and he and Georges had always had Philippe. As the oldest, Philippe was more like a father than a brother, and it was from him that Alain had gotten most of his values.

In a way, he supposed that Philippe was responsible for his having gone into family law. Philippe had always maintained that family was everything.

Too bad the Hallidays didn't feel that way. The latest case he was handling was already on its way to becoming this year's family drama. All sorts of accusations were being hurtled back and forth with wild abandon. And the tabloids were having a field day.

To be honest, it wasn't the sort of case Dunstan, Jewison and McGuire ordinarily handled. The venerable hundred-and-two-year-old firm took pride in conducting all matters with decorum and class. This case, however, had all the class of a cable reality program.

But there was an obscenely huge amount of money involved. The firm's share for winning the case for the bereaved and voluptuous widow was something only a saint would have been able to turn away from. The company had had little to keep it going but its reputation these last few years. Which was why Alain had been brought in. He was the youngest at the firm. The next in line was Morris Greenwood, and he was fifty-two. Clearly an infusion of young blood—and money—was needed.

Alain had been the one to bring the Halliday case to the older partners' attention. When they won the case—when, not if—it would also lure a great deal of business their way. Nothing wrong with that.

Like his mother, Alain was a wheeler-dealer when he had to be. He felt fairly confident that winning wouldn't present a problem. Ethan Halliday had become so smitten with his young bride that two months into the marriage, he'd had the prenup agreement torn up, and rewritten his will. The young and nubile lingerie model was to inherit more than ninety-eight percent of Halliday's considerable fortune. The will literally snatched away what the four Halliday children considered their birthright. Two men and two women, all older than their father's widow, found themselves in agreement for the first time in years, and had banded together against a common enemy: their wicked stepmother.

It had all the makings of a low-grade movie of the week. Or, in another era, a sad Grimms' fairy tale. And it looked as if the happy ending was going to be awarded to his client, if he had anything to say about it.

If he lived to deliver the deposition he'd gotten.

Another sharp skid had Alain jerking to awareness again, his mind on the immediate situation rather than the courtroom. He could all but feel the tires going out from under him.

The winds weren't helping, either. Strong gusts sporadically rose out of nowhere, fighting for possession of his vehicle. Fighting and very nearly winning. Once again he gripped the steering wheel as hard as he could just to keep the car from being shoved off the road.

It felt as if the wind had split in half, and each side was taking a turn at pushing him first in one direction, then the other, like a battered hockey puck.

Alain thought about the way the day was supposed to have gone before this sudden, spur-of-the-moment disaster had unfolded. He'd made arrangements to go antique browsing with Rachel, then grab an early, intimate dinner, after which whatever came up, came up.

Alain grinned despite the immediate trying situation. Rachel Reed was a wildcat in bed and pleasantly straightforward and uncomplicated when she was upright and dealing with life. Just the way he liked them. All fun, no seriousness, no strings. In that respect, he was very much like his mother.

He found himself struggling with the wheel again, trying to keep his car on course. Whatever that was at this point.

Where the hell was he, anyway?

Though he knew it was futile, Alain looked expectantly at the GPS system mounted on his dashboard. It continued doing what it had been doing for the last fifteen minutes: winking like a flirtatious teenager with something in her eye. One of the arrival-time readings that had flashed at him earlier had him back at his house already.

He only wished.

"What good are you if you don't work?" he demanded irritably. As if in response, the GPS system suddenly went dark. "Hey, don't be that way. I'm sorry, okay? Turn back on."

But it remained dark, as did the rest of his dashboard. He no longer had lights to guide him, and all that was coming from his high-definition radio was an endless supply of static.

Alain blew out a breath. He felt like the last man on earth, fighting the elements.

And lost, really lost.

Even his cell phone wasn't working. He'd already tried it more than once. The signal simply wasn't getting through. Mother Nature had declared war on him and all his electronic gadgets. It was as if she knew that without them, he had no sense of direction and was pretty much adrift, like a leaf in a gale.

There was a map tucked into a pocket of the front passenger door, but it was completely useless since it only encompassed Los Angeles and Orange County, and he was somewhere below Santa Barbara, on his way to Oz—or hell, whichever was closer.

He was crawling now, searching desperately for some sign of civilization. He'd left the city behind some time ago, and he knew there were homes out here somewhere because he'd passed them on his way up. But they were sparse and far apart and he'd be damned if he could see so much as a glimmer of a light coming from any building or business establishment.

He couldn't even make out the outline of any structure.

Squinting, Alain leaned forward, hunching over his steering wheel and trying to make out something—anything—in front of him.

Just as he gave up hope, he saw something dart into his path.

An animal?

His heart leaping into his throat, his instincts taking over, Alain swerved to the left in order not to hit whatever it was he'd seen. Tires squealed, brakes screamed, mud flew and he could have sworn the car took on a life of its own.

Where that tree on his left came from he had absolutely no idea. All Alain knew was that he couldn't slam into it, not if he wanted to walk away alive.

But the car that he had babied as if it were a living, breathing thing had a different plan. And right now, it wanted to become one with the tree.

A moment after it started, Alain realized that he was spinning out.

From somewhere in the back of his head, he remembered that you were supposed to steer into a spin. But everything else within him screamed that he *not* make contact with the tree if he could avoid it. So he yanked hard on the wheel, turning it as far as he could to the right.

Horrible noises assaulted his ears as the screech of the car's tires, the whine of metal and the howl of the wind became one. His usual composure melted as genuine panic gripped him. Alain heard something go pop.

And then there was nothing.

It seemed as if Winchester had been giving her problems since the day she'd found him and brought him home from the animal shelter. But she had a soft spot in her heart for the dog and cut him more than his share of slack. Of all the canines Kayla McKenna had taken in, his was one of the saddest stories.

Before she'd rescued the small German shepherd, someone had used him for target practice. When the dog had come to her attention, Winchester had a bullet in his front right leg and was running a low-grade fever because an infection had set in. Rather than go through the expense of removing the object, the local animal shelter, where she'd found the wounded dog on her bimonthly rounds, had only placed a splint on the leg.

The dog she'd whimsically named Winchester, after a rifle made popular during the winning of the West, was down to only a few hours before termination when she'd come across him. The instant she'd insisted that the attendant open up his cage, Winchester had come hobbling out and laid his head on her lap. Kayla was a goner from that moment on.

It was her habit to frequent the shelters every few weeks or so, looking for German shepherds that had, for one reason or another, been abandoned or turned out. If she could she would have taken *all* the dogs home with her, to treat, nurse and groom for adoption into good, loving homes. But even she, with her huge heart, knew she had to draw the line somewhere.

So she made her choice based on her childhood. Hailey had been her very first dog when she was a little girl—a big, lovable, atypical shepherd. As a guard dog, she was a complete failure, but she was so affectionate she'd stolen Kayla's heart from the start. Her parents had had the dog spayed, so she never had any puppies. But in a way, Kayla thought of Hailey as the mother of all the dogs she'd rescued since moving back here after getting her degree.

Kayla had all but lost count of the number of dogs she'd taken into her home, acting as foster guardian until such time as someone came along to adopt them. It didn't hurt matters that she was also a vet, so that the cost of caring for the neglected, often battered animals was nominal.

"You'll never get rich this way," Brett had sneered condescendingly. "And if you want me to marry you, you're going to have to get rid of these dogs. You know that, don't you?"

Yes, she thought now, lifting the lantern she'd brought out with her, to afford some sort of visibility in the driving rain. She'd known that, and hadn't wanted to acknowledge it. She'd met Brett in school. He was gorgeous, and she had fallen wildly in love. But it turned out she had completely misjudged him. He was *not* the man she could spend the rest of her life with.

So she'd kept the dogs and gotten rid of her fiancé and in her heart, she knew that she had made the better deal.

The wind shifted, lashing at her from the front now instead of the back. She tried to pull her hood down with her other hand, but the gusts had other ideas, ripping it from her fingers. Her hair was soaked in a matter of seconds.

"Winchester!"

The wind stole her breath before Kayla could finish calling for the German shepherd.

Damn it, dog, why did you have to run off today of all days? This wasn't the first time he'd disappeared on her. Winchester was exceedingly nervous—the result of mistreatment, no doubt— and any loud noise could send him into hiding.

"Winchester, please, come back!" The futility of her plea seemed to mock her as the wind brought her words back to her. "Taylor, we need to find him," she said to the dog on her left.

Taylor was one of the dogs she'd decided to keep for herself. He was at least seven, and no one wanted an old dog. They represented mounting bills because of health problems, and heartache because their time was short. But Kayla felt that every one of God's creatures deserved love—with the possible exception of Brett.

Suddenly, both Taylor and Ariel, the dog at her other side, began to bark.

"What? You see something?" she asked the animals.

Shading her eyes with her free hand, she raised the lantern higher with the other. As she squinted against the all but blinding rain, Kayla thought she saw what it was that Taylor and Ariel were barking at.

What all *three* of her dogs were barking at, because she could suddenly make out Winchester's shape. He was there, too, not more than five feet away from the cherry-red vehicle that, from this vantage point, seemed to be doing the impossible: it looked as if it were climbing up the oak tree. Its nose and front tires were more than a foot off the ground, urgently pressed up against the hundred-year-old trunk.

Despite the rain, Kayla could swear that she smelled the odor of smoke even from where she was standing.

One second her legs were frozen, the next she was pumping them, running toward the car as fast as she could. The rain lashed against her skin like a thousand tiny needles.

She almost slid into a rear wheel as she reached the vehicle. Rain had somehow gotten into the lantern and almost put the flame out. There was just enough light for her to see into the interior of the disabled sports car.

Dimly, Kayla could make out the back of a man's head. His face appeared to be all but swallowed up by the air bag that had deployed.

She heard a groan and realized it was coming from her, not him.

Her runaway, Winchester, was hopping on his hind legs, as if to tell her that he had discovered the man first. This had to be the canine variation on "He followed me home, can I keep him?"

The man wasn't moving.

Kayla held her breath. Was the driver just unconscious, or—?

"This is the part where I tell you to go for help," she murmured to the dogs, trying to think. "If there was someone to go get."

Which there wasn't. She lived alone and the closest neighbor was more than three miles away. Even if she could send the dogs there, no one would understand why they were barking. More than likely they'd call the sheriff, or just ignore the animals.

In either case, it did her no good. She was on her own here.

Setting the lantern down, Kayla tried the driver's door. At first it didn't budge, but she put her whole weight into pulling it. After several mighty tugs, miraculously, the door gave way. Kayla stumbled backward and would have fallen into the mud had the tree not been at her back. She slammed into it, felt the vibration up and down her spine, jarring her teeth.

She hung on to the door handle for a moment, trying to get her breath. As she drew in moist air, she stared into the car. The driver's face was still buried in the air bag, and the seat belt had a tight grip on the rest of him, holding him in place. Admitted to the party, the rain was now leaving its mark, hungrily anointing every exposed part of the stranger and soaking him to the skin.

And he still wasn't moving.

Chapter Two

"Mister. Hey, mister." Kayla raised her voice to be heard above the howl of the wind. "Can you hear me?"

When there was no response, she shook the man by the shoulder. Again, nothing happened. The stranger didn't lift his head, didn't try to move or make a sound. He was as still as death.

The uneasiness she felt began to grow. What if he was seriously injured, or—?

"Oh, God," Kayla murmured under her breath.

Moving back a foot, she nearly stepped on Winchester. The dog was hobbling about as if he had every intention of leaping into the car and reviving the stranger. At this rate, she was going to wind up stomping on one of his good legs.

"Stay out of the way, boy," Kayla ordered, and he reluctantly obeyed.

She frowned. The air bag was not deflating, but still took up all the available space on the driver's side. After having possibly saved his life, it was, in effect, smothering the man.

Kayla pushed against the bag, but it didn't give. She tried hitting it with the side of her hand, hoping to make the huge tan, marshmallow-like pillow deflate.

It didn't.

Desperate, Kayla put the lantern down on the wet ground and felt around in her pockets. In the morning, when she got dressed, she automatically put her cell phone in her pocket, along with the old Swiss army knife that had once been her father's prized possession.

A smile of relief crossed her lips as her fingers came in contact with a small, familiar shape. Quickly taking it out, she unfolded the largest blade and jabbed the air bag with it. Air whooshed out as the bag deflated.

The moment it was flat, the stranger's head fell forward, hitting the steering wheel. He was obviously still unconscious, or at least she hoped so. The alternative was gruesome.

Kayla felt the side of his neck with her fingertips and found a pulse. "Lucky," she muttered under
her breath.

The next step was to free him from the car. She'd
seen accidents where the vehicle was so badly
mangled, the fire department had to be summoned,
with its jaws of life. Fortunately, this wasn't one of
those cases. Considering the conditions, the driver
had been incredibly lucky. She wondered if he'd
been drinking. But a quick sniff of the air near his
face told her he hadn't been.

Just another Southern Californian who didn't
know how to drive in the rain, she thought. Leaning
over him, she struggled to find the release button for
the seat belt.

Was it her imagination, or was he stirring? God
knew she hadn't been this close to a man in a very
long time.

"Have…we…met?"

Sucking in her breath, Kayla jerked back, hitting
her head against the car roof as she heard the
hoarsely whispered question.

She swallowed. "You're awake," she declared in
stunned relief.

"Or…you're…a dream," Alain mumbled weakly.
Was that his voice? It sounded so high, so distant. And
his eyelids, oh God, his eyelids felt heavier than a ton
of coal. They kept trying to close.

Was he hallucinating? He heard barking. The hounds of hell? *Was* he in hell?

Alain tried to focus on the woman in front of him. He was delirious, he concluded. There was no other explanation for his seeing a redheaded angel in a rain slicker.

Kayla looked at the stranger closely. There was blood oozing from a wide gash on his forehead just above his right eyebrow and his eyes kept rolling upward. He looked as if he was going to pass out again at any moment. She slipped her arm around his waist, still trying to find the seat belt's release button.

"Definitely…a dream," Alain breathed as he felt her fingers feathering along his thigh. Damn, if he'd known hell was populated by creatures like this, he would have volunteered to go a long time ago.

Finding the button, she pressed it and tugged away his seat belt. Kayla looked up at his face. His eyes were shut.

"No, no, don't fade on me now," she begged. Getting the stranger to her house was going to be next to impossible if he was unconscious. She was strong, but not that strong. "Stay with me. Please," she urged.

To her relief, the stranger opened his eyes again. "Best…offer…I've had…all day," he said, wincing with every word that left his lips.

"Terrific," she murmured. "Of all the men to crash into my tree, I have to get a playboy."

Moving her fingers along his ribs gingerly, she was rewarded with another series of winces. He must have cracked or bruised them, she thought in dismay.

"Okay, hang in there," she told him as she slowly moved his torso and legs, so that he was facing out of the vehicle. With effort, she placed her arm beneath his shoulder and grasped his wrist with her hand.

The man's eyes remained closed, but he mumbled against her ear, "You shouldn't…put your trees… where…people can…hit them."

Kayla did her best to block the shiver that his breath created. Gritting her teeth against the effort she was about to make, she promised, "I'll keep that in mind." Spreading her feet, she braced herself, then attempted to rise while holding him. She felt him sagging. "Work with me here, mister."

She thought she heard a chuckle. "What…did you have…in…mind?"

"Definitely not what *you* have in mind," she assured him. Taking a deep breath, she straightened. The man she was trying to rescue was all but a dead weight.

Curling her arm around his waist as best she could, she focused on making the long journey across her lawn to her front door.

"Sorry…" His single word was carried away in the howling wind. The next moment, its meaning became clear: the man had passed out.

"No, no, wait," Kayla pleaded frantically, but it was too late.

He went down like a ton of bricks. She almost pitched forward with him, but let go at the last moment. Frustrated, she looked at the blond, striking stranger. Unconscious, he was just too much for her to carry.

She glanced back toward the house. So near and yet so far.

Catching her lower lip between her teeth, Kayla thought for a moment as all three of the dogs closed ranks around the fallen stranger. And then a rather desperate idea occurred to her. "There's more than one way to skin a cat."

Taylor barked enthusiastically, as if to add a coda to her words. Kayla couldn't help grinning at the large animal.

"You'd like that, wouldn't you? Okay, gang." She addressed the others as if they were her assistants. "Watch over him. I'll be right back."

The dogs appeared to take in every word. Kayla was a firm believer that animals understood what you said, as long as you were patient enough to train them from the time you brought them into your house. Just like babies.

"Oilcloth, oilcloth," she chanted under her breath as she hurried into her house, "what did I do with that oilcloth?" She remembered buying more then ten yards of the fabric—bright red—last year. There'd been a healthy-size chunk left over. She could swear she'd seen the remainder recently.

Crossing the kitchen, she went into the garage, still searching. The oilcloth was neatly folded and tucked away in a corner. Kayla grabbed it and quickly retraced her steps.

She was back at the wrecked vehicle and her still unconscious guest almost immediately. Spying her approach, Winchester hobbled to meet her halfway, then pivoted on his hind legs to lead her back.

"Think I forgot the way?" she asked him.

Winchester took the Fifth.

As the rain continued to lash at her, Kayla spread the oilcloth, shiny side down, on the muddy ground beside the stranger. Working as quickly as she could, rain still lashing unrelentingly at her face, she rolled the man onto the cloth. His clothes had been muddied in the process, but it couldn't be helped. Leaving him out here, bleeding and in God only knew what kind of condition, was definitely not a viable option.

"Okay," she said to her dogs, "now comes the hard part. Times like this, a sled would really come in handy." Winchester yipped, looking up at her with adoring eyes. She was, after all, his savior. "Easy for you to say," she told him.

Gripping the ends of the oilcloth, one corner in each hand, she faced the house. "Here goes nothing," she muttered under her breath, and began the long, painfully slow journey of pulling him, hoping that the stranger, with his upturned face, didn't drown on the way.

The first thing Alain became aware of as he slowly pried his eyes opened, was the weight of the anvil currently residing on his forehead. It felt as if it weighed a thousand pounds, and a gaggle of devils danced along its surface, each taking a swing with his hammer as he passed.

The second thing he became aware of was the feel of the sheets against his skin. Against almost *all* of his skin. He was naked beneath the blue-and-white down comforter. Or close to it. He definitely felt linen beneath his shoulders.

Blinking, he tried very hard to focus his eyes.

Where the hell was he?

He had absolutely no idea how he had gotten here—or what he was doing here to begin with.

Or, for that matter, who that woman with the shapely hips was.

Alain blinked again. He wasn't imagining it. There was a woman with her back to him, a woman with sumptuous hips, bending over a fireplace. The glow from the hearth, and a handful of candles scattered throughout the large, rustic-looking room provided the only light to be had.

Why? Where was the electricity? Had he crossed some time warp?

Nothing was making any sense. Alain tried to raise his head, and instantly regretted it. The pounding intensified twofold.

His hand automatically flew to his forehead and came in contact with a sea of gauze. He slowly moved his fingertips along it.

What had happened?

Curious, he raised the comforter and sheet and saw he still had on his briefs. There were more bandages, these wrapped tightly around his chest. He was beginning to feel like some sort of cartoon character.

Alain opened his mouth to get the woman's attention, but nothing came out. He cleared his throat before making another attempt, and she heard him.

She turned around—as did the pack of dogs that were gathered around her. Alain realized that she'd been putting food into their bowls.

Good, at least they weren't going to eat him.

Yet, he amended warily.

"You're awake," she said, looking pleased as she crossed over to him. The light from the fireplace caught in the swirls of red hair that framed her face. She moved fluidly, with grace. Like someone who was comfortable within her own skin. And why not? The woman was beautiful.

Again, he wondered if he was dreaming.

"And naked," he added.

A rueful smile slipped across her lips. He couldn't tell if it was light from the fire or if a pink hue had just crept up her cheeks. In any event, it was alluring.

"Sorry about that."

"Why, did you have your way with me?" he asked, a hint of amusement winning out over his confusion.

"You're not naked," she pointed out. "And I prefer my men to be conscious." Then she became serious. "Your clothes were all muddy and wet. I managed to wash them before the power went out completely." She gestured about the room, toward the many candles set on half the flat surfaces. "They're hanging in my garage right now, but they're not going to be dry until morning," she said apologetically. "If then."

He was familiar with power outages; they usually lasted only a few minutes. "Unless the power comes back on."

The redhead shook her head, her hair moving about her face like an airy cloud. "Highly doubtful. When we lose power around here, it's hardly ever a short-term thing. If we're lucky, we'll get power back by midafternoon tomorrow."

Alain glanced down at the coverlet spread over his body. Even that slight movement hurt his neck. "Well, as intriguing as the whole idea might be, I really can't stay naked all that time. Can I borrow some clothes from your husband until mine are ready?"

Was that amusement in her eyes, or something else? "That might not be so easy," she told him.

"Why?"

"Because I don't have one."

He'd thought he'd seen someone in a hooded rain slicker earlier. "Significant other?" he suggested. When she made no response, he continued, "Brother? Father?"

She shook her head at each suggestion. "None of the above."

"You're alone?" he questioned incredulously.

"I currently have seven dogs," she told him, amusement playing along her lips. "Never, at any time of the night or day, am I alone."

He didn't understand. If there was no other person in the house—

"Then how did you get me in here? You sure as hell don't look strong enough to have carried me all the way by yourself."

She pointed toward the oilcloth she'd left spread out and drying before the fireplace. "I put you in that and dragged you in."

He had to admit he was impressed. None of the women he'd ever met would have even attempted to do anything like that. They would likely have left him out in the rain until he was capable of moving on his own power. Or drowned.

"Resourceful."

"I like to think so." And, being resourceful, her mind was never still. It now attacked the problem of the all-but-naked man in her living room. "You know, I think there might be a pair of my dad's old coveralls in the attic." As she talked, Kayla started to make her way toward the stairs, and then stopped. A skeptical expression entered her bright-green eyes as they swept over the man on the sofa.

Alain saw the look and couldn't help wondering what she was thinking. Why was there a doubtful frown on her face? "What?"

"Well…" Kayla hesitated, searching for a delicate way to phrase this, even though her father had been gone for some five years now. "My dad was a pretty big man."

Alain still didn't see what the problem was. "I'm six-two."

She smiled, and despite the situation, he found himself being drawn in as surely as if someone had thrown a rope over him and begun to pull him closer.

"No, not big—" Kayla held her hand up to indicate height "—big." This time, she moved her hand in front of her, about chest level, to denote a man whose build had been once compared to that of an overgrown grizzly bear.

"I'll take my chances," Alain assured her. "It's either that or wear something of yours, and I don't think either one of us wants to go that route."

It suddenly occurred to him that he was having a conversation with a woman whose name he didn't know and who didn't know his. While that was not an entirely unusual situation for him, an introduction was definitely due.

"By the way, I'm Alain Dulac."

Her smile, he thought, seemed to light up the room far better than the candles did.

"Kayla," she told him. "Kayla McKenna." She saw him wince as he tried to sit up to shake her hand. Rather than a handshake, she gently pressed her palms against his shoulders and pushed him back down on the sofa. "I think you should stay there for a while. You gashed your head and cracked a couple of ribs. I sewed your forehead and taped you up," she added. "Nothing else appears to be damaged. I ran my portable scanner over you."

Other than running into someone from *Star Trek,* there was only one conclusion to be drawn. "I take it you're a doctor?"

Kayla shook her head. "Vet," she corrected.

"Oh." Gingerly, Alain touched the bandage around his head again, as if he wasn't quite sure what to expect. "Does that mean I'm suddenly going to start barking, or have an overwhelming urge to drink out of the toilet anytime soon?"

She laughed, and he caught himself thinking that it was a very sexy sound.

"Only if you want to. The basics of medicine, whether for an animal or a human being, are surprisingly similar," she assured him. "They don't even automatically shoot horses anymore when they break their legs these days." He began to stir, then stopped when she looked at him a tad sternly. "Why don't you rest while I go see if I can find my dad's clothes in the attic?"

Without his realizing it, the pack of dogs in the room had closed in on him. They appeared to be eyeing him suspiciously. At least, that was the way it seemed to him. There were seven in all, seven German shepherds of varying heights and coloration: two white, one black and the rest black-and-tan. And none of them, except for the little guy with the cast, looked to be overly friendly.

Alain raised his eyes toward Kayla. "Are you sure it's safe to leave me with these dogs?"

She smiled and nodded. "You won't hurt them. I trust you."

"No offense, but I wasn't thinking of me hurting them. I was worried about them deciding they haven't had enough to eat tonight." He was only half kidding. "Survival of the fittest and all that."

"Don't worry." She patted his shoulder, and realized it was the same gesture she used with the dogs to reassure them. "They haven't mistaken you for an invading alpha male." She looked around at them and realized, to an outsider, they might seem a bit intimidating. "If it makes you feel any better, I'll take some of them with me."

That was a start, he allowed. "How about all of them?"

"You don't like dogs." It wasn't a question, it was a statement. She felt a bit disappointed in the man, although she wasn't entirely certain why.

"I like dogs fine," he countered. "But I prefer to be standing in their company, not lying down like the last item on their menu."

She supposed, given his present condition, she could understand his frame of mind. "Okay, they'll come with me. I'll just leave you Winchester." She nodded toward the smallest dog.

The shepherd looked friendly enough. But Alain was curious as to her reasoning. "Why? Because he broke his leg?"

"He didn't break his leg," she corrected. "Someone shot him. But I thought the two of you might form some sort of bond, because Winchester was the one who found you." She left the room with the menagerie following her, closer than a shadow.

It came to him about a minute after Kayla walked

out of the room with her four-legged entourage that she was wrong. Winchester hadn't found him; the dog had been responsible for his sudden and unexpected merging with the oak tree.

But it was too late to point that out.

Chapter Three

The door to the attic creaked as she opened it. For a moment, Kayla just stood in the doorway, looking at the shadows her lantern created within the room.

Ariel bumped her head against her thigh, as if to nudge her in.

Taking a deep breath, Kayla raised the lantern higher to illuminate the space, and walked in.

She hadn't been up here in a very long time. Not because the gathering place for spiders, crickets and all manner of other bugs held any special terror for her. She had no problem with any of God's creatures, no matter how creepy-crawly the rest of the world might find them. No, what kept her from coming up here was the bittersweet pain of memories.

The attic was filled with furniture, boxes of clothing, knickknacks and assorted personal treasures belonging to people long gone. Yet she couldn't make herself throw them out or even donate them to charity. To do so, to sweep the place clean and get rid of all the clutter, felt to her like nothing short of a violation of trust. But as much as she couldn't bring herself to part with her parents' and grandparents' possessions, coming up here, remembering people who were no longer part of her everyday life, was still extremely difficult.

Kayla treasured the paths they had walked through her life, and at the same time hated being reminded that they were gone. That the people who had made her childhood and teen years so rich were no longer there to share in her life now.

Maybe if they had been around, she wouldn't have had that low period in San Francisco....

As if sensing her feelings, the six dogs that had come racing up here now stood quietly in the shadows, waiting for her to do whatever it was she had to do.

Kayla took another long, deep breath, trying not to notice how the dust tickled her nose.

An ancient, dust-laden, black Singer sewing machine that had belonged to her great-grandmother stood like a grande dame in the corner, regally presiding over all the other possessions that had found their way up here. Her grandfather's fishing rod and lures stood in a corner, near her father's golf clubs, still brand-new beneath the covers her mother had knit for them.

Next to the clubs was a body-building machine that had belonged not to her father but her mother. Kayla's mom had been so proud of maintaining her all-but-perfect body. She'd used the machine faithfully, never missing a day. Kayla pressed her lips together to keep back the tears that suddenly filled her eyes. The cancer hadn't cared what her mother looked like on the outside, it had ravaged her within, leaving Kayla motherless by the time she was sixteen.

By twenty-two, she'd become a veritable orphan.

Now the dogs were her family.

You're getting maudlin. Snap out of it, Kayla upbraided herself.

Taking another deep breath, she blew it out slowly and then approached a large, battered steamer trunk in the corner opposite the sewing machine. The trunk had its own history. Her grandfather had come from Ireland with all his worldly possessions in that trunk. When he landed in New York, he'd discovered that someone had jimmied it open and taken everything inside. Seamus McKenna had kept the trunk, vowing to one day fill it with the finest silks and satins.

These days, her parents' things resided inside the battered container, mingling just the way they had when they'd had been alive. The contents were worth far more to Kayla than the silks and satins her grandfather had dreamed of.

The attic fairly shouted of memories. Kayla could have sworn she could see her parents standing just beyond the lantern's light.

She felt her heart ache.

"I miss you guys," she said quietly, blinking several times as she felt moisture gathering along her lashes.

All of them, especially her father, had been her inspiration. She couldn't remember a time when she hadn't wanted to be just like him, hadn't planned on going into medicine because he had. He was the kindest, gentlest man ever created….

But her passionate love for animals took her in a slightly different direction, and instead of a doctor, she'd become a veterinarian. She never once regretted her decision. Being a vet, along with the volunteer work she was presently doing for the German Shepherd Rescue Organization, had given her a sense of purpose she badly needed.

And there was another, added bonus. She didn't feel alone anymore, not with all these four-footed companions eager to display their gratitude to her at the drop of a dog treat.

Crossing to the trunk, Kayla started to open it, then stopped and glanced back at the dogs.

German shepherds, despite their tough public image as police dogs, had very delicate skins and often had a multitude of allergies. The ones she had taken into her home and was presently caring for certainly did. Three of them were on daily allergy medication.

"Maybe I should have left you downstairs," she said, thinking out loud. Well, it was too late now. "Okay, stay."

She said the last word as a command. She knew that training animals was a constant, ongoing thing, and she never missed an opportunity to reinforce any headway made. The dogs instantly turned into breathing statues. Kayla smiled to herself as she flipped the lock on the trunk and lifted the lid.

A very faint hint of the perfume her mother always wore floated up to her.

Or maybe that was just her imagination, creating the scent.

Kayla didn't care. It was real to her, and that was all that mattered. A vivid image of her mother laughing flashed through her mind's eye. Her mom had remained healthy-looking until almost the very end.

Leaving the lantern beside the trunk, Kayla carefully went through the clothes and memorabilia inside. Some of her father's old medical school textbooks lined the bottom of the trunk—he'd never liked throwing anything away. Finally, she found the overalls. They were tucked into a corner near the pile of books.

Daniel McKenna had never favored suits or ties. He tended to like wearing comfortable clothes beneath his white lab coat. Ironically, the week before he'd suddenly died, he'd told her that when he was gone, she should give away his clothes to the local charity—just as he'd always given away his time and services so generously in his off-hours.

But Kayla couldn't force herself to give away every article of clothing. For sentimental reasons, she had kept one of his outfits—his old coveralls.

Taking them out now, she held up the faded denim and shook her head. The man on her sofa was going to be lost in them. But it would do in a pinch. And, after all, it was only temporary. Just until his own clothes were dry again.

She had to admit, Kayla thought as she folded the large garment, that if she had her druthers, she would vote to have Alain Dulac remain just the way he was right now. There was no denying that beneath that blanket, he was one magnificent specimen of man-hood.

Her mother would have approved of the sculpted definition in his arms, and the washboard abs. Most likely, Kayla thought with a smile, her mom would have wound up comparing workout routines with him, and giving Alain advice on how to get twice the results out of his efforts.

Not that there was really any room for improvement, she mused, her mouth curving.

Closing the lid of the trunk, Kayla stooped down and picked up the lantern again.

She hadn't seen a wedding ring on the man's hand, but that didn't really mean anything. A lot of married men didn't wear rings—and those that did could easily take them off. Although, now that she thought of it, there hadn't been a tan line on Alain's finger to indicate he played those kinds of games.

Still, she couldn't help absently wondering if there was someone waiting for Alain Dulac back home, wherever home was.

The next moment she laughed at herself. What was she thinking? Of course there was someone waiting for him. Men who looked like Alain Dulac *always* had someone waiting for them. They didn't go around creating bodies like that just because they had nothing better to do. That kind of body was bait, pure and simple. Had he reeled in his catch?

Probably more than his share.

Makes no difference one way or another, she insisted silently, leaving the attic.

She waited until her entourage had gathered around her out in the hall, then closed the door.

"Okay, gang," she announced cheerfully, "We got what we came for. Let's go."

Winchester had remained at his side, staring at him, the entire time Kayla was gone. He'd tried to pet the dog, but the very movement had sent pains shooting up and down his side.

Alain strained now, trying to hear if the woman he was indebted to was coming back. Boards squeaked overhead. She was leaving the attic, he guessed, relieved.

"Your mistress is coming," he told the dog. "You can go stare at her now."

Alain heard the sound of thirteen pairs of feet hitting the stairs, hers muffled by the clatter of the dogs'.

Damn, he wanted to sit up to greet her like a normal person, but even shifting slightly on the sofa brought the anvil devils back, swinging their hammers in double-time. Not only that, but there was an excruciating pain shooting up from his ribs.

He'd never been one to make a fuss, and he'd always thought he had a high pain threshold. When he fell out of a tree and broke his arm at the age of eight, he'd been so stoic Philippe had been certain he'd gone into shock. But this was bad. Really bad. He couldn't take in a deep breath, only shallow, small ones—which somehow fed the claustrophobia he felt. He kept trying to inhale a deep breath to hold the sensation at bay, but each failure only drew it closer.

"Why can't I take a deep breath?" he wanted to know the second Kayla walked into the living room. He was vaguely aware how the light from the lantern preceded her like a heavenly beam, illuminating her every movement. Directly behind her, her animals came pouring in.

"Because you cracked two ribs and I've taped you up tighter than a CIA secret," she answered matter-of-factly. Patient feedback—and complaints— were two things she didn't get as a vet. Being a vete- rinarian did have its perks, she thought. "It's only temporary."

Placing the lantern on the coffee table, she held up the coveralls.

It took him a second to realize that she wasn't un- furling a bolt of material, but an article of clothing. The man who had sired this petite woman had been huge. It was obvious that she must have taken after her mother.

"Wow, you really weren't kidding about your father being big, were you?" The coveralls looked as if they could accommodate two of him. "How much did your dad weigh?"

"Too much," she answered shortly. "Given his profession, he should have known better."

Trying to ignore the throbbing shaft of pain that kept skewering him, he tried to focus on the conversation. "What was his profession?"

"My father was a doctor. A general practitioner," she explained.

"Could have been worse," Alain allowed. When she looked at him quizzically, he said, "Your father could have been a nutritionist or a diet doctor." Forcing a resigned smile to his lips, he reached out for the coveralls she was holding, then suddenly dropped his hand as he sucked in what little breath he had to spare.

Concerned, Kayla set the coveralls on the coffee table. "Maybe you should just lie back. You can always get dressed later. God knows you're not going anywhere tonight."

As if to underline her assessment, the wind chose that moment to pick up again, rattling the windows like a prisoner trying to break out—or, in this case, in.

Kayla lightly placed her hand on Alain's forehead and then frowned.

He didn't like her reaction, Alain thought. "What's wrong?"

She drew her hand back, looking at him thoughtfully. "You feel warm."

He didn't like the way she said that, either. He really didn't have time for this. His schedule was full and he should have been on his way home. "Isn't that a good sign? Doesn't cold usually mean dead?"

"*Stiff* means dead," she corrected, with just a hint of amusement reaching her lips. "Wait here, I'm going to get you something to make you feel better."

"Wait here," he echoed when she'd gone. Winchester looked at him with what appeared to Alain's slightly fevered brain to be sympathy. "As if I had a choice."

The shepherd barked in response, apparently agreeing that, at the moment, he didn't.

Alain stared at the animal. He had to be hallucinating. What other explanation was there for his having a conversation, albeit mostly one-sided, with a dog in a cast?

This time Kayla returned more quickly. When she came back, she was holding a glass of water in one hand and an oval blue pill in the other.

"Here, take this," she instructed in a voice that left no chance for argument. She held the blue pill to his lips.

Alain raised his eyes warily. For the most part, he was as laid-back as they came. But he also wasn't a trusting fool. "What is it?"

"Just take it," she told him. "It'll make you feel better, I promise." When he still made no move to swallow the pill, she sighed. "It's a painkiller," she told him, a note of exasperation in her voice. "Do you always question everything?"

"Pretty much." Well, if she'd wanted to get rid of him, she could have done it while he was unconscious, he reasoned. So, with some reluctance, he took the pill from her, preferring to put it in his own mouth. "It's in the blood."

"What?" She raised one eyebrow quizzically. "Being annoying?"

"Being a lawyer." He placed the pill into his mouth.

Kayla shrugged at the reply. "Same thing," she quipped. Placing her hand behind his head, she raised it slightly so that he could drink the water she'd brought. As she did so, she could feel him tensing. He was obviously struggling not to show her that he was in pain. "This will help," she promised again.

He had nothing against painkillers, but the pain actually wasn't his main problem. "What'll help is if I can get back on the road," he told her. "I'm supposed to be in L.A. tonight." Rachel wasn't going to take it kindly if he rescheduled their date, and he was having too good a time with her to put a stop to it just yet.

And there was that impromptu get-together that the firm was holding. Dunstan had said there was no pressure to attend, but everyone knew there was.

The vibrant redhead was shaking her head in response to his statement. "Sorry, not going to happen. Your car is immobilized." She tucked the coverlet closer around him. "And so are you."

"My car." Flashes of the accident came back to him. Had he really driven the car up a tree, or was that some kind of nightmare? He tried to sit up, and felt not so much pain as an odd sort of murkiness pouring through his limbs. And the cloudiness was descending over his brain again. What the hell was going on? "How bad is it?"

Kayla pretended to consider the question. "That depends."

The town probably came equipped with a crooked mechanic who made his money preying on people who were passing through and had the misfortune of breaking down here, Alain thought. Everyone knew someone who had a horror story about being taken because there was no other alternative.

"On what?" he asked warily.

That, she assumed, was his lawyer look. But she could already see it fading away as the painkiller kicked in. "On whether you want a functioning vehicle or a very large paperweight."

He'd only had the car for a year. It was barely broken in. He should have gone with his first instincts and rented a vehicle to drive up to Santa Barbara. "It's totaled?"

This time she did consider his question. She really hadn't paid that much attention to the condition of his car; she'd been more concerned with getting him out of the vehicle and out of the rain.

"Maybe not totaled," she allowed, "but it's certainly not going anywhere anytime soon."

Suddenly the room seemed to be getting darker. Was the fire going out?

Or was he?

His ribs didn't hurt anymore. Maybe he could pay her for the use of her own car, he thought. His head began to do strange things. Alain tried to focus. "I can't stay here."

"Why not?" she asked innocently. "It doesn't look as if you have much choice." And then she added with a smile, "Don't worry, I'm not going to charge you rent."

Thinking was rapidly becoming difficult for him. He needed to stay on point. "I've got places to go, people to see."

"The places'll still be there tomorrow. And the day after that," she added for good measure. "And if the people are worth anything, so will they."

Kayla had no doubt that the pill was taking effect. She should have given it to him in the first place, she thought, but she'd needed his input to see how bad he was. He was going to be asleep in a few more minutes, she judged.

She sat down on the coffee table facing him. Taylor lowered his haunches and sat down beside her like a silent consort.

"Right now," she continued in a soft, soothing

voice, "you need to rest. The roads are probably flooded, so you wouldn't be going anywhere, anyway. Every time it rains like this, Shelby becomes an island."

"Shelby?" he asked groggily.

"The town you're passing through." It was hardly a dot on the map. Most people didn't even know they'd been through it. Leaning forward, Kayla placed her hand on his arm to make him feel secure. "I gave you something to make you sleep, Alain. Stop fighting it and just let it do its thing."

He liked the way his name sounded on her lips.

The thought floated through his head without preamble. He was drifting, he realized. And his limbs were growing heavier, as if they didn't belong to him anymore.

"If…I…fall asleep…" He was really struggling to get the words out now.

She leaned in closer to hear him. "Yes?"

"Will…you…have your way with me now?"

She laughed and shook her head. This one was something else.

"No," she assured him, not quite able to erase the smile from her lips. "I won't have my way with you."

"Too…bad."

And then there was no more conversation. His eyelids had won the battle and closed down.

Chapter Four

He was being watched.

The unshakable sensation of having a pair of eyes fixed on him, on his every move—from close range—bore through the oppressive, thick haze that was swirling around him.

Alain struggled to surface, to reach full consciousness and open his eyes. When he finally succeeded, only extreme control kept him from crying out in surprise.

Approximately five inches separated his face from the dog's muzzle.

Alain jerked up, drawing his elbows in under him.

The salvo of pain that shot through him registered an instant later. This time, a moan did escape.

In response, the dog reared up and licked him. Alain grimaced and made a noise that expressed something less than pleasure over the encounter.

"Welcome back."

The cheerful voice was coming from behind him. Before he could turn his head to look at her, Kayla moved into his line of vision.

She'd changed her clothes, he noticed. It looked as if she was wearing the same curve-hugging jeans, but instead of a T-shirt, she had on a green pullover sweater that played up the color of her eyes—among other things.

It took him a second to raise his gaze to her face. "How long was I out?"

She bent to pat Winchester on the head. The dog had spent the entire night at Alain's side. There was a definite attachment forming, at least from the dog's point of view.

"You slept through the night," Kayla told him. She had spent it in the chair opposite him, watching to make sure he was all right. "Rather peacefully, I might add." And then, because he'd mentioned a woman's name during the night, she couldn't resist asking, "Who's Lily?"

That question had come at him from left field. Did this woman know his mother? It seemed unlikely, given that she was wrapped up with her animals, and the only animals her mother liked were the two-legged kind. *In bed*.

Alain watched Kayla's face as he answered, "My mother. Why?"

"You called out to her once during the night." She cocked her head, curious. "You call your mother by her first name?" She'd been around six years old before she even knew her parents had other names besides Mommy and Daddy. She couldn't imagine referring to either of them by their given names.

"No, not really." Since he couldn't remember if he'd even dreamed, he hadn't a clue as to why he'd call out his mother's name, and he didn't know any other Lily. But he was more curious about something else. "You stayed up all night watching me sleep?" Why would she do that? he wondered, feeling oddly comforted by the act.

Kayla laughed as she shook her head. "We're a little rural here, but I'm not that desperate for entertainment. No, I didn't stay up all night watching you sleep. I spent part of it sleeping myself," she assured him.

In actuality, she'd spent very little of it asleep. His breathing had been labored at one point, and she'd worried that she might have given him too much of the medication, so she'd remained awake to monitor him. But she didn't feel there was any reason for Alain to know that.

"Nothing I wouldn't have done for any of my other patients," she continued nonchalantly. "Even if you don't have fur." And then she looked a little more serious. "How's the head?"

Until she asked, Alain hadn't realized that the anvil chorus was no longer practicing their latest performance inside his skull. He touched his forehead slowly as if to assure himself that it was still there.

"Headache's gone," he said in amazement. The way it had hurt last night, he'd been fairly certain it was going to split his head open. And now it was gone, as if it had never existed. Except for the state of his ribs, he actually felt pretty good.

Pleased, Kayla nodded. "Good." Moving away from the coffee table, she turned toward the kitchen. "Hungry?"

He was about to say no. He was never hungry first thing in the morning, requiring only pitch-black coffee until several hours after he was awake and at work. But this morning there was this unfamiliar pinch in his stomach. It probably had something to do with the fact that he hadn't had any dinner last night, he reasoned.

He nodded slowly in response to her question. "Yes, I am."

Kayla caught the inflection in his voice. "You sound surprised."

"I am," he admitted. "I'm not usually hungry first thing in the morning."

He was probably always too busy to notice, she guessed. People in the city tended to spin their wheels a lot, going nowhere and making good time at it. She should know; she'd been one of those people for a while. "Country air will do that to you."

Her comment surprised him. "So you consider this the country?"

That seemed like an odd thing for him to ask. "Don't you?"

Alain laughed shortly. "Last night, I considered it Oz," he admitted. "But usually 'country' means farmland to me."

She supposed there was an argument for that. To her, any place that didn't pack in a hundred people to the square yard was the country.

"There used to be nothing but farms around here. We've still got a few." And she loved to drive by them whenever she had the chance. Not to mention that the families on that acreage were always opened to taking in some of her dogs. "Corn and strawberries, mostly," she added.

Ariel was shifting from foot to foot behind her, silently reminding her that she had yet to be fed. Which brought Kayla full circle. "So, what's your pleasure?"

The question caught him up short. Without fully

realizing it, he'd been watching the way Kayla's breasts rose and fell beneath the green sweater with every breath she took.

As for her question, he wasn't about to give her the first response that came to his lips, because he doubted that the beautiful vet would see it as anything more than a come-on. And maybe it was, but he'd never meant anything more in his life. His pleasure, at the moment, involved some very intimate images of Kayla—sans the green sweater—and himself.

"Whatever you're having," he told her, glancing toward Winchester. The dog was still eyeing him, an unrelenting polygraph machine waiting for a slipup.

His answer satisfied Kayla. "Eggs and toast it is." She nodded.

The choice surprised him. Somehow, he'd just assumed that Kayla would be a vegetarian. Half the women he knew turned their noses up at anything that hadn't been plucked out of the ground, pulled down from a tree or gotten off a stalk. In addition, he would have thought that the cheerful vet would have been health conscious.

He watched her face as he said, "Don't you know eggs are bad for you?"

She shook her head. "They've been much maligned," Kayla countered. "The FDA says having four eggs a week is perfectly acceptable. Besides, an

egg has a lot of nutrients to offer. My great-grandfather ate eggs every day of his life and he lived to
be ninety-six."

"Might have lived to be ten years older if he'd
avoided eggs," Alain deadpanned.

His quip was met with a wide grin. Something
inside of him responded, lighting up, as well. "You
have a sense of humor. Nice," she said.

The last word seemed to whisper along his skin,
making him warmer. Since the response was something a teenager might experience, Alain hadn't a
clue as to what was going on with him. Maybe it was
a reaction to whatever she'd given him last night.

The way he was looking at her, looking right into
her, stirred up a whole host of things inside of Kayla.
His smile alone made lightning flash in her veins.
She didn't bother squelching it, because for once, entertaining these kinds of feelings was all right. She
wouldn't act on it, and at the moment, she was
willing to bet that he couldn't. By the time he could,
he would be gone.

She held off going to the kitchen to make breakfast a moment longer. "I almost forgot. I've got some
good news."

He immediately thought of the disabled BMW.
"My car's all right, after all?"

His car. She hadn't even looked at it since she'd
pulled him free of the wreckage. It was still raining

and the power was still out, which meant the phones weren't working. There was no way to call Mick's gas station to get someone out to look at the fancy scrap of metal.

"No, your car's still embracing my tree," she told him, "but your clothes are dry, so you don't have to put on my father's coveralls." Her mouth curved into what her mother had once called her wicked grin as she added, "Unless you want to."

"If I'm going to get lost inside of someone else's clothes, I'd rather the clothes belonged to someone of the female persuasion." Preferably with her still in it, he added silently. "No offense."

"None taken," she assured him.

Was it her, or was it getting warmer in here? Kayla wondered. The fire certainly hadn't gotten more intense since she'd lit it earlier this morning.

Kayla placed the clothes that she had just gotten off the line in her garage on the coffee table in front of him. "You can put them on after breakfast, if you're up to it. How *are* you feeling?" she asked, suddenly realizing that she'd only asked about his headache, nothing more.

Alain quickly took stock of his parts before answering. His ribs were still aching, but not as badly as they had last night. And while there was no headache, he was acutely aware of the gash she must have sewn up on his forehead. It pulsed.

"Good enough for me to put my clothes on now," he told her.

She opened her mouth to say that maybe he should wait until after he ate before he went jumping into his clothes, but then she shut it again. The man should know what he was capable of doing. She wasn't his mother or his keeper.

"Okay." But being distant and removed just wasn't her way. Kayla came closer to the sofa again. "Why don't I help you to the bathroom so you can change in private?" she suggested.

He thought that was a little like closing the barn door after the horse had run off, seeing as how she'd been the one to undress him in the first place. But he didn't raise the point, since it might sound like a protest. He didn't have anything against beautiful woman doing whatever they wanted with his clothes and his body. What he didn't like was the idea of being an invalid and needing help.

"I can make it on my own," he informed her.

If he meant to make her back off, he was in for a surprise, she thought. "How do you know?" Kayla challenged. "You haven't been on your feet since I brought you in."

Instead of answering, he sat up and swung his legs out from under the bedclothes. He meant to stand up and show her that he was all right. Planting his feet on the floor, he pushed himself up off the sofa—and immediately felt the room spin.

Alain blinked his eyes as if that would help him clear his head. He was feeling as weak as a kitten with a cold. Exasperated, he stole a look in Kayla's direction.

"What the hell did you give me last night?" he demanded.

He wouldn't be familiar with the generic name of the drug she'd used, Kayla thought. There was no point in mentioning it. She kept it simple. "Just something to make you sleep."

"For how many days?" He'd lost all track of time. "Twenty?"

"Do you always exaggerate?" she replied, then answered her own question. "Oh, wait, I forgot, you're a lawyer."

This time, he thought he saw her top lip curl in a sneer. Was that her reaction to what he did for a living? Most women melted when they found out that he worked for a famous firm, equating it to wealth. "You don't place much stock in lawyers, do you?"

The land the house was on used to be twice the size it was now. A boundary dispute had brought her family into court, and the judge had ruled against them. Her grandfather had come precariously close to losing everything he'd worked for his entire adult life. Watching his spirit being bent and then all but broken had been a horrible experience for Kayla. She thought of lawyers as only slightly higher on the food chain than scorpions.

The best ones had silver tongues, but the bottom line was the same: they were all vultures. "They live off the sweat of others."

Alain nodded. "I'll take that as a no."

She was surprised that he just let the matter drop like that. "Aren't you going to try to defend your brethren? To tell me all the good that lawyers have accomplished? How the world's a better place because of attorneys?"

Alain shook his head. "I never try to pry open a closed mind. Good way to lose my fingers." And then he grinned, creating a mini-whirlpool in her stomach. "Not to mention other, equally as precious body parts."

He didn't argue what he knew he couldn't win. Intelligent as well as good-looking, she decided. "Well, I'll give you this—you're smarter than the average lawyer." As she had last night, Kayla braced herself. And then she looked down at him. "Ready?"

"For what?" Certainly not her, he added silently. There was definitely more to this woman than met the eye.

Kayla nodded to her left. "The bathroom."

There seemed to be no point in arguing with her

about his ability to get around. Alain dug his knuckles into the sofa on either side of his thighs and pushed himself up and off the cushion once more. Triumph was fleeting. As he straightened, he felt wobbly—again.

So much so that he swayed even though he was trying hard not to. Preoccupied with not falling flat on his face and on his dignity, he didn't even notice that he was still wearing only the very small black briefs he'd intended strictly for Rachel's perusal.

The next moment, he felt Kayla slip her arm through his. "Shall we?" she asked brightly.

Her eyes were looking directly into his. But from the smile he saw in them, he knew that she'd allowed herself at least one long, assessing scan of his torso. He couldn't help but wonder how he'd measured up with whoever she'd taken to her bed in earnest.

He began to walk, using what felt like someone else's legs. A disembodied feeling hovered over him with each step he took.

"The last time someone walked me into their bathroom, we wound up showering together."

"I don't recommend a shower right away," she told him. "But if you want to take one later, let me know. I'll need to get some plastic wrap for you."

A vision of the two of them, naked but wrapped together tightly in plastic, materialized in his mind. "Sounds kinky."

"For your bandages," she told him, without missing a beat. God, but he was well-built, she thought again. It was like propping up a rock wall. "You can't get them wet."

He looked down at the white gauze around his chest. "How long are they going to have to stay on?"

That depended on his healing process. "Longer than a day."

He was still taking what felt like baby steps. His knees were shaky but he wasn't altogether sure if that was due to the accident he'd had or the proximity of his escort.

Alain decided it might be a combination of both. Like his brother Georges, he could never resist a good-looking woman, and the one next to him was leagues beyond merely good-looking. However, unlike Georges, he was completely confident that settling down was not in the cards for him. When it came to that, he was too much like their mother.

Once upon a time, he'd thought that Georges was, too, but that was before he'd had met what Philippe referred to as their brother's "once in a lifetime woman." Vienna was a gentle, heart-stoppingly beautiful woman who had, without trying, changed all the dynamics in Georges's life and made him long for what he'd never had before: a steadfast relationship.

Well, for Georges's sake, Alain hoped that existed. As for himself, he knew it would never happen.

Kayla stopped walking and he realized that they must have reached the bathroom. Leaning him against the wall by the door, she slipped her arm from his and took a step back. Alain would have been amused if he wasn't perspiring so much.

"Holler if you need me," she instructed. It wasn't just a throwaway line; she meant it.

Alain remained leaning against the wall. He had his suspicions that she noticed.

"I won't need you," he assured her. "Despite what you might think of lawyers, I am capable of dressing myself. I have been doing it since I was three."

She smiled, inclining her head. If she took note of the line of perspiration along his brow, she gave no indication. "I'm sure you have."

She backed away, and that was when he realized that they hadn't reached this part of the house alone. The dogs were all in the background. But Winchester, easily the runt in this eclectic litter, was right there, front and center.

The odd thing was, the dog appeared to be looking up at *him* rather than her.

"If you need an escort back," she continued, "just send Winchester to get me. I'll be in the living room, making breakfast."

"The living room?" he echoed. "Don't you usually make it in the kitchen?"

"I do," she allowed. "When the electricity is

working. But it's not and there's a fireplace in the living room."

"You're using the fireplace?" he asked incredulously. Most of the women he knew could barely turn on a stove. Roughing it meant eating at a less than five-star restaurant.

She winked just before she turned on her heel. "Think of it as camping in."

He watched her walk away. Watched and appreciated the gentle sway of her hips with each step.

Alain roused himself with effort.

It felt like an incredibly domestic scene, he thought as he entered the bathroom. He closed the door just in time, before Winchester managed to slip in with him.

Too domestic, he decided.

He never remained for breakfast when he slept with a woman. That had less to do with his rarely having breakfast than it did with the fact that he never spent the night, no matter how long the lovemaking lasted or what hour it was finally over. Literally sleeping with someone would have opencd up an entire floodgate of assumptions that had no place in his life.

The only relationships he wanted to form with the opposite sex were temporary, cursory ones. Like his mother. Lily Moreau might have been married to all three of the men who'd fathered her sons, but even those unions had dissolved for one reason or another. The other liaisons—and there had been too many to count—had all been short-lived. His mother operated by one small rule of thumb: she enjoyed her relationships, until she didn't. And then she moved on. Before they did.

Life was too short to stay in one place and wait for the inevitable pain to come.

Alain looked in the mirror. A faint, pale stubble was growing on his cheeks and chin, but otherwise, he didn't look the worse for his experience.

A noise outside the door caught his attention. He'd better get dressed before she came in to check up on him. Alain shook his head. He wasn't too sure what to make of Kayla McKenna. She was a great deal friendlier than he thought was actually prudent, given her living situation. And he couldn't help wondering why she was unattached. There had to be a story there.

Damn, just pulling on his trousers exhausted him. That accident had taken more out of him than he'd thought. Even so, he struggled to put on his socks and his shirt. For the time being, Alain left the suit jacket off.

After pausing to throw water into his face, he opened the door.

And nearly stepped on the dog with the cast.

Chapter Five

Moving back to avoid stepping on Winchester's foot, Alain grasped the door to keep from falling down himself. He swallowed a string of choice words he knew Kayla wouldn't exactly appreciate hearing.

Winchester looked up at him with adoring, liquid-brown eyes. Alain blew out a breath and shook his head, then picked his way around the animal. Winchester immediately fell into step directly behind him.

Alain glared at the four-footed shadow. "Your dog keeps following me."

Kayla was in the living room, tending to the breakfast she was making over the fire. The other dogs were patiently standing by, waiting to be fed. She smiled over her shoulder. "I noticed. I think he's adopted you."

Just what he needed, Alain thought. "Well, tell him to unadopt me." He frowned as he made his way carefully back to the sofa. Winchester hobbled right behind him, this time trying to stay out of the way and apparently get on his good side.

Kayla transferred breakfast from the skillet to a plate, placing the former out of the way so that one of the dogs didn't accidentally pull it down.

She crossed to Alain and presented the plate of bacon and eggs to him.

"Sorry, can't make toast right now," she stated, then nodded toward Winchester, who had lain down at Alain's feet and was eyeing the plate of food wistfully. Winchester knew better than to try to snare a taste unless it was offered. "He really likes you."

Taking the plate, Alain snorted dismissively. He'd never had a pet, even as a child, and had no desire for one.

"I think he just feels guilty about making me crash my car." The moment the first forkful passed his lips, he realized just how ravenous he was. It took effort not to wolf the rest down.

Perching on the arm of the sofa, Kayla smiled tolerantly at her unexpected guest. "Dogs don't feel guilt."

"I guess that puts them one up on people." Alain thought of the case he was currently handling. His client showed absolutely no shred of guilt that her share of the inheritance cut her late husband's children completely out of the will. "At least some people," he amended.

"Everyone feels guilt," Kayla countered. Ariel nuzzled her and she absently stroked the dog's head as she spoke. "It's just a matter of whether or not they act on it."

Intrigued, Alain raised his eyes to look at her. "What do you feel guilty about?"

She hadn't expected *that* question.

"Oh." She thought a moment. Taylor tried to nudge Ariel out of the way for some attention. She gave the old dog equal time. "Not being able to do enough to save these magnificent creatures."

Alain glanced toward the fireplace, where the other dogs were still eating, then back at the two who were vying for her favor. As far as he could tell, she was already doing more than enough.

"You've got seven and a half dogs," he pointed out, throwing in the "half" because of the dog she called Ginger, who looked obviously pregnant. "How many more could you be taking in?" Without being branded eccentric, he added silently.

Her eyes swept over the animals. Alain saw the affection there and wondered why she wasn't sharing that with someone who could appreciate and reciprocate it.

"For every one I save," she told him, a thread of sadness running through her voice, "I know that two or more get euthanized."

"But you choose to focus on the positive," he asked.

"I focus on the positive," she confirmed. Otherwise, Kayla added silently, she probably wouldn't be able to make it through the day.

"What else?" he prodded.

She didn't understand what he was trying to get at. "What else what?"

She'd stirred his curiosity, making him want to know things about her. It wasn't very different from his usual approach to women, except that he felt a genuine interest in this one.

"What else do you feel guilty about? In your private life, apart from dogs. What have you done or not done that creeps up on you in the dead of night to prey on your mind and haunt you?"

That was as good a description as any she'd ever heard. *And dead-on.*

"You *are* a lawyer, aren't you?" she laughed.

Now that she'd sparked his curiosity, he wasn't about to give her a chance to turn this around. "We're talking about you, not me."

When had that happened? "No, we're not."

But even so, she reflected on his question. The only thing she felt guilty about was a time in her life when she allowed herself—in the name of love—to be bullied. She'd actually believed that if she did just what Brett wanted, they could live happily ever after. And in putting up with him, she had let everyone else down. Her parents would have expected more of her had they been alive to see what was happening.

She'd allowed her fear of being alone to back her into a corner, to tolerate the intolerable and behave like someone she wasn't.

But she'd learned. Learned that there *was* no happily ever after possible with men like Brett, nor for the people in their lives.

Kayla squared her shoulders, driving the memory away. She didn't like to think about that period of her life, didn't like thinking of herself that way—weak, submissive, constantly giving and never receiving. More than guilt, it made her feel ashamed. Ashamed and almost obsessively determined never to allow something like that to happen to her again. She had her dogs, her practice and her pledge to rescue German shepherds wherever she found them being neglected and mistreated. She didn't need a man to validate her existence, to make her feel loved.

Alain narrowed his eyes, locking them on hers. His gaze was penetrating.

"C'mon," he coaxed, and she could almost see

someone on the witness stand being mesmerized by those eyes. "There has to be something," he insisted quietly.

"Okay," she said slowly, as if was considering his question. "I feel guilty that I didn't buy that generator when I had the opportunity."

She was evading the question, Alain thought, more intrigued than ever. The more she resisted answering, the more he found himself wanting to know what it was she wasn't telling him. "I'm serious."

"So am I," she replied innocently. "Power outages happen here about twice a year. Sometimes more. If I were operating on a patient…"

Her voice trailed off. Not having a generator, now that she thought of it, was a serious oversight on her part. She needed a backup power source as much as a local hospital might. Just because her patients had four feet instead of two didn't change that. The minute the roads became passable again, she should drive to the hardware store in Everett, the neighboring town, and pick up a good generator.

She decided to turn the conversation away from her and back to him. "What about you?"

Finished eating, he placed his plate on the table. Winchester looked up at him mournfully. With a sigh, Alain nodded, and the small dog went at it.

"I never thought about getting a generator," he quipped.

Oh, no, he wasn't getting out of it that easily. "I mean what do you feel guilty about?"

"Nothing." To her ear, the response was automatic. Friendly, but with established boundaries that she could tell were not meant to be crossed.

Okay, so she wasn't allowed any further enlightenment into the mystery that was Alain Dulac. But at least her point was made. He didn't like someone prying into his life any more than she did.

But even as Kayla silently congratulated herself for not being curious enough to elbow her way into his personal life, she found herself wondering about him.

"Maybe that's why Winchester's taken to you," she said carefully, watching his expression. "He senses a kindred spirit."

Alain shook his head, not buying it. "He's looking for a handout."

Kayla's eyes dipped down to the plate on the coffee table. Everything but the rosebud design in the center of the plate had been licked off. "And he has pretty good intuition," she concluded, with an easy smile.

Alain's eyes followed her line of vision. He flushed. Winchester had cleaned the plate and was looking hopefully at him again. *That's it, dog. There ain't no more.*

"It was good," he told her, hoping she wouldn't say anything about his feeding the dog the last of the scraps. "Aren't you having any?"

She shook her head. "I tend to nibble as I cook," she told him, rising from her perch, "so technically, I've already had breakfast." Picking up the plate from the coffee table, she raised her brow in a query. "Want some coffee?"

"Please." The request was made almost worshipfully. And then he stopped. If she was offering him coffee, the stove had to have come back on. Which meant that he could use the phone to get someone to drive him home. "Is the power on?"

She wished. But she'd tested the stove just before she'd begun to make breakfast, and nothing had turned on. Kayla shook her head. "Nope."

He looked at her skeptically. "Then how are you going to make coffee?"

"Same way the cowboys used to when they were out on the range," she answered cheerfully. Kayla glanced at him over her shoulder just before she stepped into the kitchen to retrieve a battered aluminum coffeepot. "Haven't you ever been camping?"

"No." The answer was given almost defensively, as if he felt that the admission unmanned him somehow in her eyes.

Kayla stopped and looked at him incredulously. "You're kidding."

His defensiveness went up a notch. "Why would I kid about something like that?"

She shrugged nonchalantly. "No reason, I guess.

I just thought everyone went camping at some point or other in their lives." She'd pegged him right. He was a city boy, born and bred. "City kids especially, just to get away from it all."

His eyes narrowed a tad. "And by 'it' you mean electricity and flush toilets?"

She took no offense at his tone or the slight note of sarcasm in his voice. Instead, she just laughed.

The expression that came over his face was positively wicked. "My sense of adventure takes me in other directions."

For a second, her eyes met his. Kayla knew exactly what he was talking about. Unless her guess was wrong, Alain Dulac's idea of adventure involved someone of the opposite sex and a minimum of clothing.

She shook off the warm feeling that invaded her. "I'll bet," she murmured under her breath, then said audibly, "So, black?"

Okay, she'd lost him again. "Excuse me?"

"Your coffee," Kayla elaborated pleasantly. "You take it black?"

Good guess, he thought. "Yes."

"Coming up," she promised.

Kayla left the room and the dogs moved right along with her.

All except Winchester. The small shepherd with the large cast remained behind, sitting by the sofa, as if he'd been placed on guard duty. Cocking his head, he managed to move it directly beneath Alain's hand.

"Not very subtle, are you?" he laughed.

He began to pet the dog. After a beat, Winchester's rear right leg started thumping. Intrigued, Alain switched from petting to scratching. Winchester's leg responded by thumping harder, as if it had a mind of its own.

"I think your dog is about to dance a jig," Alain called out to Kayla.

Rather than shouting back, she returned with a battered coffeepot, holding the handle with an old kitchen towel she'd wrapped around it. She smiled at him, or maybe it was the dog she was smiling at.

"You found his sweet spot."

What would it take to find hers? Alain caught himself wondering. "Is that a good thing?" The leg was thumping almost frantically. He half expected the dog to fall over.

"A very good thing as far as Winchester's concerned." She peered closer at the dog's face as she came forward. "I think he's smiling."

Now she was pulling *his* leg, Alain thought. "Dogs don't smile."

"Oh, yes, they do." She said it with such conviction, he began to think that she was serious. "If my computer was up, I'd show you a whole gallery of smiling dogs." She placed the two large mugs she'd brought in with her on the coffee table, then poured what looked like liquid asphalt into each cup. Picking one up, she handed it to Alain. "Here you go. Coffee, black."

Their fingers brushed as Alain took the mug from her. He could have sworn that a spark of electricity flew between them, even if it was still conspicuously absent everywhere else.

Outside, the wind had stopped howling, but the rain continued coming down, rhythmically pelting in huge drops against the window as if it never intended to halt.

Holding the mug in both hands, Alain nodded toward the window. "How long does it generally rain here?"

"Until it stops." Kayla hid the smile that came to her lips behind her mug.

Not about to accept defeat, he tried again. "And when would that be?"

Lowering the cup, she said innocently, "When the clouds go away."

Very funny, he thought. "I can't stay here indefinitely," he told her.

"No," she agreed. "But less than twenty-four hours isn't exactly 'indefinitely.'" She knew that the laid-back answer was not the one he wanted. The man definitely needed to learn how to relax a little. She nodded toward Winchester, who hadn't moved an inch since he'd planted himself in front of Alain. "Try petting him again," she suggested. "It's a proven fact that petting a dog or cat is very soothing."

"For who?" Alain challenged, with that same note of sarcasm that seemed to come into his voice effortlessly. "The dog or cat?"

"For the human—although I'm sure the animal likes it, too." She looked at the dog closest to her— Ariel—and stroked her noble head. Ariel leaned into her hand to get the full benefit of each stroke. "Don't you, girl?"

Alain could have sworn he heard the dog sigh, but that just might have been the sound of the rain hitting the windows.

He was feeling somewhat better now, and stronger for having eaten something. He was more inclined than ever to get back on the road. "I don't want to be soothed, I need to be on my way," he told her, adding, "I've got a deposition to have transcribed, not to mention a get-together tomorrow."

"She'll wait," Kayla replied knowingly.

God knew that she herself would—if she belonged in his world, she thought, then immediately discarded the idea. Kayla had learned that this was where she belonged. Cities were all right to visit, but nothing beat the warm feeling of a town small enough that people knew your name.

"It's not a she," he told her.

"Oh." Okay, she thought, he played for the other team. Nothing wrong with that, but it did seem like an incredible waste. "Then he'll wait."

Alain knew what she was thinking—that he was in a hurry to meet someone socially. He set her straight. "I have a meeting with my boss. The whole firm is getting together. Over brunch."

She wondered if that was his firm's version of an annual picnic. "If it's over brunch, it can't be that important."

The corners of his mouth curved. Her small-town upbringing was showing. "You've never been part of the corporate world, have you?"

"No. Mercifully," she added.

But this was obviously important to him. She doubted if the car would be travel-worthy for several days.

"Tell you what. Since the lines are down, I'll take a drive later to the next town to see if Mick can come out."

"Mick?"

She was getting ahead of herself, she realized. "He's the best mechanic in two towns."

Alain wasn't naive enough to take that at face value. "Let me guess. The only mechanic in two towns."

She laughed and nodded again. "I made it too easy for you. But seriously," she stated, "Mick is good."

Alain thought back to something else she'd told him earlier. "I thought you said that the roads were impassable."

There was no discrepancy in her statements. "They are. But I know an out-of-the-way route."

As much as he wanted to be on his way, he didn't want to have this woman's demise on his conscience. "Maybe the rain'll let up."

"It always does," she allowed with a smile. "The question is how long it might take." If he was willing to wait, so much the better. "We could give it a few more hours, see what happens."

He realized he was watching her lips as she spoke. And letting his mind drift to places his gut told him she wouldn't want to go. "All right."

She moved to the other side of the sofa and fluffed the pillow. "And that'll give you more time to rest."

He did feel more tired than he was happy about, but he wasn't ready to admit that to her. "I didn't exactly exert myself lifting the fork."

"And getting dressed," she added, her eyes smiling down at him as she moved away from the sofa again. "Don't forget about getting dressed."

"Not exactly considered an Olympic event in most circles," he told her wryly.

"All depends on how challenged the dresser is," she said, amused. "You play cards?"

The question took him by surprise. He thought of

the weekly poker game Philippe held at his place. "Sure."

"Good." She crossed to the side table and opened a drawer. "Then we have a way to while away the time." Holding up a deck, she flashed him a smile.

He considered himself a damn good player. "Might not be fair," he warned her.

She winked. "I'll go easy on you."

"We are talking about poker, right?"

Sitting on the edge of the coffee table, facing him, she began to shuffle. "Is there any other game?"

"No," he agreed. "There isn't."

A few hands turned into a marathon. Except for a few breaks made necessary by little things like eating, they played well into the night. Played and talked. For Alain, time had never moved so quickly. He forgot about the rain and all the places he had to be. Where he was was far more enjoyable.

Chapter Six

The next day found Alain eager to resume playing. He was down by eight hands and he wanted to get even.

"You're down by ten," Kayla corrected, putting away the plates she'd used for their breakfast. "But who's counting?"

"You, obviously," he replied. He was feeling somewhat better today, and since it was still raining and the power was still out, playing poker kept his hands busy and his mind from straying to other activities that had an even greater allure. "C'mon, stop stalling. My ego demands that I catch up."

She knew better than that. Over the course of the hours spent playing yesterday, she'd learned that while her handsome patient enjoyed competition, he liked winning even better.

"Your ego demands that you beat me." Kayla looked amused, but then her expression became slightly somber as she scanned the room, obviously looking for something.

"What's wrong?" he asked her.

Turning around, Kayla did a quick head count. "Have you seen Ginger?"

The only name that was familiar to him was Winchester, who was still by his feet. Kayla had rattled off the other names to him yesterday, after he'd asked why she had so many dogs around. She'd told him about belonging to the German Shepherd Rescue Organization, but for the life of him, he couldn't recall the dogs' names now. "Which one's Ginger?"

She opened the hall closet. No Ginger. "The pregnant one."

"Oh, right." He couldn't recall when he'd last seen her. "I've been meaning to ask you. Why is she pregnant? I thought you'd spayed them all."

"I can't spay them all. Some I have to neuter," she teased. People confused the two terms all the time. "But to answer your question, I found her that way. With child." She walked toward the bathroom and looked in. Still no Ginger. "Or puppies, as the case may be. I wasn't about to terminate them once they were on their way."

Alain felt he had to point out the obvious. "That just means you're going to wind up with more unwanted dogs."

"I'll find people who want them," she said with confidence. "People love puppies. Just like everyone loves babies."

"Yes, but puppies grow up faster."

"By then, they've already entrenched themselves in your life and it's too late to back out." Retracing her steps, she went off in another direction, searching with no success. Where *was* that dog? "Ginger," she called as she walked out of the living room. "This is no time to play hide and seek. Get your little pregnant butt in here. Now."

Kayla's voice was growing distant as she made her way to the back of the house. And then he heard her exclaim, "Oh, damn."

He winced as he sat up straight, one hand pressed against the bandages around his ribs.

"What's wrong?" he called. "Did you find her?"

"Yes." And then he learned the reason for her dismay. "She's giving birth."

"But that's a good thing, right?" After all, Kayla was a vet. Birthing animals was part of what she did, wasn't it?

She didn't answer his question; Ginger did. A high-pitched, mournful howl pierced the air.

Gritting his teeth, Alain pushed himself up off the sofa. Winchester, who had sunk down near his feet a few minutes ago, instantly popped up, alert and ready to hobble anywhere that the man he'd surrendered his affections to was going.

"Watch your head, dog," Alain warned. He was thrown off balance as he tried his best not to trip over Winchester or step on him.

As if he understood him, the shepherd obligingly took a step back, out of the way.

Coincidence, Alain thought. Steadier now, he followed the sound of the howling. It led him to the kitchen, where he found Ginger scrunched up beneath a rectangular table. She wasn't alone. Kayla was right beside her.

"Anything I can do to help?" he offered a little uncertainly. "Aren't dogs supposed to do this by themselves? They've been doing it since the beginning of time, long before there were vets to tend to them."

"So have women," she countered. "Squatting in the field and giving birth, then going on with whatever farm chore they were doing before they went into labor. But most women do a lot better with help instead of going it alone, don't you think?"

She wasn't about to get an argument from him about that, he decided. His brother Georges was a

doctor. Still, Alain was hard-pressed to try to visu-
alize the German shepherd taking deep breaths and
panting in between pushes—although now that he
noticed, she did seem to have the panting down pat.

Trying not to pay attention to the pain radiating
from his ribs, he squatted down to be face level with
Kayla. "What do you want me to do?"

It was on the tip of her tongue to say, "Stay out
of the way," because there was only so much room
beneath the table. Besides, if he exerted himself he
might wind up making his own condition that much
worse. There was no way she would be able to attend
to Ginger and help him at the same time.

But one look at Alain's face told her that he was
sincere. Maybe he could save her a few steps, she
decided. That seemed harmless enough.

"If you could get the basin that's under the sink for
me, rinse it out and fill it with warm water, I would
appreciate it." The second she mentioned the temperature, she remembered. With the power out, the
water heater wasn't working. "Oh, damn, there isn't
any warm water," she amended. There was only one
thing to do. "Well, fill it with cold water—and towels.
I need towels," she told him. Glancing over her
shoulder at him, she could see his next question
forming. "There are clean kitchen towels in the cabinet
right next to the sink." She pointed in that direction.

Placing a hand on top of the table, Alain drew

himself up. It took him a couple of seconds to locate the cabinet she was referring to. When he opened it, he saw that it was stuffed with towels.

"How many?"

"Two, three, whatever you can grab."

It was happening, Kayla thought. The miracle. Ginger was ready to give birth. She didn't care how common it was or how often it happened before her eyes, it was still a miracle, each and every time. But even miracles needed a helping hand every now and then.

"Hurry," she told him.

"Hurrying," Alain assured her.

He grabbed a handful of clean towels from the cabinet and brought them over to Kayla as fast as he was able.

There was a large damp spot on the floor beneath the table and he could have sworn he saw something emerging from Ginger's nether region, accompanied by a low, moaning noise.

He glanced at Kayla for confirmation. "Is that—?"

She didn't wait for him to finish. The puppies were definitely coming. "Yes. Basin. Water." The words shot out like bullets. Her eyes were riveted on the animal in labor.

By the time he got the basin filled—and avoided colliding with his four-footed, furry shadow—Alain saw that Kayla had a tiny, scrawny, hairless bit of life in her hands. It looked more like a little rat than a puppy.

"That's what they look like when they're born?" he asked incredulously.

She could tell by his tone that he found the puppy less than appealing. *Pagan*.

"Yes," she said, carefully drying the tiny black puppy. "Beautiful."

When he looked at the newly minted animal, it wasn't the first descriptive word that occurred to him. Or the second. But Alain had a feeling that was something best kept to himself.

"There's another one!" he cried, watching a second puppy emerge.

His reaction tickled her. "Where there's smoke…" She allowed her voice to trail off as she took possession of the second puppy, also black, and wiped him clean. She set both puppies down beside her.

They continued coming like clockwork, one after the other. Twenty minutes later, there were nine of them.

"Is that it?" he asked her, amazed that so many puppies had come out of a relatively small German shepherd.

"I think so."

He heard something in her voice. A note of distress he hadn't heard before. "What is it?"

"This one isn't breathing." The last puppy, the tiniest one of the lot, lay still in her hand.

"Isn't there something you can do?" he asked. It seemed wrong, somehow, to mar this celebration of birth with a death at the same time.

Holding the puppy in her hand, its spine resting against her palm, Kayla began to gently massage the tiny chest. Ever so delicately, she blew into the puppy's nostrils. It was all she could think of. This had never happened to her before. With all the litters she'd delivered, there had never been a stillborn.

She didn't want there to be one now.

"Here," Alain offered, "let me try. My hands are bigger."

As if that made a difference.

Kayla wanted to ask him what he thought he could do that she couldn't, but she knew how agonizing the futility of facing death could be. So she handed over the puppy and watched Alain do exactly what she had been doing—but less gently and with more vigor.

"That's not going to—" She was going to tell him to stop when she saw the slight movement. The puppy's chest had moved. And again. Stunned, she looked up at Alain. "He's breathing. The puppy's breathing."

Alain grinned. "Yeah, I know. I can feel it in my hand." He looked down at the small creature in his palm. "Almost lost you there, didn't we?" He felt a sense of triumph, a rush that he'd never experienced before, even when winning a case in court. There was something pure and unadulterated about being part of bringing a life into the world.

Kayla smiled, touched by the way he'd responded to the puppy, and impressed by the way he'd responded to the emergency.

Alain glanced up and saw how she was looking at him. Again he was aware of the crackle of electricity between them. But this time, it felt softer, more intimate.

Rousing herself, Kayla looked down at Ginger and stroked the dog's head. "You did good, Mama. Now it's time to feed your babies."

Alain was still on his knees, and he helped her round up the small, wobbly litter. There were nine tiny puppies in need of sustenance, vying for position at a bar where only eight could be seated at any one time.

Holding the puppy he'd saved, and another one against him, Alain raised his eyes toward Kayla. "She's only got, um, eight…" He was really out of his element here, he thought.

Kayla grinned. "Nothing gets by you, does it?" Rising to her feet, she crossed to another cupboard. When she turned around again, he saw that she had an empty baby bottle in her hand. She filled it with milk from the refrigerator and then crawled back under the table, next to him.

Alain had gently ushered eight of the puppies toward their first meal, and they were doing the rest. She noted that he was still holding the puppy he'd breathed life into. Kayla offered the bottle to him. She would have preferred warming the milk, but this would have to do for now.

"Want to do the honors?" she asked.

He glanced at the bottle and then the puppy. It didn't really look like a good fit; the bottle seemed almost as large as the puppy. The tiny creature was mewling, sounding more like a kitten than a canine.

Taking the bottle, he looked at Kayla. "He'll drink this?"

"Why don't you put the nipple near his mouth and see?" she suggested.

He had no idea why her innocent words conjured up the image within his head that it did. An image that had far less to do with nourishing a puppy and a great deal more with nourishing something within him. It took him a couple of moments to clear the picture from his mind.

Nodding, he said, "Okay."

The second he brought the nipple to the puppy's mouth, the newborn began sucking madly, as if starving.

Alain smiled at the way the puppy ate with such

gusto. And then he realized something. "His eyes are shut."

Kayla nodded, watching over the other eight even as she kept glancing over her shoulder at Alain and the puppy he was feeding. "That's how they come, wiggly, hairless and sightless." She continued to stroke Ginger's head. "Something only a mother could love," she added softly.

"And you."

Her eyes met his. She smiled and something stirred inside of him. "And me," she agreed.

Outside, the wind howled and the rain lashed at the windows again, as if unleashing round two. Caught up in the miracle of the moment, neither one of them noticed.

"Where are you going?"

It was several hours later. Ginger and her brood had been moved over by the fireplace to keep them all warm. Alain had spent most of his time watching over the new mother and her puppies. Winchester had placed himself in close proximity to both man and new mother. Winchester was there, at Alain's feet. Ginger tolerated him. As for Alain, he was amused by the microdynamics of this small society.

Kayla's crossing to the front door, a rain slicker draped over her clothes, instantly roused him from this uncomplicated, domestic scene. Was she going out in weather like this?

She fished out the keys to her truck. "I'm going to see about getting Mick to come out and at least take a look at your car, see if it can be salvaged."

The birthing process and the business of caring for Ginger and the new puppies—especially Nine, which was what he'd called the one he'd saved—seemed so surreal it had knocked out all sense of time. He felt like he was someplace where the minutes just stood still. But the mention of his car brought reality—and his shot-to-hell schedule—back to Alain.

"And if it can't?" he asked. "Is there a car-rental agency around here?"

She smiled. "You might be able to pay Mick or one of his people to drive you wherever you have to go—once the weather clears up a little."

Alain groaned. That didn't sound promising. From where he sat, it looked like the kind of weather in which a man with a flowing beard would feel called upon to collect two of everything and push them onto his boat.

"How long do you think that'll be?"

Kayla shook her head as she raised her hood to cover her hair. "Haven't a clue," she confessed. "It doesn't usually rain at all this time of year." About to walk out, she hesitated, then looked at him over her shoulder. "There's dry dog food in the garage if you want to bribe any of them. I'm taking Taylor and Ariel, but the rest are staying with you."

He looked uneasily at the dogs she was leaving behind. There were three besides Winchester and Ginger. Not counting the puppies. He couldn't help feeling vastly outnumbered.

"You think that's wise? I'm a stranger to them."

Not after forty-eight hours, she thought. The number struck her. Had it really only been that long? It certainly felt longer.

"The dogs are smart. They can sense things. They know you're not here to steal the silverware." She grinned. He still looked somewhat uncertain. "I'll be back as soon as I can," she promised.

"Sure the phones aren't working?" he called after her.

Instead of leaving, Kayla doubled back to the kitchen. Picking up the receiver from the wall unit, she held it toward him without saying a word. Even with the distance between them, he could hear that there was nothing but silence coming from the receiver.

"I'm sure," she said. Then she smiled at him, resurrecting that same odd tightening inside his gut. As she passed him, she patted his shoulder. Much the way, he noted, that she'd stroked Ginger's head. "You'll be fine," she assured him.

And then she was gone.

* * *

He kept checking his watch, wondering if Kayla was all right. Shouldn't she have gotten back by now? It felt like an eternity since she'd left.

Where was she?

As a lawyer, he was worried that something might have happened to her in the storm, and since he'd sent her out, he was liable for her. He could be sued on a number of counts if she—or her estate— were savvy enough to think like lawyers. As a man, he just worried about her welfare and wanted her back, safe and sound. And presiding over her dogs. He didn't feel too comfortable about the way two of them had begun pacing. Did they know something he didn't?

Or were they just doing that to intimidate him?

He hadn't a clue.

Each time he rose to his feet, whether to look out the window or to get something from the refrigerator, he couldn't shake the sensation of having five pairs of eyes trained on him. Even the puppies seemed to raise their heads in the direction of the sound he made. Definitely unnerving.

When Kayla finally walked through the door, the five dogs who rushed to her were not the only ones who were happy to see her. Walking across the threshold, she shed her slicker and sent a mini-shower onto the floor as she laughed at the greeting, petting two dogs at a time.

"How were they?" she asked, looking at the puppies.

"They survived my care," he answered. He noticed that aside from the two dogs Kayla had taken with her, she was alone. "Couldn't get him to come, I take it?"

Kayla looked at Alain quizzically for a second before she realized who he was asking about. "Oh, you mean Mick. Yes, I got him to come."

"And he's where, in your pocket?"

"No, he's outside, looking over your car." The rain had subsided a bit, no longer coming down at an all-but-blinding rate.

Alain crossed to her, not bothering to hide his eagerness. What he did hide was that he still felt incredibly achy.

"And?"

"And he's outside, looking over your car," she repeated. Alain lived in a faster-paced world than she did, where everything was done yesterday. She'd sampled that world, and been more than happy to leave it behind when she came back here. "That's all I know for now."

He was pushing, Alain realized. He'd been driven all his adult life, and it wasn't something he could easily brush off. "Sorry, I'm not usually this antsy."

He didn't want her thinking of him as another man who lived in the fast lane. Why, he wasn't sure.

Kayla inclined her head. "This isn't exactly your typical, run-of-the-mill situation," she admitted.

Crouching, she quickly looked over the puppies, just to satisfy her own concerns. To her delight, they really were fine. These she could find a home for. As she'd told Alain before she left, everyone loved puppies.

Before he could agree with her assessment, he heard the front door opening again. Turning, he saw a tall thin man, with long, dirty-blond hair—currently wet—walk in. The smell of oil and gasoline followed him. Small, intent brown eyes looked him over before the man finally offered his hand.

"Mick Hollister," he introduced himself. "Pretty fancy car for these parts."

Alain derived his own interpretation from the man's words. It wasn't admiration so much as a lack of knowledge in the man's voice. Disappointment reared. "Then you can't fix it."

"Oh, I can fix it, all right," Mick assured him. "They haven't invented a machine I can't fix. But it's gonna take awhile," he warned Alain. "Gotta get parts, that kind of stuff. Not something I usually stock."

Alain could see this stretching out to two, three weeks. And as much as he found himself liking this feisty vet's company, he needed to get back. "I don't have awhile."

Mick nodded, absorbing the information. Keeping his judgments simple. "Then I guess you've got a problem."

Alain was nothing if not a problem solver. Maybe not as good as Philippe, but he could hold his own. "How about if I leave the car with you to be fixed, and meanwhile, you drive me to Orange County?" He could see that the other man was not keen on the idea. "I'll pay you."

But Mick shook his head. "Sorry, can't leave my shop. Too much work to do," he explained.

Alain couldn't see much money being made in a small town like this, or the neighboring vicinity. "I'll pay you twice whatever it is you're making working on the cars."

Instead of jumping at the chance the way he thought the mechanic might, the older man shook his head. "That wouldn't be right. I'd be robbing you."

Alain had never run into honesty as a stumbling block before. In his line of work, the opposite was usually the case. Stunned, he looked at Kayla. "He's serious."

"As a thunderstorm," she replied simply. She picked up Nine and stroked him as she spoke. "Is there anyone you can call to come pick you up— once the phone lines are back up?"

He sighed, frustrated. There were his brothers and several cousins he could call—if he could call. Which he couldn't in this backward town. He was stuck, he thought. Alain didn't think that anyone would miss him until some time next week, when he had to file papers regarding another case he was handling. He doubted that Rachel would call either of his brothers to say he hadn't shown up for their date, or that anyone from his office would think to check why he had missed the meeting and wasn't in the office today. Which left him as stranded as the Prisoner of Zenda.

"Yes," he finally said, "there are several people I could call—if I could call," he repeated. "How long before the lines are back up?"

Kayla shrugged casually. "Hard to say. On the average, it's not more than a few days."

A few days. That translated to an eternity in his world.

As if sensing his agitation, Winchester hobbled next to him, planted himself on his rear and looked up at him adoringly while his tail moved back and forth like a deranged metronome.

"If I were you, mister, I'd just relax and make the best of it," Mick suggested. And then he followed his words with what sounded like a wicked laugh.

Alain couldn't help noticing that the man with the dirt-stained fingers had deliberately looked toward Kayla as he tendered his advice.

Chapter Seven

Outside, it was growing dark. The rain had finally stopped, but the sky looked ominous, as if another storm was in the making. And the power still had not made an appearance.

Alain was stranded, which ordinarily would make him agitated. Not having control over something usually did that to him. Yet as he sat at the kitchen table with the candles casting elongated shadows about the room, he felt calm inside. Since he couldn't do anything to change the situation, he'd come to terms with it.

After all, the power outage couldn't last forever.

At least he hoped not. And rather than get frustrated because he couldn't do anything about it, he made himself relax and take in the moment.

And the woman who was so much a part of it.

Right now, Kayla was busy getting their dinner ready. He'd offered to help, but she had told him just to sit and relax, that too many people milling about the fireplace would get in each other's way. He assumed that "two" constituted "too many."

So here he sat, watching her.

And he liked watching her.

Alain's mind drifted back to his situation. He doubted if he'd be replaced on the case he was currently assigned to at the firm. Bobbie Jo Halliday liked him, and money talked. Besides, it really hadn't been *that* long. Maybe by tomorrow the power would be restored, and, more importantly, the phones lines would rise up from the dead.

Periodically he'd take his cell phone out of his pocket and check to see if it was finally receiving some sort of signal. Every time he flipped it open, the tiny screen gave him the same message: *Searching for a network*.

Obviously the network had decided to take a holiday.

The mechanic that Kayla had brought back with her was long gone. Mick had taken Alain's BMW back to "the shop," wherever that was.

It occurred to Alain that he was placing a great deal of trust in this woman he hadn't even known existed seventy-two hours ago. Maybe that was a mistake.

He thought of some of the mysteries—his favorite form of entertainment—that he'd read. What if this Mick character was really stealing his car? And he was stripping it in order to sell the vehicle for parts. Kayla could be in on it, she could even—

Alain reined in his thoughts. The woman was not the devious, mastermind type. She was—

Suddenly he felt something wet and rough against the back of his hand and fingers. He looked down to see that Winchester had made his way over again and was licking his hand.

Alain didn't bother restraining the smile that rose to his lips. He'd even begun to feel a small measure of affection for the injured dog—one injured creature relating to another, he mused.

The stew she'd put together had been simmering nicely and, if the dissolving diced potatoes were any indication, it looked as if it was finally done. Time to eat.

Kayla glanced over her shoulder toward the kitchen and Alain.

She smiled fondly at Winchester. Her smile took in Alain, as well. "He's just trying to get you to pay attention to him." She wasn't sure, but she thought she saw Alain raise a quizzical eyebrow. "He thinks you've been won over by Nine and his crew."

"I haven't been 'won over' by anything," Alain protested, although, reflecting back, he had to admit that saving the last puppy had been a rather emotional experience.

Kayla moved away from the fireplace, dusting off her hands on the back of her jeans. The grin on her face as she spared him another look told Alain that she knew otherwise.

She made her way to the cupboard and took down two large bowls. "Oh, I think you have. Nothing wrong with having a soft spot in your heart for animals—dogs especially."

She began to ladle out equal portions of stew. Taylor and Ariel took an extreme interest in her every move, anticipating a handout. She deliberately avoided making eye contact with the dogs.

Kayla brought both bowls to the table and set them down. Turning, she went to another cabinet and retrieved a bottle of wine, then two glasses.

"Didn't you have a favorite pet when you were growing up?"

He waited for her to sit down opposite him before picking up his fork. The stew smelled incredible and he could feel his appetite spiking.

In more ways than one, he thought, watching as

she pushed her hair back out of her eyes. He took a sip of wine.

"I didn't have a pet," he answered, "favorite or otherwise."

She raised her eyes to his. Even in this dim light, he thought they were mesmerizing. "You're kidding."

Alain forced himself to look down at his dinner and not at her. He took another sip of wine before responding. A warm, mellow feeling began to slip over him. "Why would I kid about that?"

When she gave no answer, he raised his eyes to her face. She was looking at him as if she'd suddenly realized how deprived he was.

"I'm sorry," she told him softly.

He wasn't sure he followed her. "Sorry you thought I was kidding?"

"No, sorry that you didn't have a pet." He'd missed out on a lot, she thought. "Everyone should have at least one pet in their lives." She looked over to where Ginger was lying, her puppies in a semicircle around her. Kayla's sweeping glance took in the other dogs, as well, ending with Winchester, who was standing at Alain's left like a small, furry bodyguard. "There's nothing like the feeling of having a set of adoring brown eyes looking up at you."

Alain laughed before he could think better of it and stop himself. Her description pretty much summed up the way Rachel always looked up at him—he was almost a foot taller than she was. The woman had to have the softest eyes he'd ever seen. That is, they had been until he'd looked down at Winchester.

"You're thinking of your girlfriend, aren't you?" Kayla asked.

The knowing tone, breaking into his thoughts, took him by surprise. Without thinking, he dropped his left hand and began to stroke Winchester's head. A peacefulness seeped into him.

"How did you know what I was thinking about?" he challenged.

That was easy, she thought as she swallowed another forkful of her stew. "You smirked."

"No, I didn't," he protested, then realized he was becoming defensive when there was no reason to. He liked Rachel, but there wasn't anything lasting between them. Just as there had never been anything lasting between him and any of the other women he took out. He couldn't get serious about a woman. He wouldn't allow it. "And besides, I wouldn't call her my girlfriend."

So there was a "her" in his life, Kayla thought. Finding that out shouldn't have made a difference, one way or another. The fact that it bothered her both intrigued and worried her.

She did what she could to bank down her feelings.

"Then what would you call her?" she asked mildly, aware that she was marginally flirting with him and enjoying it.

He shrugged his shoulders. It felt a little strange discussing his personal life with this woman. Especially since he was having difficulty drawing his eyes away from her. "Rachel."

Rachel. Pretty name. Probably a very pretty girl. Why did that even matter? "Does this Rachel know she's not your girlfriend?"

"Yes," he answered firmly. In case Kayla was casting him in the role of some heartless womanizer, he added with feeling, "I don't make a secret of how I feel about relationships."

This was getting very, very interesting. "And how do you feel about relationships?"

Alain narrowed his eyes as he looked at her. "What are you, my shrink?"

She countered with another mild question. "Do you have one?"

His question had been intentionally sarcastic, not intended as some sort of revelation. He didn't believe in baring his soul to a stranger.

Then what the hell are you doing right now?

Alain frowned. "No."

"Then, no," Kayla replied whimsically, looking back at her dinner, "I'm not."

Winchester was nudging him. Alain fished out a

bit of meat from his bowl and offered it to the dog. No sooner was it in his hand than it was gone. Winchester's teeth had never even touched his skin.

"Why all the questions?" he asked.

Kayla's expression when she looked up at him was innocence personified. "It's called conversation, Alain. You might have noticed, the radio and TV are out and talking is the only form of entertainment that's left to us at the moment. We did it last night over cards. Why can't we do it over dinner?" She shifted slightly in her seat, ignoring the begging animals on either side of her. The other dogs knew better than to beg, but Taylor and Ariel were her newest charges, and they were still hopeful. "Now, unless you'd rather just sit there like a statue, it's your turn to answer." She could see by his expression that she'd lost him in the maze of words. "You were going to tell me how you felt about relationships."

"No, I wasn't."

She leaned forward a little, and a soft, sensual fragrance tickled his nose. Moved his soul. "Humor me. I saved your life."

Alain made a show of trying to hold his ground, all the while knowing that he'd answer her in the end. "People don't die from cracked ribs."

"They do if the rib punctures a lung," she countered, growing serious for a moment. "Now you really have me curious," she admitted, still sitting on the edge of her seat. "You're obviously against relationships. Why?" Could it be for the same reason that she'd been steering clear of men these last couple of years? "Did someone hurt you, Alain?"

The woman was getting way too personal, and yet he couldn't bring himself to tell her that. Maybe because there was something almost surreal about being trapped here like this, in the middle of a storm, he allowed himself to purge his soul. This place would be in his past soon, as if it had never existed.

"No," he told her and it was the truth. He'd never allowed anyone the chance to hurt him. Because his mother had taught him that, by example.

Kayla wasn't sure if she quite believed him. "Then you're just a carefree, confirmed bachelor?"

Finished eating, Alain moved the bowl away from the edge of the table and Winchester's wistful gaze. "Something like that."

She paused for a moment, studying his face. And then she shook her head. "You're too young to be a confirmed anything."

She kept surprising him. "How do you know how old I am?"

Kayla shrugged carelessly, avoiding his eyes. "Your driver's license."

"You looked at my driver's license?"

She raised her head, looking at him as if she hadn't done anything out of the ordinary.

"While you were unconscious. I like knowing who I'm dragging into my house." Then, because he was still frowning, she added, "You could have been a serial killer."

"They don't put that on driver's licenses," he pointed out.

"True," she allowed, "but I did learn your name. And if you were wanted for anything, I'd know."

He didn't see how. "Are you one of those police program junkies?"

Watching *Cops* was a guilty pleasure she allowed herself, but judging from his tone, he looked down on things like that. So she said, "I wouldn't go so far as calling myself a junkie—I just like being informed, and I make myself aware of who's wanted for a crime."

He decided there was no point in arguing about what Kayla had done. Instead, he turned it to his benefit. "Okay, so you know my age. How old are you?"

"A gentleman never asks that of a lady," she countered smoothly.

The woman had more moves than a welterweight champion. "I'm just looking for a trade of information here."

She reconsidered. "Fair enough, I suppose. I'm twenty-seven."

She looked younger, he thought. "Ever been married?"

"No." Her eyes held his as she asked, "You?"

He thought they'd covered that when she asked about relationships. Was she intentionally trying to trip him up? "No. Siblings?"

"None. You?"

He thought of Philippe and Georges, both now settled. Unlike him. It seemed to him as if the dynamics in his life had changed rather quickly. "I've got two brothers."

"You're lucky."

The longing in her voice was hard to miss. He wouldn't have traded positions with an only child for the world, even though there had been knock-down, drag-out fights in his past, mostly with Georges. "At times," he allowed.

She envied his memories. If she'd had siblings, maybe Brett would have never been in her life, would have never had a chance to upend it the way he had. "Parents still alive?"

The way she phrased it told him that hers weren't. "Just my mother."

Kayla caught the inflection in his voice. Finished eating, she pushed her bowl away and leaned her elbow on the table, her chin on her palm. Humor curved her mouth. "What is it about your mother that makes you roll your eyes?"

For a second, he thought of brushing off her question, but then, he was no longer embarrassed by his mother. Certainly not the way he'd been when he was growing up, and her free-wheeling lifestyle had mortified him. As an adult, he could understand his mother's quest to have someone in her life who would adore her. And he understood her fickleness.

"My mother is Lily Moreau." Even as he told Kayla, he had his doubts she would recognize the name. This wasn't exactly the hub of culture.

One look at Kayla's face told him he'd guessed wrong. A skeptical look had entered her eyes. "Lily Moreau is your mom?"

He couldn't tell by her tone if she liked or disliked his mother. Something protective stirred in his chest. All of them had grown protective of Lily.

"Yes."

He was pulling her leg, Kayla thought. But if that was his intent, wouldn't he have used someone more famous, less controversial? "Lily Moreau, the artist."

"You've heard of her."

Now *that* she took offense at. "This isn't Briga-doon. We're small, but we're only about a hundred and twenty miles from L.A. County. We get *People* magazine around here, and next month," she told him brightly, "they say we might even get indoor plumbing."

He'd insulted her, he realized. "Sorry."

Kayla ignored the apology, more taken with the information he'd just given her. She'd seen photographs of the famous woman. The handsome blond man at Kayla's table didn't look a thing like the raven-haired artist.

"She's really your mother," she said again, disbelief lingering in her voice.

"I'll e-mail you a photograph of the two of us when I get home if you want proof." And then, because he'd been toying with the thought of seeing her again, he said, "Better yet, if you come down, I'll introduce you." He knew he had to qualify that, in case Kayla took him up on the invitation. His mother was nothing if not unpredictable. "Provided that she's in town. She has a habit of taking off and flying around the world on a moment's notice." At least, it had always seemed that way to him. "Though not as much as she used to."

Because she admired strong, independent women, Kayla knew more than a little about the famous artist. "What's it like, having such a famous mother?"

When he had been very young, it had bothered Alain that his mother was always taking off, that she wasn't like the mothers his friends had. But over the years, he'd made his peace with that. These days, now that he understood her better, he was rather proud of what she had accomplished. A lot of women would have surrendered in defeat, especially after their husband had practically sold the house out from under them—as Philippe's father had, to fund his gambling addiction.

"Apart from sharing her with the world, it has its moments," he murmured succinctly.

He was holding something back, Kayla thought. She tried to read between the lines. "You must have had an interesting childhood, traveling all over the globe, wherever there was an art gallery."

He'd wanted to, but Philippe had always been the voice of reason, pointing out that the trips would get in the way of Alain's schooling. He'd hated his brother for that. And hated his mother for listening. Now, Alain was grateful. He wouldn't be where he was if it hadn't been for Philippe.

"Not really. Most of the time, we stayed home, wherever home was at the time."

Philippe and even Georges had gone through more turmoil than he had. With each new husband, a new return address would appear in the corner of the envelope. As far as touring the different art galleries, he and the others remained home, technically under the care of nannies. But it was really Philippe who took care of them, Philippe who had handled the assignment his mother unwittingly thrust on him: being his brothers' keeper and surrogate father.

"Is that why you don't have relationships?" Kayla asked suddenly. "Because of your mother?"

The question caught him off guard, and hit much too close to home. "I thought you said you were a vet, not a head doctor."

She shrugged. "In a small town, you get to stretch beyond your boundaries, be a little of everything."

"I don't belong in this town," he reminded her. Which negated her right to analyze him.

Kayla didn't back away. "You're here now. That's all that matters."

She made it sound like a life sentence. He took it a step further. "You mentioned Brigadoon. If I'm here past midnight, does that mean I have to stay for the next hundred years?"

"Maybe you hit your head harder than I thought," she said. Getting up, she rounded the table and went through the motions of looking for a bump on his head. "You've already stayed here over night," she pointed out. "In fact, you're going on three."

She was standing so close to him, Alain could feel the heat coming from her body. Could feel the urges being aroused in his own.

All he had to do, he thought, was reach up and pull her down to his lap.

And kiss her.

He wanted to kiss her in the worst way, he finally admitted to himself. And something told him that if he did, she'd be receptive. But if he kissed Kayla, it would mean something to her. He doubted if he was ready for that. If he'd *ever* be ready for that.

But he still wanted to kiss her.

"Just a joke," he told her, turning his head to look at her. Brushing his arm against her leg.

"Oh." Kayla inhaled sharply when his eyes touched hers.

She shouldn't have put that bottle of wine out, she told herself. Or she shouldn't have had any of it. Wine always did things to her. Made her vulnerable as well as exceedingly fluid. She felt as if she could easily melt into his hands if he touched her.

Then why aren't you backing away? Why are you just standing here, waiting for him to reach for you?

Rousing herself, Kayla took a step back. Or tried to. It felt as if she were trying to walk through glue.

And then he did it. Hands bracketing her hips, Alain drew her onto his lap.

"You shouldn't be doing this," she warned. When he looked at her, waiting for her to elaborate, she told him, "You could hurt yourself."

He laughed. "You don't weigh that much."

"I wasn't thinking about weight," she replied. "A man in heat doesn't always think straight, and you do have cracked ribs."

He slowly ran his thumb along her lower lip. A thrill of anticipation ran through him, leaving no part untouched. He felt as if his whole body had suddenly gone on alert.

"It's a kiss, Kayla," he whispered softly, "just a kiss, nothing more."

Her breath was already caught in her throat. "You never know how these things will turn out," she stated, barely aware that the words were leaving her lips.

Get off his lap, something inside her cried. *Now. Before it's too late.*

But it was already too late.

Chapter Eight

It was too late, because his lips had found and captured hers.

Too late, because her body was already melting into a sizzling puddle.

Too late, because she was responding. Responding to him, to the kiss, with such intensity that had she had any breath to spare, it would have been sucked away immediately.

As it was, she was swiftly becoming light-headed even as she felt her pulse racing faster than the lead car at the Indianapolis 500.

She could no longer remember when she'd last been kissed by a man, or kissed one back.

She was kissing back now.

It was as if every single logical process that went on in her mind had suddenly opted to take a holiday.

She was melting faster than a handful of snow in the month of July.

Kayla wrapped her arms around Alain's neck and lost her way.

Lost herself in the heat, in the anticipation. In the excitement that leaped through her veins.

Damn, but he was a good kisser.

The best she'd ever had by a long shot. She found herself grateful to Brett and his mean streak. Had he not had one, she would have never found herself here, going up in smoke and thrilled about it. She would have gone on thinking that Brett was as good as it got.

She would have been so wrong.

Alain deepened the kiss, amazed at the sensations he was feeling. He wasn't drunk—it took far more than two glasses of wine for that to happen—but he certainly felt drunk. And drugged. And wildly aroused.

This feisty little vet with the soft lips made his heart race and the air in his lungs all but disappear.

Trying to get his bearings, he cupped her face in his hands and gently drew back so that he could look at her.

His eyes caressed her. "We're not in Kansas anymore," he murmured.

"Not even in Oz," she whispered back, surprised that her lips worked. She'd been fairly certain they'd been singed off.

Alain fought the very real, very strong temptation to go on kissing her. His palms itched and he wanted nothing more than to touch her, to trace the outline of her body with his fingertips and memorize each curve, each contour.

Hell, he wanted everything. Wanted to make love with her until he was too numb to move. She was turning him inside out and he was willingly allowing it to happen.

Alain drew in a long, deep breath. "We seem to have a new development here." His mouth suddenly felt so dry, he might have been gargling with sand.

She didn't want to hear about it, didn't want to hear about logic, or pause to weigh and measure consequences. Didn't want to think at all. She just wanted this to continue to its rightful conclusion. Otherwise, she was going to burn up in frustration.

"Stop being a lawyer," she told him, her voice low and husky.

Before Alain could reply, she was kissing him again, slanting her mouth against his over and over to prevent the parade of words from escaping. Kayla wasn't interested in his philosophies or his ability to reason things out. Wasn't interested in his legal mind or his rhetoric. What she was interested in was having the wild rush in her veins continue. She wanted him to kiss the hollow of her neck and make her crazy with desire.

Okay, crazier.

"Yes, ma'am."

She felt rather than heard his response, felt his smile ripple against her skin as he pressed his lips to her throat.

She moaned and gave herself up wholeheartedly to the feeling.

Somewhere during the heated, moist tangle of tongues, lips and teeth, Alain slowly rose to his feet. In sync with him, Kayla slid off his lap and planted her feet on the floor. Arms still entwined around his neck, she pressed herself against him.

She sucked in her breath and reveled in his hard, firm body. Her very core felt as if it were on fire. It took everything she had not to just leap up into his arms and wrap her legs around his waist. But in Alain's bruised condition, that could only hurt him.

Yet it was oh so hard to be reasonable when she burned like this.

Kayla didn't know which of them started the process first—whether she began tugging his clothes off or he hers. All she knew was that clothing began piling up on the floor beside the table as items were stripped off, one by one.

With each, her body temperature went up a degree, until she felt utterly fevered. And nude.

And then momentarily airborne. Alain caught her up in his arms and lifted her onto the table.

"Your ribs," she protested. She didn't want him reinjuring himself.

Ever so gently, he pushed her down on the table. The main course for his feast.

"You taped them up damn well," he told her, just before he began to conduct a complete inventory of her body. He covered every single inch first with his hands, then his lips.

She twisted beneath him, absorbing every touch, aching for more.

Kayla could feel the scream of pleasure bubbling up in her throat, and pressed her lips together as hard as she could. Any sudden cry from her could be misconstrued and instantly bring at least six dogs to her rescue, if not Ginger, too. They were very protective of her. She was taking no chances on Alain getting hurt—or the delicious assault on her body being halted.

Climaxes were rocking her, one exquisitely flowering into another as she arched against his mouth. But even as her head swam and she craved more, her sense of fair play broke through. It didn't seem right for this to be so one-sided.

Drawing on a great deal of strength, she raised her head to look at him. "What about you?" she panted.

Busy tracing a warm, moist trail between her thighs, Alain glanced up at her. She'd never seen a more sensually wicked look than the one on his face.

"I'm doing fine," he assured her. As he spoke, his breath brushed against her skin, all but driving her to the brink of distraction.

Another climax exploded within her.

She was swiftly losing the last shred of rationality and didn't want that to happen until they came together.

With superhuman effort, Kayla pushed herself up to a sitting position and then slid off the table. Before he could ask if she'd changed her mind, she wrapped her fingers possessively around his and tugged him down to the floor.

"I want you," she murmured thickly.

It was all he needed to hear. All he wanted to hear. The next moment, they were lost in each other's arms as he kissed her again. Kissed her as if he'd never done it before.

Kissed her until she felt her very soul leaping for joy.

And then, her back flat against the floor, his mouth sealed to hers, he entered her. They were joined, becoming one, instantly moving to a shared rhythm that they both felt beating within their chests.

They climbed together, faster and faster, until suddenly streamers of starlight burst over them.

Gripped by a feeling of euphoria, Kayla hung on to the afterglow as long as she could. Then he was pivoting his weight onto his elbows as he looked down into her face.

He was smiling.

"Something funny?" Her effort not to sound breathless was a failure. She wasn't expecting the answer that he gave her.

"Life," Alain told her. "If I'd paid for Halliday's valet to come down to L.A. to give his deposition, instead of driving to him, I'd never been caught in this storm, never wrecked my BMW." His fingers feathered along her cheek, moving a strand of hair away so that he could look at her unobstructed. She thought he was lamenting the events he was citing, until he added, "And I would have never been saved by you."

The way he said it made it seem as if he was talking about more than just her dragging him from the vehicle.

She was reading too much into it, Kayla decided. It was all just wishful thinking on her part, nothing more. Everyone knew that fantastic lovers did not make faithful lovers. It was a law written some-where.

The next moment, his body still pressed to hers, Alain jerked and stiffened.

Her eyes widened. "What's the matter?"

He laughed and then pointed behind him. Taylor was standing there, looming very close to his posterior. "I've just been goosed. I think he's jealous." And then he looked at her, his expression growing serious. "I think maybe we should take this to your bedroom."

"You want to do it again?"

Alain couldn't tell by her expression if his suggestion appalled her. Until this second, he'd thought that the pleasure was mutual. "It wasn't that bad, was it?"

"Bad?" Is that what he thought? She was quick to set him straight. "No. Oh, God, no. It's just that…" How could she put this without sounding as if she slept around? "I thought men could only do it once a night."

His smile was amused, and somehow still managed to seem incredibly intimate to her. "Lady, you've had the wrong lovers."

Lovers. Did he think she had sex casually? Well, what else would he think? They hadn't exactly known each other from the first grade, had they? He hadn't been in her life three days, and here they were, making love. So what did that make her?

Incredibly glad, a small voice whispered in her head.

When Alain extended his hand, she wrapped her fingers around it and allowed him to help her to her feet. Her knees didn't quite feel solid at the moment.

* * *

They made love two more times. Each time felt as exquisite as the last.

After the third time, Kayla wasn't sure if she could move anymore, not even if someone set fire to the house. And then Alain surprised her again by gathering her into his arms. He didn't turn from her and just go to sleep, the way Brett had. The way she assumed most men did. Alain was actually *holding* her.

Oh, God, was he real? Or was she just dreaming?

"A penny for your thoughts," he said, noting the dazed expression on her face.

Busted. Kayla raised one shoulder in a shrug. "I'm just wondering why you're not being stalked."

He wasn't sure what he'd expected her to say, but it certainly wasn't that. "What?"

"Well," she began slowly, trying not to come off as a mindless idiot, "I'm assuming I'm not the first woman you've ever made love to. And given the insensitive lovers out there, someone like you would be quite a catch for any woman."

Did she have any idea how adorable she was? He smiled at her, his eyes softly caressing her face. "Maybe I was just inspired this time."

A content sigh escaped her before she could stop it. She knew he was probably just feeding her a line, but she pretended that he was telling her the truth.

So rather than go on talking, she nestled against him, taking comfort in the beat of his heart against her cheek. Indulging in a fantasy that this was going to go somewhere, beyond tonight.

And then, as her eyes began to drift shut, she suddenly found herself assaulted by a wave of lights, accompanied by a battalion of sounds as everything within her bedroom and the rooms beyond came to life. Every appliance, every light fixture, the TV, the radio, everything she'd turned on when the power had gone out, hoping to find a spark of electricity, came on at the same moment, generating a swirling tornado of light and noise.

Startled, she bolted upright. Alain was right beside her, as surprised as she was.

"And then there was light," he said, looking around. His gaze returned to Kayla, who was sitting up, nude to the waist. His smile grew sensual as he reached for her. "This time," he said to her, "I get to see what I'm doing."

But just as he leaned in to kiss her, the phone on the nightstand began to ring.

His face an inch away from hers, Alain's eyes widened as the sound registered. "The phone." He looked up at it. "Your phone's ringing."

She knew what he was thinking. Phone service had been restored along with the power. That meant he could call someone to come get him.

And take him from her.

She knew that was inevitable; she just hadn't thought it would happen tonight. A huge wave of disappointment washed over her.

"So it is." Resigned, Kayla turned away from him and reached for the phone. She brought the receiver to her ear. "Hello?"

"Kayla, where've you been? I've been calling your number for over a day and no one's been answering." The deep male voice on the other end of the line was loud enough for Alain to make out.

It was Jack Brown, one of the volunteers she occasionally worked with at the rescue center. She struggled to focus.

"We had a power failure here," she told him. They didn't socialize, so this had to be about dogs. "Is something wrong?"

"Yes, something's wrong," he told her, although his voice no longer sounded as upset as it had. "I have a couple of shepherds in the Riverside shelter that aren't going to live out the week unless someone comes to claim them."

It was a familiar story. She'd traveled up and down the length of Southern California and beyond, going to the city shelters and rescuing German shepherds marked for extermination. At times, it felt like a never-ending battle.

Nodding as Jack gave her a few more details, she

interrupted and asked for the address, just to be sure she had the right shelter. "All right, tell them I'm coming. I'll be there as soon as I can manage. Probably around noon tomorrow. Thanks for calling."

Business as usual, Kayla thought, hanging up. Then, picking up the phone, she shifted in the bed and offered it to Alain. She tried to sound cheerful as she said, "Your turn."

But he didn't take it from her. Instead, he asked, "Who was that? Someone needing a vet?"

She shook her head. "Someone needing an angel of mercy," she corrected. That was the way they saw themselves, the members of the rescue team. Angels of mercy for a constant stream of furry orphans. "Two German shepherds were located at a Riverside shelter—they're usually euthanized within two weeks after arriving at one of the city shelters. There are just too many stray and abandoned dogs out there to keep them all alive."

That was the excuse, but he could see how much the reality of it bothered her.

"And you're riding to the rescue?" He assumed that from her end of the conversation.

A self-depreciating smile played on her lips. "It's what I do."

Nodding, Alain glanced at his watch. It was a little after 10:00 p.m. Not late by his standards, but he knew that Philippe liked to get to bed early so he didn't drag the next day. His eldest brother had always been an early riser, unlike Georges. *And him.*

Making up his mind, Alain shook his head and gently pushed away the phone that Kayla was holding out to him.

"It'll keep until morning," he assured her. He watched as she struggled with the sheet she'd wrapped around her breasts, replacing the phone on the nightstand. When she turned back to him, he grinned at her. "Now, where were we?"

"Again?" she asked incredulously. The man was absolutely incredible, she thought.

"Unless you're too tired," he qualified.

His thoughtfulness touched her. Most men wouldn't have worried about whether she was as keen on another go-around as they were. But making love with him had taken on a new urgency for her. This would be the last time, she realized. Tomorrow, he would make his call to his brothers or a friend, and once they came for him, he would be out of her life within a matter of hours, if not less.

Granted, his car was in Mick's shop, but he could always send someone up for it. And even if he did return for the vehicle himself, there was no guarantee that he would stop by her place. Most likely he wouldn't.

They were from two different worlds. No one had to tell her that.

But she forced a smile to her lips as she slid down against the pillow and looked up at him. "Too tired?" she echoed. Her eyes softened. "Alain, I'm just getting warmed up."

"Good," he said, pulling her to him. "That makes two of us."

Chapter Nine

When morning with its bright, glittering sunshine crept into the bedroom, Alain found himself experiencing a strange reluctance to stir or even open his eyes.

His reluctance had nothing to do with the aches and pains still riding roughshod over him. They were purely physical, and he knew that once he started moving, they would work themselves out relatively soon.

No, his reluctance to acknowledge morning stemmed from the fact that once he did, he was going to have to resume his life. Placing a call to Philippe, which was the first thing on his agenda, would instantly connect him with that life, and this adventure would, in essence, end.

He'd be leaving.

Leaving a simpler way of life, one he'd thought would quickly drive him up a wall—but hadn't.

Leaving Kayla.

The long and short of it was, he didn't want to leave her. Not yet. Not when he'd only just begun to enjoy being around her.

The fact that he did was nothing new. He'd always enjoyed being with women, enjoyed the company of vibrant, independent females who knew what they were about.

But he'd learned never to require the company of any particular woman for long. Because, for one reason or another, they would leave. The nannies he grew attached to had always left, some sooner than others. Throughout his childhood and adolescence, his mother was always leaving. So Alain became very good at not needing them to remain. Eventually, he became the one who left first.

But his time with Kayla had been much too brief. Barely three days, and the first really didn't count, inasmuch as he really hadn't been himself.

Still, maybe it was better this way. Better because he had a feeling that, though it hadn't happened for more than a decade and a half, he could become attached. Attached to this woman with the laughing eyes, the killer smile and the heart as big as all outdoors. And he'd long since learned that attachments were only unions begging for severance. For disappointments. He knew this as well as he knew his own name. There was no reason to expect anything else, anything different.

Damn it, he needed to shake off this malaise. He needed to get on his way.

Alain forced himself to open his eyes, to take the first step that would set him on the path to the rest of his life.

He was alone except for the dog in a cast staring him in the face.

Winchester.

But not Kayla.

Absently, he petted the animal as he sat up. Opening his mouth to call out to her, Alain thought he heard noises coming from somewhere in the house. Pots being moved. A refrigerator being opened and closed.

Kayla.

A warmth spread over him. He fought a desire to get up and go looking for her. A desire to bring her back to bed and go through a reenactment of last night.

Damn it, what was wrong with him?

Annoyed with himself, Alain reached for the phone instead. First things first.

Picking up the receiver, he held it to his ear. It was

then that he realized he was holding his breath. Waiting to find out if the phone was actually still working? Or hoping that it wasn't?

The latter seemed foolish, but he really couldn't have said with any amount of certainty which direction his hopes were aimed.

This place had scrambled his brain.

Just as she did.

Maybe this town *was* like the fictional Brigadoon, seducing whoever came upon it into remaining, committing his soul to a timeless world where life was a great deal simpler.

But the world beyond Kayla's home was beckoning to Alain. His fingers punched in Philippe's phone number on the keypad before he could talk himself out of it. The phone on the other end rang only twice before someone picked up. And then he heard Philippe's deep voice say hello.

There'd been a time, whenever his older brother picked up the phone, that he would sound incredibly grumpy. Philippe didn't like being interrupted. The oldest of Lily Moreau's sons worked at home. He had made his fortune and his mark on the software world by withdrawing into his home office and wrestling with concepts that completely mystified the rest of the family. Because it took so much deep concentration, he hated having to focus on anything else while he was working. This included incoming calls, even from the companies that he was dealing with.

But J.D.—Janice—had changed all that, had completely remodeled Philippe's house and his world. These days, his brother was positively sunny and damn near unrecognizable.

So it was a remarkably cheery voice that said, "Zabelle here."

"Philippe."

"Alain!" The concern in his brother's voice was palatable. "Where *are* you?"

"Funny you should ask," Alain murmured. "I'm not in Bedford."

"I already know that," Philippe answered with a touch of impatience. "You haven't been home the last three nights."

Alain knew he could tell that simply by walking out his front door. They lived next door to one another, he and his brothers, in houses that, to the passing eye, formed what appeared to be a single sprawling mansion. In reality, there were three attractive homes made to look like one huge estate.

That had been Philippe's idea. He'd grown up caring for his brothers, and it was a habit he didn't seem to want to break. In truth, though neither Alain nor Georges admitted it aloud, they liked the arrangement, liked being close, yet able to maintain separate lives. Again, all Philippe's doing.

Taking a deep breath, Alain forged ahead. "I was in an accident."

The concern was immediate. "Are you all right?"

"Yes," he quickly assured him. "But that's more than I can say for my car."

He heard Philippe sigh. Material things had never been a priority with him. "All right, tell me what happened."

Alain knew that there was no way he was getting off the phone until he gave Philippe every single detail of the accident, what led up to it and what had transpired afterward. He summarized the events as quickly as he could, talking faster and faster. Trying to outrun the reluctance that was mushrooming through him.

And when he was through, he concluded, "So I need a ride."

It was obvious the request was nothing less than Philippe had expected. "I'll be there as soon as I can," he promised.

Why did that make Alain's heart sink a bit? "You don't have to leave immediately," he told him. "Wait for the traffic to die down."

His brother would have to drive through the snarl of L.A. traffic to get to him. Traffic that, at its peak, crawled rather than flowed—if that. Alain felt bad enough already about asking him to come get him. He didn't want him stuck in bumper-to-bumper congestion.

"I'm on my way," Philippe replied firmly.

"Right." Obviously, his mind was made up. "Thanks."

No sense in trying to talk his brother out of it. No one, Alain thought, letting the receiver fall back into the cradle, could tell Philippe what to do— with the possible exception of Janice, or Kelli, her pint-size daughter.

There'd been a lot of changes in the family of late. Philippe was getting married next month, and Georges wasn't going to be lagging far behind, now that he'd lost his heart to a woman with the improbable name of Vienna. And Alain wouldn't be surprised if Gordon, Janice's older brother, wasn't going to be making an announcement soon himself. Georges's cousin Electra had set her cap for the man, and both she and Gordon seemed exceedingly happy about the arrangement.

Alain's cousins, Remy, Vincent and Beau, were still very much ensconced in the bachelor life, so he wouldn't feel like the last holdout. But it wasn't exactly the same thing as having his brothers unattached, without the responsibilities of hearth and home, and all that entailed.

Funny, when he was a kid, he'd been convinced things would never change—except for the faces of their mother's "companions."

It was, he knew, a foolish fantasy, and yet he couldn't quite help the longing he felt....

"Coffee?"

The cheerful voice broke through his thoughts, scattering them like mist. Roused, Alain looked toward the doorway.

Kayla was standing there with a large mug in her hand, a faint curl of steam rising above it. The scent of coffee began to fill the room.

The scent of coffee and the light perfume she wore.

"Sounds great."

Alain shifted in the bed as she crossed to him. He was about to reach out for the mug when he realized he was still very much unclothed beneath the sheet spread haphazardly over him. The second the realization hit him, temptation sprinted through him.

"You know what sounds even better?" Accepting the mug, he placed it on the nightstand.

Her eyes were wide. "What?"

Alain curled his fingers around her wrist. Her warmth spread into him. "Guess."

"Breakfast?" she asked innocently. Or at least she tried to sound innocent. In actuality, her heart was racing like a yearling at its first major event.

She'd thought that she could pull this off, that she could sound blasé and sophisticated, like the women she assumed populated his world. She knew he was going to be leaving this morning, or at the very latest, this afternoon. She'd thought she'd made her peace with that. But obviously, she hadn't.

What was going on here? She had no desire to fall into any tender trap. No desire to get caught up again in all the briars and brambles that were part and parcel of being with someone. With caring about someone.

And yet here it was, uninvited. She didn't seem to have any say in the matter, any say in what she felt or didn't feel.

She didn't *want* to feel anything.

But she did.

All the worse for her, because he *was* going to be leaving, Kayla told herself. And she didn't want his last thoughts about her to be filled with pity.

"Not even close." Alain gently drew her down onto the bed. His eyes held hers. "That's not the appetite that's stirring."

"You called your brother." He'd made no effort to lower his voice, so she'd overheard his part of the conversation. *Because you were straining for the sound of his voice, idiot,* she upbraided herself. "Shouldn't you be getting ready? Or isn't he coming?" Oh, God, did that sound as hopeful as she feared it did?

"Oh, he's coming. The sun will stop rising before Philippe stops being dependable. But it'll take him more than two hours to get here." Alain found himself actually rooting for the traffic. How strange was that? "Maybe three."

"Two hours," Kayla echoed, the last bit of any resistance ebbing away. She'd turn off the eggs she was making, because part of her had hoped...

"Maybe three," he repeated softly, beginning to unbutton the blouse she was wearing. Sending hot tongues of desire radiating all through her. "And seeing as how I'm already 'dressed' for the occasion..."

He gently tugged the ends of her blouse out of her jeans. Leaning forward, he feathered a kiss along the side of her neck. Her eyes fluttered shut as she released the last of her grip on decorum.

Wild things began to happen within her. Wild, delicious things. She scarcely remembered helping him, scarcely remembered tearing off her clothes and slipping, sleek and naked, back into her bed.

For one last visit to paradise.

Kayla couldn't readily recall the last time she'd felt this awkward. As far back as she could remember, she had always felt comfortable in her own skin. Oh, there was that short period of time when she'd allowed herself to be sublimated into the kind of woman that Brett had wanted, a person he could order around. She'd allowed it to happen because she'd loved him, or told herself she did. But she'd quickly snapped out of it the second she'd come to her senses.

Other than that, she'd always been confident in any given situation, confident in her own abilities.

She felt at loose ends right now.

It had nothing to do with the tall, good-looking man standing in her living room. He had a kind smile, and she found herself liking him instantly. Alain's older brother radiated authority, but in a good way.

Philippe Zabelle had Patriarch written all over him, even though he didn't appear to be that much older than the brother he'd come to fetch.

He'd already thanked her twice for rescuing Alain. Not only that, but he'd looked genuinely interested when she'd shown him her "foster" dogs. Especially Ginger's puppies.

"I'd like to come back and adopted one of them when they're ready to leave their mother," he'd told her. Alain had looked at him quizzically, but he'd addressed his words to her. "My daughter would just love a puppy."

My daughter. Not "my fiancée's daughter," or "my stepdaughter," but "*my* daughter," even though, from what Alain had told her, the wedding was still more than a month away. He'd obviously taken the little girl to his heart. Yes, Kayla had found herself instantly liking this man.

The awkwardness stemmed from the fact that she found herself missing Alain even though he was still standing here.

What was she going to do about that?

Move on, she told herself firmly. Because life was going to do just that, move on. Whether or not she chose to come with it.

Alain noticed that Philippe seemed to be retreating, edging toward the front door. They had to get going.

"I'll wait for you outside," he told him, then nodded at Kayla. "Nice meeting you. And thank you again for taking care of Alain."

Before she could brush his thanks away again, Philippe closed the door behind him. Leaving the two of them to say goodbye.

Alain felt his breath catch in his throat, blocking the words. Why did she have to look so damn desirable again? It wasn't like he could just stay here, making love with her three times a day. He had a life to get back to. A rich, full, *busy* life.

The word *goodbye* refused to emerge.

"Um, look…" He pulled his checkbook out of his jacket pocket. "I'd like to pay you—for your help," he added quickly, when he saw her eyes widening in shock and something he couldn't fathom.

Kayla drew herself up, squaring her shoulders. Had he just insulted her? That was the last thing he wanted to do.

"I didn't do it for your money." She took a breath, as if trying to quell a flash of temper. "Just pass it on. Help someone else in trouble if you get the chance."

Her voice suddenly sounded distant, as if she was closing off from him. But he needed to do this. Whether it was his conscience or something else at play, he didn't know, but a small token of appreciation would make things better.

Wouldn't it?

"At least let me make a donation to your organization." She began to demur again, but he was already writing out a check for a generous amount. Tearing it off, he held it out to her. "You can fill in the correct name. I'm afraid I don't remember it."

She glanced at the amount. That couldn't be right. "You put in too many zeroes," she told him.

Alain looked at the check, then shook his head. "No, I didn't."

"That's for a thousand dollars." The most she'd ever gotten was a hundred. Most donations were in the tens and twenties.

"Yes, I know."

It was guilt money, she thought. Somehow, he was trying to soothe his conscience.

About what? The man didn't owe her anything. No promises had been exchanged. Just a good time.

She forced herself to smile. The money would go a long way toward the care and feeding of needy animals. God knew they could use it. It would certainly buy a lot of dog food. Besides her seven-plus, there were currently forty-five unadopted dogs living with a handful of volunteers, and that number fluctuated on a regular basis, usually growing rather than decreasing.

"All right, to help the dogs," she said, taking the check from him.

He found himself wanting to do more for her. And to postpone leaving for at least another minute or so. "Look, my mother knows a lot of people," Alain said suddenly. "Maybe, around the holidays, she could throw a fund-raiser, get some *real* money for your organization."

Kayla nodded, but she really didn't believe a word he was saying, and doubted that he did, either. It was like that old line, "we'll stay in touch," uttered at parting, by kids still in the throes of a summer romance. The intent was there, but it wouldn't happen. There'd be no fund-raiser, no Alain. This was it. He was leaving and she'd never see him again.

Still, she tried to look as if she believed him. "Sounds good," she murmured.

Before he could stop himself, Alain took her into his arms. Damn, but she felt good. As if she belonged there.

What the hell are you thinking? Just how hard did you hit this head of yours?

Taking a deep breath, he allowed himself one quick, fleeting kiss. Not a lingering one, but a fast brush of lips. And then he was letting her go, and the emptiness was seeping in.

"Thanks for everything."

His parting words hung in the air long after he shut the door and left.

Chapter Ten

"She seems like a nice woman."

The comment splintered the silence that had infiltrated the interior of his car. Philippe didn't know what to make of it. Ordinarily, he was the quiet one in the family.

Thinking back, he had never known a time when Alain *wasn't* talking. Which was why, when he'd announced at the tender age of ten that he intended to become a lawyer, it really seemed like the natural choice for him. Though Georges was no shrinking violet, of the three of them, it was Alain who truly had the gift of gab. He had always been as talkative, as outgoing, as their mother. Maybe even more so.

Which made his silence now almost eerily unnatural.

Alain took in a deep breath before answering. "Yes," he said quietly. "She is."

Something was definitely wrong here, Philippe thought. This just wasn't like Alain. They were on a two-lane road, making their way to the coast and Interstate 5. He spared his brother a glance, looking at the bandage on his forehead covering the gash that had been sewn up. Was there a concussion that had been overlooked?

"Maybe I should drive by Blair Memorial when we get back home, take you to the emergency room," Philippe suggested. He'd never been an obsessive worrier, but there was nothing wrong with being thorough.

Lost in his own thoughts, trying to extricate himself from a quagmire of emotions that threatened to pull him under, Alain frowned. Philippe's suggestion seemed to come out of the blue. "Why?"

"To get you checked out," he answered simply. "You don't sound like yourself." He thought of the uncustomary silence. "Hell, you don't 'sound' at all. I've never known you to be quiet. You even talk in your sleep—at least you did when you were a kid." The road straightened and he pressed down on the accelerator, speeding up in order to pass a truck.

"I'm all right," Alain told him, his voice flat. "I don't need to go to any hospital."

Philippe debated turning on the radio to ward off the quiet, but decided that it would only be a distraction. They had at least an hour before they would reach Orange County and more before they got home. They might as well have this out now.

"Convince me." It was a softly spoken order.

Alain bristled, surprised at how short his temper was. He didn't usually have one. "What do you mean, convince you? Why do I need to convince you?"

The answer to that was simple. "Because if you don't, I am taking you to the hospital." It didn't matter that his passenger was a full-grown adult and slightly taller than he was. Philippe had always been the patriarch and he didn't intend to relinquish the role anytime soon.

Alain dismissed his brother's words. "What I need is to get to work—" he looked down at what he was wearing "—and a change of clothes. I've been living in these since Friday…." He saw Philippe glance at him. And sniff to check if the air around him was ripe. "After Kayla washed them," he added.

Little pieces were being nudged into place in Philippe's head. "What did you wear while that was happening?" He asked, his tone innocent.

"A blanket."

Alain saw a hint of a smile curve the corner of his Philippe's mouth and knew exactly what he was thinking. That he and Kayla had gotten it on. After all, that was the reputation he had. He felt defensive, not for himself but for her.

What the hell was that all about?

"Don't give me that look. She was just being practical. I was soaking wet and unconscious. She was afraid I'd get pneumonia. She's the one who bandaged me up and stitched my head."

He couldn't read Philippe's expression. Surprise? Skepticism? A bit of both? "She's a doctor?" he asked.

Alain turned his head, presumably to look out the window, before he answered.

His voice was so low that Philippe couldn't hear what he said above the rumble of traffic. They'd just gotten on the freeway. "What?"

Alain didn't turn his head, and made no attempt to speak up as he repeated his answer.

If Philippe was frustrated, he didn't show it. He just inclined his head toward Alain and said, "One more time."

"A vet, a vet, a vet," he fairly shouted, this time turning toward his brother. Trying to rein in his temper, he glared at him. "All right?"

Philippe acted as if his answer had been tendered

in a voice several decibels lower. "Being a vet is fine. What's not fine is your attitude." And then a small spark of annoyance was evident. "What the hell's gotten into you?"

Alain crossed his arms, thinking that he was acting like a jackass, but unable to stop himself. "Nothing." He knew that he had to give Philippe some kind of an excuse for his lapse in temper, so he thought of work. "I just don't like losing time, that's all. I was supposed to be at Dunstan's brunch on Sunday to talk over strategy, and I needed to be in touch with Bobbie Jo Halliday over this weekend, as well." He still hadn't told the woman about the valet's favorable testimony. That, along with everything else, clearly had them winning their case.

Why didn't that make him happy? Winning always made him happy.

Philippe had heard about the case his little brother had landed. "Ah, right," he said evenly, "the trophy wife trying to stick it to her late husband's kids."

Alain knew how Philippe felt about the matter. It was Philippe who had tried to instill a sense of fair play in him and in Georges. But this was different. This was the real world and his career they were talking about. "The will is in her favor."

Philippe nodded, signaling to change lanes and get away from a tanker truck. He'd never liked driving alongside a possible death trap. "Doesn't make it right," he countered.

Funny, he could almost hear Kayla saying the same thing, Alain thought. The woman probably had more in common with his brother than she had with him....

Why was he even thinking about something like that? What did it matter what they did or didn't have in common? She was just someone he was probably never going to see again. Except, maybe, if the fund-raiser came into being.

Where the hell had this wave of sadness come from? Maybe Philippe was right, maybe he did need a checkup.

"The law's the law," Alain replied belatedly, suddenly realizing that his brother was waiting for a response.

"Maybe," Philippe allowed. "But 'justice' is a whole different concept." He spared Alain a quick look. It was suddenly very important to him that Alain understood what he was saying—and agree with him. "What if Mother were to marry that juvenile who's wrapping her around his finger?" He was referring to Kyle Autumn, her latest protégé. Kyle had hung around longer than any of the others—except for her three husbands—and that was beginning to really concern Philippe. "And he got her to leave all her money to him. I have got a feeling you wouldn't be talking about 'the law being the law' then."

Alain shook his head, dismissing the comparison. "Mother wouldn't do that."

"But if she did?" Philippe pressed, not wanting to drop the matter. "If Kyle turned her head and made her feel that if she didn't change her will, he'd think she didn't love him. So she changes it and conveniently dies, what then?"

Alain didn't like thinking about things like that, didn't like being pressed or pushed to the wall. His thoughts were jumbled enough as it was. "Look, I don't want to talk about the case right now."

"All right," Philippe said indulgently, "what do you want to talk about?" He wasn't a big believer in sharing his own thoughts, but that didn't apply to the rest of them.

"Nothing." It was meant as a final response, a letting down of the curtain to announce that the show was over.

Except that it wasn't.

"That is definitely not like you," Philippe stated. He was silent for a couple of minutes. But just when Alain thought he'd gotten a reprieve, Philippe spoke again. And it wasn't about something innocuous, like the weather or sports. "It's that vet, isn't it?"

Alain could feel his back going up. Why couldn't his brother just drop it? How many times had they been in the car when *Philippe* didn't speak?

"What are you talking about?"

Philippe didn't answer his question. "What happened up there during the power failure?"

Alain reined in his thoughts, refusing to think about any of it right now. But he knew Philippe wouldn't back off until he gave him something. "We lived like pioneers."

Philippe waited. "And?"

Alain waved his hand impatiently. "And then the power came back on."

Philippe slanted a knowing look at him. "Yours or the electric company's?"

"What are you getting at?"

"Only that I've known you your entire life, watched you Romeo your way through an ocean of women, flashing that sunny smile of yours, and staying pretty much unaffected."

Alain had no idea why his guard was up, but it was. "Your point?"

"My point," Philippe stated patiently, determined to get to the bottom of all this, "is that you don't seem like the carefree bachelor you always were. Did something happen between you and that lady vet while you were waiting for the power to come on?"

Alain's answer was immediate and firm. "No."

Philippe read between the lines. "You slept with her, didn't you?"

He began to deny it again, then reconsidered. There were times he thought that Philippe probably knew him better than he knew himself. So he merely shrugged his shoulders. "There wasn't a whole lot of sleeping going on."

Philippe had lost count of the women who'd floated through Alain's life. But his brother had never been like this. Philippe drew the only conclusion he could. "And she got to you, didn't she?"

"No," Alain insisted, annoyed that he wouldn't just didn't let the subject drop. "She didn't 'get' to me." Philippe gave him a knowing look, causing him to protest, "We only made love last night. A person can't 'get' to you over the space of a few hours."

Philippe knew better. Janice had gotten to him the first moment he laid eyes on her. It just took him awhile to stop fighting it. "If you say so."

Alain loved and respected his brother and could sincerely say he was grateful Philippe had been in his life to steer him straight those times when he'd almost run aground. But this time, he was dead wrong. Alain refused to believe anything else. "I say so."

Philippe merely smiled.

Rather than take a few days off to recuperate and deal with his aches and pains, Alain threw himself back into his work. But to his dismay, the zest he'd always had for his cases just didn't seem to be there anymore. It was as if he was seeing everything in a different light.

It wasn't about winning anymore, it was about doing the right thing, just as Philippe had said.

As Kayla would have said had she known what he was about.

Memories of Kayla, of those few simple days he'd spent housebound with her, would sneak up on him unannounced, ambushing him when he least expected it. Interfering with his thought processes. Alain did what he could to banish the images, to place her and everything about her in a neat little box and shove it aside, the way he'd always done with the women he slept with.

He tried to forget about it, about Kayla, going on dates with a few women. No matter how good they looked, how much they tried to please, they all failed to measure up.

Failed to have the same effect on him, on his pulse, that Kayla had had.

That fact alone left him in a progressively worsening mood. He didn't want her to have that kind of effect on him, because if she did, that gave her a power over him. He'd seen what caring deeply about someone could do to a person, and he refused to let that happen to him.

That both Philippe and Georges were in love and firmly on a path that would lead them to marriage didn't convince Alain that happy endings were actually possible.

But he missed Kayla.

How could you miss someone you'd known for less than four days? he silently demanded as he stared, unseeing, at the Halliday case file. What was wrong with him? He was acting like some lovesick middle-school adolescent. Even when he'd been that age, he hadn't behaved like one.

Alain sighed and turned his chair away from his desk to stare out the window at a sky pregnant with dark, ominous clouds. Rain was coming, a storm by the looks of it. Just like…

This had to stop.

He was building her up in his mind. Making her into something larger than life, into something she wasn't. What he needed, he told himself, was to see her again—and see that he'd gotten carried away. That he had turned her into some sort of goddess in his mind.

What he needed, he decided, was to have her here, on his home turf. That would be his wake-up call.

The promise he'd made to Kayla just before he'd left came back to him. He'd told her that he would hold a fund-raiser for her organization. He grinned to himself. A fund-raiser. She couldn't turn that down. She'd *have* to come down for it.

He felt something quicken in his stomach and did his best to ignore it as he turned his chair back around and reached for the phone.

* * *

"A fund-raiser?" Lily repeated.

She'd been in her studio, agonizing over her latest effort, when her youngest son knocked and asked for permission to come in. Because inspiration was eluding her, she'd set down her brush and beckoned him in. She studied him now, surprised by the request. None of her sons ever asked her for anything.

"And it has nothing to do with art?" she asked.

Maybe he'd made his case too quickly. Lily always needed time to digest things, to mull them over as if she were staring at pieces of a puzzle.

"Not this time. It would be for an animal rescue organization. Volunteers find abused and abandoned German shepherds, take care of them and then place them with people."

Lily nodded. She'd always liked dogs, although she preferred little ones she could carry around and cuddle when the mood hit her.

"Well, that sounds straightforward enough," she commented. She looked at him curiously. "Why would they need a fund-raiser?"

It had been a long time since Lily had needed money. Both her paintings and her last two husbands, especially Georges's father, had made her a very wealthy woman.

His mother had forgotten what it meant to do

without, Alain thought. "To pay for food and medical expenses. Some of these dogs are boarded out until someone comes to adopt them. And some require a great deal of medical attention."

She cocked her head, curious. "Don't they have vets who volunteer their time? I thought I read something about that once."

He was certain that Kayla gave a hundred-and-ten percent of herself, probably using money she made as a practicing vet to help care for the animals she took in. But there were still limits.

"Their time, yes, but the supplies they use cost money." He knew his mother worked best with examples, so he decided to tell her about Winchester. As he thought of the dog, he couldn't help but wonder if Kayla had placed him yet, or if she still had him. It'd been close to three weeks since Alain had seen the dog—and her.

Rousing himself, he said, "There's one dog who was shot—"

That got his mother's attention. "Shot?" Her violet eyes opened wide. "Why on earth would someone shoot a poor dog?"

Alain gave her the answer that Kayla had given him. "Target practice."

Lily covered her mouth with her hands, genuinely appalled. "How awful. That poor creature." Her eyes flashed. She had always been on the side of the downtrodden. "Whoever did that should be drawn and quartered."

"No argument," he agreed, and quickly brought the conversation back on track. "But about the fundraiser… Do you think you could use your considerable influence to get some of your friends to attend and donate toward the cause?"

She smiled at his choice of words. They both knew he was flattering her, but she enjoyed it nonetheless. "Darling, you pour enough liquor and I can get them to donate to anything." Standing on her toes, she took his face between her hands, affection shining in her eyes as she looked at him. "I could never say no to you," Lily told him.

Alain didn't quite remember it that way, but now wasn't the time to remind her of all the junkets she'd taken, leaving the three of them behind with paid strangers. All the times he'd called to her to stay. That was in the past and he was none the worse for it now.

So he smiled, covering her hands with his own. "I was counting on that."

She studied him for a moment. "This means a lot to you, doesn't it?"

Alain thought it best not to admit to that, not even to himself. He didn't answer directly. "I gave my word to someone."

He was too much like her for her to believe it was only that. Lily smiled. "You're being a lawyer, Alain.

Be my son." And then her expression turned serious. "I know that perhaps I don't have the right to ask that of you, considering I was never much of a mother."

He'd stopped blaming her a long time ago. As Philippe had pointed out, she was just being Lily. And they all loved her.

"Oh, I wouldn't—"

Lily pressed a forefinger to his lips. "Don't interrupt, dear," she chided. "I don't apologize very often. I do want you to know that I was the best mother I could be."

Alain kissed the top of her head. "You were fine, Mother. And we always had Philippe. Let's see…a software engineer, a doctor and a lawyer." They'd all chosen a productive career rather than growing up to be spoiled, rich blots on society. "I'd say the three of us turned out pretty well."

"Yes," she agreed with affection, "you did." She looked back at her canvas and felt a rush. It was time to paint. But first, she needed to put this to rest. "All right, when do you want this fund-raiser?"

He knew his mother was mercurial, and her attention span had a tendency to shift without warning. "As soon as possible."

"Then it'll be as soon as possible," she agreed with a laugh. "A week from Saturday suit you?"

He hadn't expected it to be *that* fast. Alain grinned at his mother. "Perfect."

She raised her head and patted her hair, a wicked smile curving her lips. "So they tell me."

"C'mon, Winchester, you have to eat," Kayla begged. The forlorn dog lay listlessly on the floor at one end of the sofa. He'd pulled down the small cushion earlier, and now had it between his paws, resting his muzzle on it. The choice had mystified her, since the dog was nothing if not well behaved. And then she remembered that Alain had laid his head on the cushion, using it as a pillow. Winchester was just looking for his scent.

Makes two of us, she thought.

The next moment, she roused herself. She must have been under some kind of spell. There was no other way to explain her actions. She had never, ever gone to bed with a man she'd known only a matter of days. That was tantamount to a one-night stand.

Well, wasn't that what you had? A one-night stand?

They'd only had that one night. Why was she making such a big deal out of it? He obviously hadn't. It had been more than three weeks and he hadn't called her, hadn't tried to get in touch with her in any way. He hadn't even phoned about his precious car—which was taking Mick longer than he'd anticipated to fix. He was waiting for a part to be flown in, meanwhile working on the vehicle on good faith.

Kayla placed a dish of food beside the dog, who merely turned his head away.

"That's beef stroganoff," she told Winchester, just in case his keen sense of smell had deserted him. "Your favorite, remember?" But as she tried to coax him to sample at least a little, the dog turned his head to the other side. He had been eating less and less, ever since Alain had left. "Look, I know how you feel, but starvation isn't the answer. Don't make me force-feed you, Winchester."

His only response was to sigh.

That made two of them.

Chapter Eleven

When Alain first placed the call to Kayla, to his annoyance, he experienced all the nervous anticipation of the town geek asking the town beauty to the prom. So when he got her answering machine instead of her, he found himself doubly frustrated.

Assuming she was out on call, he waited until the following morning to try again. And again. And still again. Each time, her phone rang ten times, then her recorded message came on, calmly asking for details and a phone number where the caller could be reached.

He didn't want to talk to a machine, even if it was

her voice on the recording. He wanted to talk to her, to hear Kayla say his name. To hear the surprise in her voice because he'd hunted down her phone number and made good on his promise to get back to her about the fund-raiser.

Where was she? Out on a call involving some sort of lengthy emergency with someone's beloved pet? Or was she out all night with another man? Lying in someone else's arms the way she'd lain in his?

He knew he had no right to be feeling what he was right now. After all, the woman couldn't be expected to sit by the fireplace, pining away for him.

It didn't change how he was feeling.

No strings, remember? The way you always want it, right?

He slammed his briefcase shut on the kitchen counter. The lid bounced a little before settling down again. If there were no strings, why the hell did he feel so damn tangled up inside? And why, when her answering machine came on after his fifth attempt to get her, did he feel something akin to molten lava bubbling up within him, ready to spill out on anyone and anything? She could just be out with a friend, not a man. Alain hadn't a shred of evidence to support the wild, half-formed thoughts in his head.

It was as if despite all his legal training, his sharp mind had somehow turned to pudding, of absolutely no use to him.

He picked up the receiver again, then with a curse, let it drop back down in the cradle. There was no point in hitting Redial: he'd only get the machine.

Disappointment infiltrated, leaving a larger imprint than he thought possible. He'd been anticipating giving Kayla the good news that he had gotten his mother on board about the fund-raiser, and that Lily was even now pulling it together. He wanted, he realized, to reappear in Kayla's life, galloping up on a white charger and being her knight in shining armor.

He wanted Kayla to be grateful to him. Hell, he wanted Kayla, pure and simple. Ordinarily, the impressions left by women who passed through his life faded rather swiftly. But this time, nothing had faded. If anything, it had increased. He vividly remembered every moment of their lovemaking.

Remembered and longed for more.

Maybe he was coming down with something, Alain thought. Even so, he picked up the receiver one more time. This time, when he got the recording, he left a message, doing his best not to sound as put out that she wasn't there as he felt.

Just as he started to speak, he heard the doorbell. He ignored it and left his message.

"Kayla, this is Alain Dulac. I've got an update on that fund-raiser I mentioned to you. Give me a call back when you get in."

Whoever was at his door was now knocking. Alain quickly rattled off his cell number into the phone, then hung up.

The knocking grew louder. He needed to get going or he'd be late for work. He was definitely *not* in the mood to deal with whoever was on the other side of his door. Probably some impatient fool who was going to offer to do his gardening for him at a cut rate.

Or worse, it could be someone out to save his immortal soul by trying to convert him to the only true religion. He knew what his soul needed right now, and it had nothing to do with converting.

Alain was feeling far less than friendly as he picked up his briefcase and crossed to the front door, ready to go out. Whoever was there had damn well picked the wrong morning to throw a sales pitch in his direction.

A few cryptic words intended to send the intruder on his way hovered on his lips as Alain swung open the front door. He stopped dead, the words aborted.

Kayla. And a dog.

She summoned all her energy into her smile, wondering why she felt so nervous. This was only an errand of mercy.

For who, you or the shepherd?

"You need a dog."

Stunned, Alain stared at Kayla, the sunlight filtering through her red hair, creating an aura about her as if she were Venus surfing on a half shell.

For a second, he was convinced that he was hallucinating. But she was still standing there after his heart had slammed twice against his chest. And hallucinations didn't come with overly eager German shepherds, reared up on their hind legs, madly licking his face while their tails doubled as metronomes set to triple-time.

Alain stumbled backward, whether from the force of the dog, or the surprise of having her materialize on his doorstep, he wasn't completely sure.

"Winchester, down," Kayla ordered, giving the leash one hard tug. The dog reluctantly obeyed, dropping down to all fours again, but never took his eyes off the object of his affection, and his tongue remained at the ready to deliver another prolonged, hearty greeting.

"You're here," Alain heard himself saying in disbelief.

"Yes, I am." She tugged on the dog's bright-red leash again as Winchester, newly separated from his cast, gave every indication that for once he was going to openly disobey one of her commands.

"How did you find me?" Alain asked in stunned surprise. He looked down at the barely harnessed ball of energy. "Did your dog track me?"

"Your address was on the check you gave me for

the organization," she reminded him. As a lawyer, this man was not the sharpest she'd ever encounter. Winchester began to tug again, and she wrapped the leash around her hand twice. "And he isn't my dog." She saw Alain raise his eyebrow quizzically, and decided that made him look sensuously adorable. "Apparently, he's yours."

"I don't understand."

Out of the corner of his eye, Alain saw his neighbor from across the street on her way to deposit garbage into one of the dark-green pails at the side of her house. She was blatantly watching them, as if she'd tuned into her own private soap opera. The woman had always taken a very active interest in both his and his brother Georges's life.

Alain stepped forward and placed his hand on the small of Kayla's back, gently urging her into his house. "Why don't you and Winchester come in?"

She was beginning to wonder if he was ever going to invite her inside. Why did he have to look so good? She was kind of hoping that the dire circumstances of their encounter had been what made him seem so attractive to her. But in the light of the Orange County sun, he looked even better than he had in Shelby.

With a nod, she stepped inside his house, careful to keep herself between Winchester and him until the dog calmed down a little and got accustomed to seeing Alain again.

That might go for both of you, she told herself wryly. "Thanks," she said aloud.

Alain closed the front door. He could almost hear the woman across the street sigh in exasperation. For the time being, he deposited his briefcase by the door. Looking down at the prancing German shepherd, he realized that the dog no longer had any bandages on his right front leg. "He's all healed."

Kayla nodded. "I took the cast off on Friday." She petted the animal, though Winchester hardly noticed. He was trying to get closer to Alain.

With a grin, Alain ran his hand over the dog's head. If he had any intention of stopping, Winchester wouldn't allow it. The dog kept repositioning his head under his hand each time it passed over his fur. Alain laughed and continued petting.

He looked back at Kayla, and something else occurred to him. There were no other dogs with her. "Where's the rest of your posse?"

"With friends." She'd divided up the animals among other volunteers in the group, the way she always did whenever her rescue missions took her out of town. This time, she wasn't all that certain she was going to be back before nightfall. "All except Winchester." She nodded at the dog. "He wanted to come see you."

Alain's mouth curved and the next words out of his mouth told her he was humoring her. The man didn't understand animals. But he would. Winchester would teach him.

"He told you that?"

"As a matter of fact—" she smiled down at the dog, then raised her eyes to Alain's face "—yes."

The second she looked at him, Alain felt something tighten within his gut. Damn, but he could get lost in those green eyes. He rallied as best he could. "I had no idea he was such a talented dog. How long has he been talking?"

She shook her head. "You don't need words to make yourself understood. He all but stopped eating when you left, and now he just mopes around all day." She could see the denial forming on Alain's lips, but she had more proof. "You left a handkerchief behind, and he carries it around with him wherever he goes." To prove her point, she dug into a pocket of her jeans and produced a very mangled scrap of cloth.

Alain looked at the handkerchief skeptically. "Is he sick?"

Winchester grabbed the handkerchief from her hand, then let it drop at Alain's feet, raising his head and looking at his adopted master soulfully. "Lovesick, maybe."

Suddenly eager and playful, Winchester began to run in circles around him. Only Kayla's sternly voiced command of "Winchester, sit. Stay," finally stopped the whirling dog. Alain looked at him, stunned. "And I'm the object of this lovesickness?"

She felt as if she was answering for both Winchester and herself. But he didn't need to know that. Didn't need to know that standing here, looking at him, was making her stomach knot. Nothing could come of this. They were from two different worlds, belonged to two different spheres.

And yet...

Kayla inclined her head. "Apparently."

Alain scratched behind the dog's ear and Winchester slipped into dog heaven, thumping his foot in rhythmic ecstasy. "But I'm not a dog."

"Maybe lovesick's the wrong word," she allowed. *It's more applicable to me than the shepherd.* "But he's been listless ever since you left. Doesn't play, doesn't really eat, hardly drinks. Here." She dug into her pocket and placed a few dog treats in his palm, closing his hand with both of hers. For a second, something leaped up inside of her. It stayed, levitating, as his eyes held hers. She reminded herself to breathe. "Offer him this."

"All right." Alain no sooner held out the treats than Winchester snapped his jaws over the two bone-shaped crackers—taking care not to injure the fingers that held them.

Alain instinctively pulled back his hand, then examined it. No marks, no pain. He looked down at the munching dog. Winchester devoured the treats like the hungry dog he actually was. "Wow."

Kayla folded her arms before her chest. "I rest my case."

Alain studied the dog for a moment. Granted, Winchester was a handsome animal, now that he looked at him, but that didn't alter anything. "So what are we going to do about this?"

She gazed at him, her conviction clear in her eyes. "I think that's pretty obvious. He's your dog." And she doubted if anything would readily change that. The German shepherd had adopted Alain, instinctively knowing he would have a good home with him.

But Alain was shaking his head. As if he believed he had a real say in the matter. "I don't have any room for a dog."

Kayla didn't answer immediately. Instead, she slowly looked around the space she was standing in. The living room had vaulted, cathedral ceilings that gave the impression of vast, open spaces. To the left was a staircase leading up to the second floor. Beyond the living room was a formal dining room. The kitchen, she imagined, was beyond that, and who knew how many rooms there were in total. When her gaze returned to his face, she didn't try hiding the fact that she thought he was dead wrong.

"You could fit my place in here twice over, with room to spare, and I have six dogs and nine puppies," she pointed out.

But Alain liked being free. That meant not having anyone depending on him for anything. He didn't bother trying to reconcile this with the fact that he'd always felt he would be there for either of his brothers—or his mother—should the need arise. Be that as it may, he wasn't ready to take on more.

He tried again, knowing, somehow, that this might be a losing battle. "I don't know the first thing about owning a dog."

There were books for that. And she could offer her services in the short run. The biggest hurdle had already been vaulted: the dog loved him.

She grinned, stooping down to Winchester's level and running her hands over his back affectionately.

"That's because you don't own the dog, the dog owns you. I can give you a few pointers if you like, and he is housebroken and trained. Besides that, I'd say that Winchester pretty much made up his mind about you. If I take him back with me, he just might waste away, pining after you."

"You really think that?"

There was no hesitation on her part. She was dead serious. "I really do."

Alain looked at her for a long moment. It was on the tip of his tongue to say he'd missed her. That he was actually indebted to Winchester because the dog had brought her back into his life, for however short a period. But he couldn't. Something—self-preservation?—kept the words from coming out.

The best he could do was fall back on an excuse. "I've been trying to get ahold of you."

She wanted to believe him, but if that was the case, if he had been trying to get her, what had kept him from succeeding? "Oh?"

He shrugged, suddenly feeling awkward. He *never* felt awkward. What was she doing to him? "I guess you were on your way here."

"You called this morning?" When he nodded, she was more than willing to believe him, even as she told herself that the man was a smooth talker and was probably only saying what he thought she wanted to hear.

And she did; she wanted to hear that so badly. Wanted to hear that he missed her. That he had felt at loose ends, the way she had ever since he'd left.

"Why?" she asked, holding her breath, telling herself that she was an idiot—but she just couldn't make herself run for cover. Not yet.

"That fund-raiser I mentioned." Was it his imagination, or did she look a tad disappointed? He'd thought for sure this was the best way to get on her good side. Alain forged on. "My mother thinks it's a great idea."

Try as she might, Kayla couldn't quite picture the very flamboyant Lily Moreau heading up a fund-raiser for abused, abandoned German shepherds. But if the woman was actually willing, who was she to question that? Heaven knew they could use the money. Kayla's own bank account was swiftly dwindling because the animals needed so much. So many who came to her attention were sick, hurt or both.

She nodded. "That's great. Any idea when it might be?"

"Saturday night."

The man was nothing if not full of surprises. She couldn't have possibly heard him correctly. "*This* Saturday night?"

"Yes." Alain gauged her tone. There was a note of hesitation in her voice. "You have plans."

"No, nothing out of the ordinary," she qualified quickly, not wanting him to know that she spent the most social night of the week at home, grooming her dogs.

If the truth be known, she hadn't gone out with a man, much less to bed with one the way she had with him, since she had left Brett. She had no time to invest in a relationship, only to be disappointed. Her dogs gave her all the affection she needed.

Or had, until Alain set her bed on fire.

She squared her shoulders like a warrior. "But I

would have appreciated a little bit of a warning ahead of time."

"I did try calling you this morning," he reminded her. His eyes narrowed just a touch as he added, "And last night."

She hadn't gotten in until almost midnight. When she'd walked through the door, the dogs had surrounded her. All except Winchester. That was when she'd more or less made up her mind to bring him with her on her run down to the shelter in Anaheim. "Last night Jake Walton had a sick cow."

He supposed that made sense. Still, the type of animal surprised him. "You treat cows?"

"I'm a vet," she reminded him.

"Sorry, I thought you just worked on dogs." Damn, that sounded lame. *He* sounded lame. Where was all that charm that came so easily to him? Where was that magnetism that he'd been told all but radiated from him? Why did he feel like some awkward schoolboy because the woman who'd kept popping up in his head when he'd least expected it had done the same on his doorstep?

Kayla supposed, if she lived in a city, she would have narrowed her field. But she was the only vet for miles, and that broadened her playing field. "Dogs are my specialty, but I pretty much treat any animal that needs me."

"And lawyers," he interjected.

She had no fondness for lawyers. Brett had been a lawyer. "I wasn't treating a lawyer, I was treating an injury."

Winchester had turned his attention to the brief-case on the floor. Rescuing it, Alain remembered what he'd been doing when he opened the door. Leaving.

"I've got to get to work, but why don't you make yourself at home? I should be able to be back before six." He would make sure of that. "We could—"

Kayla stopped him before he continued and got completely entangled in the wrong idea. She didn't want him thinking that she'd used Winchester as an excuse to see him. That would be putting all the cards in Alain's hand.

"This isn't exactly a social call," she told him.

The way she said it had him pulling up short. "Oh?"

"I had to come down to see about a German shepherd they're holding at the Anaheim shelter. She's scheduled for termination—" God, she hated the way that word tasted in her mouth "—by the end of the week. Since I was going to be down here anyway, and it seemed like you were the cure for what ailed him, I thought I'd drop off Winchester with you first."

This time, Alain put his briefcase down on the side table. "So you really are serious about giving him to me?"

"What made you think I was kidding?" She didn't

wait for an answer. "I really don't think you have a choice in the matter."

He supposed that having a pet around wouldn't be so bad. It would give him an excuse to see her after the fund-raiser. He grinned at her. "You always come on so forcefully?"

She'd never had to bully anyone into taking one of the dogs. There were plenty of people who loved animals. She supposed she *was* coming on a little strong here, but only because she really did think that Winchester would begin to waste away if he was separated from Alain.

Kayla played along. "It works better than saying 'pretty please with a cherry on top.'"

"Oh, I don't know." He drew a little closer to her. "Maybe you could try it."

She was about to tell him he was crazy, but then she shrugged, and pursed her lips to form the first word.

She never got the opportunity to say it out loud.

When her lips puckered, Alain swept her up in his arms and kissed her. Hard. The way he'd been wanting to all these weeks.

He felt her surprise and then her surrender. And then he felt her kissing him back. Just as hard as he was kissing her. The little moan that escaped sent shivers up and down his spine. And a desire for more.

Her head was spinning again. Just the way it had the first time he'd kissed her at her house. That night in Shelby hadn't been a fluke. He really did make her feel as if she was intoxicated.

Kayla wrapped her arms around his neck and sank into the kiss, drowning in it.

Her pulse hammered wildly when she finally drew her head back to look at him. It took her a second to catch her breath. "I was wondering when you were going to get around to that."

He held her close for a moment, enjoying the way the rhythm of her heart matched his. "Didn't want to grab you the second you turned up on my doorstep. Well, I did," he allowed, "but I didn't want to frighten you away." It was bad enough that one of them was scared beyond words—because he'd never felt an impact like this before and he was afraid it was going to undo him completely if he wasn't careful.

"I think if I ran," she told him, "Winchester would fetch me back."

He grinned. "Well, that seals the deal for me. How can I refuse a dog that can fetch women?"

"Woman," she emphasized. "Not women."

"Even better." He leaned over, about to kiss her again. She put her hands up on his chest, looking a little hesitant.

"I really have to get going." But even as she said it, she made no effort to draw farther away.

"Yeah, me, too." Still holding her to him, Alain glanced at his watch over her head.

Her body was heating at an alarming rate. She needed to leave, but her feet wouldn't obey. "What are you thinking?"

He wrapped his arm back around her again. "That I could call in late."

"But I can't." She needed to remember that she was a responsible person, not some neo-hippie who could gratify her whims at will and damn the consequences. "The shelter is expecting me, and I hear the traffic on the way is awful."

"Traffic *is* awful," he agreed. "It gets better by ten. You could leave then."

"Ten." She grasped his wrist and looked at his watch. "That's two hours away."

"Yes." His smile was nearly blinding. "I know."

Her eyes were wicked as she looked up at his face. "What'll we do until then?"

"We could show Winchester his new backyard and then…" His voice trailed off.

"Then?"

"Then," he repeated.

Abandoning words, he showed her. He pressed a kiss to the side of her neck. When he heard her draw in her breath, the sound excited him to the point that he wanted to take her right there, on his living-room floor. Take her the way he'd fantasized about over and over again.

He began to unzip her jacket. Her breath came more

heavily. With effort, she put her hands on his to stop him. "Don't you have to call your office first?"

He nodded, taking out his cell phone. He pressed one of the preprogrammed numbers, and when he got the machine on the other end, left a message that he was going to be delayed that morning.

Kayla was doing the same on her cell phone, leaving word at the shelter that she was stuck in traffic, but would be there by around ten or so.

The second she closed the lid, terminating the call, she found herself being caught up in his arms.

The kiss that followed rocked her to her toes, which were no longer touching the floor.

Chapter Twelve

The delicious euphoria began to dissipate, quietly tiptoeing into the navy-blues and whites of Alain's coolly decorated bedroom. Unwilling to release her grasp on the joy that had been feeding her very soul, Kayla struggled to hold on to the feeling a little longer. But reality being what it was, the euphoria was even now slipping through her fingers.

With a reluctant sigh, she turned toward Alain in the rumpled bed. Her heart insisted on lighting up again, and she grinned. "You know, we have to stop meeting like this."

He laughed softly, drawing her into his arms. He

liked holding her, just holding her and having her close like this.

Definitely not business as usual, he thought, and that did worry him. But for now, he wasn't going to think about it, wasn't going to think that he was letting himself get in too deep too fast. He was just going to enjoy the surge that making love with her created within him.

He shifted his head slightly and the bright-blue numbers on his digital alarm clock all but jumped up at him. How had it gotten that late so quickly? He should have been on the road long before now.

"I hate to love and run," he told her. Then, because temptation reared its head, he allowed himself one more kiss. It was quick but potent, and pregnant with promise of things to come.

And, oh, it was such an argument for staying right where he was.

"I *really* hate to love and run," he told her with feeling, "but a client's coming in and I've got to be there or my head is going to be served on a platter." Alex Dunstan, senior partner and a friend of his late father, was counting on him to be there this morning—or what was left of it. And Bobbie Jo Halliday absolutely refused to deal with any of the other members of the firm. She'd confided in him that she found them all inflexible. Alain wasn't sure if she meant emotionally or physically.

Kayla nodded. "The trophy wife with the newly changed will." There'd been a lot on the Internet and on the news about the woman lately. None of it overly flattering, except for the photos. The woman was built like a proverbial Greek goddess.

Alain looked at her in surprise. "You were listening."

That was a first, he thought. If he did happen to "talk shop" around any of the women he went out with, it always seemed to breeze in one ear and sail right out the other. Not that he had an overwhelming desire to bring his work out of the office with him, but being a lawyer was part of who and what he was. Then again, it had never mattered to him that none of his dates cared about that, because he'd always kept things nice and loose.

So why did he feel so pleased that Kayla had paid attention? That she took an interest in his work? He wasn't making any sense.

Kayla looked surprised that he was surprised. "Why wouldn't I be listening? You were talking."

He wasn't going to think about this. "No reason," he said quickly, then pressed a kiss to her bare shoulder, which suddenly looked incredibly sensual to him.

Warm tongues of desire began to radiate out from where his lips touched her skin.

"Stop right there," she ordered, moving her hand to block his mouth. When he raised his eyes, looking at her quizzically, she said, "You trail those lips along my collarbone and neither one of us is going to get to where we're supposed to be going, not for a long, long time."

His eyes swept over her body and she saw hunger flicker in them.

Right now, the only place he wanted to go was where he'd just been. "That might be a matter of opinion," he told her.

Her own longing threatened to get the better of her, but she had a dog to rescue. And Alain had a bimbo to counsel.

"Don't make me push you out of bed," she warned.

Keeping the sheet discreetly wrapped around her, Kayla bent over the side of the bed to retrieve her clothing. Garments were haphazardly strewn on both sides, his on one, hers on the other. Luckily, hers were where she could reach them.

Rather than risk getting up and suffering what could be the delicious consequences of appearing utterly nude in front of him, Kayla pulled her clothes under the sheet and began wiggling into them.

When he realized what she was doing, Alain laughed. "You know, in some countries, that would be considered a very enticing prenuptial dance."

Having successfully pulled on her underwear and bra, Kayla went to work pulling her jeans up her legs, one eyebrow raised in amusement. "But not in this one."

Rather than follow suit, Alain rose from the bed. Looking at him, Kayla felt the insides of her mouth transform into sun-dried cotton. He was as gloriously naked as the day he was born, and far better endowed.

She couldn't draw her eyes away.

Aware that she was watching, Alain shrugged nonchalantly. "It's faster this way."

"I doubt it."

If they'd both started to get dressed that way, naked and facing one another, Kayla was willing to bet they wouldn't have gotten very far. Even now, she found breathing evenly a challenge.

Kicking the sheet aside, she rose. As she did so, she pushed her arms through the sleeves of her shirt, then quickly buttoned it up.

She felt his eyes skim over her body, and felt naked all over again.

"Do you want a key so you can come back when you're finished rescuing that dog?" he asked in a husky voice.

She couldn't help wondering how many keys to his house were floating around out there, and how many other women he'd offered them to.

Don't ruin it. You know it's not going to last, but don't hurry it along. Don't examine things too closely, she warned herself.

Glancing in the mirror over the bureau, she took a deep breath as she ran her hand through her hair in lieu of a comb. Kayla did her best to sound nonchalant. "I'm not coming back."

She saw the confusion in his face reflected in the mirror. "But the fund-raiser—"

Kayla's eyes met his in the glass. "Isn't, according to you, until Saturday. I can't stay here until then."

He didn't see what the problem was. Alain found himself rather liking the idea, since there was a ready excuse in place: she'd be only there until the fund-raiser. They'd have a few nights to enjoy each other without the threat of it being more serious.

"Why not?" he pressed. "You shared your place with me."

"There was a power outage at the time." Kayla stepped into her shoes. "And," she reminded him, "you were stranded."

He leaned over her, his engaging grin making her stomach whirl counterclockwise. "I could have a friend drive into the power grid for me," he offered. "And there's a utility pole not too far from here. I could try merging your truck with it." His expression was the soul of innocence.

It was hard not to laugh. Harder not to fall into his arms. With effort, she managed to remain steadfast. "I'll pass, thanks."

She looked so serious, he realized he wasn't sure exactly what it was she was turning down. The tongue-in-cheek offer, him, or everything.

"You don't want the fund-raiser?"

"Yes, yes I do." *For more reasons than one.* But she couldn't stay here until then. "How could I turn down something so generous? I'll be back on Saturday for it. Early," she promised. "But right now, I have a dog to pick up and take back with me." She already had foster parents waiting to take in the neglected animal.

Fully dressed, Alain looked down at Winchester. The dog had stationed himself by the doorway, as if guarding who came and who went. He'd been there for the last hour. "What about Winchester?"

She didn't quite follow. Kayla glanced over her shoulder at the dog. Winchester had eyes only for Alain. "What about him?"

"Are you taking him with you?"

She thought they'd been over this. "No, I already said he was yours."

"It's not that I don't want him," he argued, "but I don't have anything that a dog needs." He had no dog food, no dish for the animal, nothing.

Kayla begged to differ. She'd seen the way Alain had interacted with Winchester at her place.

"You have love. The rest can be bought at a pet store. And," she added, feeling that she was sealing the deal, "I brought some things with me in the truck. A bowl, his food, some of his toys. And a simple new-owners instruction booklet."

The last item caught his attention. And made him feel a wee bit better about the situation. "They have things like that?" he asked incredulously.

"Probably." However, this particular one wasn't anything he'd find in a bookstore. "I just wrote down answers to a few of the basic questions you might have." She smiled. She intended to make this as easy as possible for Alain—and Winchester. "I figured you might need help, and this'll make you feel better."

"I'd *really* feel better if you stayed," Alain declared.

So would she, Kayla thought. But for a completely different reason. Which was why she needed to go.

She forced a smile to her lips. "You'll be fine."

He looked doubtfully at the dog, then at some of his more expensive pieces of furniture. The house definitely wasn't doggy-proof.

"But I'm going to be gone for the next eight hours," he protested.

She assumed he was gone that amount of time five days a week. "And this is different from any other day how?"

That was his point exactly. "It isn't. It's not fair to a dog to be alone all the time."

Half the people who had pets were gone the bulk of the day. "It won't be all the time. And he'll adapt to your routine. You just have to pet him and show him that he's appreciated."

He wasn't going to talk her out of giving him the dog, he thought. And he supposed he was warming to the idea. Committing to a pet wasn't the same thing as committing to a woman. The dog wouldn't suddenly pack up and leave on a whim or after an argument, unwilling to work things out. A dog represented loyalty and unconditional love.

But Alain couldn't just surrender. Not all at once. "Got an answer for everything, don't you?"

"Pretty much," she agreed, without a trace of smugness or vanity. She paused to pet Winchester. "We can put him out in the yard for now."

Alain looked down at the German shepherd. He supposed it would go well, but for now, it suited his purposes to play the uncertain new owner.

"Maybe you should come back when you're finished at the shelter." His voice was soft, coaxing. "For Winchester's sake."

She saw right through him. And she had to admit it amused her. "I'm sure Winchester will be just fine." She patted the dog's head. "Won't you, boy?" In response, Winchester wagged his tail enthusiastically. "See?"

"That's just a reaction to being petted," Alain protested. He followed her as she went down the stairs. Winchester wriggled past them, then bounded down the rest of the steps energetically. Reaching the bottom, he turned and looked back, waiting for them to join him.

Kayla turned around to look at Alain when she reached the landing. "Winchester understands what you tell him, and some things you haven't even said out loud."

Alain didn't bother hiding the skeptical look on his face. His expression all but said, *Yeah, sure.* "You're giving me a mind-reading dog?"

He'd learn, she thought. "Make fun if you like, but dogs are very intuitive, and German shepherds are the smartest of the lot."

Alain nodded, seeming to take in what she was saying, but she wasn't fooled. He didn't easily give up his convictions.

"Fine. Then maybe in between doing long division in his head, he'll come up with a plan to make you stay."

She paused to brush her lips against his. When all else failed, she could always fall back on her tried-and-true excuse. "Can't leave my dogs for that long."

He thought he'd found an inconsistency. "You said they were with other people."

"They are." Kayla picked up her purse from where she'd dropped it by the front door, and slung it over her shoulder. "But all of those people have German shepherds of their own. I can't ask them to be overwhelmed indefinitely."

When she'd first told him about what she did, he'd thought of it as a hobby, or a limited one-woman crusade. Now it sounded like some monumental undertaking, the logistics of which could rival the blueprints for the undertaking of D-day. "Just how many of these dogs are out there?"

Kayla only needed a second to do the tally in her head. "Currently, we have forty-nine that need permanent homes, although the number fluctuates daily."

"And until then, until someone adopts these homeless dogs permanently, you and your friends are caring for them?"

She grinned as she patted his cheek. "Now you're catching on."

He caught her hand, pressing it against his cheek a moment longer before he released it. "So why go out of your way to pick up another one?"

Kayla looked at him for a long moment, trying to gauge if he was serious. If it was the lawyer or the man asking the question, and if the latter, whether she was wrong about him.

"The dog is going to be put to sleep by the end of the week," she reminded him quietly. "How can I not?"

Alain didn't have an answer for that, or even a

comment. She realized that she'd wanted him to agree with her without hesitation. While he hadn't done that, at least he hadn't said anything to try to talk her out of it. She supposed that was something. A baby step in the right direction.

"I'll be here before four on Saturday," she promised him, opening the door. "Be good," she told Winchester.

And then she was gone.

"You *have* to help me, Hannah."

On her knees, Hannah Martingale Peters looked up from the display she was trying to rearrange, recognizing the voice before she saw Kayla approaching her.

Because of its small size, Shelby was one of the few holdouts when it came to chain stores. Martingale's had been opened by Hannah's great-grandfather, and everyone in her family had worked here at one time or another. Each generation had improved or expanded the store, leaving its mark.

While still only a single story, the building was sprawling, and the store offered a little bit of everything, the way a five-and-dime once might have.

Leaning a hand on the counter to help her gain her legs, Hannah softly cursed the arthritis that kept her from leaping to her feet the way she had once been able to.

She anticipated what was on the vet's mind. "Honey, Ralph and I have as many dogs now as we can handle. I'd like to help you out, but what with Jonas and Corky and—"

Kayla was quick to stop the outpouring of words. Hannah, a big-hearted woman loved by all, had the ability to go on and on about nothing for hours.

"No, it's not about the dogs. At least, not directly," she qualified. She saw interest pique in Hannah's blue eyes. "I have to attend a fund-raiser—"

Her mouth dropped open. "A fund-raiser? My, my, that is impressive."

Kayla knew the woman wanted details, and she was more than willing to give them—but only after her problem had been tackled and put to rest.

"I need a drop-dead-gorgeous dress to wear." She'd already gone through the ones on the racks and found nothing that suited her purpose.

Hannah gave her a tolerant look. "Well, darling, we don't stock dresses that might kill people. Have you checked out our newest collection? There are a few very pretty ones straight from L.A." A tall woman, Hannah eyed the town vet, thinking her a tiny thing that needed fattening. That was what happened when you had no family to look after you, she mused. "I think one of them might suit you just fine."

Kayla shook her head. "I've already looked,

Hannah." She caught her lower lip between her teeth, hoping against hope. Time was getting short. "Is there anything in the storeroom that you haven't put out yet?"

Hannah began to shake her head and then stopped, suddenly remembering what had accidentally arrived in the last shipment. The order had been a mistake.

"Well, there was one. I told Ralph to send it back. Nobody here has any need for a dress that sparkles." She laughed, recalling her own reaction to the slinky gown. "Can you just see it at a barbecue, or the fall fair? The hem would get all dirty—"

"Can I see it?" Kayla asked, hoping that for once, the woman wasn't exaggerating.

Hannah lifted one wide shoulder and let it drop. "If it's still here. Like I said, I told Ralph to send it back. Ordinarily, the man never does what I ask him to, but probably, just this one time—"

Kayla couldn't wait through Hannah's diatribe about the failings of her husband of thirty years. "Can you check?"

"Well, of course I can." She paused to straighten a sign, then looked at Kayla again. "You mean now?"

She nodded vigorously. "Please."

Rather than go, Hannah peered at her, squinting through her glasses. "I don't think I've ever seen you this excited about a dress before." With a heavy sigh, she abandoned the display and waddled toward the rear of the store.

No, she'd never been excited about a dress before, Kayla thought, but that was because she'd never had a man to impress. It had suddenly occurred to her, on the drive back to Shelby with the newest rescued German shepherd riding in the back, that a lot of women Alain had gone out with might be attending this fund-raiser. The last thing Kayla wanted was to look like a hayseed next to them. And she would if she wore any of the dresses in her closet. They were functional, not fancy.

Kayla raised her voice and called out, "Find it?"

"Still looking," Hannah responded.

She mentally crossed her fingers. She wondered if she'd have time—should Ralph have proved to be dependable this one time—to drive up to Santa Barbara for the sole purpose of buying a dress that threatened to melt the eyes of the beholder.

Probably not.

She said a small prayer that Ralph had not deviated from his normal slothful pattern.

Chapter Thirteen

For the umpteenth time, Alain pushed back the sleeve of his jacket and looked at his watch. As if staring at it could somehow make the small hour hand move backward of its own accord.

She was supposed to be here by now.

He distinctly remembered Kayla telling him that she would be here on Saturday at four o'clock. *Promising* to be here at four. Well, it wasn't four anymore. Or five, or six. It was ten after six. The fund-raiser was scheduled to begin at eight o'clock sharp, at his mother's house. The printed invitations said so.

To his amazement, Lily had moved at incredible

speed, contacting people and verbally twisting arms as she called in favors in that deep, honeyed-whiskey voice of hers.

He knew she wasn't doing it for an organization she'd never heard of; she was going to all this trouble for him.

Now, for some reason, Lily felt the need to try to make up for lost time. To make it up to all of them. She was bent on living life to the fullest, not as the toast of the art community, or the most celebrated hostess on four continents, but as a loving, doting mother.

She'd already thrown Philippe and Janice an embarrassingly ostentatious engagement party, and was just waiting for Georges to make a formal announcement—or even a whispered one—to do the same for him and Vienna. Lily had even taken on, rather enthusiastically, the role of Kelli's grandmother. Although everyone knew that to call her that to her face meant being the recipient of a world of hurt, where medieval tools of torture were involved.

But even though she'd seemingly undertaken this new role with gusto, Alain knew his mother well enough to know she would be far from pleased if Kayla didn't show up at the gala.

The legendary Lily Moreau did not suffer being embarrassed.

Why wouldn't Kayla show? he silently demanded,

beginning to pace about the living room. It didn't make any sense. She seemed so devoted to those dogs. The organization stood to make a lot of money. She wouldn't turn her back on that.

Pivoting on his heel to retrace his steps, Alain almost tripped over Winchester, who had become in only a few days his ever-present shadow.

"You know her, Winchester. Why isn't she here? If she was running late for some reason, why wouldn't she call to tell me?"

And why, he wondered silently, was he so wound up about a woman he hardly knew? Why was he all but dancing attendance this way? Why was he worrying?

He'd never done anything like this before, never gone so far out of his way to try to please a woman. Hell, pleasing women came easily to him, but that usually involved dinner, some form of entertainment and then a few hours of complete, pure physical pleasure. And that was it. Nothing more.

But this was different. *Felt* different.

This felt like involvement.

And with involvement came problems. A whole slew of them.

Alain didn't want to go that route, didn't want to feel the kind of pain he knew his mother had felt.

Damn it, what had he been thinking, asking her to do this? What was wrong with him? If it was Kayla's intention to—

His train of thought abruptly derailed. Winchester was suddenly alert, his head turned toward the front of the house. Every bone in his body appeared to stiffen in complete concentration.

"You hear something?"

Before the question was out of his mouth, Alain heard the doorbell ring.

He crossed to the door in record time.

As he pulled it open, Winchester suddenly nudged him out of the way. The next moment, the dog was prancing excitedly on his hind legs, his front paws on Kayla's torso, welcoming her the only way he knew how.

Alain could only stare. "You're all right."

"Which is more than I can say for this freeway system of yours," Kayla exclaimed. Her eyes blazed as she declared, "There are way too many people stuffed in down here."

She was obviously struggling to subdue an enormous case of road rage. She'd been stuck in traffic for an unforgivable amount of time, and cut off three times.

His relief at seeing her gave way to amusement. She looked adorable with smoke coming out of her ears.

"I'll see what I can do about sending them to another county." Abandoning the banter, he closed the front door and then physically moved Winchester out of the way. "My turn," he told the animal, pulling Kayla into his arms.

"You don't want to hug an uptight woman," she warned him.

There wasn't anything he wanted to do more. "Yes, I do," he retorted, tightening his arms around her just a bit. "I want to kiss one, too."

Oh, no, she wasn't about to let him lead her astray. She'd moved heaven and earth to find the right gown to wear to this thing, and she wasn't going to get sidetracked into not wearing it. "I've got to get dressed."

"We'll make up for lost time," he promised her, kissing the side of her throat. "I'll help you, I swear."

She was still struggling, but not nearly as much. "Yeah, right. That's like asking a coyote to watch the sheep."

"They've got a very strong union, I hear. The coyotes."

Whatever Kayla was going to say in protest was muffled as his lips came down on hers.

The frustration she'd brought into the room with her died a swift, painless death, swept away by the surge of feelings that erupted the instant their kiss began to flower.

On the long trip down from Shelby, she had done her best to talk herself out of feeling anything for Alain. She'd even listed all the reasons why nothing could come of her seeing him. Over and over, she told herself that she was investing in something that had no future. Heaven knew she didn't need to feel the pain of heartache, didn't need to once more court abandonment.

And abandonment would surely come. He was a playboy, emphasis on the word *play*. Granted, she didn't exactly have one foot in the grave, and there was still time to enjoy the lighter side of life before she settled down. But the truth was, she just wasn't built that way. She didn't know how to dally, how to have an interlude and just walk away. She didn't have sex, she made love. There was a huge difference. Her heart, despite all her internal lectures, was bent on settling down. On nesting.

And the more she was with Alain, the more she wanted to be with him.

The more she wanted the impossible.

Kayla realized that she was digging her fingers into his arms. Damn him, he was turning not just her knees into liquid, but her whole body, as well. Any second now, she was going down for the third time.

With effort, Kayla placed her hands against his chest and pushed. Or tried to. Her strength seemed to have deserted her. She'd never felt so feeble in her life.

She all but sucked in air the moment she pulled her head back. "Have you registered that mouth of yours yet?" she quipped. "It really is lethal."

Her stomach was fluttering like a flag in a hot Santa Ana wind.

"I never had complaints before," he told her.

"I bet you haven't."

And there it was in a nutshell. He'd kissed a legion of uncomplaining women. He was first and last a playboy. And right now, he was playing in Kayla's yard. But not for long.

As if it was going to hurt any less when he returned to his life, Kayla silently scoffed. She was already a goner and she knew it.

Well, if she was a goner, she might as well just enjoy the time she had, however short that might turn out to be.

Willing her pulse to stop scrambling, she said, "My dress for the fund-raiser is in the trunk. Where can I change?"

The look in his eyes was nothing if not wicked. "Right here would be nice."

The traffic had made her late, despite the fact that she had left early. There wasn't much time for her to turn into a butterfly. "Seriously."

"Seriously," Alain echoed, doing his best to keep a straight face.

They both knew what would happen if she took him up on that. "I change in here and odds are we won't make the fund-raiser on time."

All his earlier concerns had burned to a crisp the

second he'd kissed her. All he wanted now was to make love with her. "My mother'll understand. She's a romantic at heart."

I'll bet. For an intelligent man, he could be almost sweetly simple. "With everyone but her sons," Kayla told him.

"What makes you say that?" she hadn't even met his mother yet. There was no way she could come to that kind of a conclusion.

"Well, for one thing, the old 'do as I say, not as I do' rule." From everything she'd read about her—a great deal in the last few days—Kayla had a feeling that Lily Moreau didn't like sharing the spotlight— or her men—with another woman. "Your mom might have led an incredibly Bohemian lifestyle, but that doesn't mean she'd like the fact that her son's excuse for being late to a function she was presiding over was that he was making love to some woman."

It was, he thought, an interesting choice of words. "Is that how you think of yourself? As 'some woman'?"

Kayla had never had a problem with self-esteem. She was comfortable with who and what she was. But that was in her world, in Shelby. This was a whole new universe, filled with competitors.

She looked at him for a long moment, trying to pretend that there wasn't a great deal riding on his reply. "Don't you?"

The answer that came to mind unsettled him. Alain wasn't ready to share it with her. And because he wasn't, he suddenly realized just how serious this was. Because if it hadn't been, he would have suavely said no, adding a few lines about how special, how unique she was. Charming her. Tossing words into the wind.

But these words had weight, had substance and meaning, and that really unnerved him.

Made him feel vulnerable for the first time in a long time.

So instead, he smiled and said, "Let's go get your outfit out of the car and I'll show you to the guest room."

For a second, everything stood still. What had just happened here? Kayla wondered. Had Alain retreated? Was it happening already, his rethinking the situation and wanting to create a safe amount of distance between them?

She drew in a long breath, reminding herself that nothing was transpiring that she hadn't already anticipated twice over. She did her best to sound unaffected, even as she felt the ground crumbling beneath her.

"By the way, Mick said to tell you that your car is ready."

Her words didn't register for a beat. Right now, the sports car was the furthest thing from his mind. "Oh, right, I'd almost forgotten."

Just how rich was this man that he could forget about an expensive sports car like that? She *really* didn't belong in this world, Kayla thought.

Alain opened the front door again. "I'll have to make arrangements to pick it up."

Arrangements. Not, "I'll be there next week to get it." Arrangements.

That meant he was going to send someone else to get the car. So much for seeing him back in her neck of the woods, she thought cynically.

Kayla had no doubt, as she led the way back to the truck parked by the curb, that after tonight, more than likely, she would never see Alain again.

Lily Moreau's house, like the woman herself, was awe-inspiring. Lavish, it stopped just inches shy of overstepping the boundaries and being overdone. Made to look like a home along the French Rivera, the building stood three stories high.

The driveway of Mediterranean-blue-and-gray paving stones, circled a fountain that would have easily dwarfed most structures. Here, it appeared to fit right in. The tennis court in the back shared landscaping with an Olympic-size pool she'd expressly built for guests.

Everything both inside and outside the impressive building was pristine. White was her trademark and it was everywhere. It made the blasts of color that much more dramatic when they appeared.

"Ready?"

Alain's question penetrated the haze in Kayla's brain as she tried to take everything in at once—and tell herself that the woman got dressed the same way as everyone else. Kayla realized that he had come around to her side and was holding the passenger door opened.

A valet had slipped in on the driver's side to take his rented vehicle away.

"Ready," Kayla replied, with far more conviction than she felt.

Taking her arm, Alain tucked it through his own. "Don't think of her as a celebrity," he whispered into her ear. "Just think of her as my mother."

And that, Kayla thought, was exactly the problem. The celebrity she could deal with. The mother…

He's not bringing you home to Mother, this is just a party with an excuse. It doesn't matter whether or not she likes you. A week from now, this'll all be a faint memory, nothing more.

The knot in Kayla's stomach loosened a little.

The moment she walked into the foyer, Kayla saw it was a house built around Lily Moreau's paintings. The same splashes of color on the canvases that graced the entryway and the walls beyond were reproduced in the marble floor and the furnishings.

There was beauty everywhere she looked. It was a little like heaven—with a twist.

"You look gorgeous," Alain whispered in her ear. He was repeating himself, but thought she needed the reassurance. As if dropping his jaw when he first saw her emerge from the guest room in the slinky, silver-and-blue gown that lovingly hugged every curve she had wasn't enough.

She flashed him a grateful smile and he struggled with the surge of desire that fought to take possession of him. There would be time enough for that after the gala.

It couldn't get here soon enough for him.

And then, as if on cue, he saw his family moving forward, en masse, converging all around them. "Brace yourself," he whispered.

It seemed to Kayla that half the room had suddenly descended on her. She tightened her grip on Alain's arm, even though she'd promised herself not to let this event make her feel like a fish out of water. Catching her reflection in a mirror that hung on one side, she decided the smile she forced to her lips looked genuine enough.

And then it froze.

Lily Moreau was coming her way. Though barely five foot two, in person she appeared larger than life. Wearing a flowing, winter-white silk caftan with threads of purple shot through it to highlight her eyes, the renowned artist looked like an empress descending upon her court.

Before Kayla could murmur a heartfelt "Save me" into Alain's ear, Lily had taken her hand in both of hers, trapping her not just physically, but with her eyes.

"So this is the woman who saved my son's life." She smiled, and it seemed to Kayla as if the sun was rising across a dark lake, its rays reflected in the shimmering waters.

Kayla was relieved that she hadn't begun to shift from foot to foot. "That's a little dramatic," she replied quietly.

Lily laughed. "They tell me so am I."

Alain stepped in. "Let the others meet her before you overwhelm her, Mother."

"It is not my intention to overwhelm her, Alain. I just wish to thank her." She made no effort to release Kayla's hand.

Kayla looked down at their clasped hands, then at Lily. "I'm not going to run away, I promise."

The woman laughed and, inclining her head, stepped back. Alain was quick to draw Kayla to his side. "Kayla, you've already met Philippe. This is his fiancée, Janice. And this is my brother, Georges—"

"The doctor," Kayla stated, shaking his hand.

"You've researched us," Philippe commented.

"I like knowing things," she replied with a smile.

Lily nodded. "Very commendable." Then she glanced at Alain. "You're too slow." With that, she rattled off the names of the others, sweeping over Vienna, Janice's brother, Gordon, and the assorted nephews-in-law that three husbands had netted her. "Done," she declared, turning her attention back to Kayla. "Now, let's chat." With that, she tucked Kayla's hand through her arm and led her off to a more private area of the large room.

"Don't you think you should save her?" Georges murmured.

But Alain merely watched the two women as they took over a corner. "Kayla can hold her own." He saw Philippe studying him. "What?"

"Nothing," his older brother responded, then smiled that all-knowing smile that used to get under Alain's skin when they were teenagers.

"Don't give me 'nothing,'" he retorted. "You've got that I-know-something-you-don't look on your face."

Philippe's smile only widened. "Maybe I do," he allowed, "if you don't realize that this girl is different."

"Woman," Janice interjected patiently. "We're called women."

"Yeah." Kelli chimed in, tugging on the bottom of Philippe's jacket until he looked down at her. "We're women."

"Well, 'little woman'—" he bent down to pick up the child he'd already adopted in his heart "—let's see about getting you some cake to keep that mouth of yours busy."

Kelli tucked her arm around his neck and happily nestled in. "Okay."

Philippe glanced over his shoulder at Alain just before he walked over to the table laden with desserts. "She has my approval."

"Mine, too," Georges echoed, clapping him on the back.

Alain had suddenly become the center of attention, and he wasn't all that sure he liked it. "Not that I need it, but exactly what does Kayla have your approval for?"

"Joining the family," Georges answered, since Philippe was out of earshot. He threaded his fingers through Vienna's. "I've got to say I never thought it would happen."

Alain could feel himself growing defensive. That in itself was unusual. He'd never felt the need to before. "It's not happening now. This is a fund-raiser for homeless dogs, not a meet-Alain's-future-wife party."

"Keep telling yourself that, Alain," Georges laughed.

Remy joined the conversation, draping an arm over his younger cousin's shoulders. "If I were you, I'd take a look in the mirror."

"Why?" Alain looked down at his shirtfront, assuming that he'd gotten it dirty somehow.

Remy's grin grew wider. "Well, from where I'm standing, you look like a pretty smitten guy."

"Smitten?" Alain echoed. He stopped watching Kayla and his mother and now looked from his brother to his cousin. Behind Remy, his other cousins, Beau and Vincent, were both nodding their heads. "What are you talking about?"

Vienna surprised him by joining the conversation. She affectionately pressed her hand to his cheek. "The look in your eyes," she told him. "It does say a lot."

He was fond of Vienna, the same way he was fond of Philippe's fiancée. Both of his brothers had lucked out. But *he* was not about to be talked into anything. Even if there was a slight chance that what they were all suggesting was true.

"It says that you're all imagining things."

But even as Alain said it, he had the uncomfortable feeling that he was protesting too much—and that they all knew it.

Chapter Fourteen

Despite the attempts of several women at the fund-raiser to entice Alain to leave with them, he continued to mingle, always keeping Kayla in his line of sight. In case she needed him.

From where he stood, she seemed to be doing fine, but that could just be an act. The famous were intermixed with the not-so-famous at this last-minute gathering his mother had thrown together. Many of these people had drifted in and out of his life, as they had his mother's, for as long as he could remember.

But until tonight, he had never realized how unusual seeing all these celebrities in one place might seem to someone who'd lived most of her life in a small town where the most well-known person was probably the town sheriff.

Was she overwhelmed? Starstruck? Gilbert Holland was very hot on the Hollywood scene, and right now, the handsome actor was giving Kayla the benefit of his charismatic smile.

The surge of jealousy that washed over Alain surprised him. It took him several seconds to bank it down.

Craning his neck, he continued watching the trio. Gilbert was dominating the conversation, gesturing and looking particularly seductive. Alain couldn't tell if Kayla was responding. Well, responding or not, this had been going on for over an hour. It was high time that he rescued her, he decided.

Besides, he wanted Kayla to himself before Gilbert or someone else decided to sweep her off her feet.

Shouldering past several people who called out to him, Alain made his way to where Kayla and his mother were standing. Gilbert, he noted, looked mildly curious as he glanced up.

An image of two male bucks locking horns flashed through Alain's mind. Reaching Kayla, he placed his hand on her shoulder, his message clear as he nodded a greeting to the actor.

Gilbert took his cue and withdrew, but not before saying, "Add my pledge to the tally, Lily. Wonderful meeting you, Kayla."

Alain kept his hand where it was, drawing Kayla closer to him. "All right, Mother. Let her up for air." His tone was mild, but he wasn't about to take no for an answer.

Lily had spent the last hour-plus steering her son's young woman from one circle of friends to another, becoming increasingly more taken with Kayla as she listened to her speak. She liked the streak of steely determination she detected just beneath the surface. Alain was the most like her, and he would need a strong hand to keep him close to home.

"Air?" she echoed, looking at the young woman who was so artfully championing these dogs she and her associates rescued. "She's breathing just fine. And we're networking, aren't we, Kayla?"

Part of Kayla felt as if she was dreaming. This *had* to be the way Cinderella had felt walking into the ballroom filled with elegantly dressed people who belonged to a world she could only fantasize about. The house was littered with individuals she had read about in the pages of *People* magazine. And Alain's mother was introducing her around as if she were one of them. Very heady stuff. It took some effort to remember why she was here.

In response to Lily's comment about networking, she grinned as she looked at Alain and said, "Yes, we are."

His mother, Alain noticed, seemed exceedingly

pleased with herself. But there was something more going on, something he couldn't quite get hold of yet. He continued studying her.

"Tell him how much we've gotten in pledges so far," Lily urged.

Numbers had been flying at her right and left. The generosity overwhelmed her even more than the people did. "I lost count at fifty thousand," Kayla confessed.

"I didn't," Lily announced. Born to poverty, she was ever conscious of money. The fact that she was given to spending it lavishly when the mood hit her didn't alter that. Despite having an accountant, she kept her own tallies. "Sixty-two thousand, seven hundred. So far," she added smugly. It was obvious she thought they would do much better by evening's end. Her next words confirmed it. Leaning her head toward Kayla, who was several inches taller, she said, "The night is still young."

"Only if you're in Hawaii, Mother," Alain patiently pointed out. It was past eleven, and despite her beaming smile, Kayla looked a little worn around the edges. "I'd still like to claim her."

Lily sighed and gestured for him to take the young woman from her side. "If you must. If we played tug-of-war with this lovely creature, tongues would wage and words would somehow leak to those horrid tabloids."

Alain hadn't stopped studying his mother. The

glimmer of sadness in her eyes became apparent as she delivered her last line. Ever the dramatic grande dame, she had underlying seriousness to her tonight.

He glanced around the gathering, swiftly scanning the guests. Ordinarily, he wouldn't have to look more than a few feet to find who he was searching for.

"Where's Kyle?"

Lily took a breath, as if to launch into a long tale, then apparently changed her mind. "Not here," she said simply.

"I can see that." Alain lowered his voice so that only his mother and Kayla could hear him. "Why?" The young, so-called artist had been his mother's shadow ever since he had come into her life. He wouldn't have missed a gathering like this. "This is his element."

Lily made a disparaging sound under her breath. "I found Kyle 'in his element' earlier today." She saw Alain raise an eyebrow, urging her to elaborate. To buffer the pain, she clung to her anger, using it like a shield. "That little groupie who's been coming to the gallery every day to admire his work. She decided to 'admire' it a little closer today." Lily's carefully made-up lips twisted in disgust. "When I came by to surprise him, I was the one surprised." And then a strange smile curved her mouth, devoid of humor, tinged with triumph. "Although, I must say, it was probably a toss-up as to who was more surprised.

His groupie lost the ability to speak. So did some of the people in the immediate vicinity of the gallery." Alain was about to ask why when she told him. "Usually you have to go to Venice Beach to see a naked man running down the street." Her tone changed, as if she was talking about someone who was merely an acquaintance and not the man she had taken into her heart.

"The last I saw of Kyle, he was trying to make a policeman understand how he came to be separated from his pants." She raised her chin, a queen sharing a not-so-amusing anecdote with her court. "I hope, for his sake, he was more forthcoming with the officer than he tried to be with me."

As much as he and his brothers held Kyle suspect, Alain felt bad about the situation. Not for Kyle, but for his mother. He *hated* seeing her hurt. Even though she would never say as much, he could feel it.

Turning his back to block the view of other people in the room, he put his hand on her arm. "Are you all right?"

Lily tossed her head, her famous black mane flying over her shoulder. "I am wonderful," she declared. "I have just lost a hundred and seventy-two pounds of unnecessary weight and—" her eyes shifted to Kayla "—I have a cause to sponsor."

Out of the blue, Kayla suddenly asked, "Would you like a dog?"

The question took Lily by surprise. "Darling, you don't have to try to sell me—"

"No, I'm serious," she interrupted. "There is nothing like the unconditional love you get from a pet." Because she had been so wonderful to her tonight, Kayla decided to share something very personal with this dynamic woman. "I don't know what I would have done without mine when I had my breakup."

Alain's ears perked up at this mention of a man in her past. He had no idea why he'd imagined himself the first to have discovered her, but he had. "Break-up?"

Kayla had an uneasy feeling that she was suddenly walking on a tightrope and working without a net. But she needed to say this to Lily. "I was really shaken up, stunned that I could have misjudged someone so much."

Lily laughed shortly. "There is a lot of that going around."

Kayla deliberately avoided looking at Alain. "The man I thought I was going to spend forever with didn't turn out to be anything like I thought he was."

Lily rolled her eyes heavenward. "Amen," she murmured.

"I already had a dog to comfort me, but then someone from the rescue society asked me if I'd be willing to take in a couple of German shepherds until permanent homes could be found for them. They thought that being a vet, I wouldn't mind doing it for a few weeks. Well, my dog would lick my tears off my face, but Lenny and Squiggy wouldn't let me feel sorry for myself. And they were so tremendously grateful for any attention, any affection I showed them. I think we all kind of healed each other."

"Lenny and Squiggy?" Alain echoed. He couldn't contain the laughter that followed. Why would she have called the dogs after two hapless characters from an old classic sitcom?

"I didn't name them," Kayla protested. "The society likes to give them new names to signify their new life. But they just about saved mine." And then she got down to the heart of the matter. The people at the fund-raiser were generously giving money, but she needed homes for the dogs as much as she needed donations. "I have a lovely purebred who's eighteen months old and needs a loving home. She was abused by her owner. He all but starved her to death. Audrey is yours for the asking. I promise you, she can fill up a lot of space inside you, until you don't feel empty anymore."

Lily was silent for a long moment, and Kayla became uneasy that she might have crossed the line with her enthusiasm. "I come on strong sometimes," she began to apologize, but got no further.

"And that, my dear, is a very good trait," Lily declared in no uncertain terms. "Don't let anyone tell you otherwise. You have to push in this world to get anywhere." It was obvious that she was thinking of her own journey, as well. "All right," she said with feeling, "I'll take this—Audrey, did you say?" Kayla nodded. "I'll take Audrey in—as long as you let me pay for her," she qualified.

"There's no fee," Kayla protested. Especially not after the amount of money Lily had raised for her.

The woman didn't seem to hear. "I can write you a check for five thousand dollars. Will that be satisfactory?"

Kayla opened her mouth to protest, but Alain interrupted. "That'll be fine, Mother," he assured her as he began to steer Kayla away. "Just make it out to the German Shepherd Rescue Society, like all the other donations tonight."

His arm around Kayla's waist, Alain ushered her toward the buffet table. As he forged a path through the wall of people, he deliberately swung past Philippe and Janice. He scarcely broke stride as he told his brother, "Kyle's been eighty-sixed. Go talk to Mother, tell her something to make her feel good, the way you always do."

Philippe, holding a sleeping Kelli in his arms, turned around, surprised. "What happened?"

"From what she said, this Kyle person cheated on

her," Kayla said, before Alain had a chance to. Her heart went out to Alain's mother. She hated seeing anyone in pain.

"Oh, your poor mom." Putting down her glass of punch, Janice turned on her heel and began to make her way toward Lily. Philippe fell into step behind his fiancée.

Kayla watched the duo until they reached Lily. "How long were your mother and Kyle together?"

Alain thought for a second, working his way backward. "About six, seven months. She was with him longer than a lot of the others." He tried to sound casual about it, knowing that a lot of people judged his mother and saw her actions in a less than flattering light. But there was no way to sugar-coat it. "Mother goes through men like someone with a head cold goes through a box of tissues. But we all thought—worried—that this one was serious. I know that he thought he was." Alain would have been willing to bet on it. He'd seen it so many times before, especially in the cases he handled. An older person, trying to hang on to youth, ultimately being taken advantage of by a younger con artist.

The case he was working on now fit the bill, he thought abruptly.

"So did she," Kayla said, looking toward the artist. Philippe and Janice had just joined her.

"Listen, I'm a stranger to her, but if you want to go and be with her, I'll understand."

Alain shook his head. Philippe was better at that sort of thing than he was. "I think that pet you offered to give her will do more good than I could. Besides, this has an upside to it—other than not having to call a money-hungry SOB 'daddy,'" he qualified. "My mother will probably paint something utterly magnificent and move on."

Kayla had read that some of the world's greatest artists did their best work while in the depths of distress. "Is that how she usually handles her heartache?"

He nodded. One of her most famous paintings had been created right after she'd heard that Georges's father had died. That was when he'd realized that she never quite stopped loving any of the men who'd been in her life. "Pretty much."

"Maybe I should give her Audrey after she finishes the painting." A smile played on Kayla's lips. "We don't want to deprive the art community."

He knew she was kidding. But the concern he saw in her eyes about a woman she hardly knew, touched him. The bantering words faded from his lips.

"You're a really nice person," he told her softly, "you know that?"

"Yes, that much I know."

The way she said it, it sounded like something she

had taken to heart after having gone through a learning experience. "About that breakup you mentioned—"

She waved a hand, as if to dismiss it. "Happened a long time ago."

Ordinarily, he didn't pry. He believed in privacy, his own most importantly. Besides, not knowing made things less personal. But he didn't want to be less personal, not with Kayla. "How bad was it?"

Remembering was like walking on glass, barefoot. But if she was evasive, he was going to think that she was hiding things. The only thing she wanted to hide was her own stupidity.

"On a scale of one to ten?" she finally asked.

He nodded. "If that works for you, okay."

She sighed. "Twelve."

Something inside his chest sank. "You loved him that much?"

She looked at Alain sharply. Lost in her own thoughts, she hadn't realized how he might interpret her answer. "Oh, no. No," she repeated with feeling. "The twelve rating is based on how hard it was for me to get rid of him—physically. I had to move." *Flee* would have been a better word, she thought.

The facts weren't fitting together for him. "I thought you said you lived in that house forever."

"I have." She'd been born there, and now it was her haven, as well. "But there was a break in time when I went upstate to get my degree." She'd been accepted by several veterinary colleges. Fate had her deciding to attend the one she'd chosen. "I met Brett in San Francisco." She could see Alain was waiting for more. "And I lived there with him even after I graduated."

Jealousy snaked through his belly, burrowing in. "How long?"

"Long enough to learn I'd made a mistake." A rueful smile played on her lips. What would life have been like for her had she gone to school in San Diego? Or even out of state? "First seven months were very good. Perfect." And they had been. Which made the months that followed even more awful. "He was warm, funny, attentive." The rueful smile faded as she remembered, even as she tried to keep her thoughts at bay. "And then he began to relax."

Alain didn't follow her. "Relax?"

Kayla nodded. Music began to softly play in the background. In the distance, a dance floor was being cleared. But she stood there, on the edge of her past, trying not to let the memory of that period of time draw her into darkness.

"His facade. There was a temper, a rather bad one, that he'd been keeping under wraps. Once he thought he had me, he stopped trying to bank it down." She frowned. "He had a tendency to shout when he was angry, and he was angry almost all the time," she remembered.

Alain wanted to ask her why she didn't leave, but he wanted to know something else even more. "Did he hit you?"

Kayla hated this, hated remembering a time she was ashamed of. It was a side of herself she hadn't known existed, a side that was weak. Vulnerable. Dependant. After it was over, after it was behind her, she'd sworn to herself never to be weak again. Not like that. Not to the point where her self-respect was sacrificed.

Shrugging, she looked away, not wanting to see pity in Alain's eyes.

"A shove here, a slap there. Nothing to really leave marks," she added quickly, knowing that was no justification. "I told myself it was stress doing it to him, that he didn't mean it. That if I only made life easier for him, he wouldn't lose his temper, wouldn't get so angry." What an idiot she'd been. It wasn't anything that countless other women didn't think, didn't feel, but it made it no easier to live with.

Alain wanted to protect her, to gather her in his arms and make her forget it ever happened. More than that, he wanted to beat into a bloody pulp the snake who'd made her feel this way.

"What made you finally leave?"

The rueful smile was back as she raised her head and looked at him. "He hit the dog."

"Your pet?" he guessed. It made sense. She wouldn't put up with his doing something to a defenseless animal.

She nodded. "A stray I'd brought home with me. He was pathetic," she remembered fondly. "Skinny, malnourished, with sores on half his body. I knew I had to save him, to make him better. Brett almost lost it when I brought the dog home, but I managed to convince him to him stay.

"That last night I was there he really lost his temper over something. I can't remember what anymore." She shrugged. "Something stupid. It was always something stupid. Anyway, he swung, and I moved out of his way. He wound up hitting the dog. The dog whimpered, Brett yelled some more, and something just snapped inside of me. The next morning, I waited until he was at work and then I cleared out my stuff from the apartment, took Petey and never looked back."

Alain assumed Petey had to be the dog. "He didn't try to find you?"

She shook her head. "I don't think his ego would have been able to process the fact that I'd left him. And he never asked where I'd lived before, so he couldn't track me down." Nevertheless, she'd spent a very edgy twelve months before she felt remotely safe.

"How long ago was that?"

"Five years." She knew it down to the day, but

didn't bother adding on the months, weeks and days. "I got involved in the rescue society shortly after that." She smiled and the serious aura around her vanished. "And the rest is history."

"What happened to Petey?" Alain was pretty sure he hadn't heard her refer to any of the dogs in the house by that name. Had her pet died?

"I gave him to a little girl who'd just lost her mother." Kayla shrugged casually. "Seemed like the thing to do. She needed him more than I did. They're inseparable now," she added.

Moved, Alain found that words failed him. She seemed to do that to him, make his stock-in-trade disappear. So instead of talking, he leaned over and kissed her.

It was a soft, sweet kiss that nonetheless made her pulse jump in anticipation. When Alain drew back, she looked at him, stunned but pleased. "What was that for?"

He slipped his arm around her waist, a bevy of emotions all elbowing each other out of the way. "For being you."

That confused her. But it was a nice confusion, she thought. "All right."

It had been one hell of a party. By the time it was over, they'd garnered, according to Lily, close to ninety-five thousand dollars in pledges. Hailing from an area where people thought five thousand dollars was a great deal of money, the sum was staggering to Kayla.

But even more important than the money was the fact that she had also managed to place nearly thirty dogs with people on the strength of her recommendations—sight unseen.

"You're quite a saleswoman." There was admiration in Alain's voice.

Even though the words were flattering, Kayla found it really hard to concentrate.

They were back at his place, in his bed, and as he spoke, he was slowly stroking her. They'd already made love once, but she could feel herself responding to him all over again. Wanting to make love again. Never wanting to stop.

God, but it was glorious, being here with him like this.

"I'd rather think of myself as a matchmaker," she told him, doing her best to sound as if she didn't have a care in the world. "Matching up people with pets that are going to make their lives warmer, nicer." She turned toward him, smiling. "There's nothing as soothing as stroking a dog's fur."

He played his fingers along her body and grinned. "You might be onto something there," he agreed. "Because I don't feel soothed right now." He propped himself up on his elbow. "I feel exceedingly aroused."

"So what are we going to do about that?"

"Guess."

She didn't have to. He was already showing her.

Chapter Fifteen

Ever since he could remember, Alain had been an extremely heavy sleeper. Thunderstorms and sirens were known to leave him unaroused. When they were much younger, Philippe had commented more than once that Alain could probably sleep through the Apocalypse if it happened in their lifetime.

Which was why he hadn't woken up when Kayla left his bed.

The midmorning Sunday sun had long since pushed its way into every corner of the bedroom, warming it and him, before he finally, reluctantly, opened his eyes.

And immediately saw that the space beside him was empty.

"Kayla?"

When there was no answer, Alain raised his voice and called her name again. With the same results.

Winchester was on the floor next to his side of the bed, pressed flat on the rug as if he'd been run over by a steamroller. When Alain swung his legs down, the dog was instantly awake, instantly ready to go.

But as eager to please as the he was, the German shepherd couldn't answer the question his master shot in his direction. "Where is she, boy? Where's Kayla?"

Kayla had certainly made a believer out of him, Alain thought, mildly amused. She had him asking the dog to take him to her.

Winchester's only response was to wag his tail and present his head to be petted. Alain spared him one quick scratch behind the ears before he padded across the rug to investigate Kayla's whereabouts.

The bathroom door was wide open. He didn't have to look in to know she wasn't there, but did, anyway.

With a sigh, he grabbed a pair of jeans from the closet and pulled them on. Closing the snap, he noticed that the clothes he'd worn last night and discarded with abandonment were no longer flung every which way on the floor. Instead, they were neatly folded and piled on his bureau. Nesting instincts? He could hope so.

But then he saw that her gown, which had adhered sensuously to her body like a glimmering second skin, and which he'd more than happily peeled off, was nowhere to be seen. Had she decided to wear it again this morning, to make last night's enchantment spin out a little longer?

Something told him he was building castles in the air.

"Kayla?"

Alain checked the guest room and saw that the clothes she'd worn when she had arrived yesterday were gone, as well.

Uneasiness began to skitter through him like an insect across a checkered linoleum floor.

Was this the answer she'd promised to give him? The one in response to the proposal that had popped out of his mouth?

Somewhere in the dead of night, after the lovemaking had left him enveloped in a sweet, seductive afterglow, he'd heard himself whispering words to her he never thought he'd say to any woman.

"Will you marry me?"

The moment the question was out, he'd felt Kayla stiffen against him, as if she was expecting a physical blow. And then she'd laughed as she relaxed again. "You've had too much to drink."

He'd caressed her face, wanting to make love with her again. But he was far too exhausted to attempt it. As for the alcohol, maybe he'd had a tiny bit more than usual. He'd let her drive them home, but he was by no means too intoxicated to know what he was saying.

"Maybe that's what's giving me the courage to ask," he'd told her. And maybe, in hindsight, that had been a wee bit too honest. But he felt he could be open with her. Felt he could be himself—without consequences. She'd made him feel so differently about everything.

"So," he'd finally pressed, when she gave him no answer, "will you? Marry me," repeated, in case she'd lost sight of the question during the silence.

"I'll let you know in the morning," she'd promised, and he'd heard the smile in her voice. A smile that warmed him from the inside out. "If you still want to ask me."

"I will," he guaranteed with feeling, slipping his arms around her.

He fell asleep holding her.

And now here it was, morning. And he couldn't find her.

Was this her way of giving him his answer?

He felt upset; he felt relieved. He felt damn confused.

Maybe this was for the best, after all.

No, damn it, it wasn't. He *wanted* to marry her. For the first time in his life, he wanted to get married.

The irony of the situation was not lost on him.

Alain called her name again, a little more urgently this time, as he hurried down the stairs. Winchester bounded down beside him and, as always, made it to the landing first.

"Kayla!"

Alain's voice echoed back to him. "I think she left us, boy," he murmured dejectedly, striding to a window that faced the front of the house.

Her truck was no longer parked by the curb. Rather than face him, rather than face his proposal again, she'd left before he woke up.

He'd never been rejected before. Alain couldn't say he liked it.

Dragging a hand through his hair, he went to the kitchen to make coffee. If he was going to figure things out, figure out how he felt about this turn of events and what his next move was going to be, he needed coffee. Lots of coffee. Black, like the mood that was swiftly descending over him.

Kayla tried to go about her life as if it were business as usual. As if her painfully reconstructed world hadn't just experienced an 8.9 earthquake, knocking out all the foundations beneath it.

Alain had asked her to marry him. And scared the

hell out of her. Because he was asking her to risk everything, to risk having her heart ripped out of her chest again and used for soccer practice.

She sighed, shaking her head as she continued grooming Audrey, the dog she'd promised to Lily.

Brett had done a number on her, Kayla admitted. He'd made her leery of trusting her own judgment. Because of him, she was afraid to savor the simple joy of falling in love. Her fear of disappointment blocked out everything else.

So, when faced with Alain's proposal, she'd run. Run instead of answering him. Run back to what she knew.

And he hadn't tried to call her, hadn't come after her. Hadn't sent out carrier pigeons to try to get in contact with her.

It wasn't as if she'd just disappeared into thin air. She'd gone home. Alain knew where that was. And he hadn't followed her.

Which told her that it *had* been the alcohol talking that night when he'd proposed. Alcohol and nothing more. Certainly not his heart. And as each day faded into night without him calling or coming by, she grew more and more certain that she'd been right not to say yes, not to ask "How high?" when her heart had told her to jump.

And with each passing day, the gaping hole in her life just seemed to grow larger.

Unlike the last time, or whenever she was monumentally upset, working didn't help.

Nothing took her mind off Alain, or the pain she felt because he didn't care.

The way she did.

"What's the matter with me, Audrey?" she asked, annoyed with herself. She rubbed a towel against the wet fur. "I didn't even know him for that long." She rocked back on her heels, the towel in her hand. "How can you fall in love with someone so fast? I don't believe in love at first sight. Lust, maybe," she allowed, "but not love."

But it had been love, pure and simple, because she was fairly certain that lust didn't hurt this way. It didn't make you feel as if the sun had suddenly been extinguished, leaving you to find your way in the dark.

God, this felt terrible.

She realized she was crying again, and blinked, wiping away the stray tear that managed to reach her cheek.

"The next guy who crashes into a tree on my property I'm leaving there," she said, looking into Audrey's big brown eyes. The shepherd's response was to raise up on her hind legs and lick Kayla's face, and she laughed despite herself. "That was my first problem. I let him kiss me." And that was the beginning of her downfall, she thought. Because the man made the world fade away.

With a sigh, she frowned, thinking about what she had to do. She'd promised to bring Lily her new pet. And Philippe had asked for one of Ginger's puppies. The dogs needed a home more than she needed to hide. But how was she going to face these people and act as if everything was all right?

She pressed her lips together, thinking. Alain's family probably had no idea that there was anything out of the ordinary going on. Kayla was willing to bet he hadn't told any of them that he'd proposed. Or that he'd willingly let her go.

There was no question in her mind that she was going to keep her word. And she had to do it *now*. It was, she told herself, like pulling a thorn out of your hand. You had to do it quickly. The longer you delayed, the more frightening the proposition seemed, and the longer it was before you could begin healing.

With a sigh, she went to get the puppy she'd selected for Philippe, a mischievous, affectionate female she'd mentally dubbed Duchess.

She forced herself to focus on the dogs and on nothing else.

His pride hurt, Alain tried his best to forget about Kayla. But his best wasn't good enough. He just couldn't seem to shake off her influence. She'd made him see everything through different eyes. Even the cases he worked. It wasn't about winning anymore. It was about, God help him, doing the right thing.

Which was why he found himself paying a visit to Bobbie Jo Halliday. He was determined to appeal to her better nature. Even if he had to bribe her to do it.

And he wasn't about to back down until he'd hammered out something acceptable to his client that was still generous to the deceased's children. Despite what his firm might say to the contrary, this was only fair.

And Kayla had taught him how important it was to play fair.

Kayla first went to Lily's house and then to Philippe's, all the while hoping against hope that she might run into Alain, even though she told herself she'd be better off if she didn't.

Well, she didn't, and God knew she didn't feel better off. What she felt, damn him, was bereft.

The song on the radio annoyed her. All the songs on the radio annoyed her. Why did people have to keep singing about finding "the right one"?

With a huff, she switched it off.

She wished she'd brought another dog along. As it was, the loneliness was eating holes in her. Making her feel empty.

Kayla's hands tightened on the steering wheel.

The freeways were moving at a good, fast pace and she was making incredible time.

Time to do what? Return home and be hit between the eyes with how empty everything was there, as well? Despite the fact that the place was now packed with eight puppies and six adult dogs?

Why did everything feel so empty just because Alain wasn't in it? She'd lived all this time without the man. Why was it so hard to continue doing that now?

Taking the turn to her house, Kayla suddenly felt her heart leap into her throat. Joy, anticipation, excitement all vied for top position.

Someone was sitting on her doorstep. Someone who, from this distance, looked just like Alain.

But it couldn't be him. He was supposed to be at work. Wasn't he?

It *was* him, she realized, drawing closer. Her pulse was racing. Why was he here? Had he missed her, or—

And then her heart sank again. His car. He was probably in town to pick it up. But if that was the case, how had he gotten to her house? And where was the vehicle, anyway?

Sliding out of the front seat, she had to brace her wobbly knees. Kayla held on to the door a second before she finally slammed it shut. She never took her eyes off Alain, afraid that he might disappear if she did.

"Hi."

"Hi," he echoed, getting up. He'd been sitting there for almost an hour, waiting for her to come back, wrestling with his thoughts. Was he being an idiot waiting for her, or was this the smartest thing he'd ever done?

When he saw her get out of her car, he had his answer.

As he crossed to her, she asked, "Come about your car?"

His car. He'd completely forgotten about the vehicle that was languishing at the mechanic's shop. More proof that he was in love. Thoughts of this woman had taken center stage in his life, completely pushing everything else into the background.

But in order not to look like a complete fool, he lied. "Among other things."

Her heart leaped up again. *Stop hoping, idiot. If he cared, he would have been here way before this.* "What other things?"

And then, suddenly, he was blocking out the sun, blocking out everything as hc looked into her eyes. "You. We have some unfinished business."

Be strong, damn it. You know this isn't going to work. She squared her shoulders. "No, we don't," she informed him quietly. "I told you I'd give you my answer in the morning." Kayla raised her chin. "And I did."

"When? How?"

"I left you a note."

"I never found a note." Although he hadn't been looking for a note, he'd been looking for her. Paper had never entered into it.

"Typical male," she murmured.

She was stalling, he thought. "So, will you repeat what you wrote, so I can hear it with my 'typical male' ears?"

It was going to be a lot harder to say this face-to-face, which was why she'd written it in the first place. She felt her courage flagging. "I don't remember exactly what I wrote—but for the record, I said something to the effect that I wouldn't hold you to a proposal that was given while you were drunk."

"I wasn't drunk," he insisted. "I had a pleasant buzz on."

Semantics, she thought. "Well, you were buzzing in my ear and—"

He wasn't about to get waylaid by rhetoric. He had to hear her say this. Maybe then he'd back away. But until he did, he was going to nurse this hope—just as his mother did each time she entered a new relationship, he realized. "You don't want to marry me?"

How could Kayla make him understand, when she didn't fully comprehend this herself? "It's not that I don't *want* to marry you. I can't marry you."

He was doing his best to understand, but it was like trying to read words through a layer of mud. "Are you already married?"

"No."

"Engaged?"

She looked away, her voice growing smaller, more distant. "No."

Then she was free, he thought. Anticipation moved to the front of the line. "Betrothed at birth to the prince of some tiny country?"

She laughed despite herself. "No."

Alain took hold of her shoulders, afraid she was going to bolt on him. "What, then?"

"I can't marry you because you weren't serious when you asked me."

That made no sense whatsoever, he thought. "Would you like me to write it in blood?"

"No, I just wanted you to mean it." But she'd learned that there was no such thing as forever. And she was afraid that the hurt would be too much for her.

He looked at her, his face completely serious. "I have a cousin who works for the FBI. He could score a lie detector machine for me for about an hour. You could hook me up."

"I—"

He took her hand in his, knowing he had to show her what was in his heart if he was ever going to win her over. He was going to have to be vulnerable in order to be strong. It made no sense to him, but he knew it was true.

"Look, I admit that I'm scared. I probably look like a deer caught in the headlights—"

She followed the unflattering metaphor to its conclusion. "And I'm the truck about to run you down?"

"Don't interrupt," he chided. "You get to make your closing argument later."

With a laugh, she shook her head. "Ever the lawyer."

"Shh." He got back to his main point. "I'm scared because I never made a commitment before. You know what I'm *more* scared of?"

"Oh, you're asking a question." A smile played on her lips. "Do I get to answer?"

He went on, never more serious in his life. "I'm more scared of living without you. I tried it and I don't like it. You've made an impression on my life, Kayla. You've placed your imprint everywhere, and nothing is the same anymore. I want you in my life. I want you right there in the morning when I wake up."

She was a realist when she had to be. And she knew she had no choice right now. Her roots were here. His were not. "And you're willing to give up your work, everything you know, to be with me? Because I can't leave here, Alain. Everyone's dependent on me. We're a small community and everyone is necessary here."

She couldn't read the look in his eyes. "Did I say

you could talk yet?" he asked her. When Kayla shook her head, he continued. "I'm not going to give up everything."

Which meant that he wanted her to pick up everything and relocate in his world. She couldn't. As lovely as it was, she couldn't. "Well, then—"

"Still no talking," he reminded her. "The firm has a helicopter. I've made inquiries, and because I just put them on the map with this settlement dealing with Ethan Halliday's will—I'll tell you about that later—they're willing to let me use the copter to fly up here at night and back to the firm's landing pad every morning. That way I won't be stuck in two hours of traffic each way, and you get to stay here."

A helicopter. "You can fly a helicopter?"

"Yes."

She was impressed. "You have an argument for everything."

For the first time since he'd begun pleading his case, Alain grinned. "I'm a lawyer, I have to. And this is the most important argument of my career." He took her into his arms. "I'm in love with you, Kayla, and I can truly say I've never been in love before. So, what about it?"

The corners of her mouth curved. "I get to talk now?"

Alain nodded. "You get to talk now—but only if you say the right thing."

She batted her eyes at him innocently. "Which would be?"

"'Yes,'" he told her.

"Then it's yes, since you're not accepting any other answers. Now let's go pick up your car."

But he wasn't about to release her just yet. There was all this unbridled desire ricocheting in his chest. Just before he lowered his mouth to hers, he assured her, "The car can wait."

And it did.

* * * * *

A sneaky peek at next month…

By Request

RELIVE THE ROMANCE WITH THE BEST OF THE BEST

My wish list for next month's titles…

In stores from 17th January 2014:

☐ Ruthlessly Royal — Robyn Donald, Annie West & Fiona Hood-Stewart

☐ Millionaire Magnates — Katherine Garbera, Brenda Jackson & Charlene Sands

3 stories in each book - only £5.99!

In stores from 7th February 2014:

☐ Australian Quinns — Kate Hoffmann

☐ Pregnancy Surprise — Barbara McMahon, Susan Meier & Jackie Braun

Available at WHSmith, Tesco, Asda, Eason, Amazon and Apple

Just can't wait?

Visit us Online

You can buy our books online a month before they hit the shops! **www.millsandboon.co.uk**

0114/05

Meet The Sullivans...

Over 1 million books sold worldwide!

Stay tuned for more from **The Sullivans** in 2014

Available from:

www.millsandboon.co.uk